SUPER PANCAKE

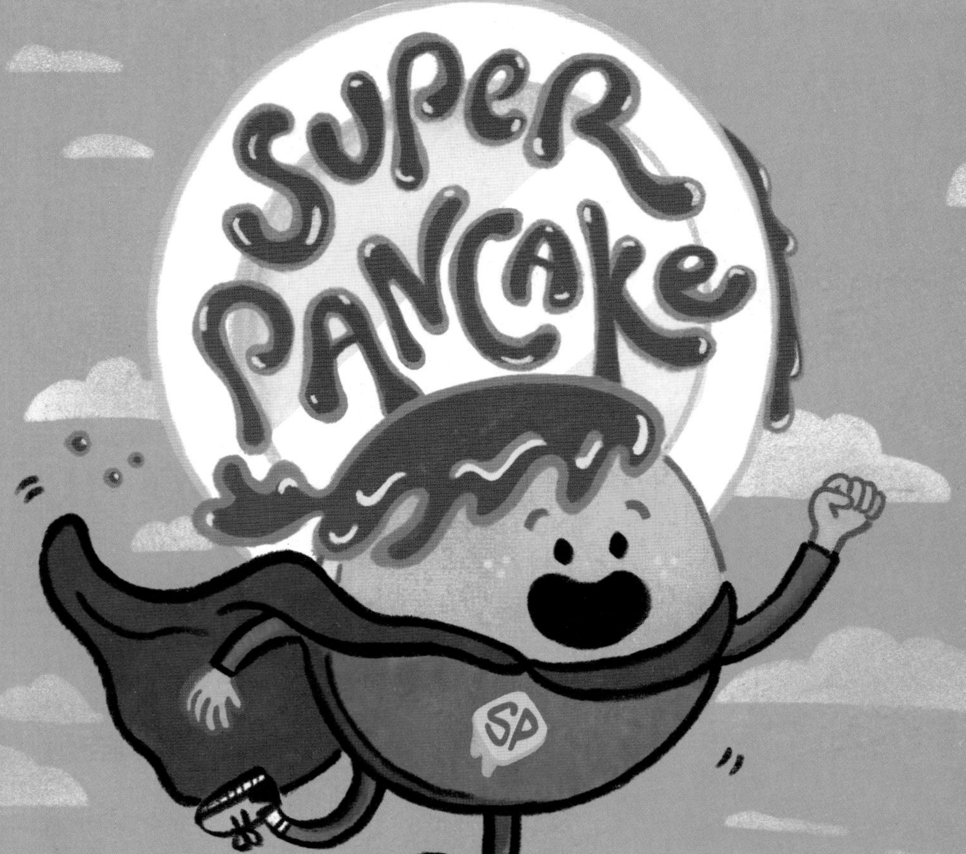

written by MEGAN WAGNER LLOYD

illustrated by ABHI ALWAR

ALFRED A. KNOPF NEW YORK

THIS IS A BORZOI BOOK PUBLISHED BY ALFRED A. KNOPF

Text copyright © 2023 by Megan Wagner Lloyd
Jacket art and interior illustrations copyright © 2023 by Abhi Alwar

All rights reserved. Published in the United States by Alfred A. Knopf,
an imprint of Random House Children's Books,
a division of Penguin Random House LLC, New York.

Knopf, Borzoi Books, and the colophon are
registered trademarks of Penguin Random House LLC.

Visit us on the Web! rhcbooks.com

Educators and librarians, for a variety of teaching tools,
visit us at RHTeachersLibrarians.com

Library of Congress Cataloging-in-Publication Data is available upon request.
ISBN 978-0-593-37844-1 (trade) — ISBN 978-0-593-37845-8 (lib. bdg.) —
ISBN 978-0-593-37846-5 (ebook)

The text of this book is set in 9.5-point Sugary Pancake.
The art in this book was created using Procreate and Photoshop.
Book design by Carol Ly

MANUFACTURED IN CHINA
February 2023
10 9 8 7 6 5 4 3 2
First Edition

For Lucy

—M.W.L.

For Prakrit,
my sweet nephew and biggest fan

—A.A.

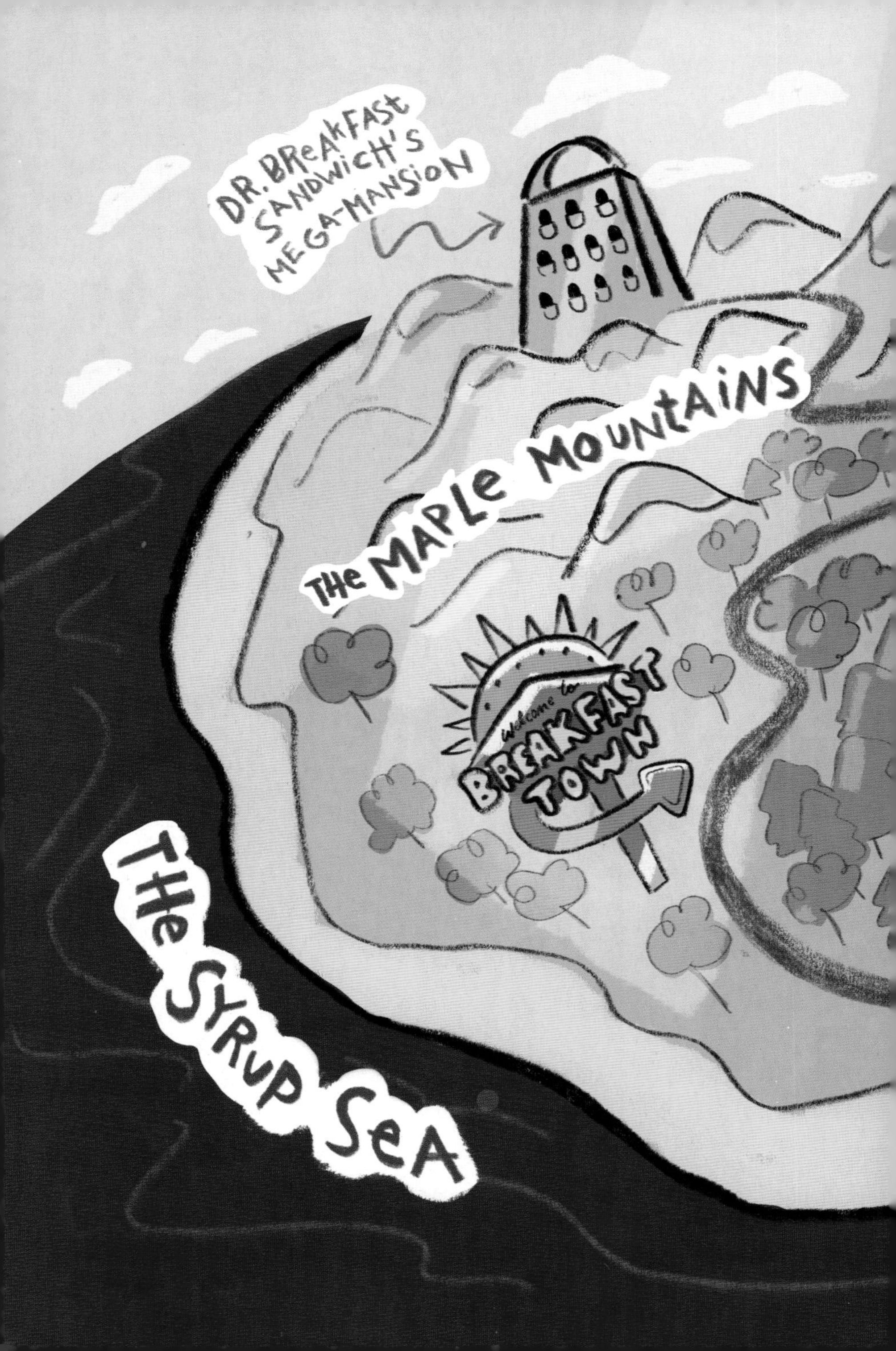

DR. BREAKFAST SANDWICH'S MEGA-MANSION
THE MAPLE MOUNTAINS
Welcome to BREAKFAST TOWN
THE SYRUP SEA

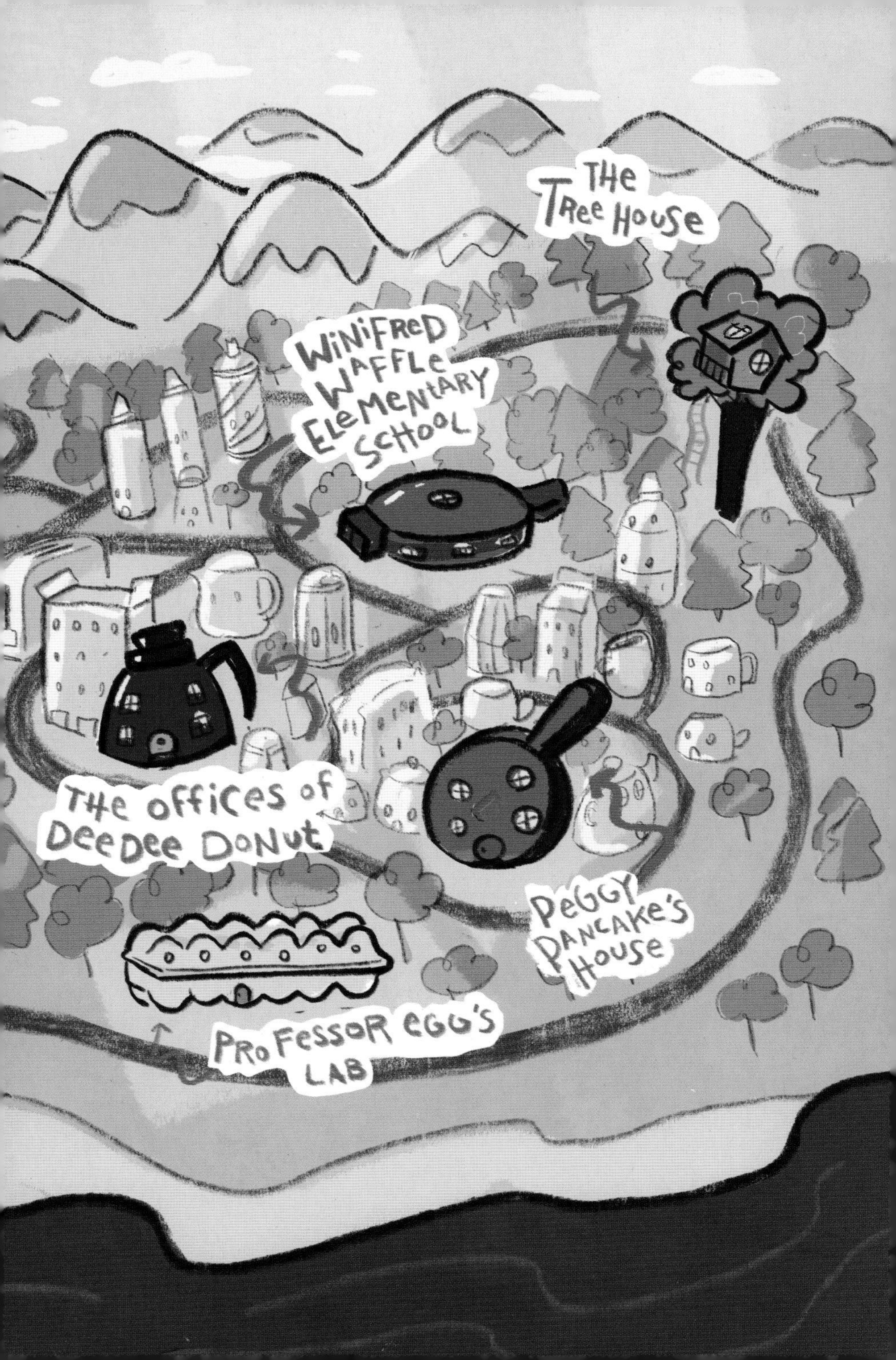
THE TREE HOUSE
WINIFRED WAFFLE ELEMENTARY SCHOOL
THE OFFICES OF DEEDEE DONUT
PEGGY PANCAKE'S HOUSE
PROFESSOR EGG'S LAB

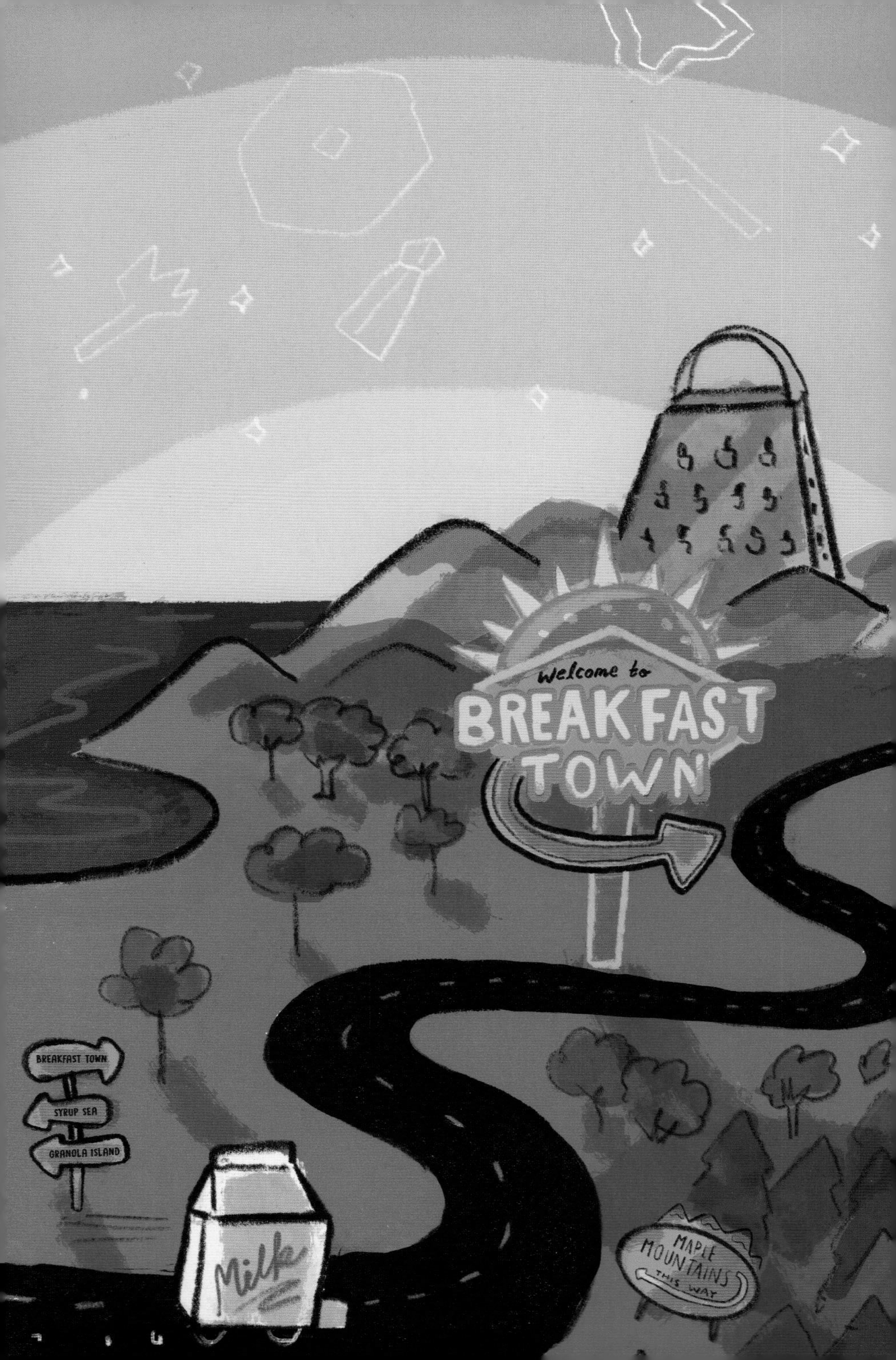
Welcome to
BREAKFAST
TOWN
BREAKFAST TOWN
SYRUP SEA
GRANOLA ISLAND
Milk
MAPLE
MOUNTAINS
THIS WAY

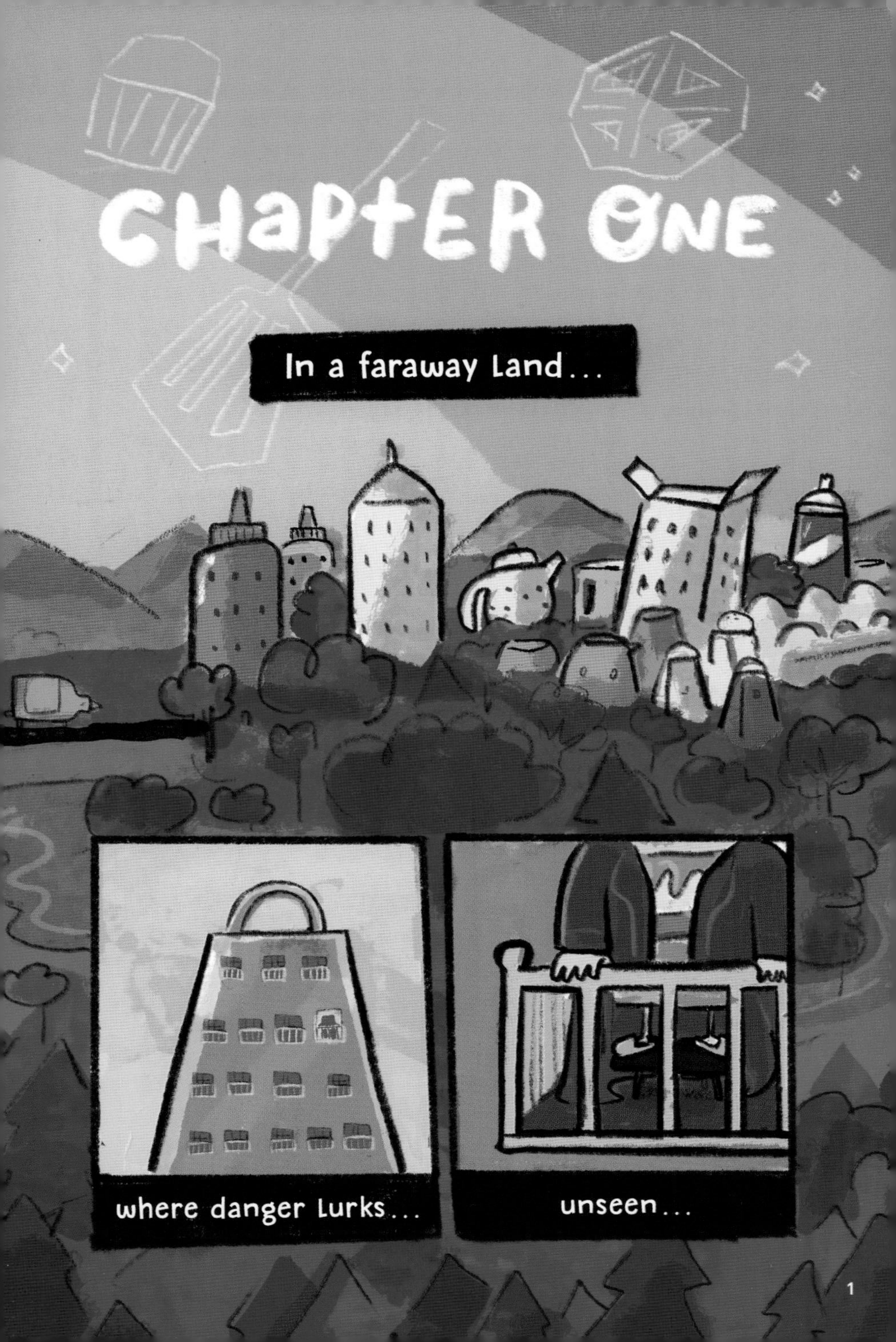
CHAPTER ONE
In a faraway land...
where danger lurks...
unseen...

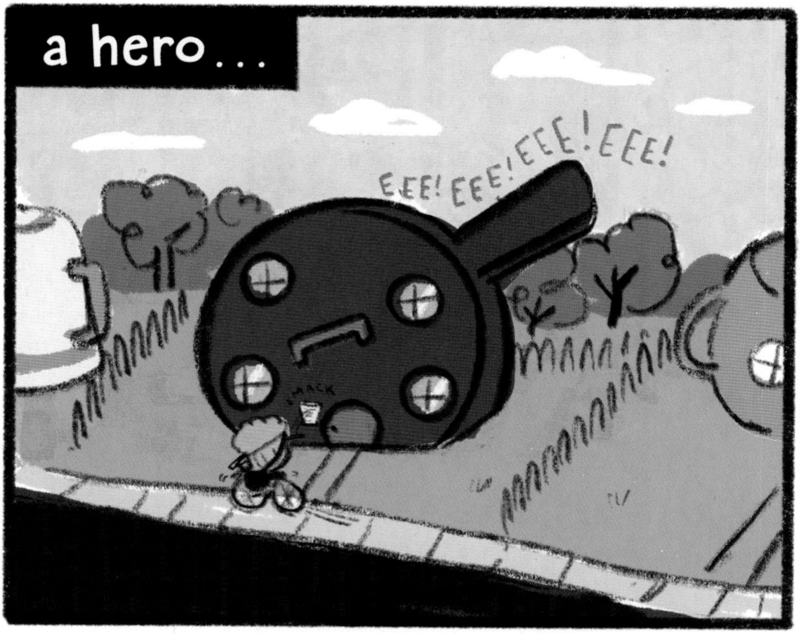
a hero...
EEE! EEE! EEE! EEE!
SMACK

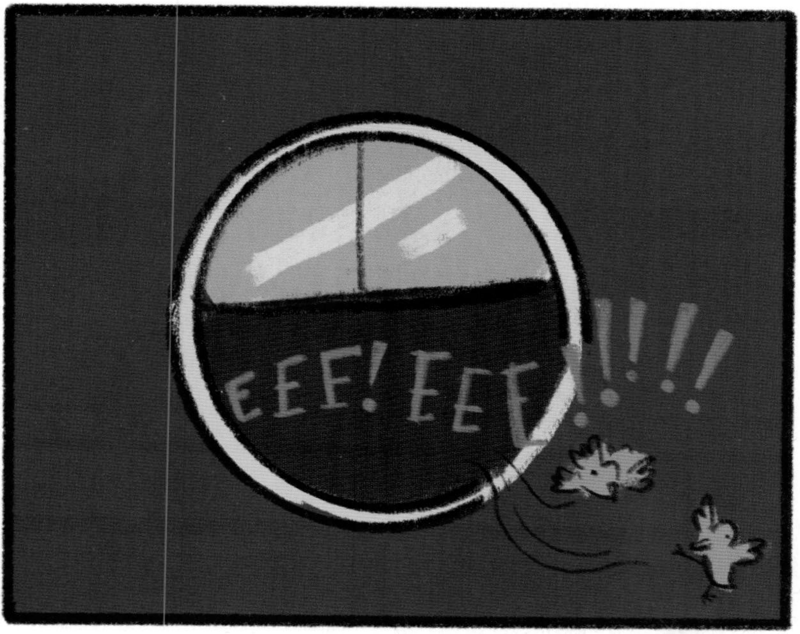
EEE! EEE!!!!!

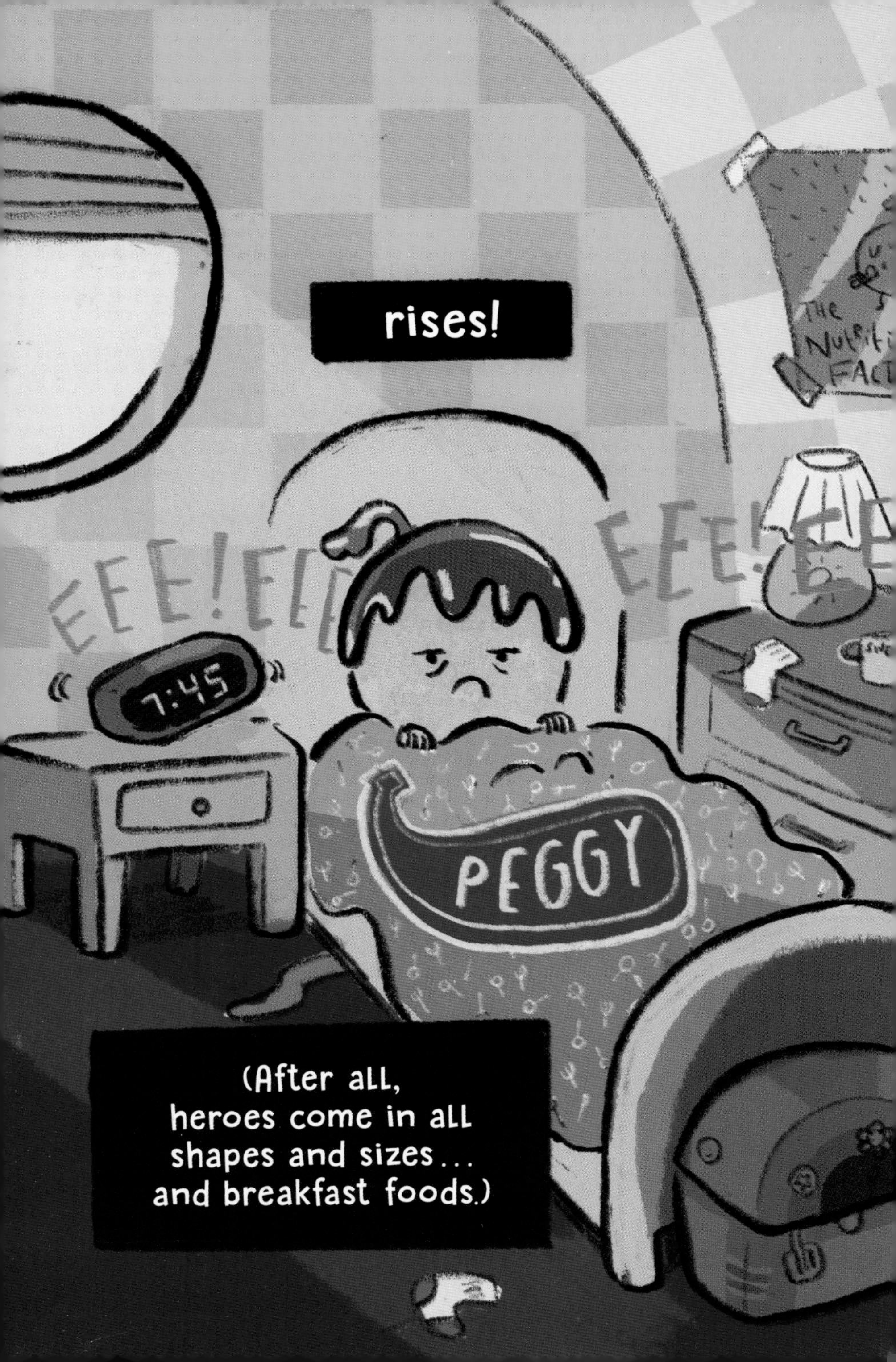
rises!
EEE!EEE
EEE!EEE
7:45
PEGGY
(After all,
heroes come in all
shapes and sizes . . .
and breakfast foods.)

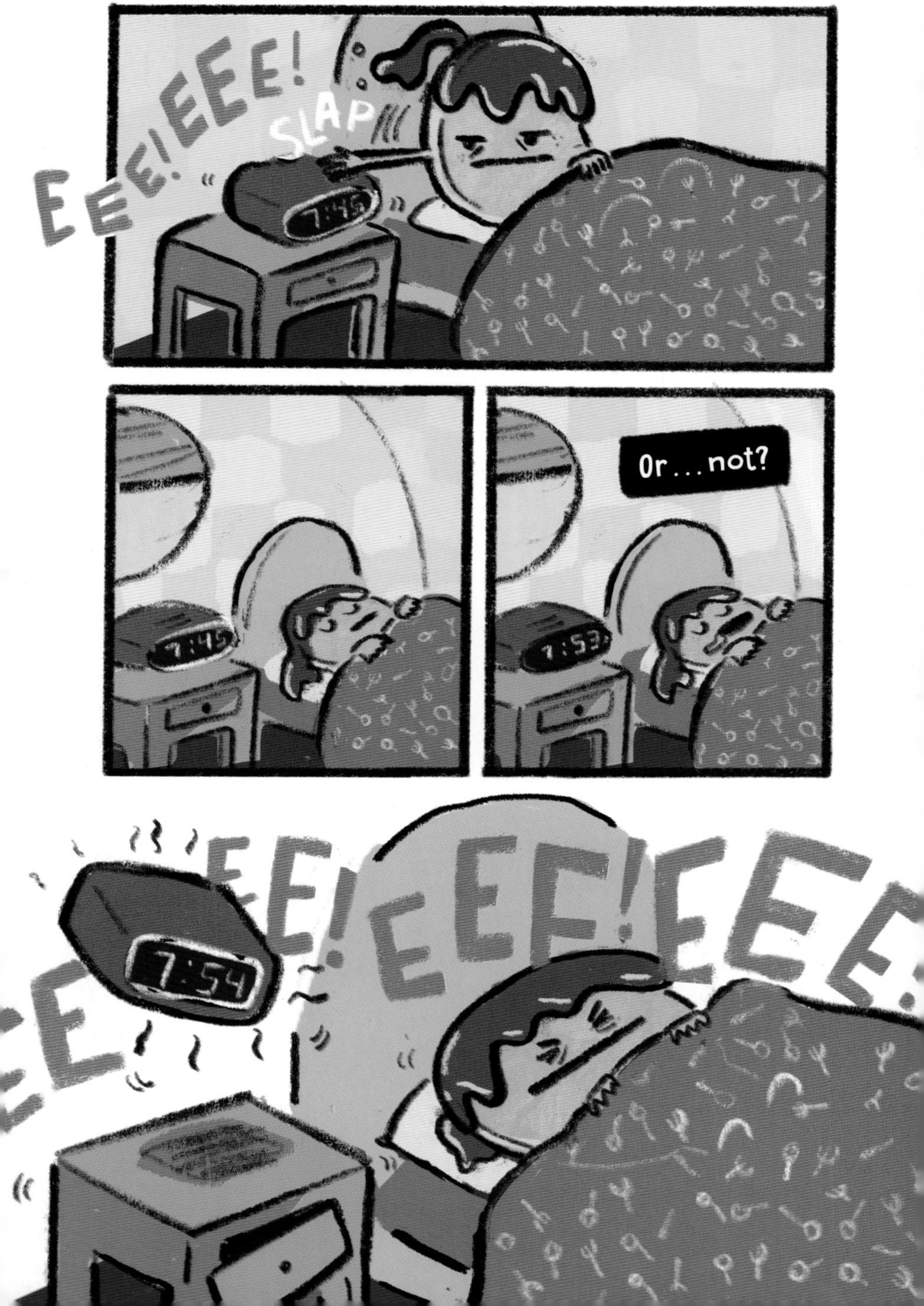
EEE!EEE!
SLAP
7:45
7:45
Or... not?
7:53
7:54
EE!EE!EEE!EEE!

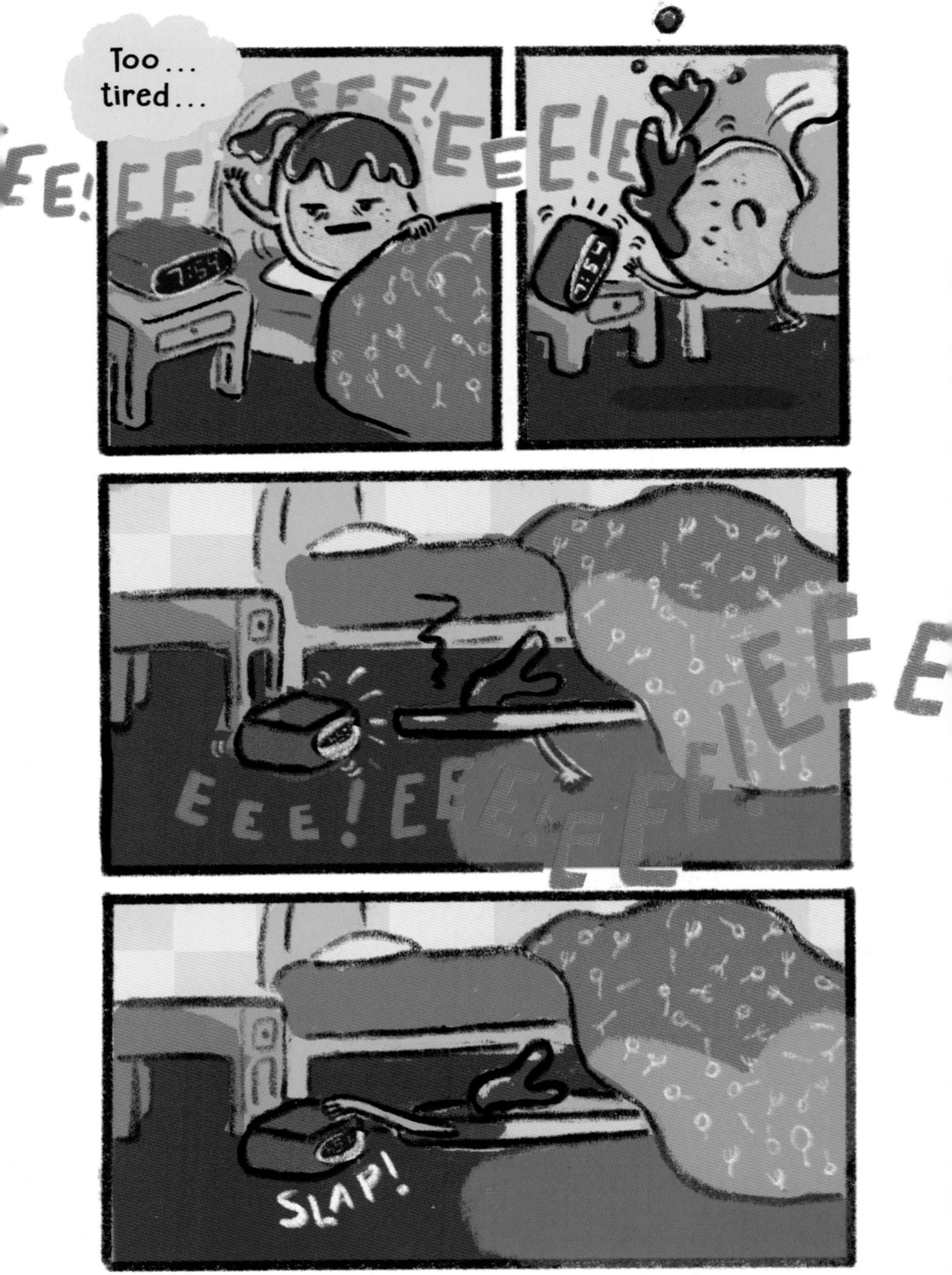
Too... tired...
EEE!EEEE!EEE!E
EEE!E
EEE!EEEE
SLAP!

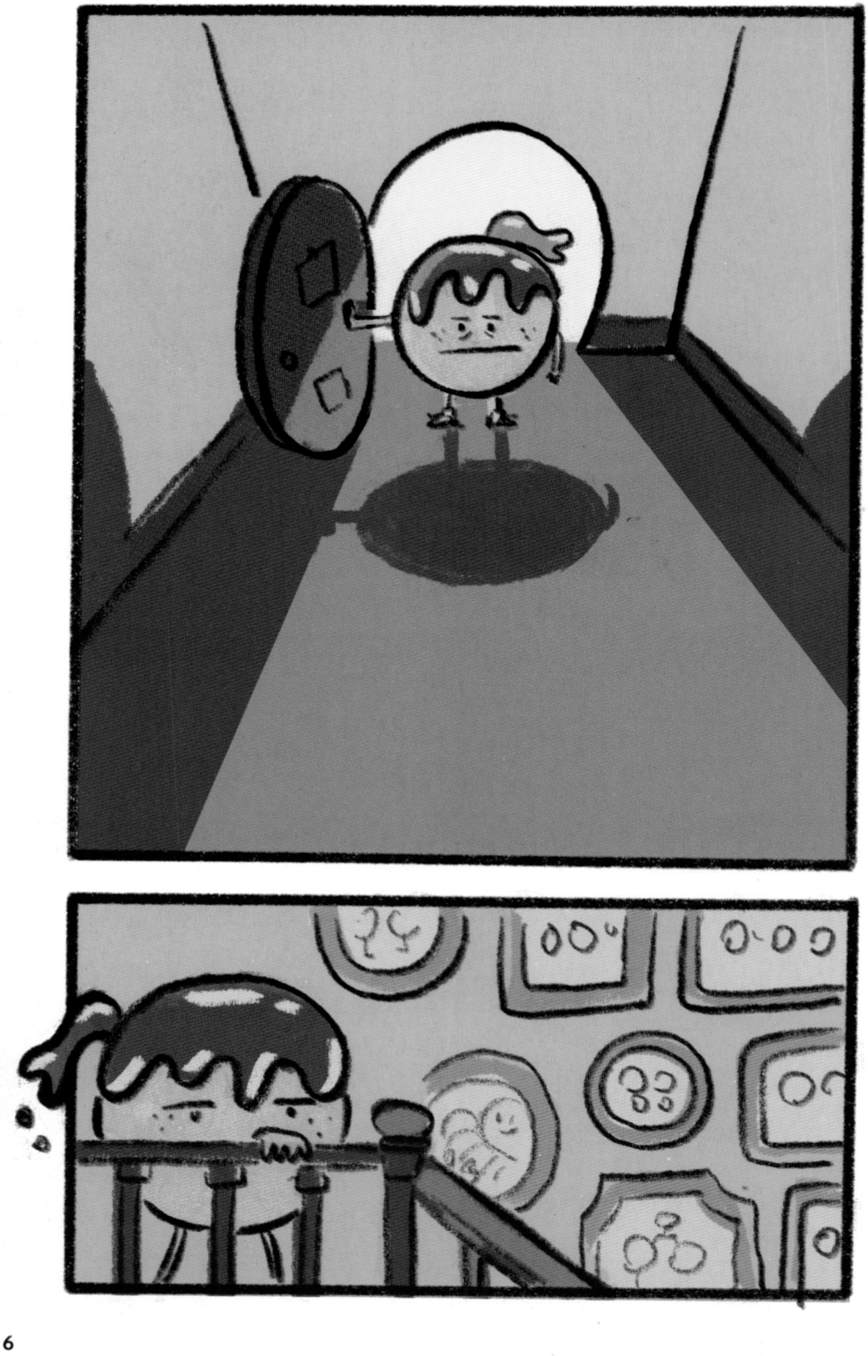

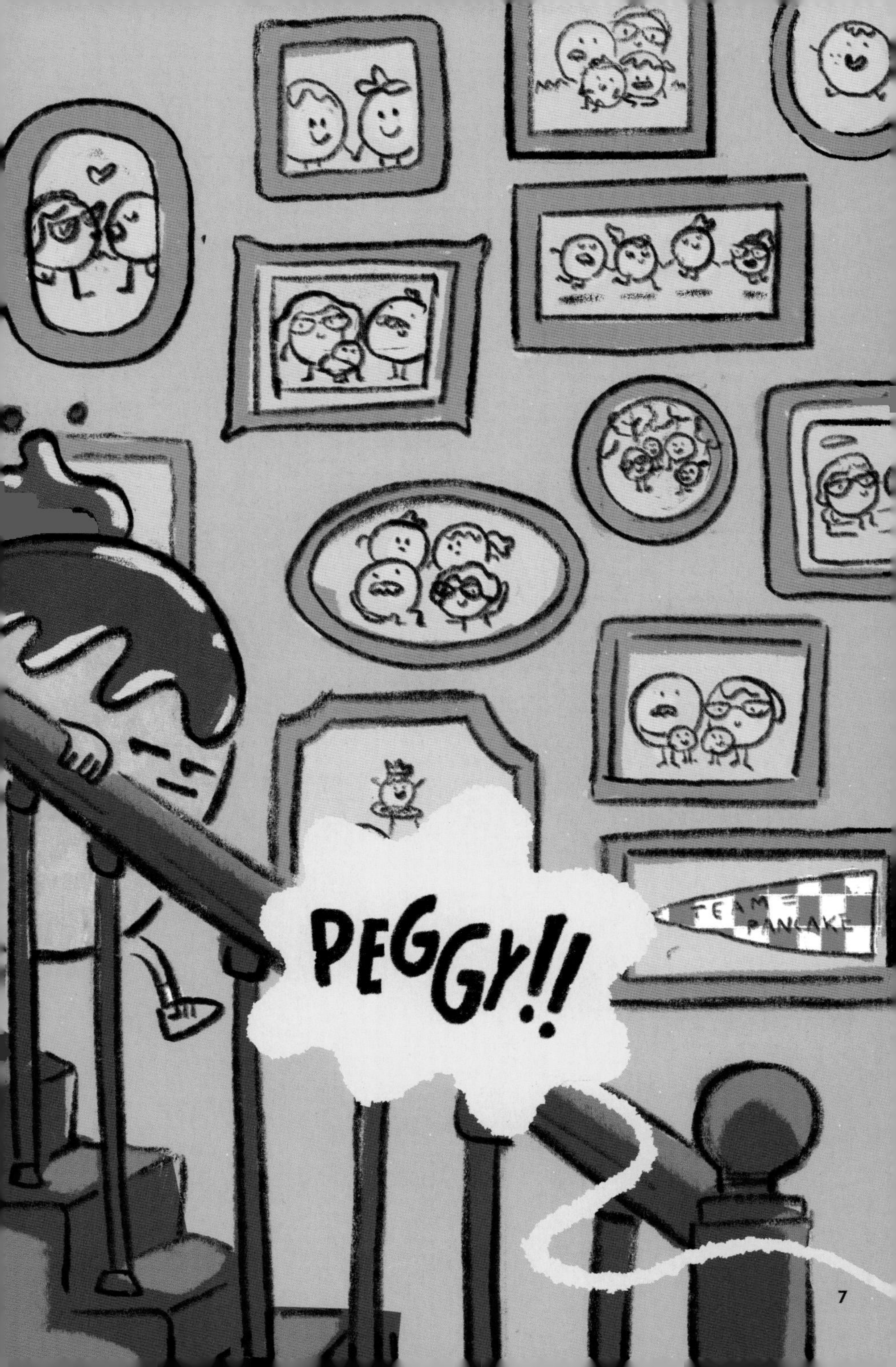

PEGGY!!
TEAM PANCAKE

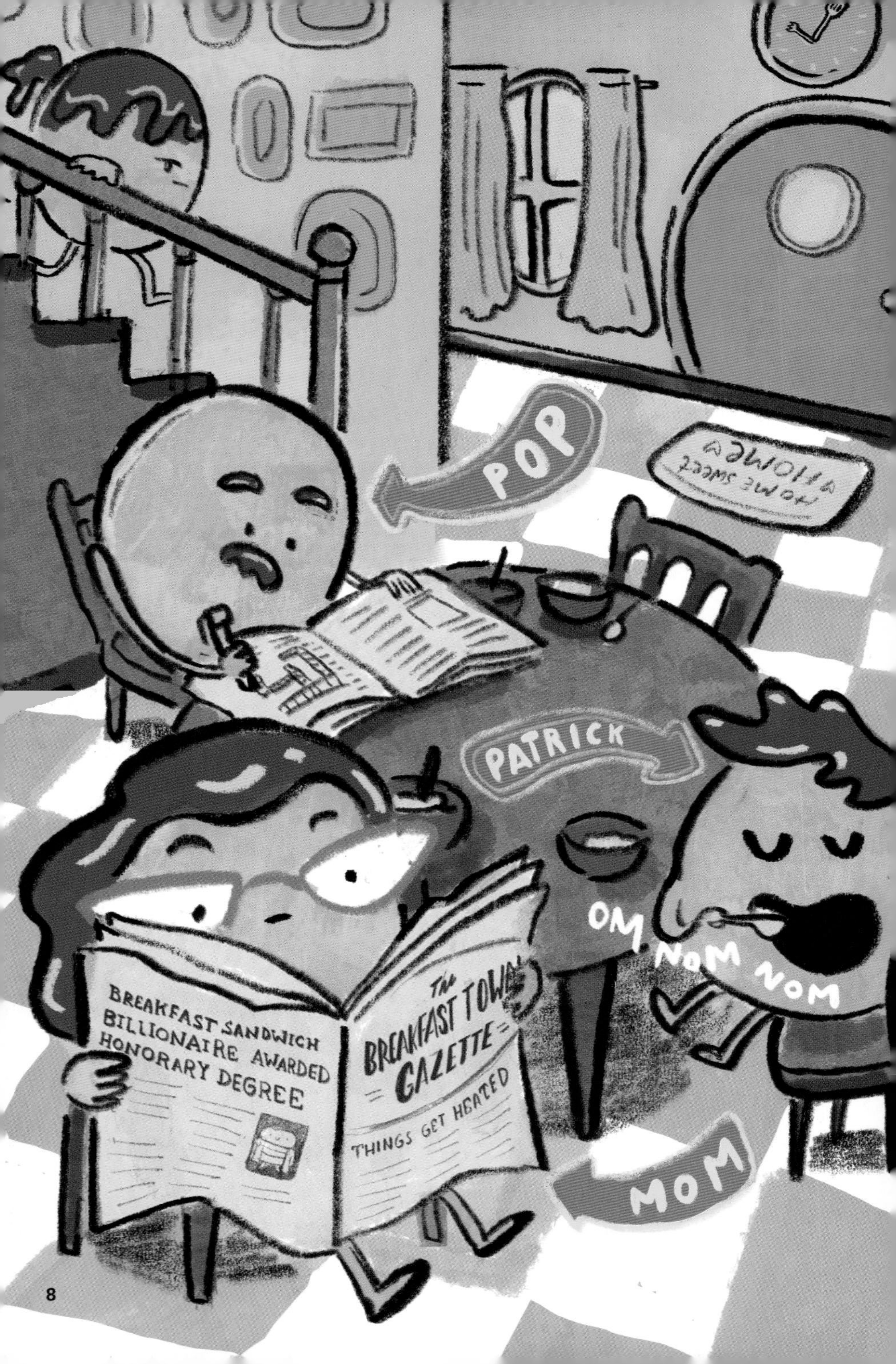
POP
HOME sweet HOME
PATRICK
BREAKFAST SANDWICH BILLIONAIRE AWARDED HONORARY DEGREE
The BREAKFAST TOWN GAZETTE
THINGS GET HEATED
OM NOM NOM
MOM

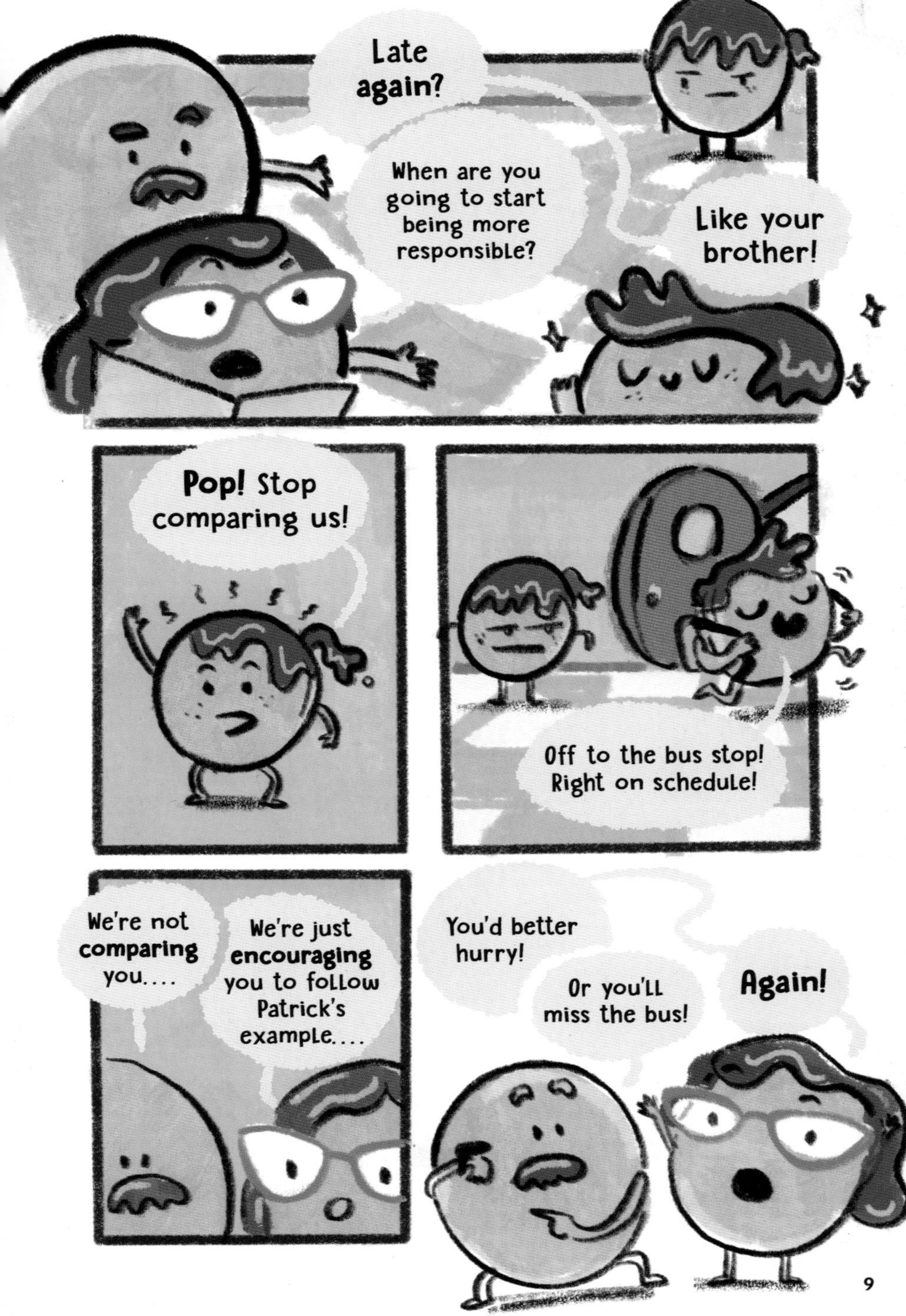
Late again?
When are you going to start being more responsible?
Like your brother!
Pop! Stop comparing us!
Off to the bus stop! Right on schedule!
We're not comparing you....
We're just encouraging you to follow Patrick's example....
You'd better hurry!
Or you'll miss the bus!
Again!

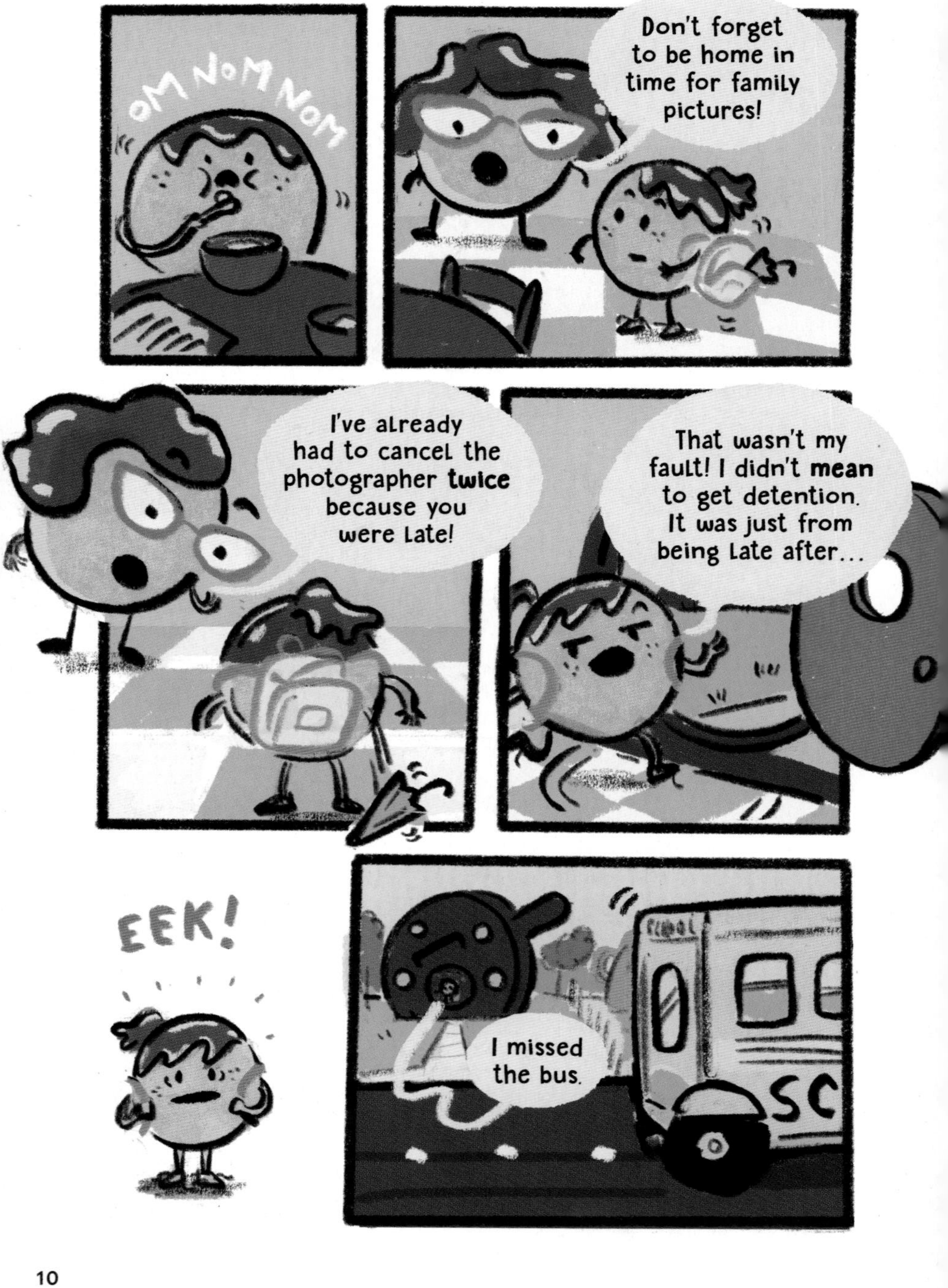
OM NOM NOM
Don't forget to be home in time for family pictures!
I've already had to cancel the photographer **twice** because you were late!
That wasn't my fault! I didn't **mean** to get detention. It was just from being late after...
EEK!
I missed the bus.
SC

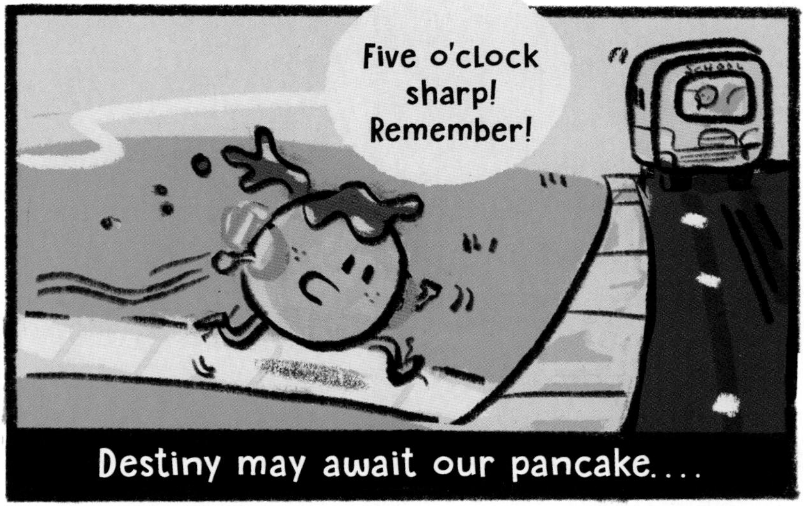
Five o'clock sharp! Remember!
Destiny may await our pancake....

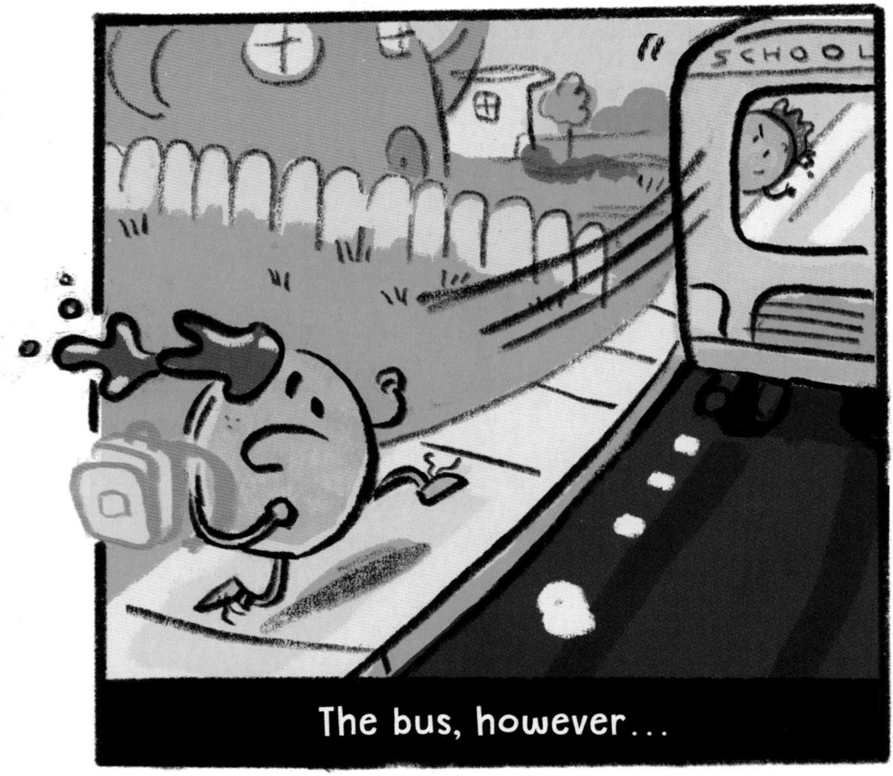
SCHOOL
The bus, however...

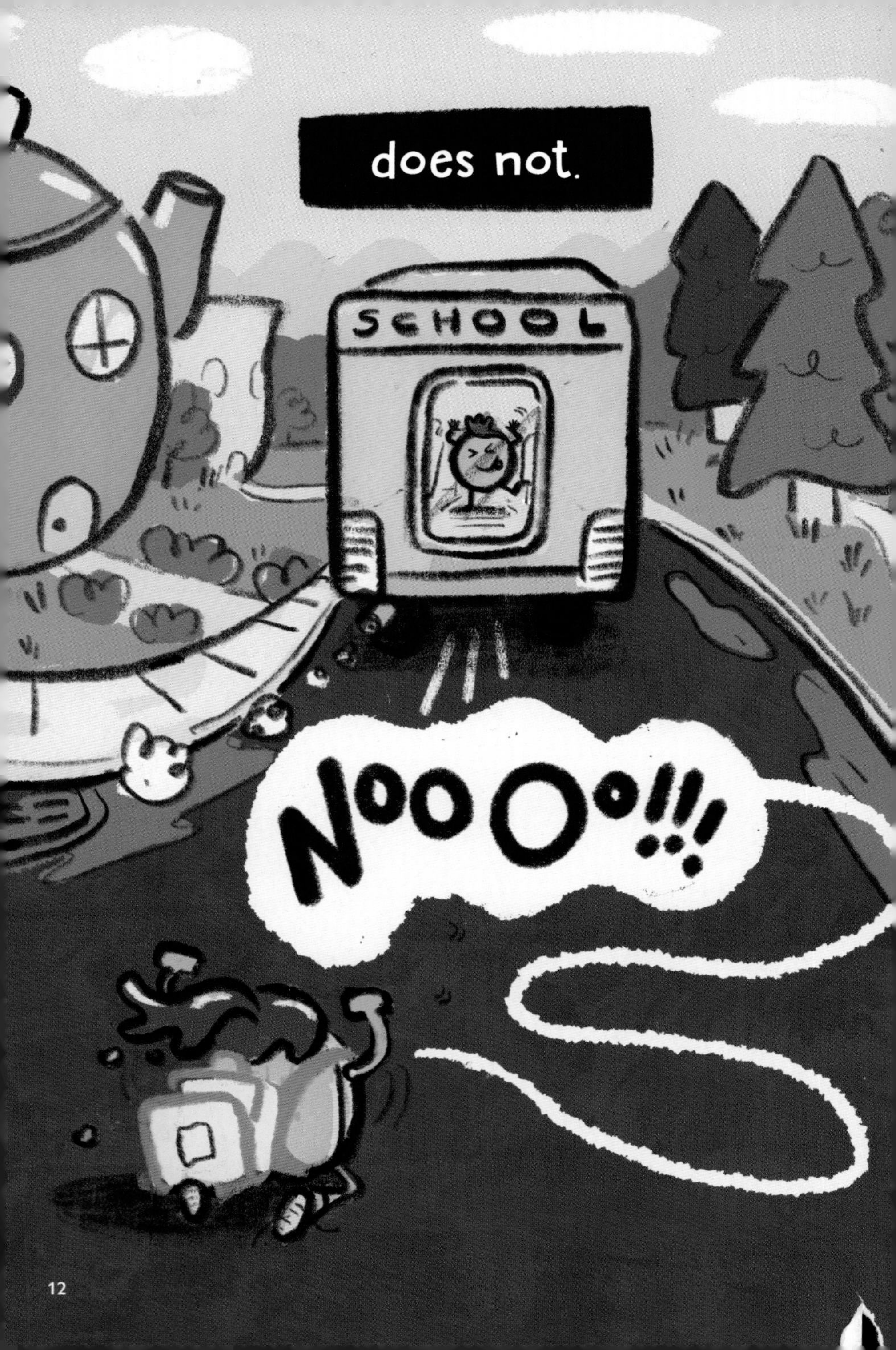
does not.
SCHOOL
NOOOO!!!

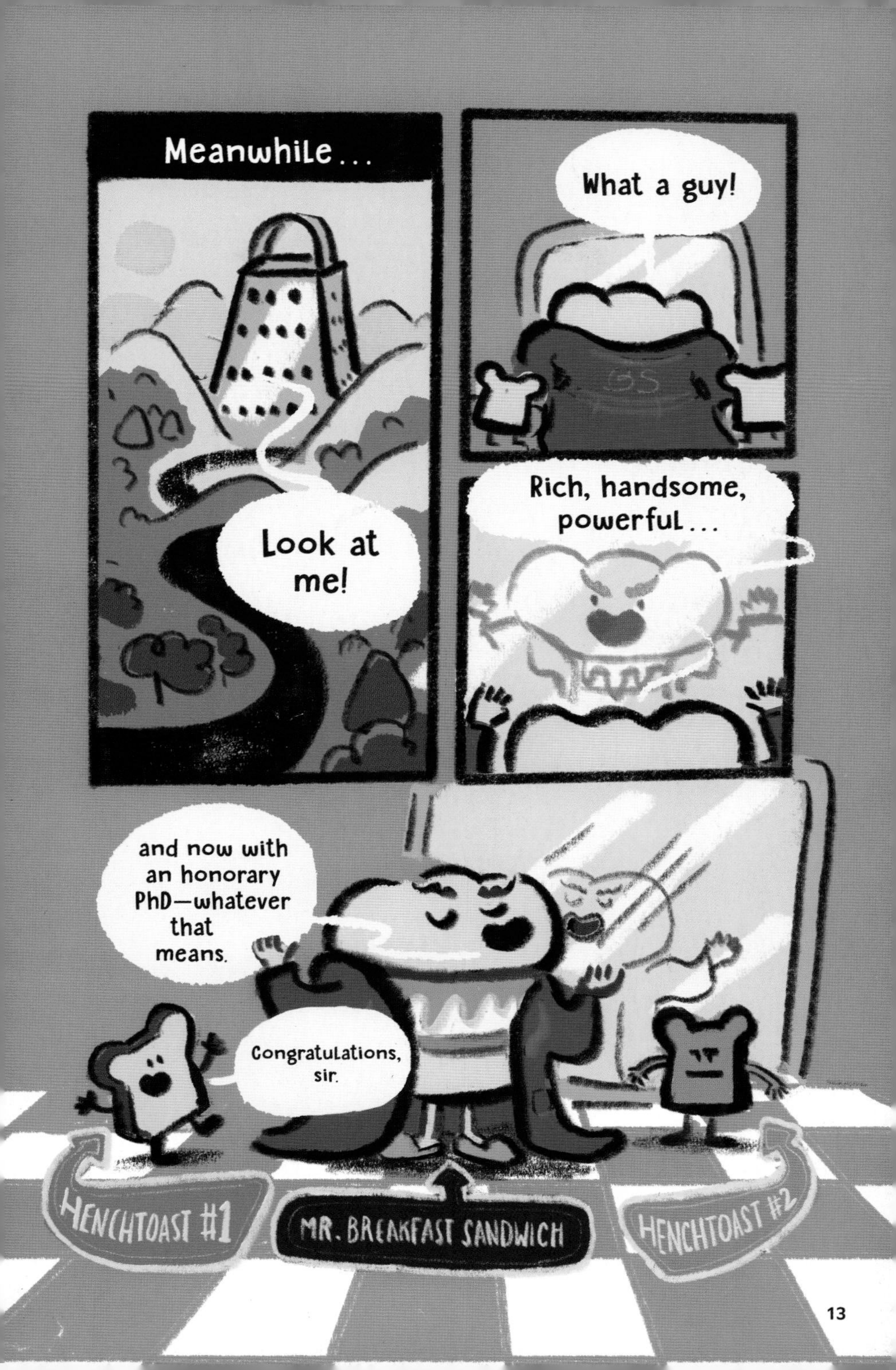

Meanwhile...
Look at me!
What a guy!
Rich, handsome, powerful...
and now with an honorary PhD—whatever that means.
Congratulations, sir.
HENCHTOAST #1
MR. BREAKFAST SANDWICH
HENCHTOAST #2

Sir?

I think you mean doctor.

Con-con-congratulations, **D-D-Doctor,** sir.

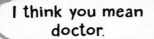

DR. BREAKFAST SANDWICH

PANT PANT

That's more like it. Yes, I'm officially a doctor now!

Those fools gave me a PhD because I gave **stolen** money to a **made-up** charity!

Just like I planned...

HA HA HA HA!

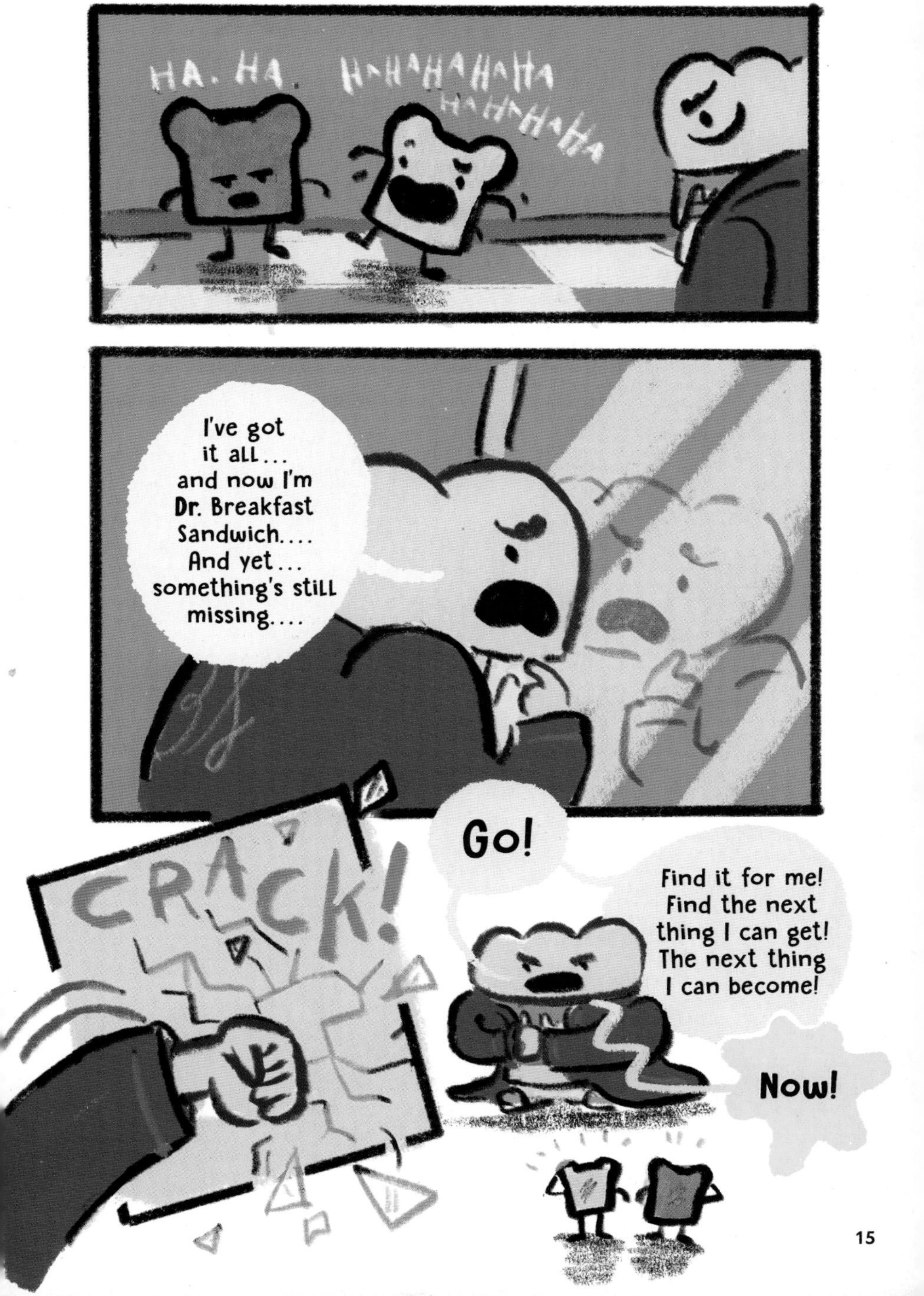
HA. HA.
HAHAHAHAHAHA HAHAHAHAHA
I've got it all... and now I'm Dr. Breakfast Sandwich.... And yet... something's still missing....
CRACK!
Go!
Find it for me! Find the next thing I can get! The next thing I can become!
Now!

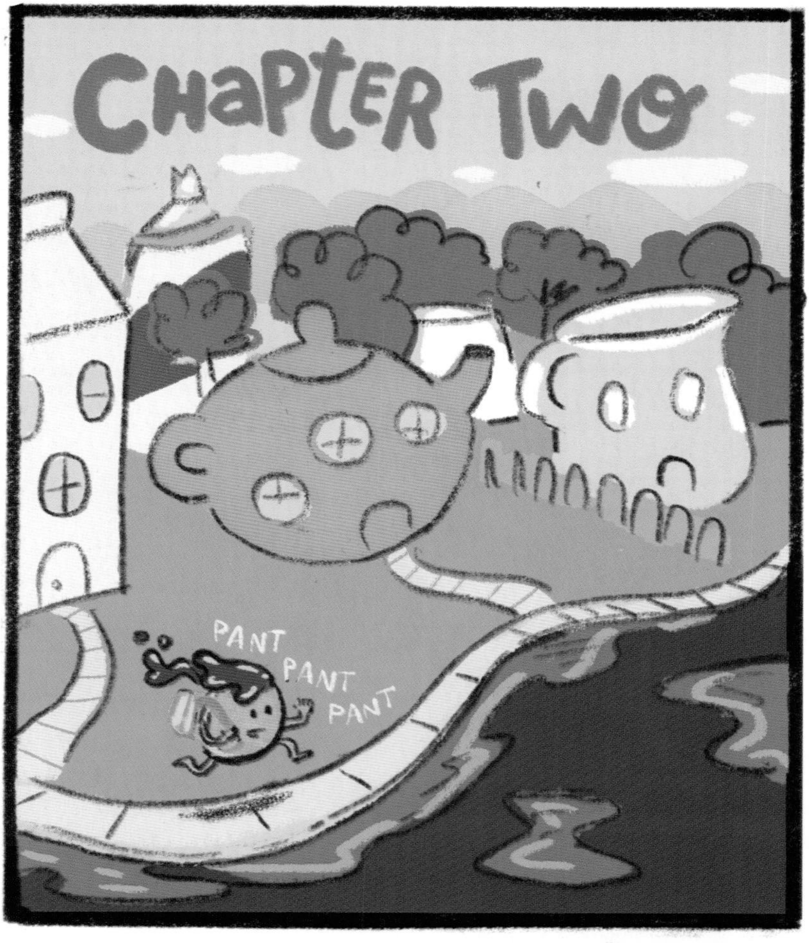
CHAPTER TWO
PANT PANT PANT

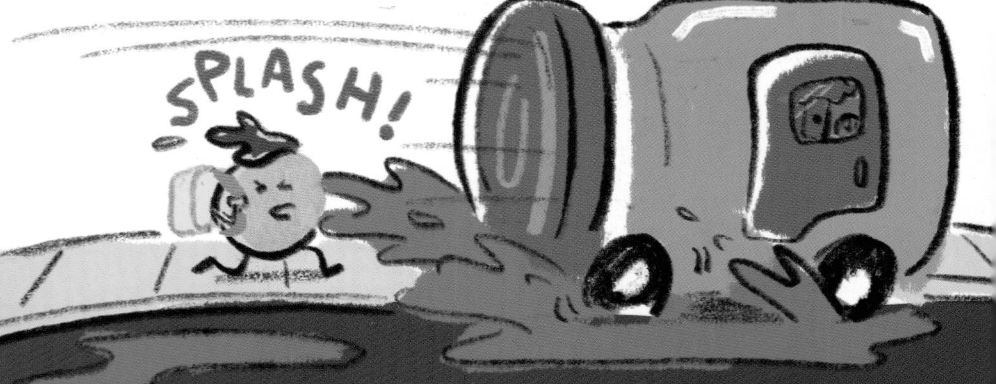
SPLASH!

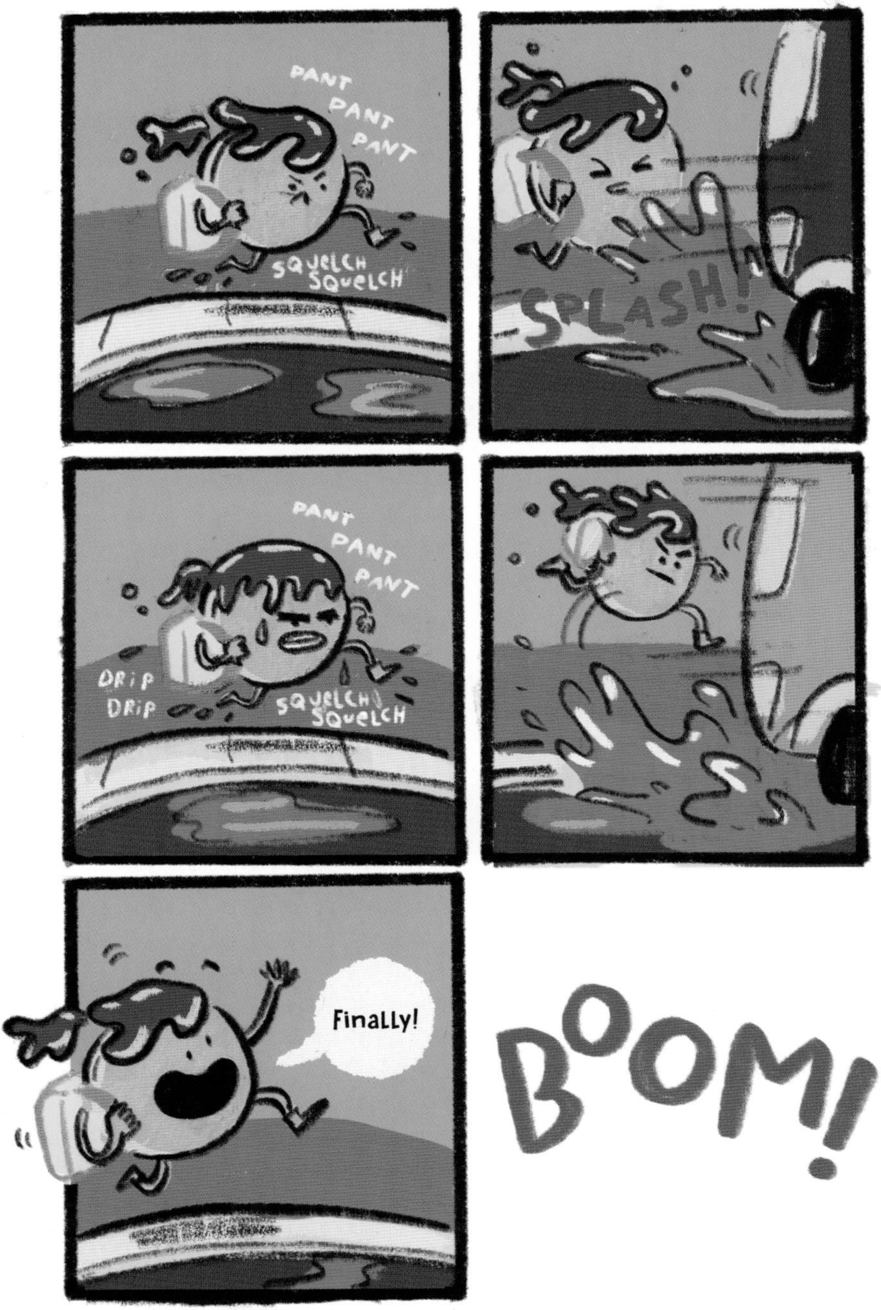
PANT
PANT
PANT
SQUELCH
SQUELCH
SPLASH!
PANT
PANT
PANT
DRIP
DRIP
SQUELCH
SQUELCH
FinaLLy!
BOOM!

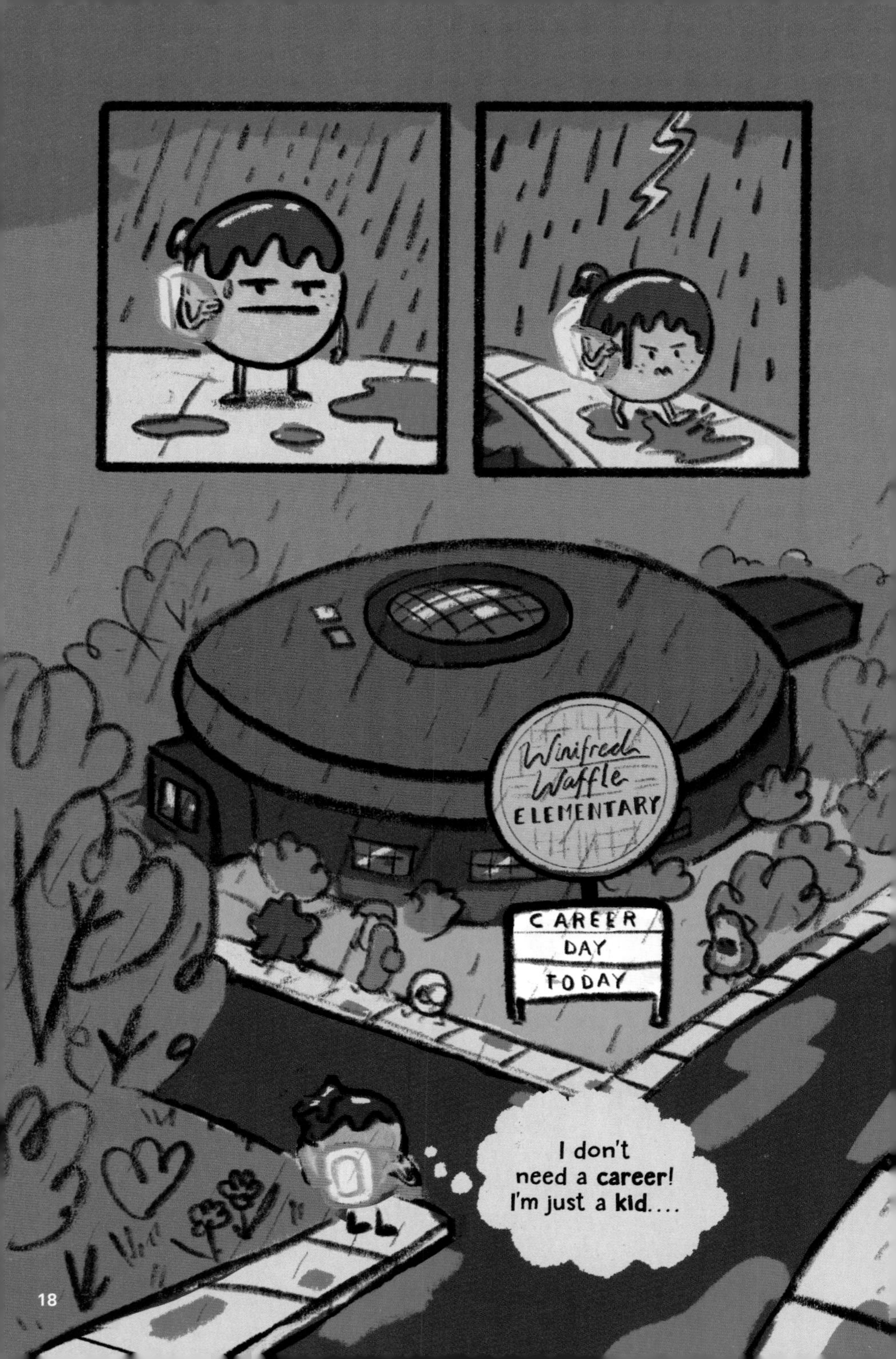
Winifred Waffle ELEMENTARY
CAREER DAY TODAY
I don't need a career! I'm just a kid....

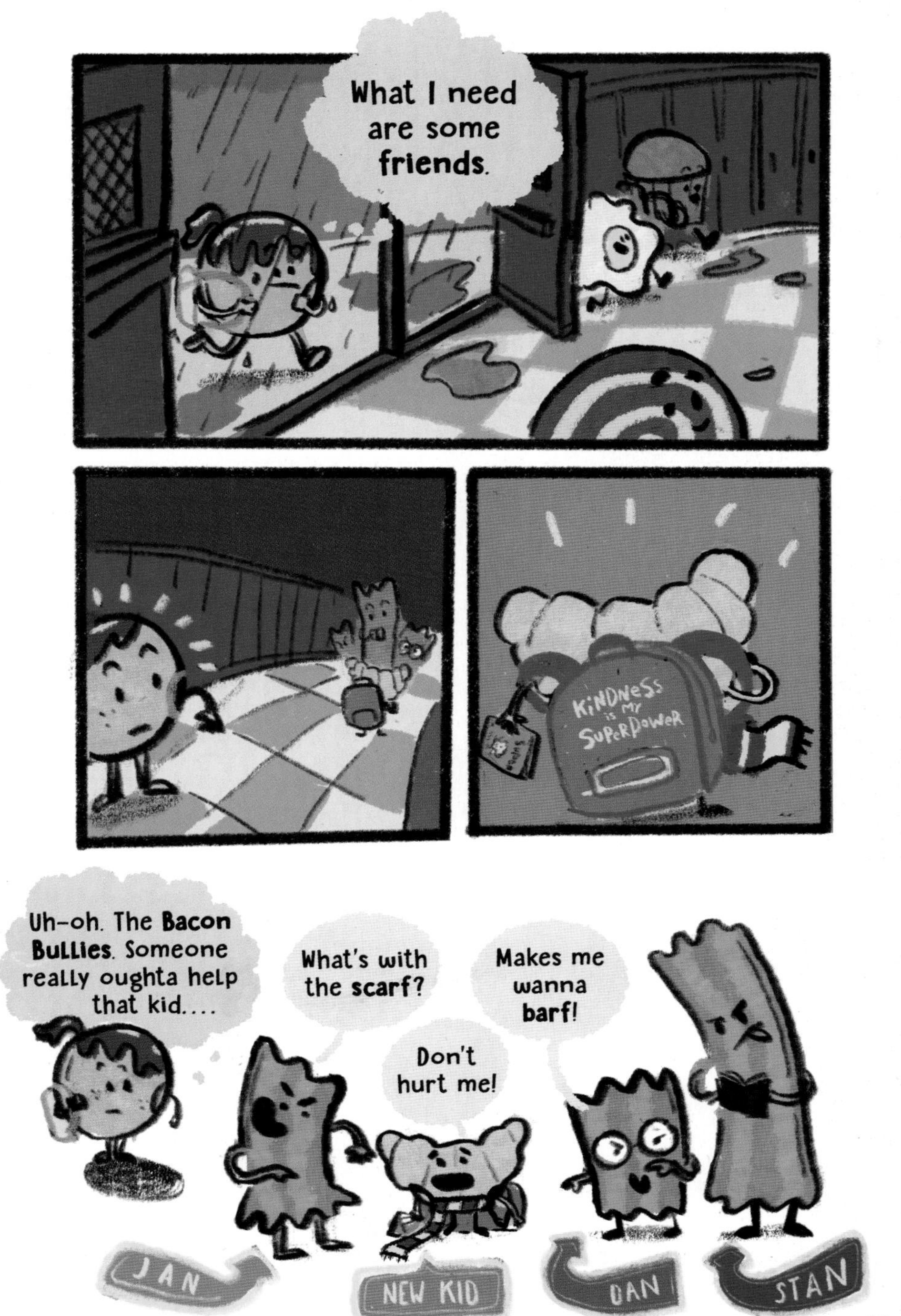

What I need are some **friends**.
KINDNESS is MY SUPERPOWER
Uh-oh. The **Bacon Bullies**. Someone really oughta help that kid....
What's with the **scarf**?
Don't hurt me!
Makes me wanna **barf**!
JAN
NEW KID
DAN
STAN

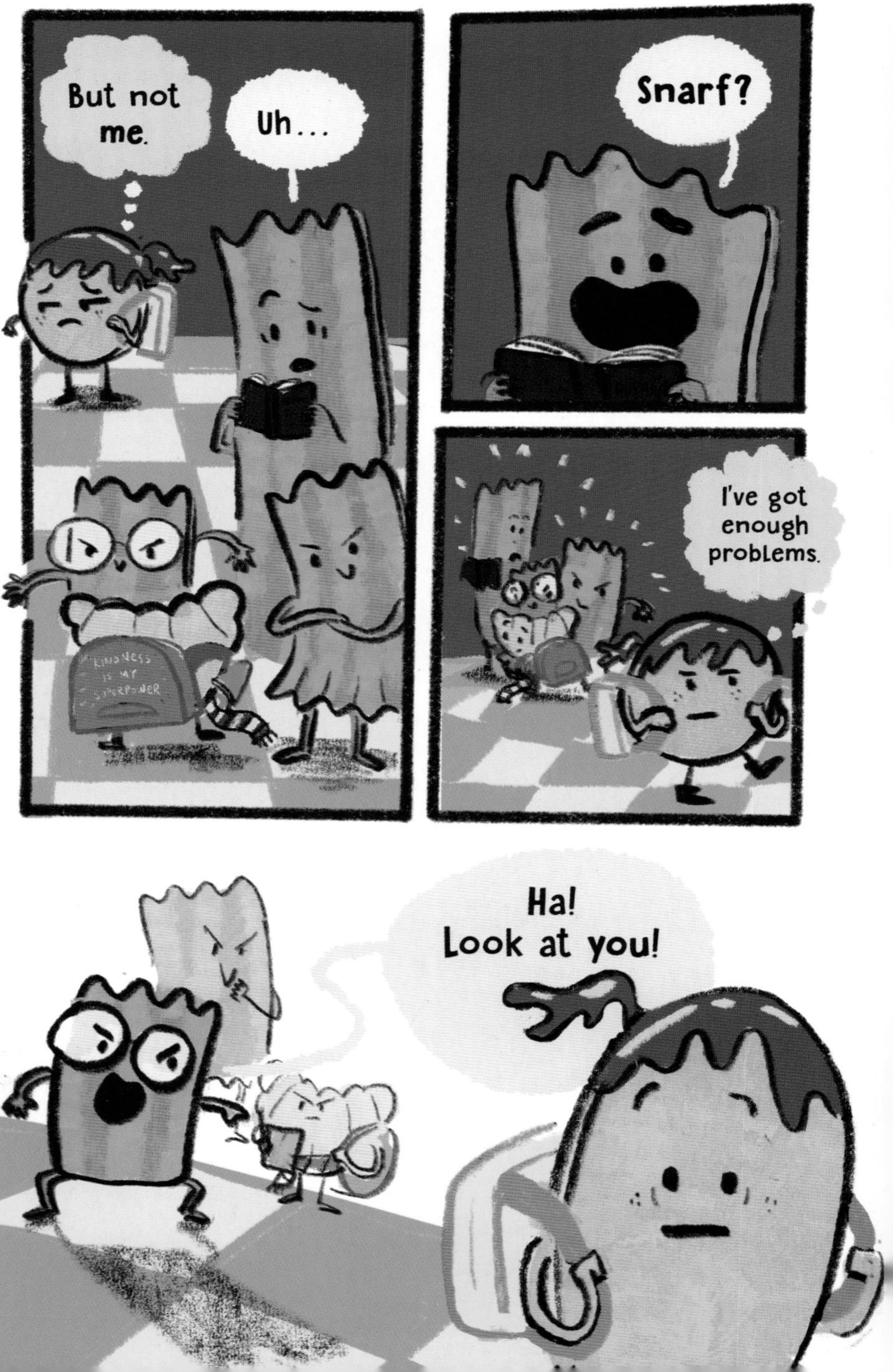
But not me.
Uh...
KINDNESS IS MY SUPERPOWER
Snarf?
I've got enough problems.
Ha!
Look at you!

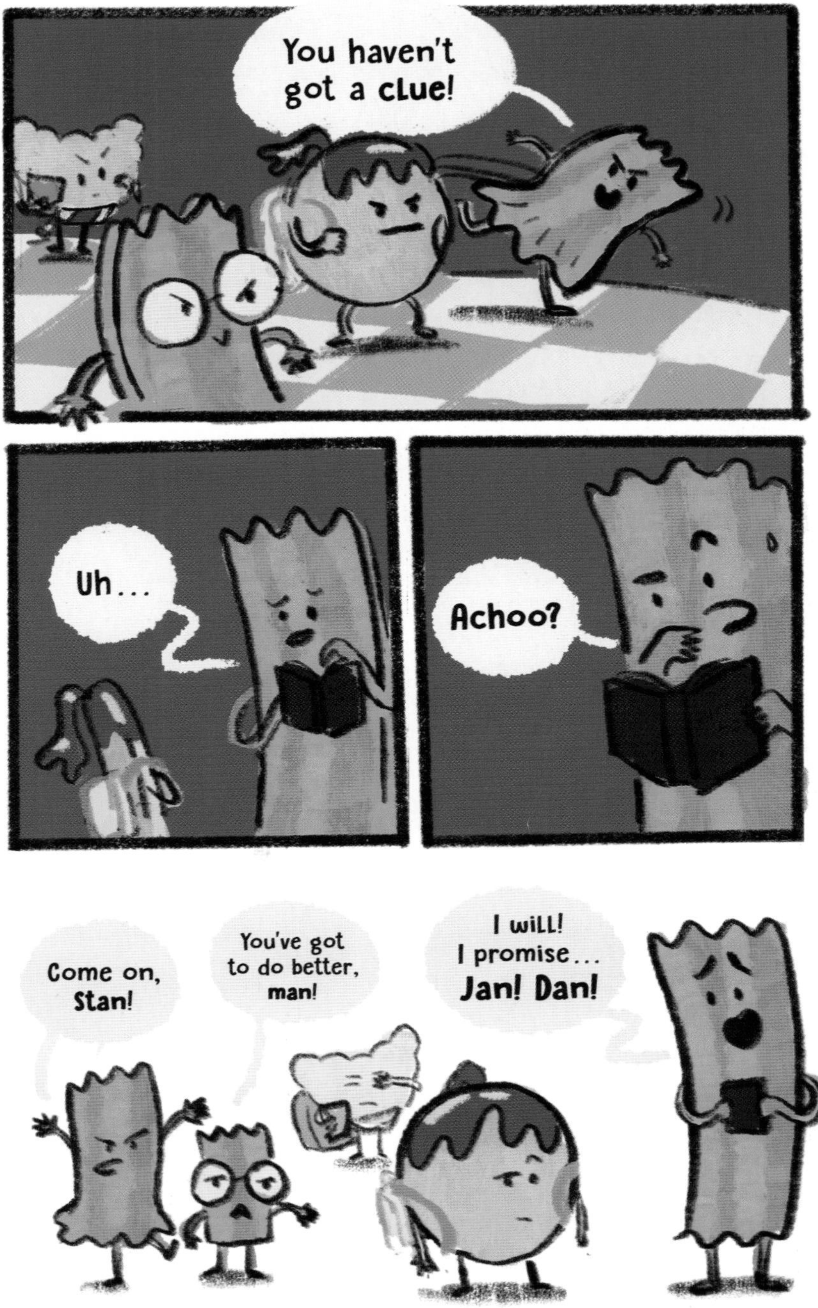

You haven't got a clue!
Uh...
Achoo?
Come on, Stan!
You've got to do better, man!
I will! I promise... Jan! Dan!

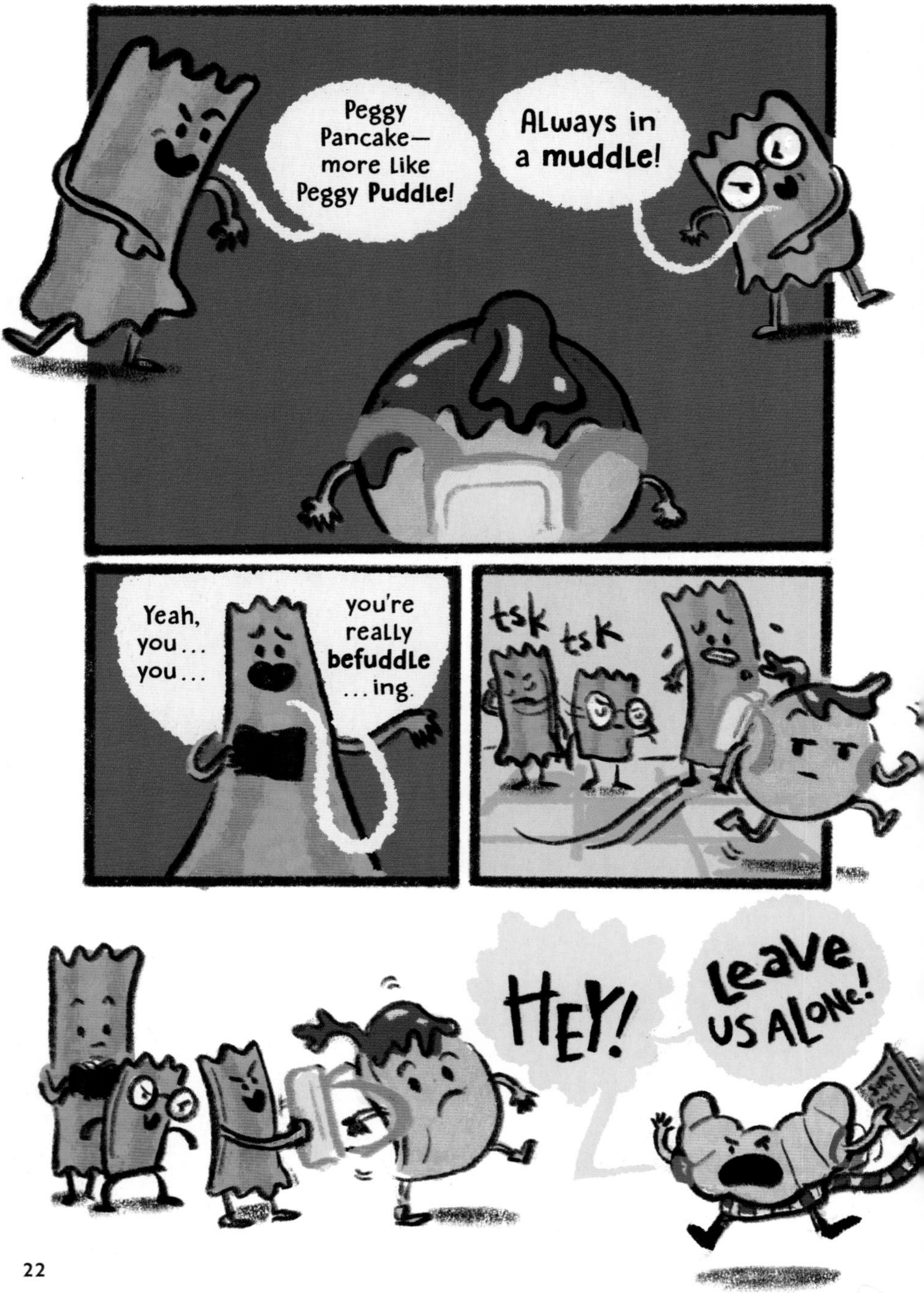
Peggy Pancake— more like Peggy Puddle!
Always in a muddle!
Yeah, you... you...
you're really befuddle ...ing.
tsk
tsk
HEY!
Leave us alone!

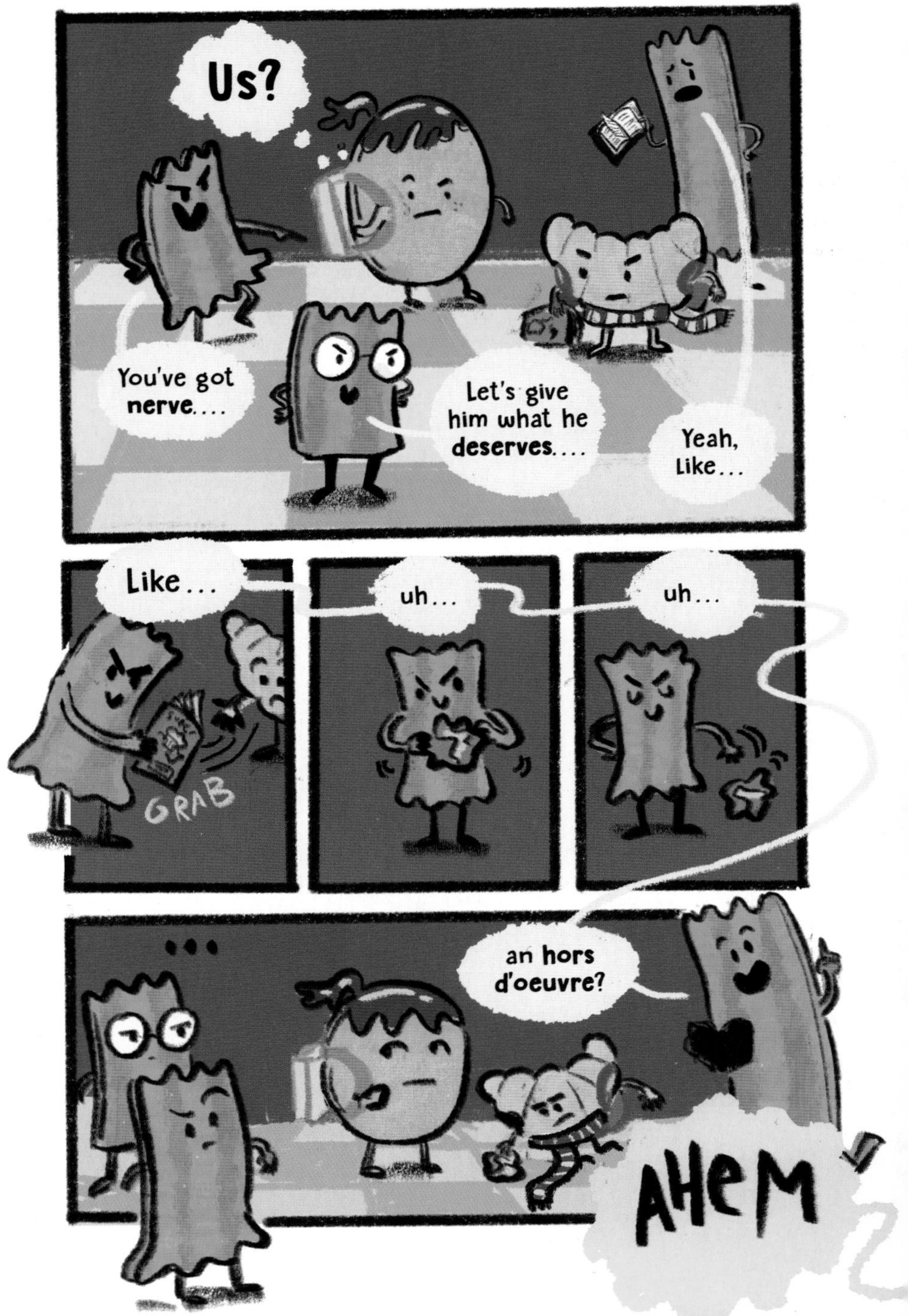
Us?
You've got nerve....
Let's give him what he deserves....
Yeah, Like...
Like...
GRAB
uh...
uh...
...
an hors d'oeuvre?
AHEM

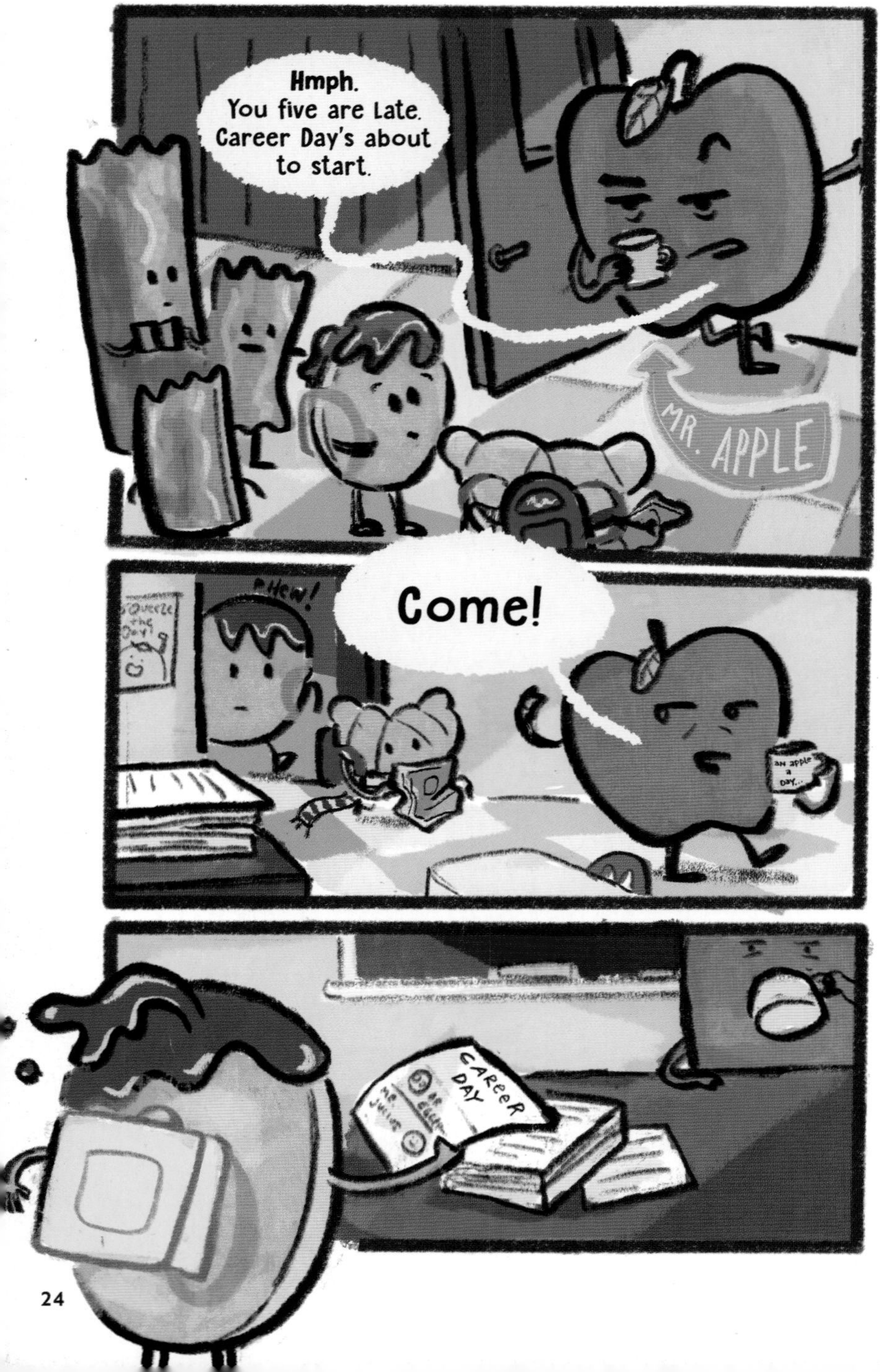
Hmph.
You five are Late.
Career Day's about
to start.
MR. APPLE
PHEW!
Squeeze the Day!
Come!
an apple a day...
CAREER DAY

Chapter Three

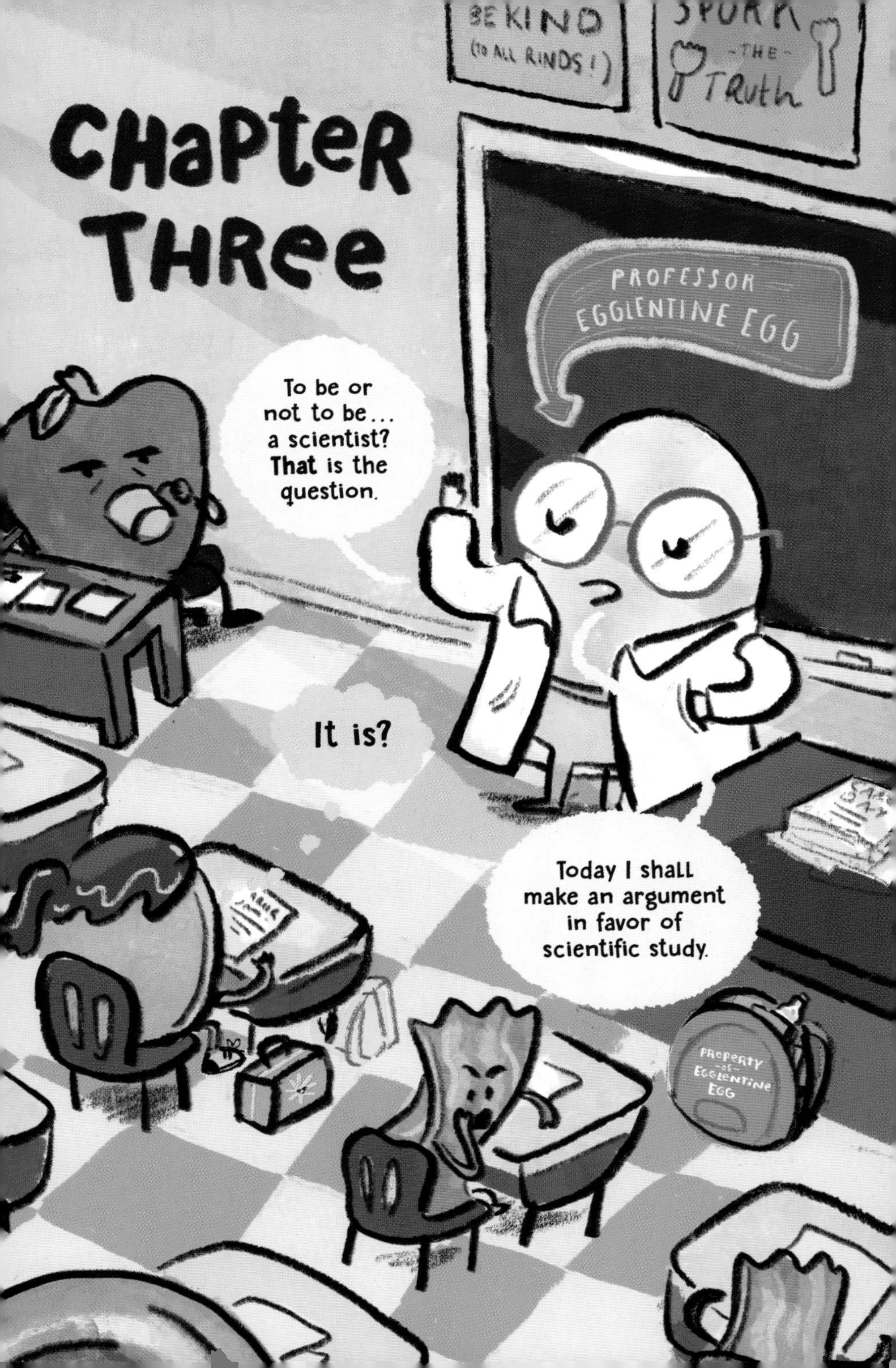

BE KIND (TO ALL RINDS!)
SPOON -THE- TRUTH
PROFESSOR EGGLENTINE EGG
To be or not to be... a scientist? That is the question.
It is?
Today I shall make an argument in favor of scientific study.
PROPERTY -OF- EGGLENTINE EGG

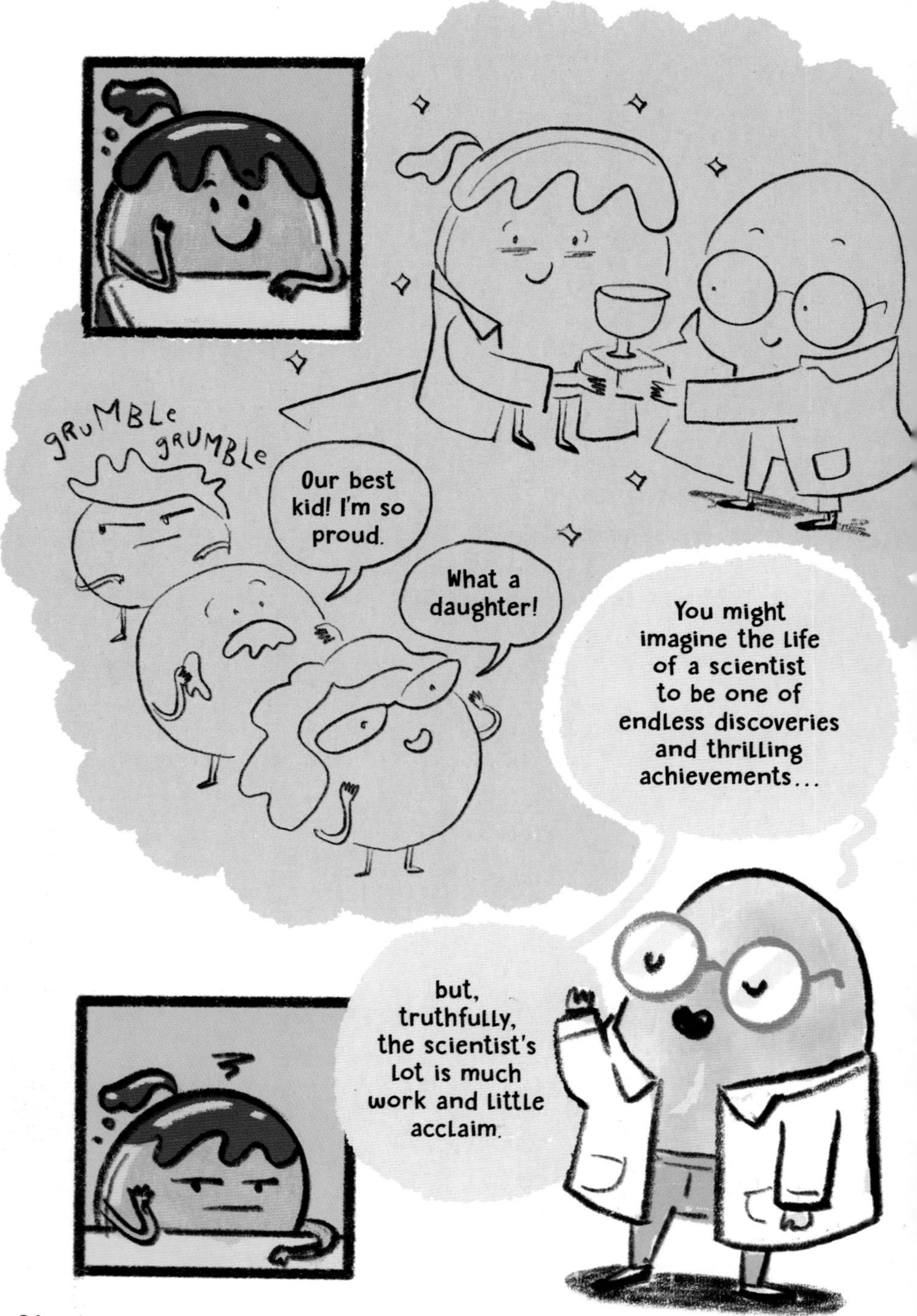
grumble grumble
Our best kid! I'm so proud.
What a daughter!
You might imagine the life of a scientist to be one of endless discoveries and thrilling achievements...
but, truthfully, the scientist's lot is much work and little acclaim.

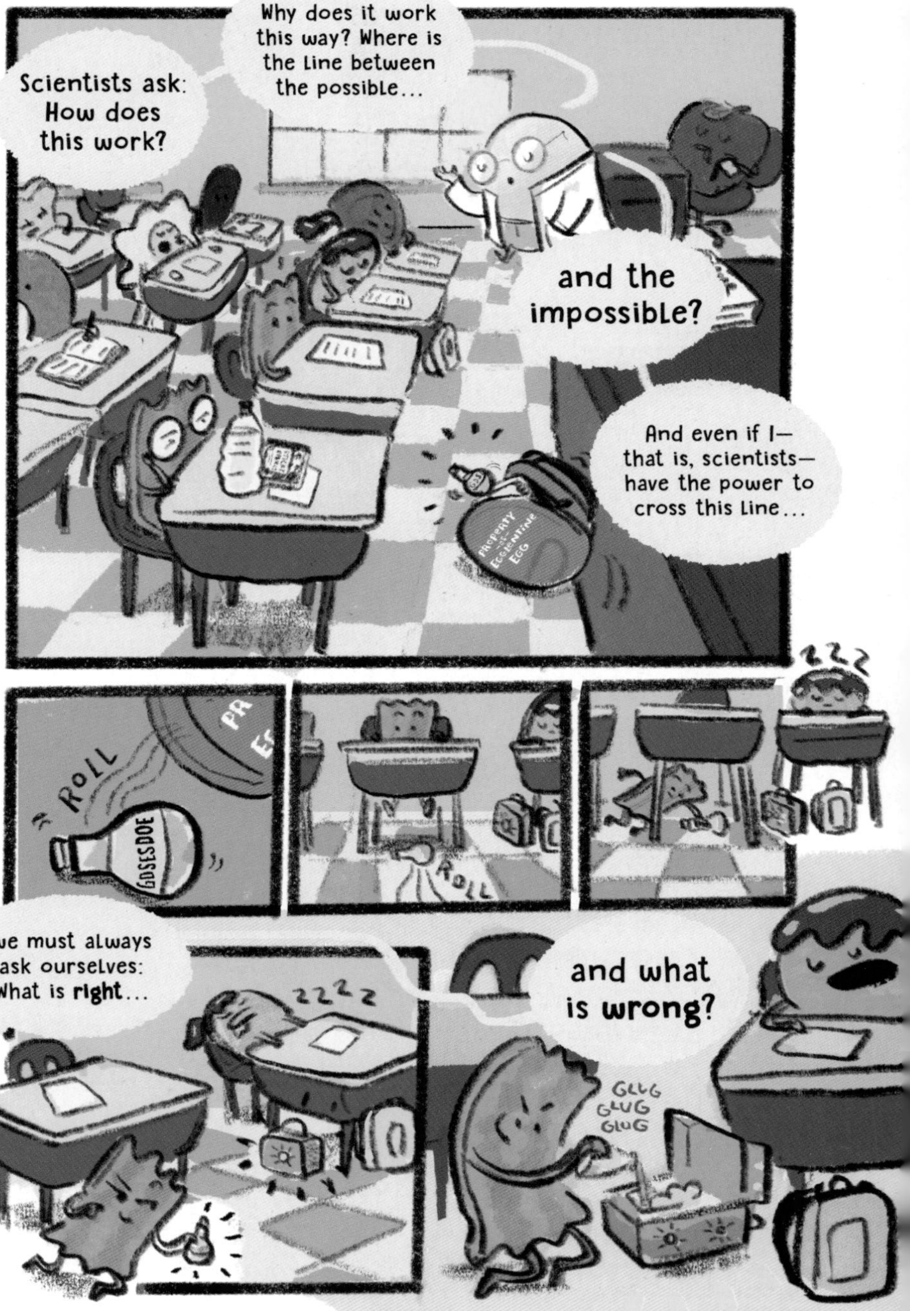
Scientists ask: How does this work?
Why does it work this way? Where is the line between the possible...
and the impossible?
And even if I—that is, scientists—have the power to cross this line...
PROPERTY OF EGGLENTINE EGG
ROLL
GOSESDOE
ROLL
ZZZ
we must always ask ourselves: What is right...
and what is wrong?
ZZZZ
GLUG GLUG GLUG

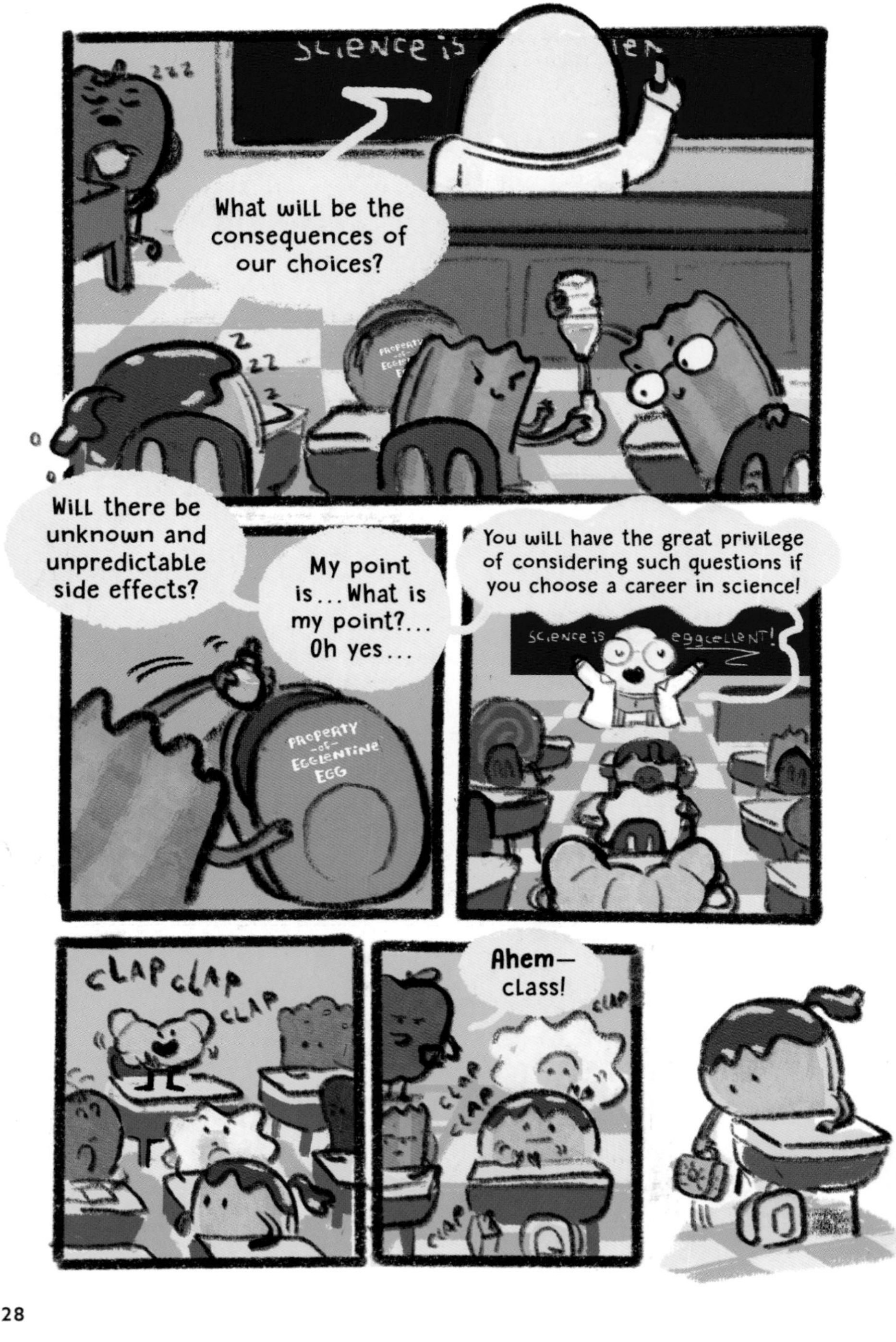
What will be the consequences of our choices?
Will there be unknown and unpredictable side effects?
PROPERTY -of- EGGLENTINE EGG
My point is... What is my point?... Oh yes...
You will have the great privilege of considering such questions if you choose a career in science!
SCIENCE IS EGGCELLENT!
CLAP CLAP CLAP
Ahem— class!
CLAP
CLAP CLAP
CLAP

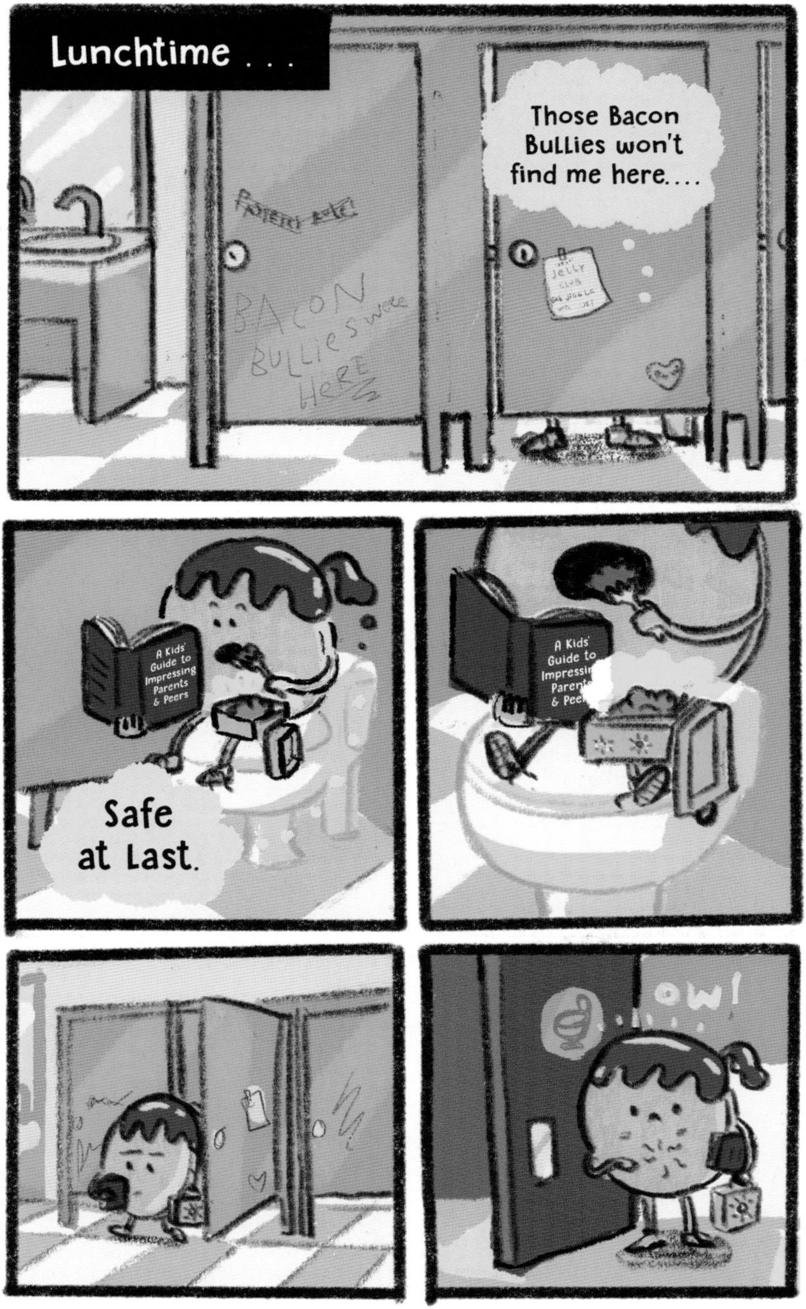
Lunchtime . . .
Those Bacon Bullies won't find me here....
BACON BULLIES WERE HERE
A Kids' Guide to Impressing Parents & Peers
Safe at Last.
OW!

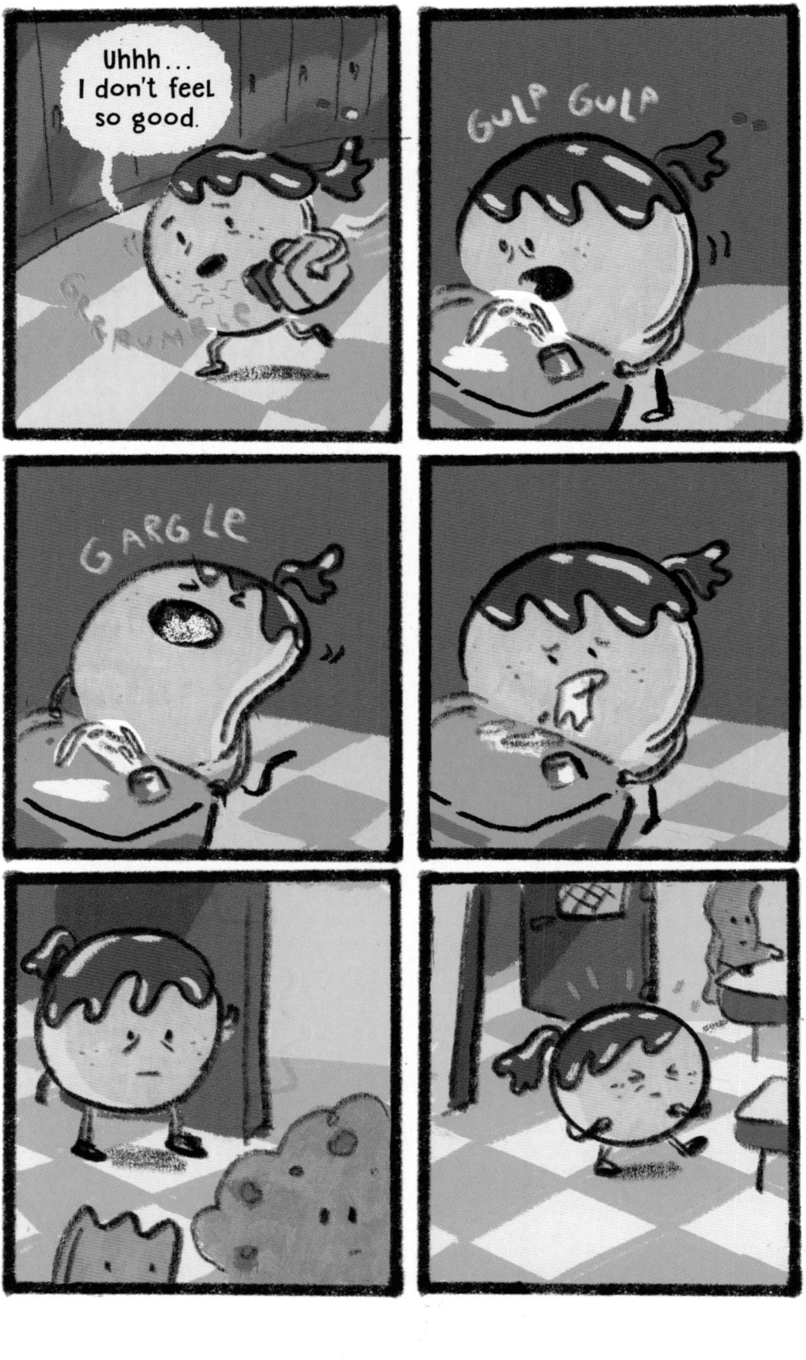
Uhhh... I don't feeL so good.
GULP GULP
GARGLE

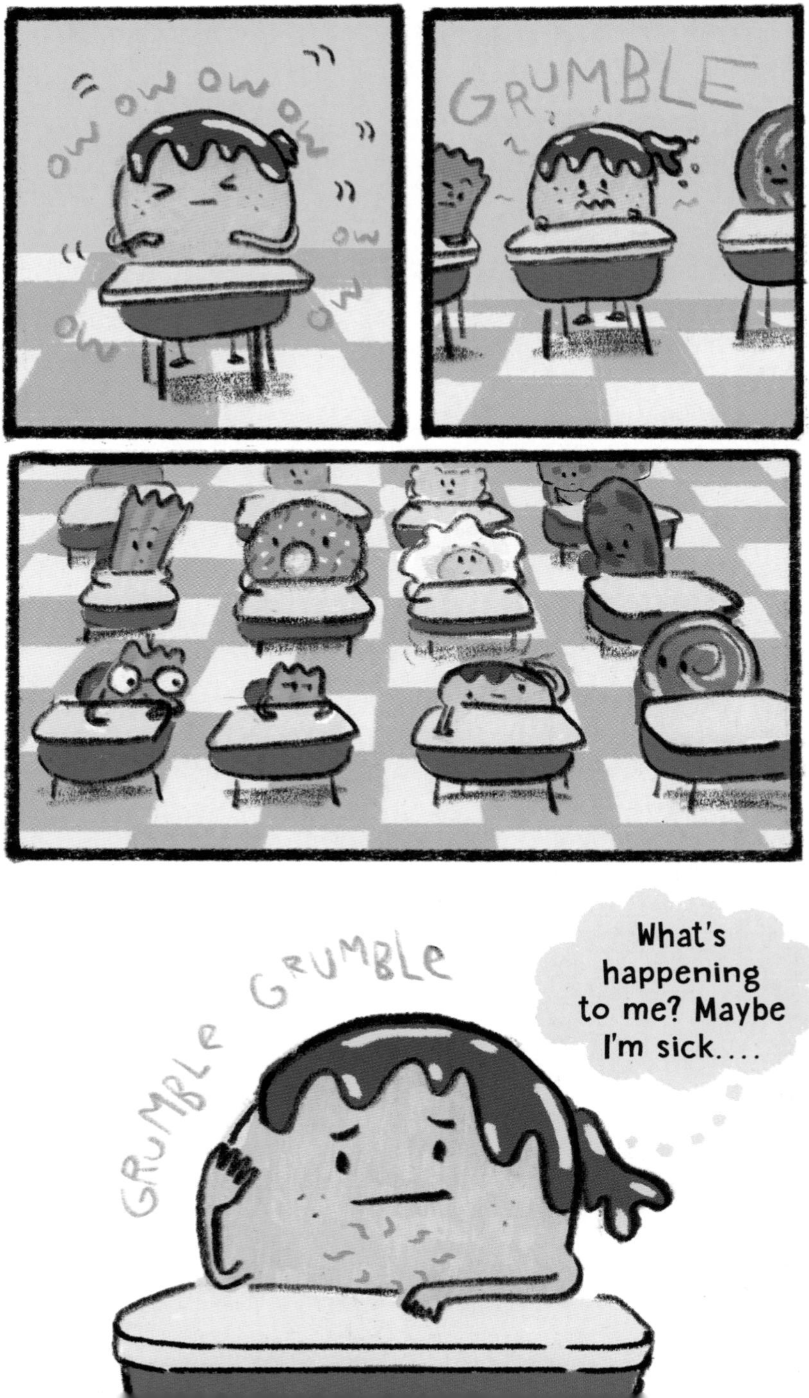
OW OW OW OW
OW
OW
OW
GRUMBLE
GRUMBLE GRUMBLE
What's happening to me? Maybe I'm sick....

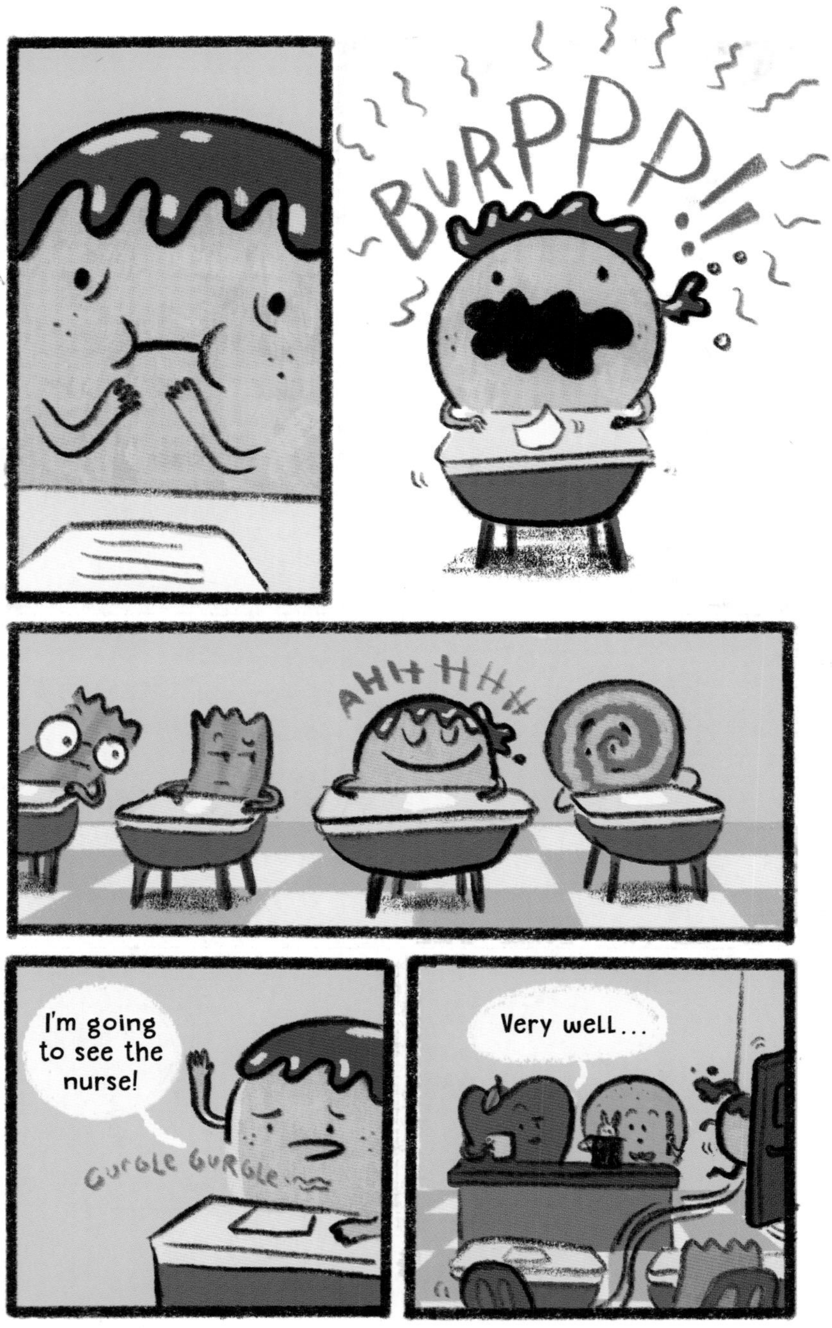
BURPPP!!
AHHHHHH
I'm going to see the nurse!
GURGLE GURGLE
Very well...

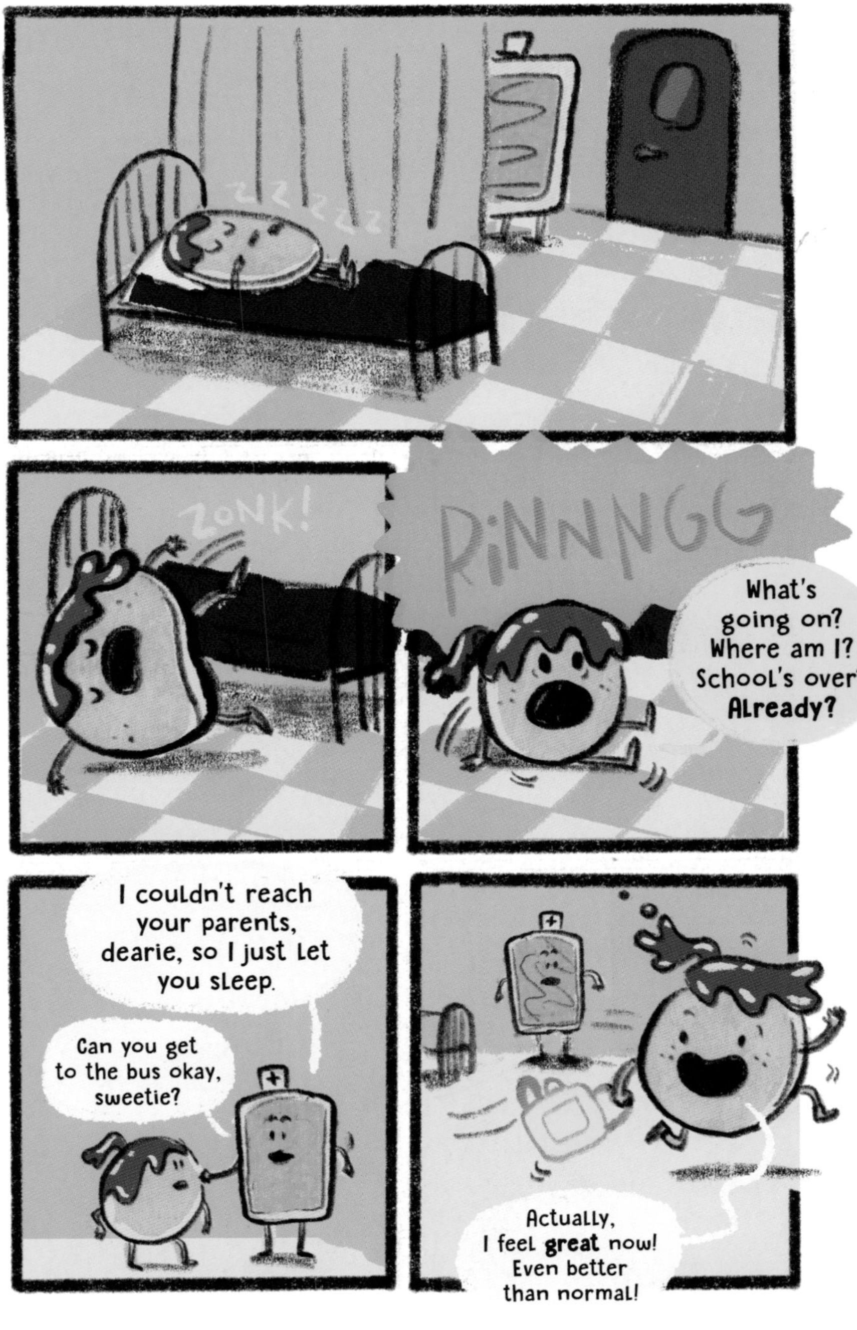
ZZZZZZ
ZONK!
RiNNNGG
What's going on? Where am I? School's over? **Already?**
I couldn't reach your parents, dearie, so I just let you sleep.
Can you get to the bus okay, sweetie?
Actually, I feel **great** now! Even better than normal!

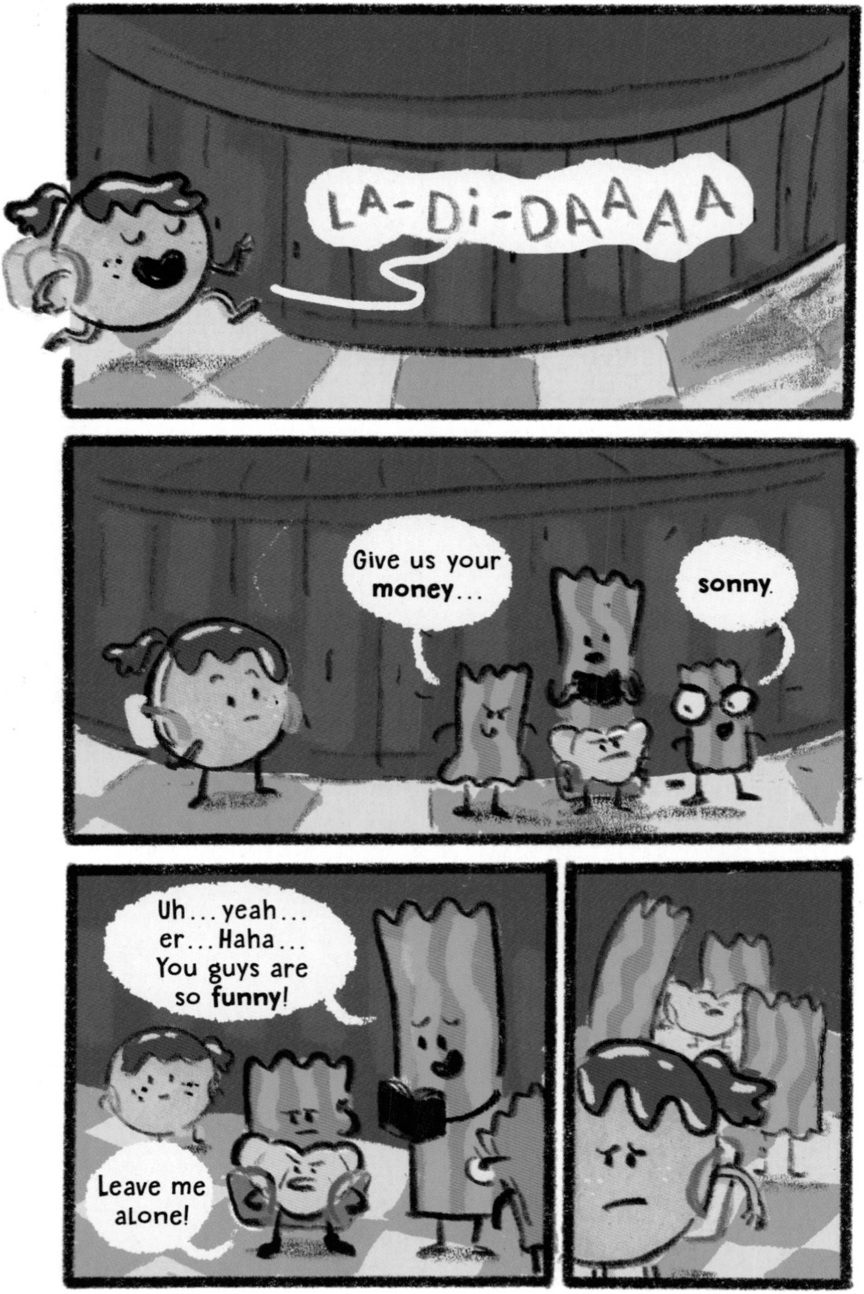
LA-DI-DAAAA
Give us your money...
sonny.
Uh... yeah... er... Haha... You guys are so funny!
Leave me alone!

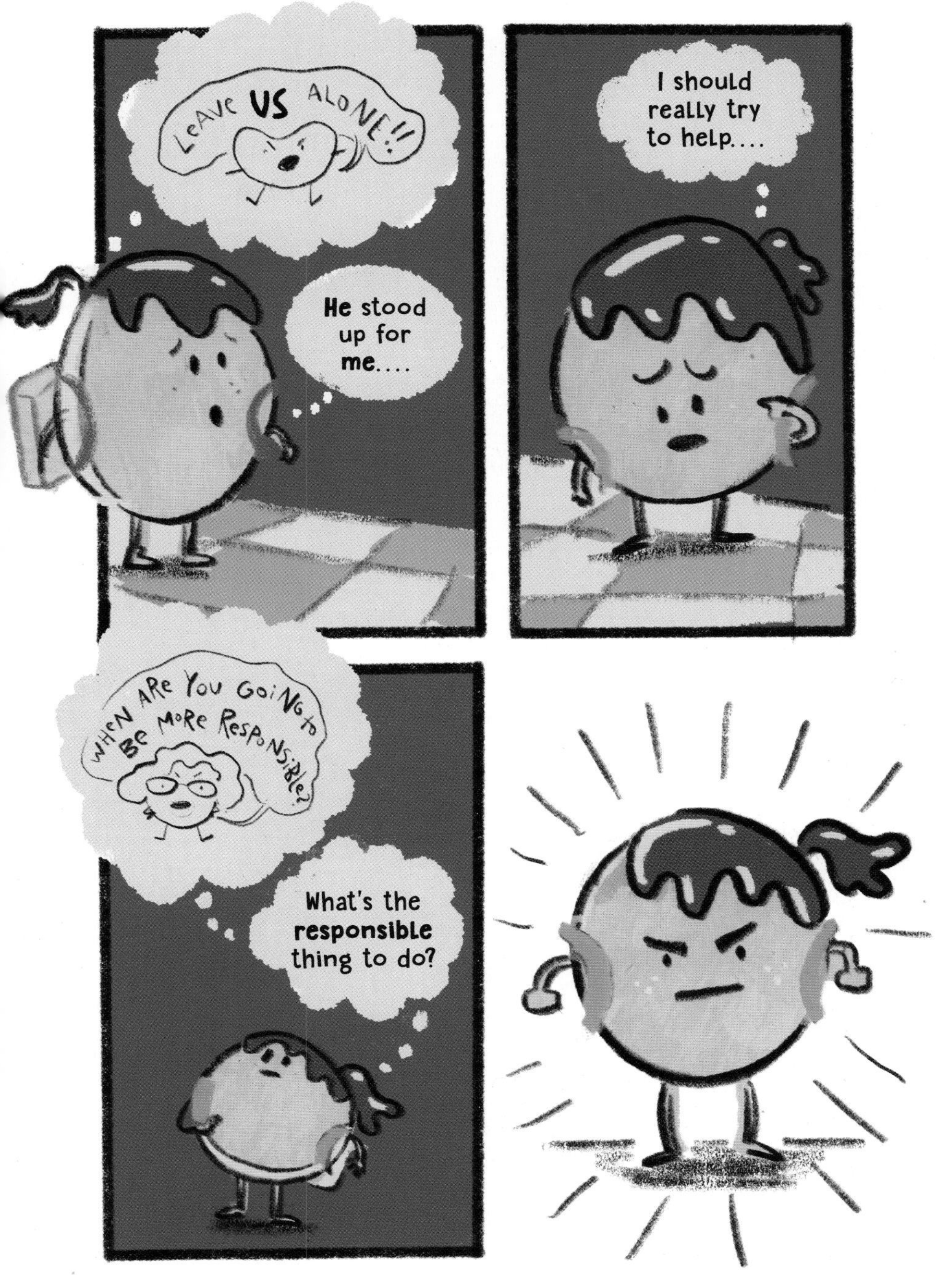
LeAVe US ALoNE!!
He stood up for me....
I should really try to help....
WHEN ARe YoU GoiNG to Be MoRe ResPoNSiBle?
What's the responsible thing to do?

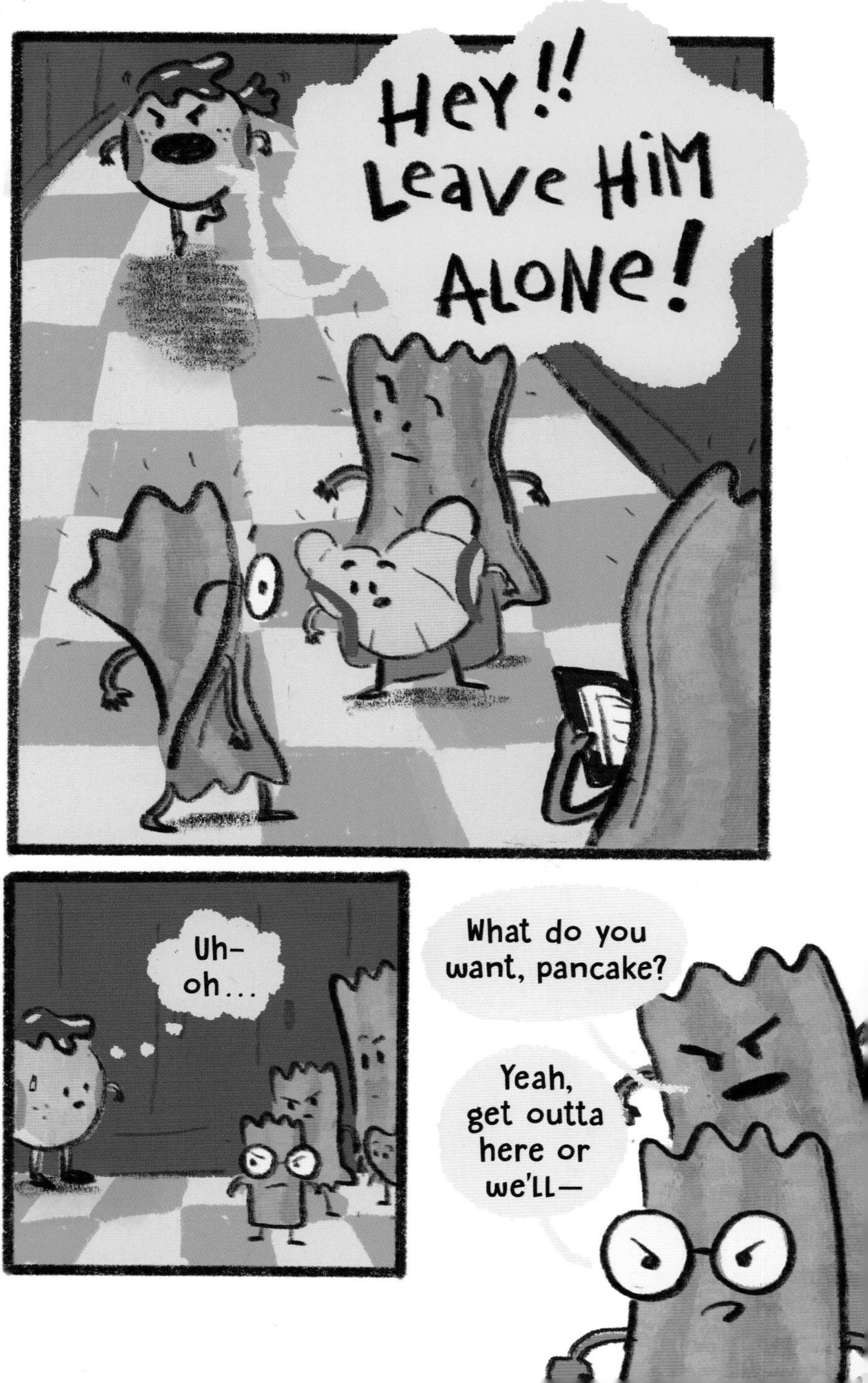

Hey!! Leave HiM ALONE!
Uh-oh...
What do you want, pancake?
Yeah, get outta here or we'LL—

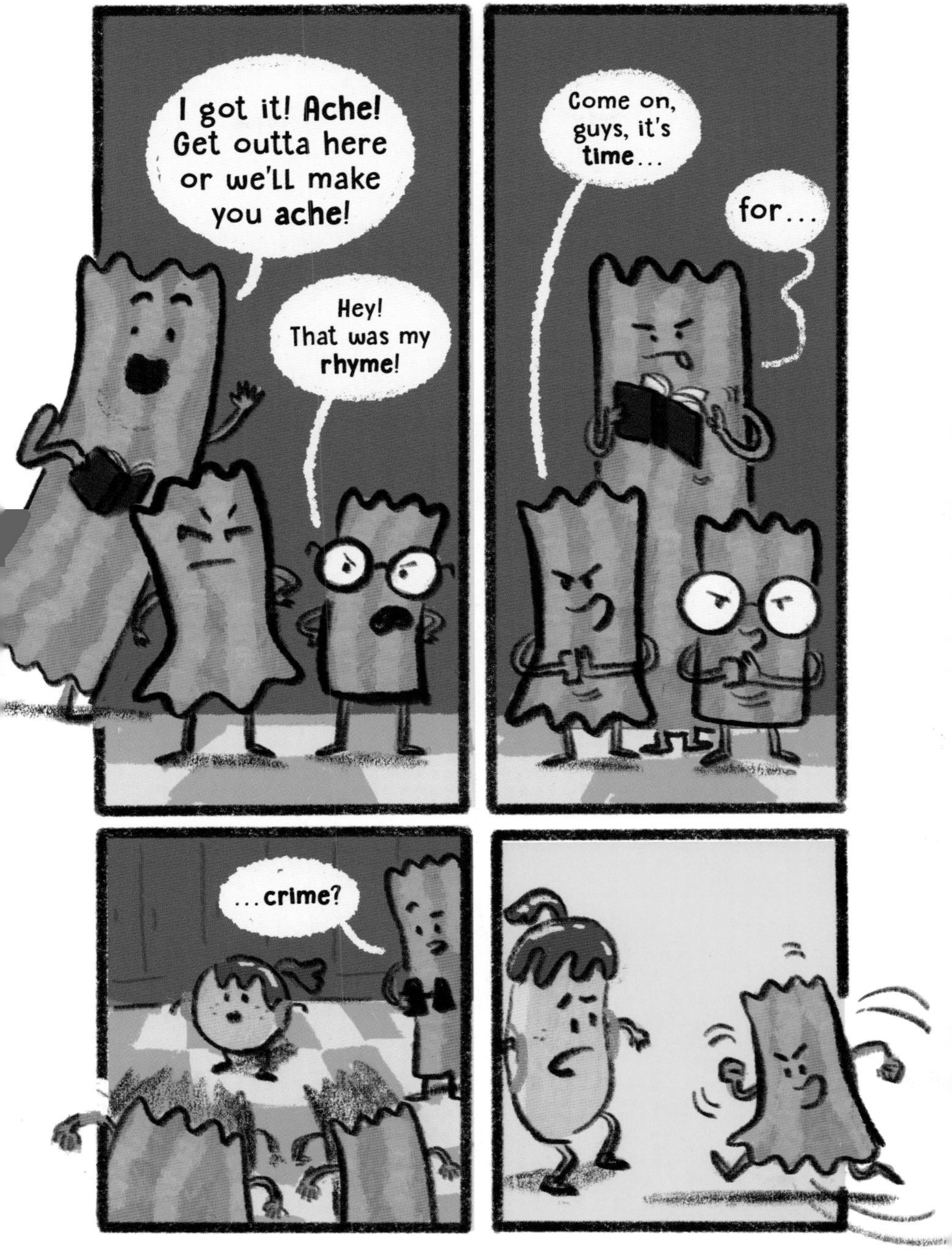
I got it! Ache! Get outta here or we'LL make you ache!
Hey! That was my rhyme!
Come on, guys, it's time...
for...
...crime?

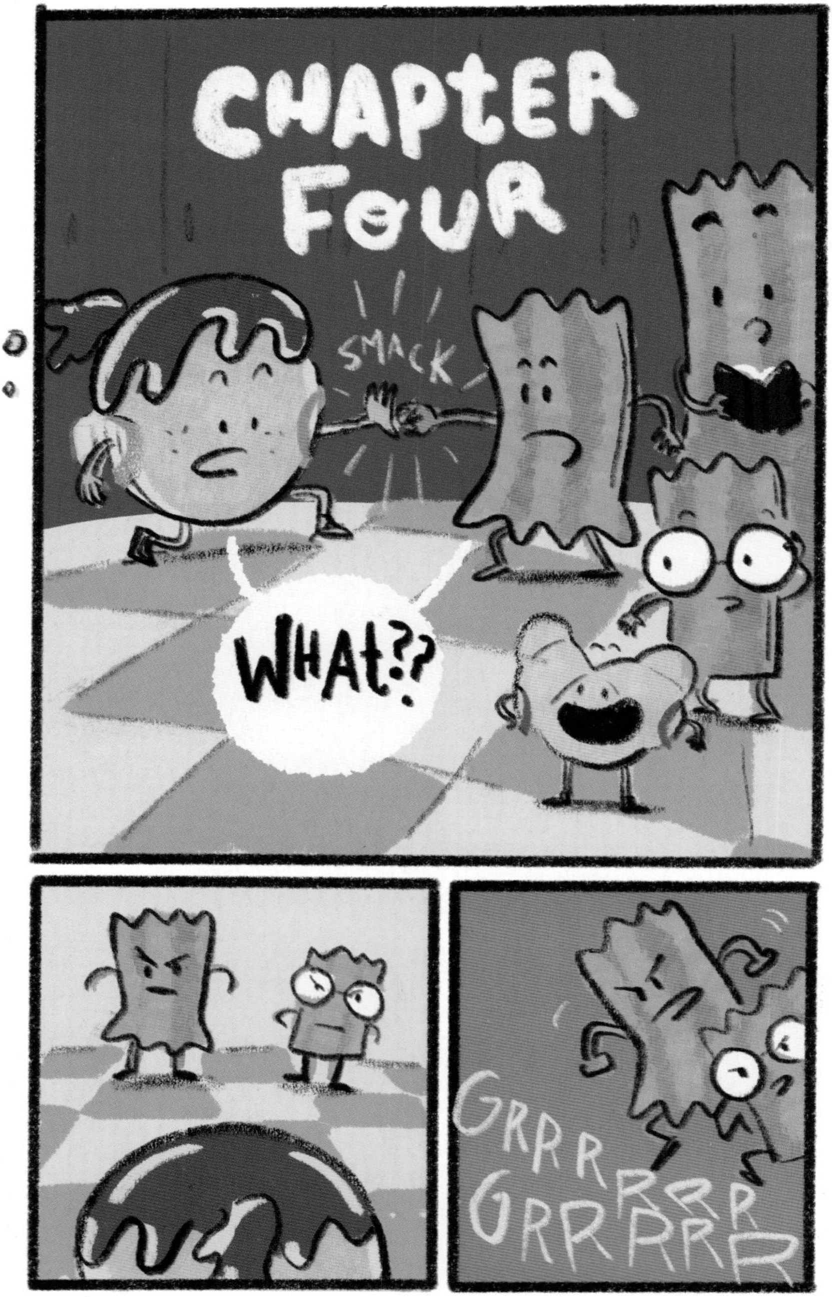
CHAPTER FOUR
SMACK
WHAT??
GRRRR
GRRRRRRRR

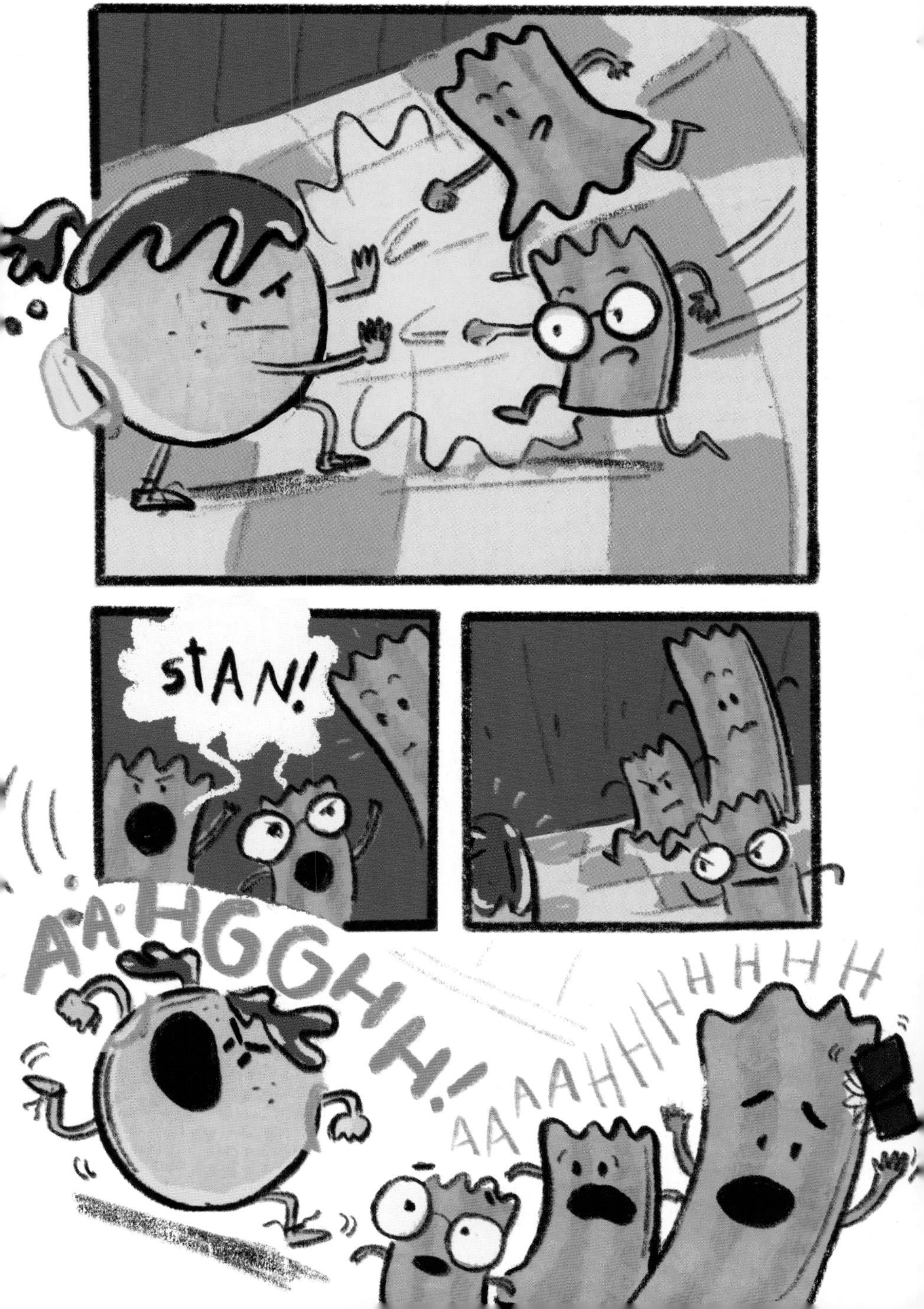
STAN!
AAHGGHH!
AAAAHHHHHHHH

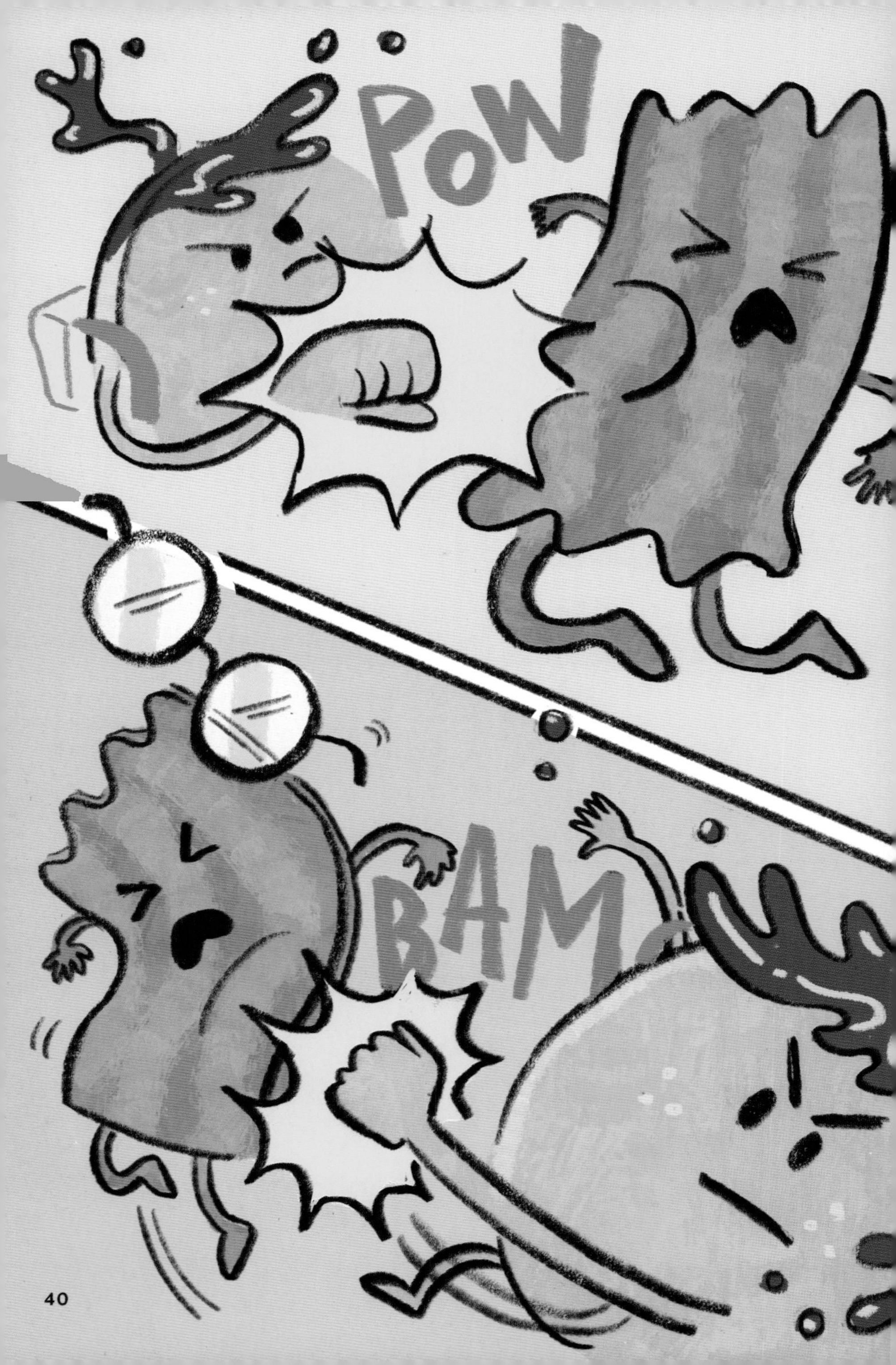
POW
BAM

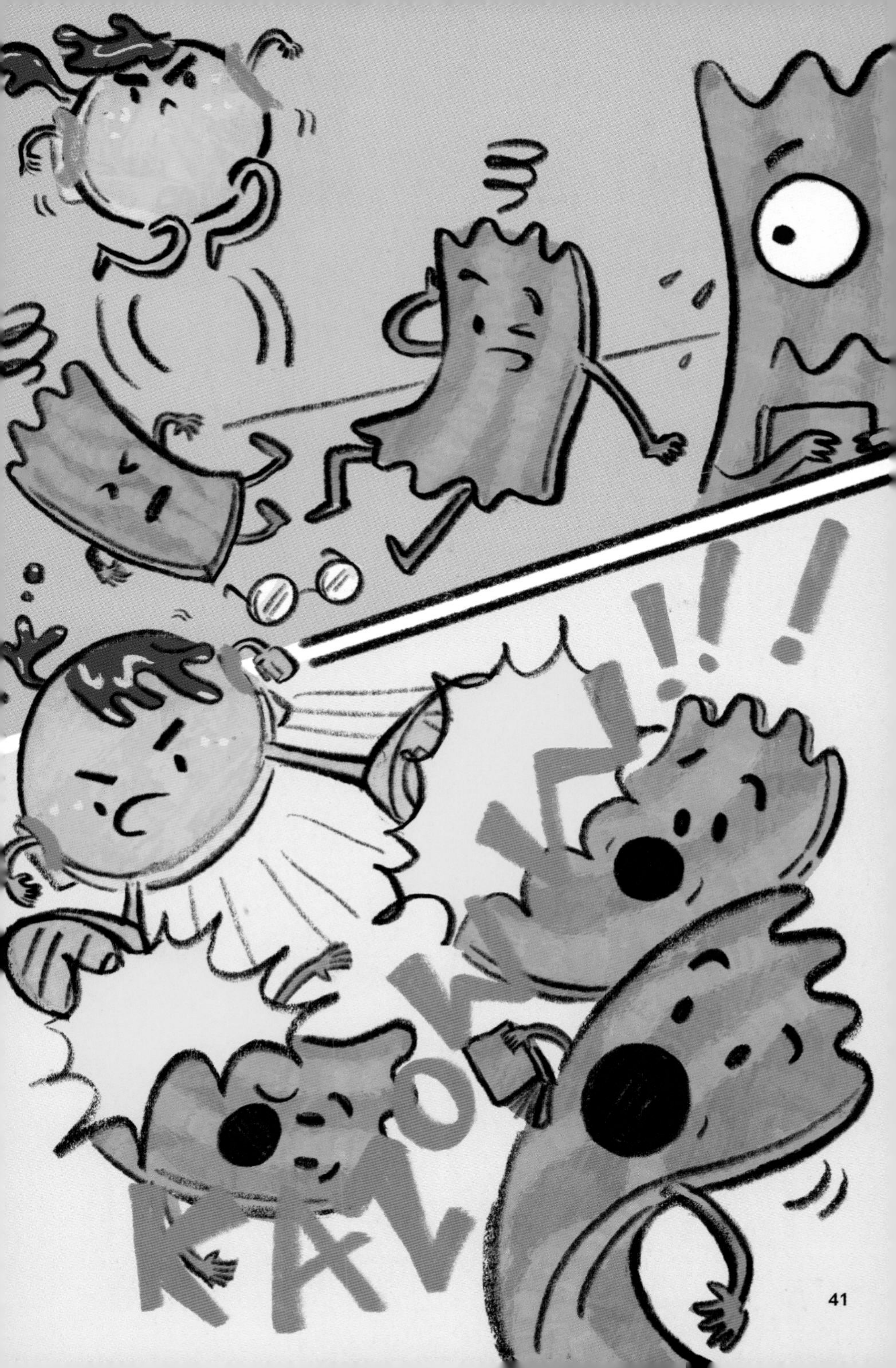
KAVOWW!!!

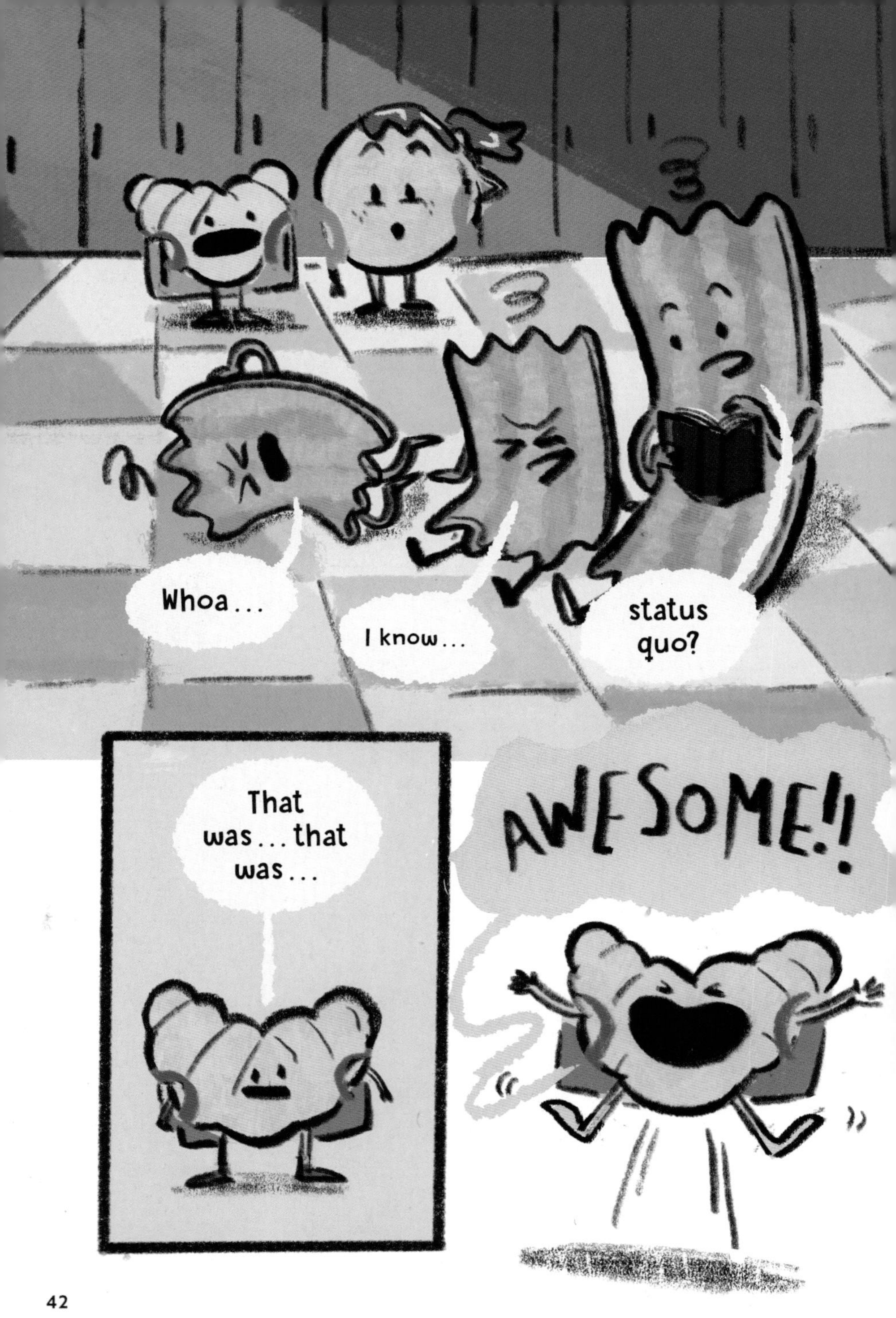
Whoa...
I know...
status quo?
That was... that was...
AWESOME!!

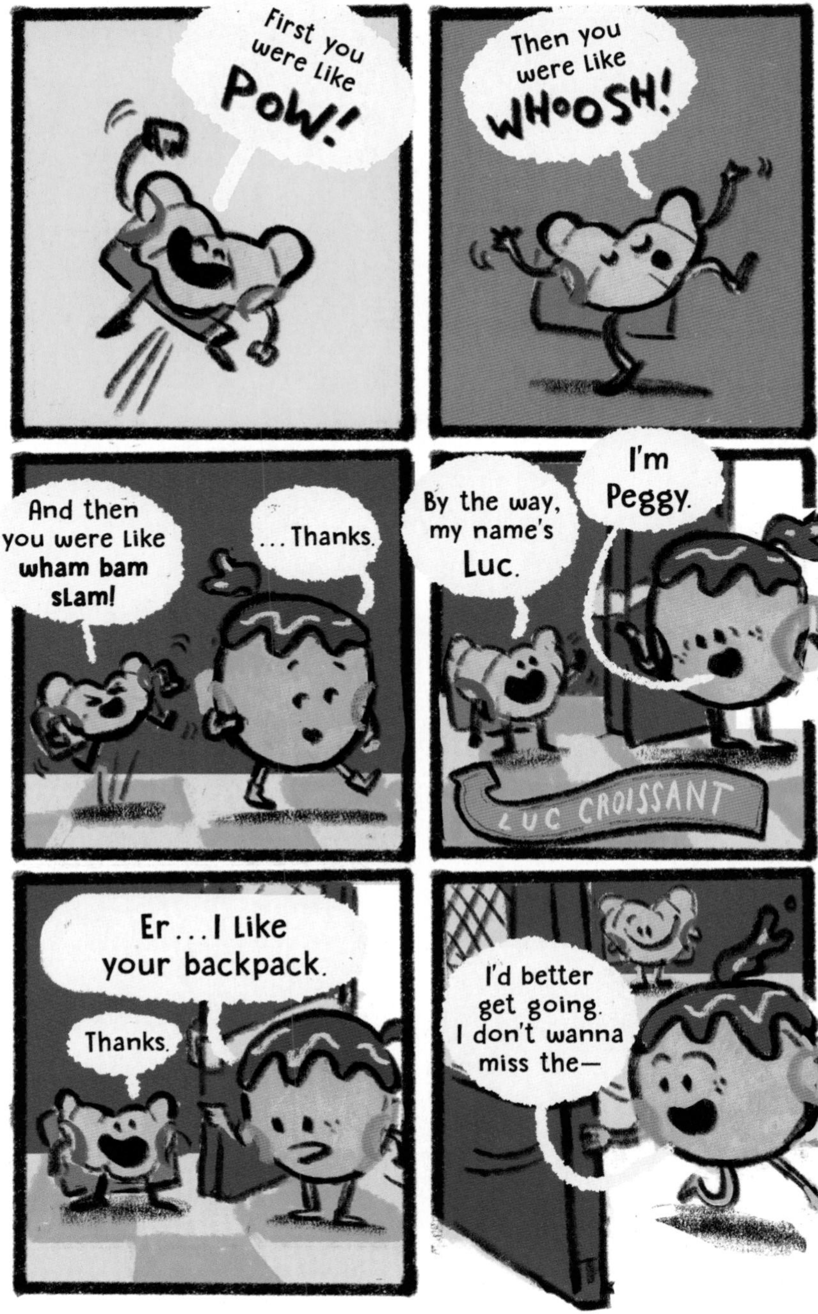
First you were like POW!
Then you were like WHOOSH!
And then you were like wham bam slam!
...Thanks.
By the way, my name's Luc.
I'm Peggy.
LUC CROISSANT
Er...I like your backpack.
Thanks.
I'd better get going. I don't wanna miss the—

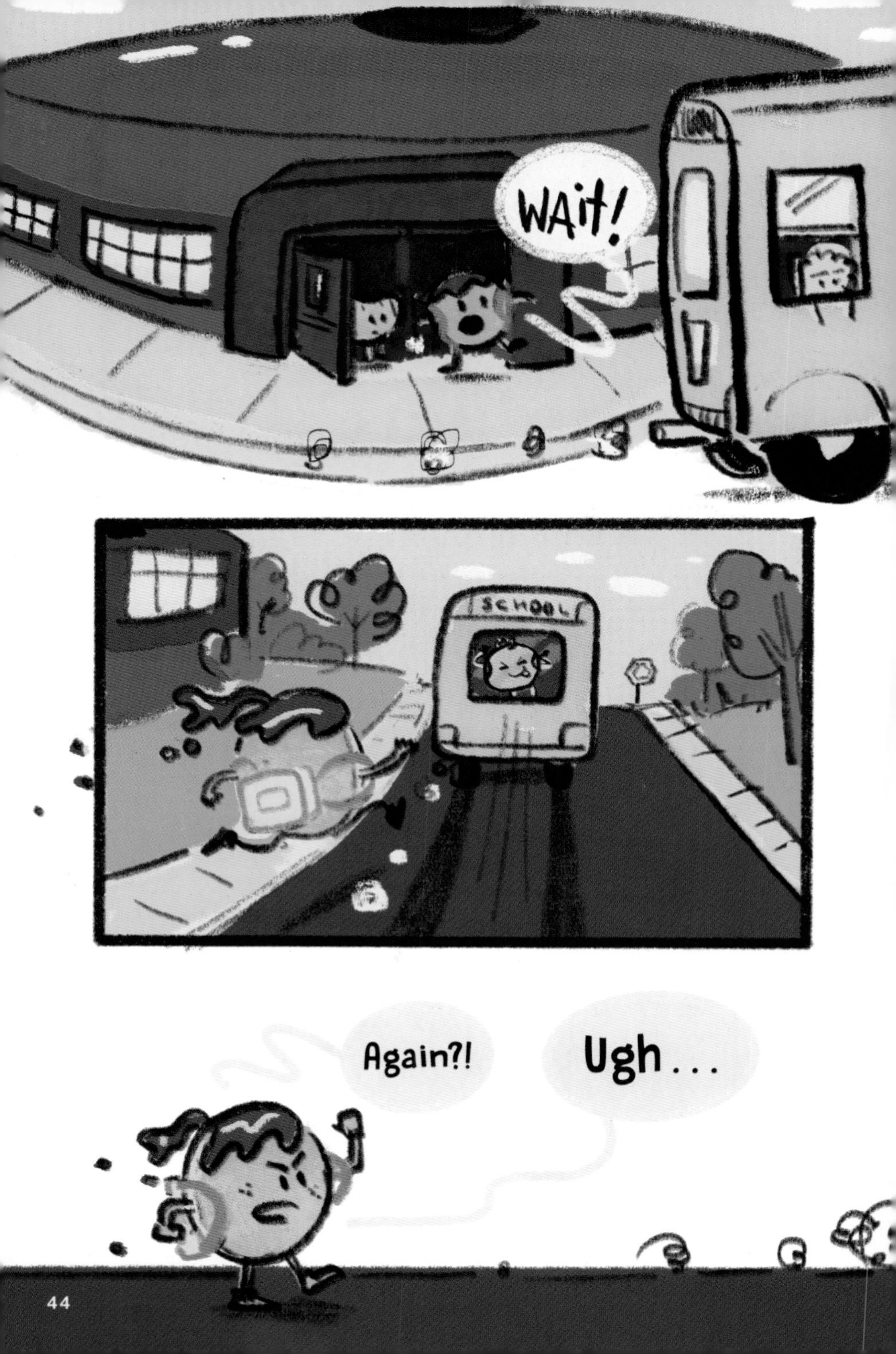
WAIT!
SCHOOL
Again?!
Ugh . . .

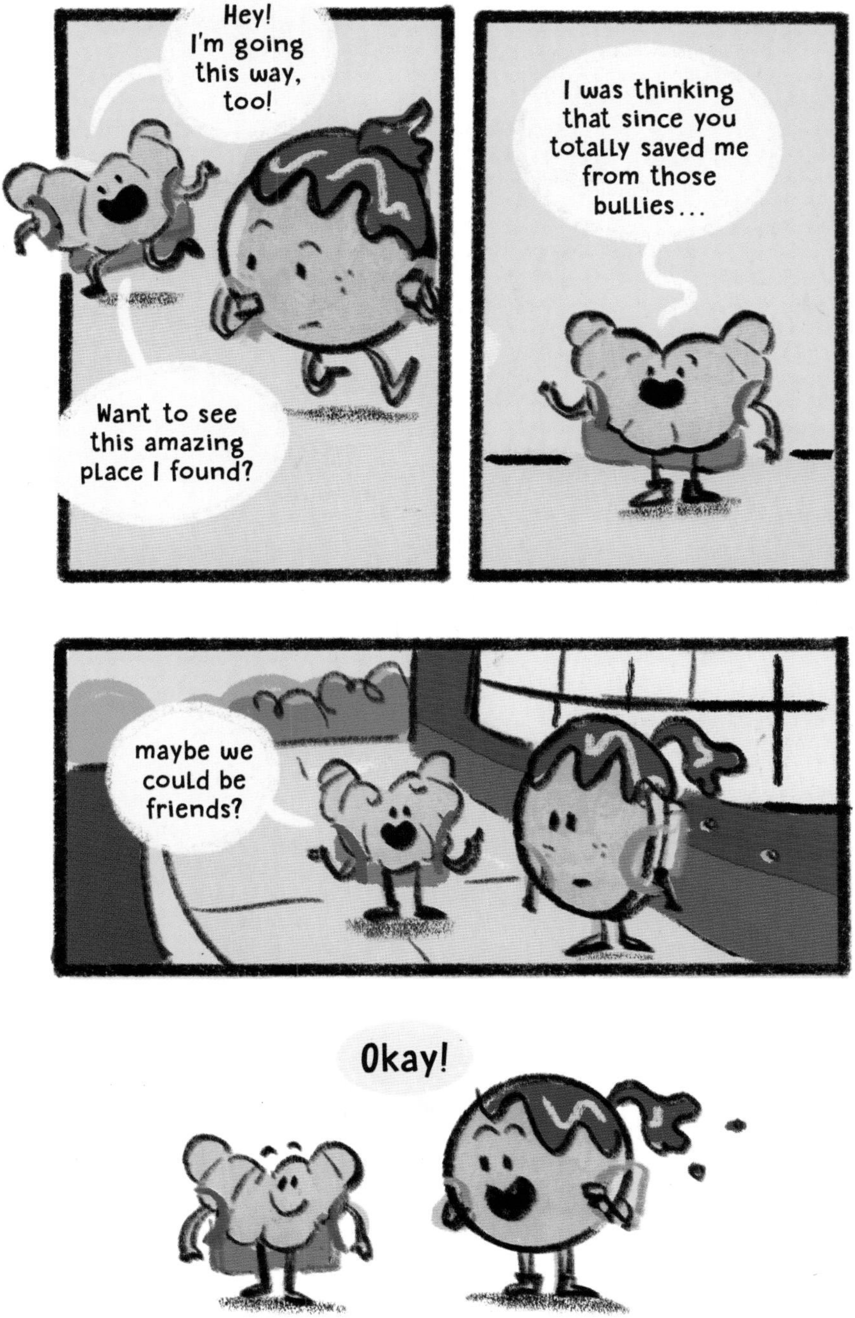
Hey! I'm going this way, too!
Want to see this amazing place I found?
I was thinking that since you totally saved me from those bullies...
maybe we could be friends?
Okay!

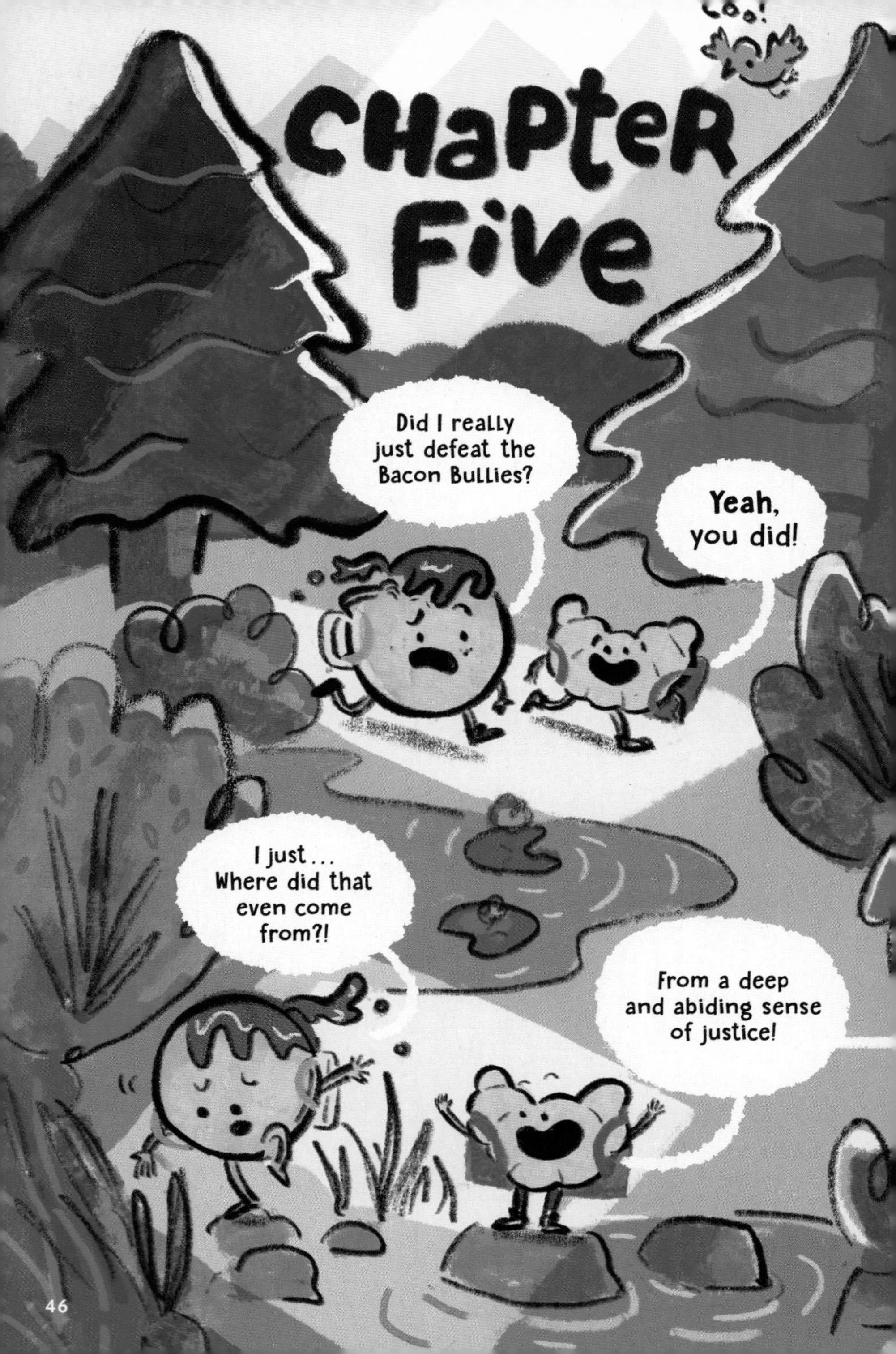
COO!
CHAPTER FIVE
Did I really just defeat the Bacon Bullies?
Yeah, you did!
I just . . . Where did that even come from?!
From a deep and abiding sense of justice!

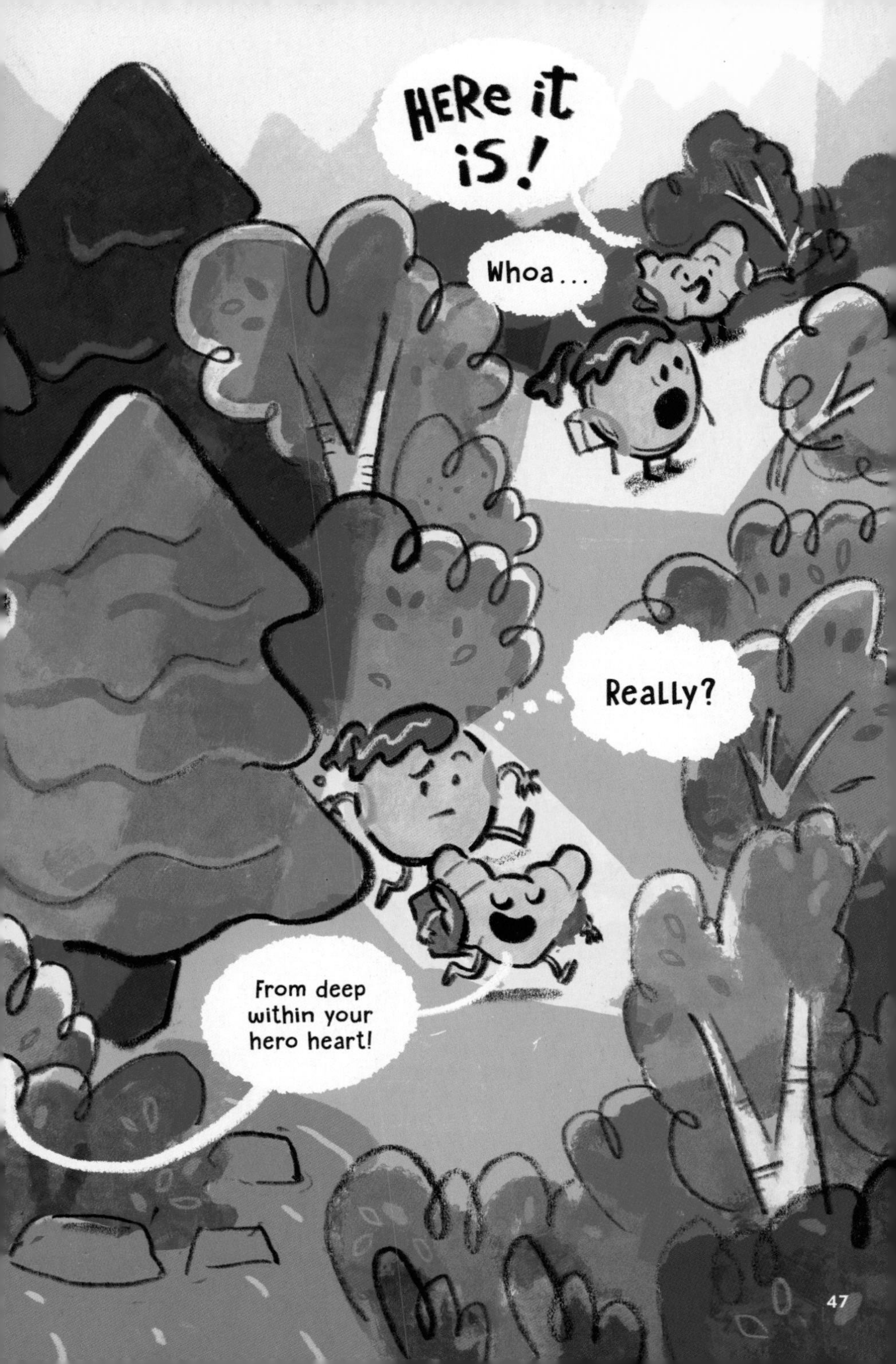
HERE it is!
Whoa...
Really?
From deep within your hero heart!

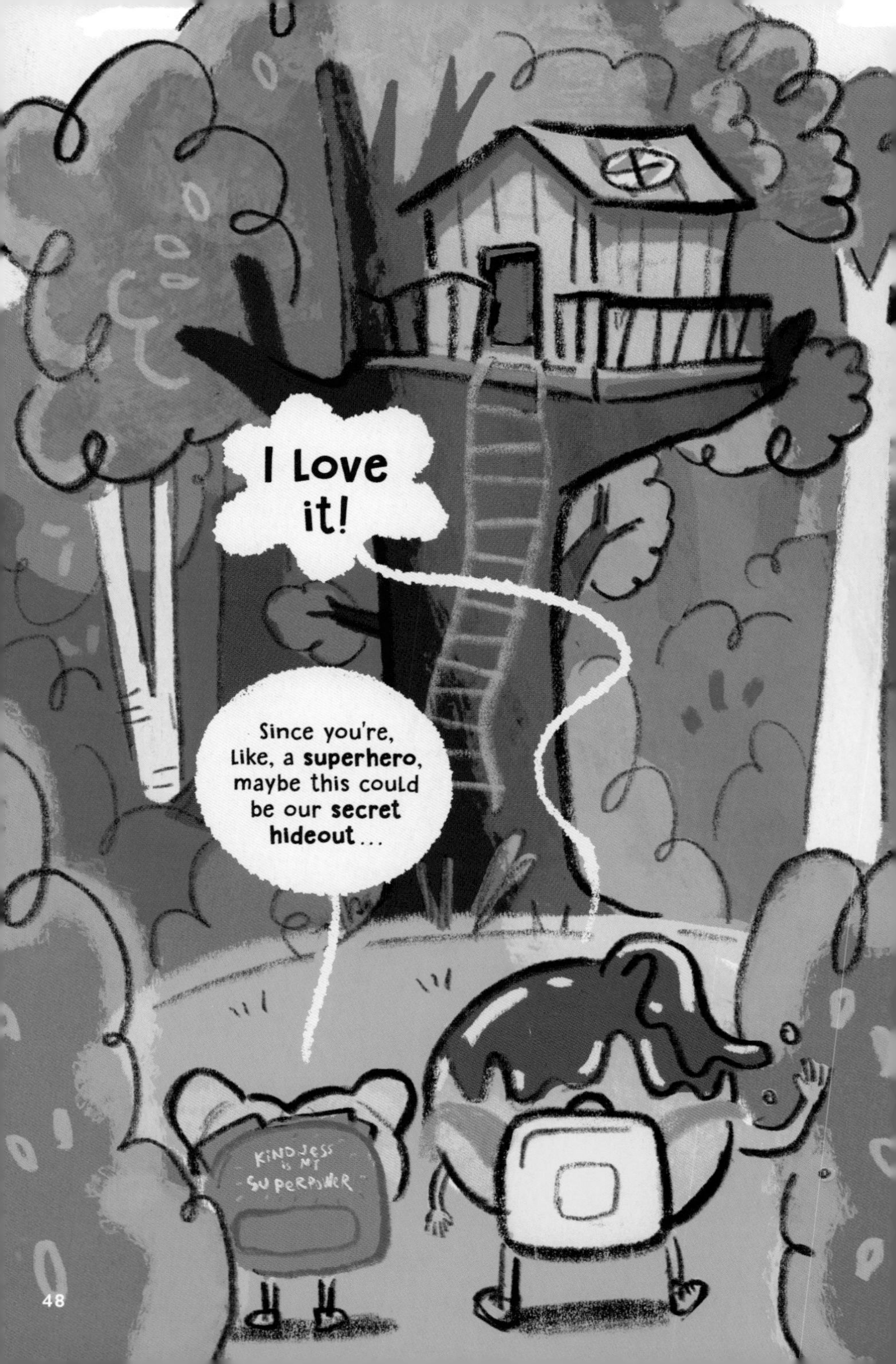
I Love it!
Since you're, Like, a **superhero**, maybe this could be our **secret hideout**...
KINDNESS IS MY SUPERPOWER

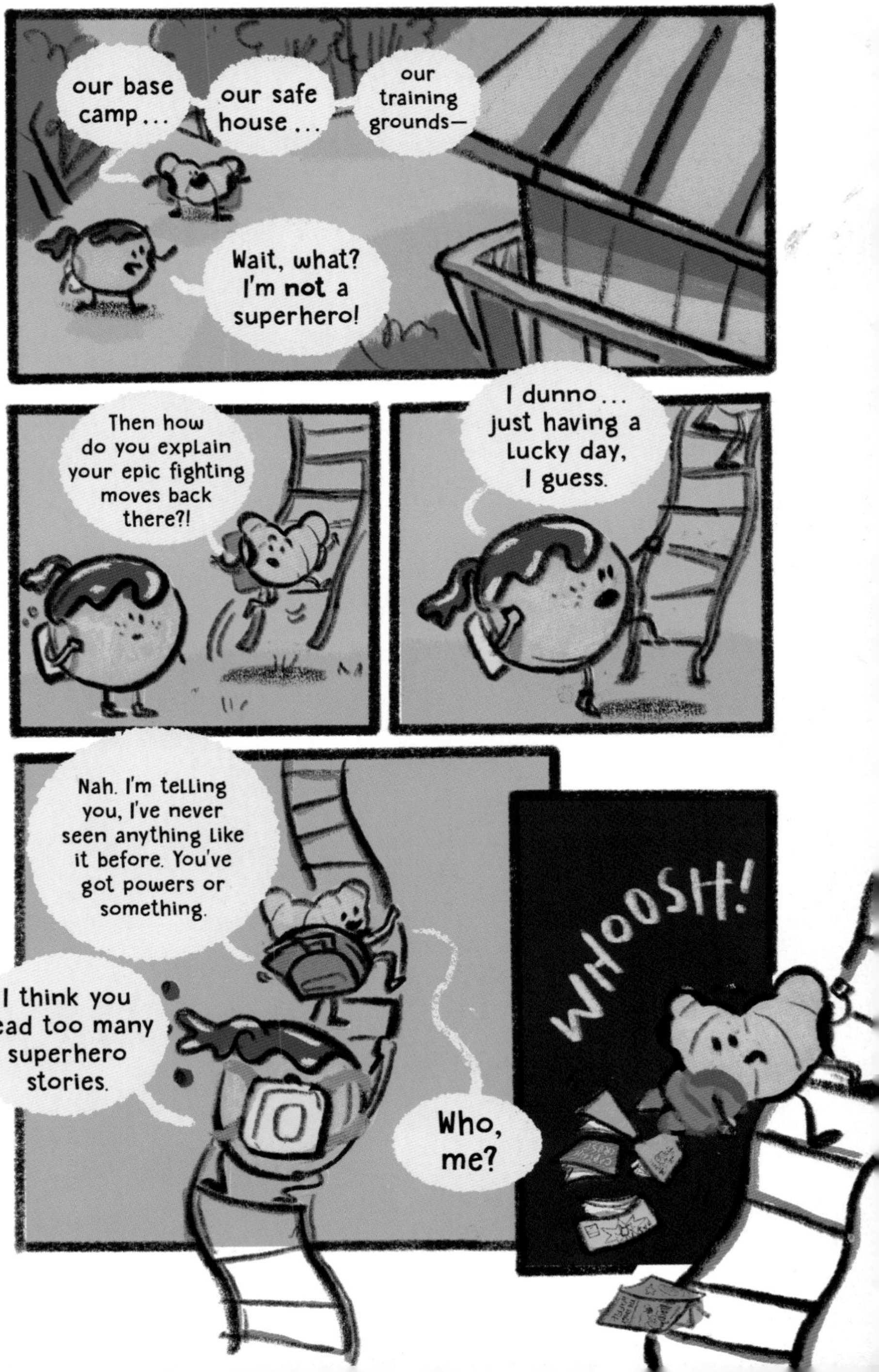
our base camp...
our safe house...
our training grounds—
Wait, what? I'm **not** a superhero!
Then how do you explain your epic fighting moves back there?!
I dunno... just having a lucky day, I guess.
Nah. I'm telling you, I've never seen anything like it before. You've got powers or something.
I think you read too many superhero stories.
Who, me?
WHOOSH!

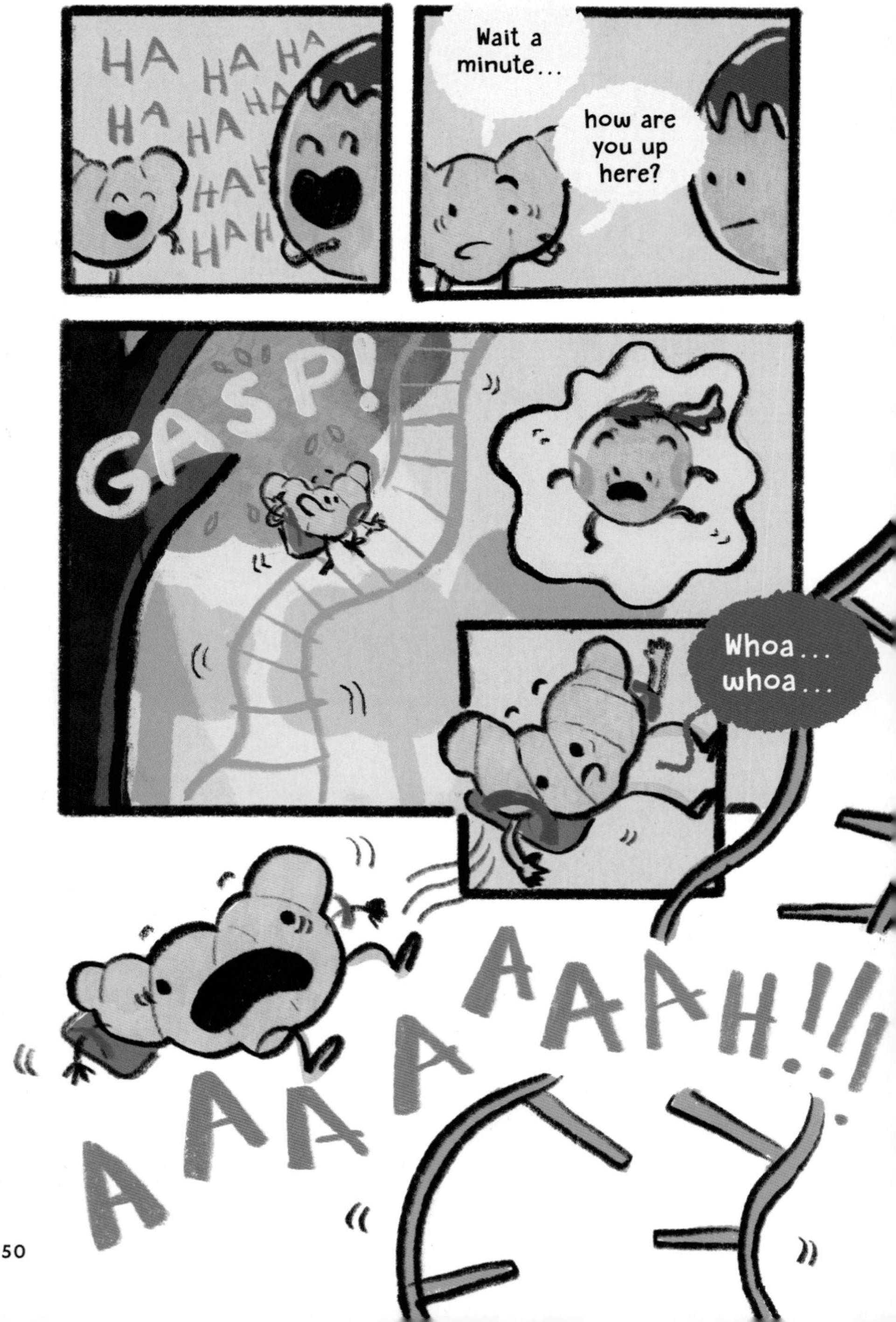
HA HA HA
HA HA HA
HA
HA
Wait a minute...
how are you up here?
GASP!
Whoa... whoa...
AAAAAAAH!!!

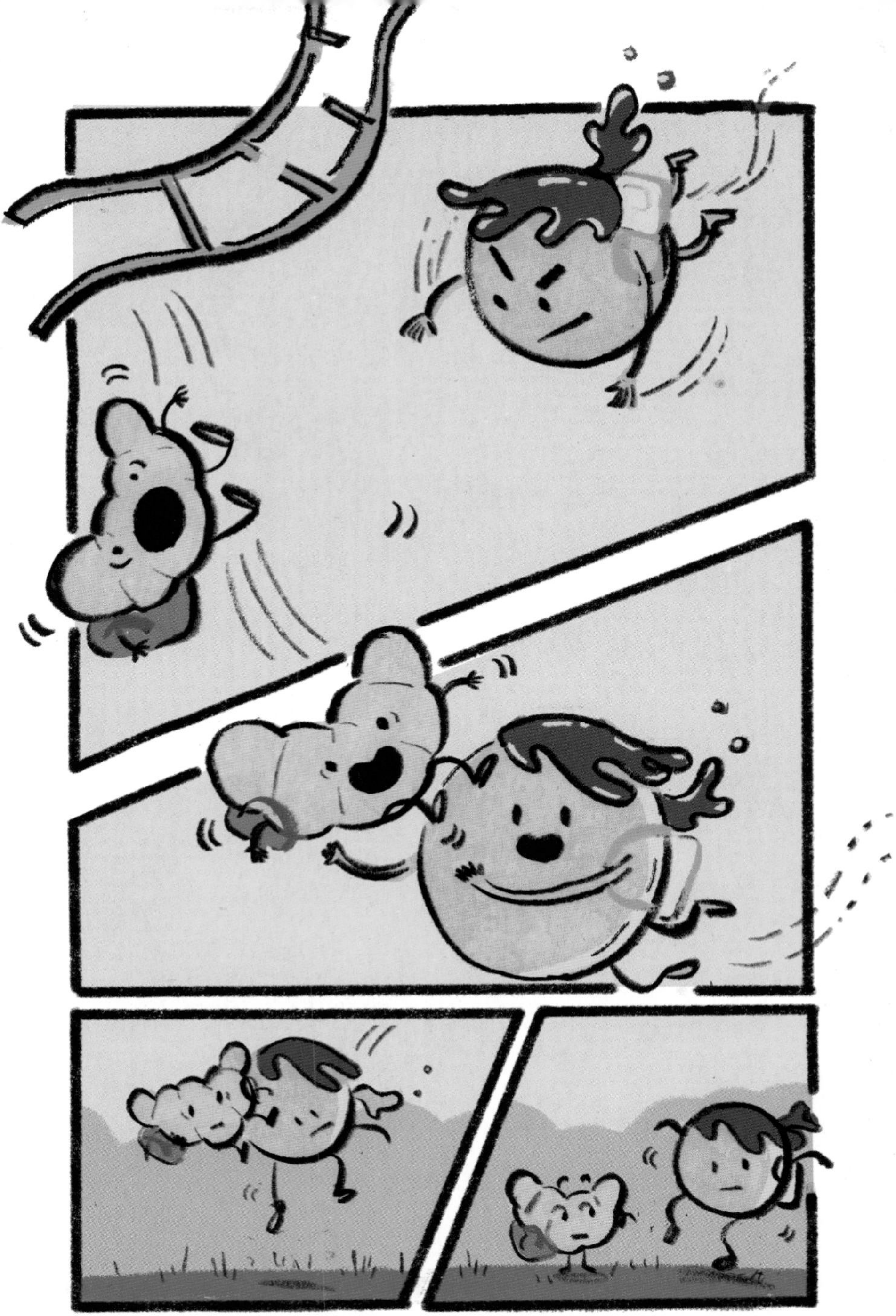

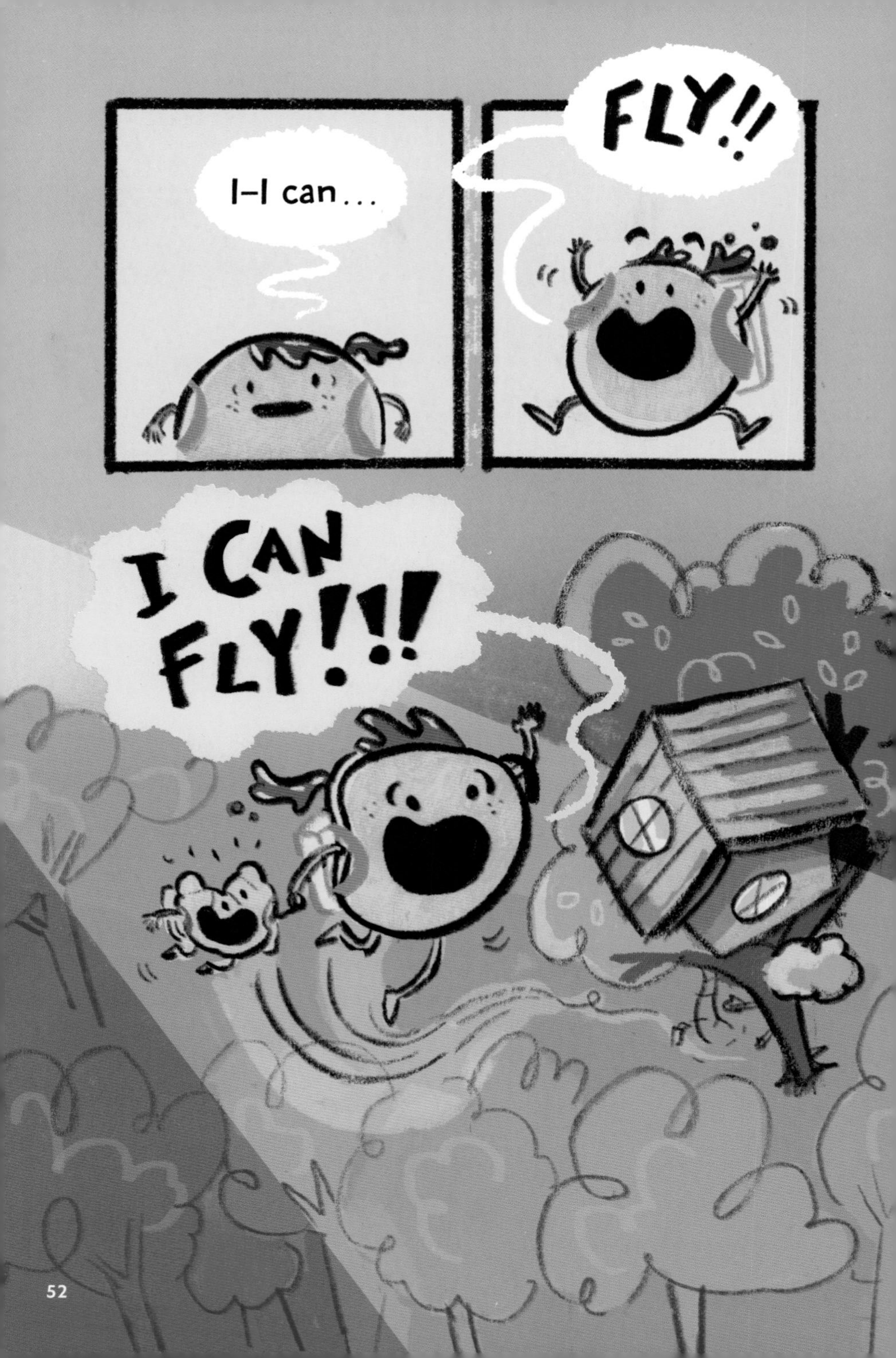
I–I can...
FLY!!
I CAN FLY!!!

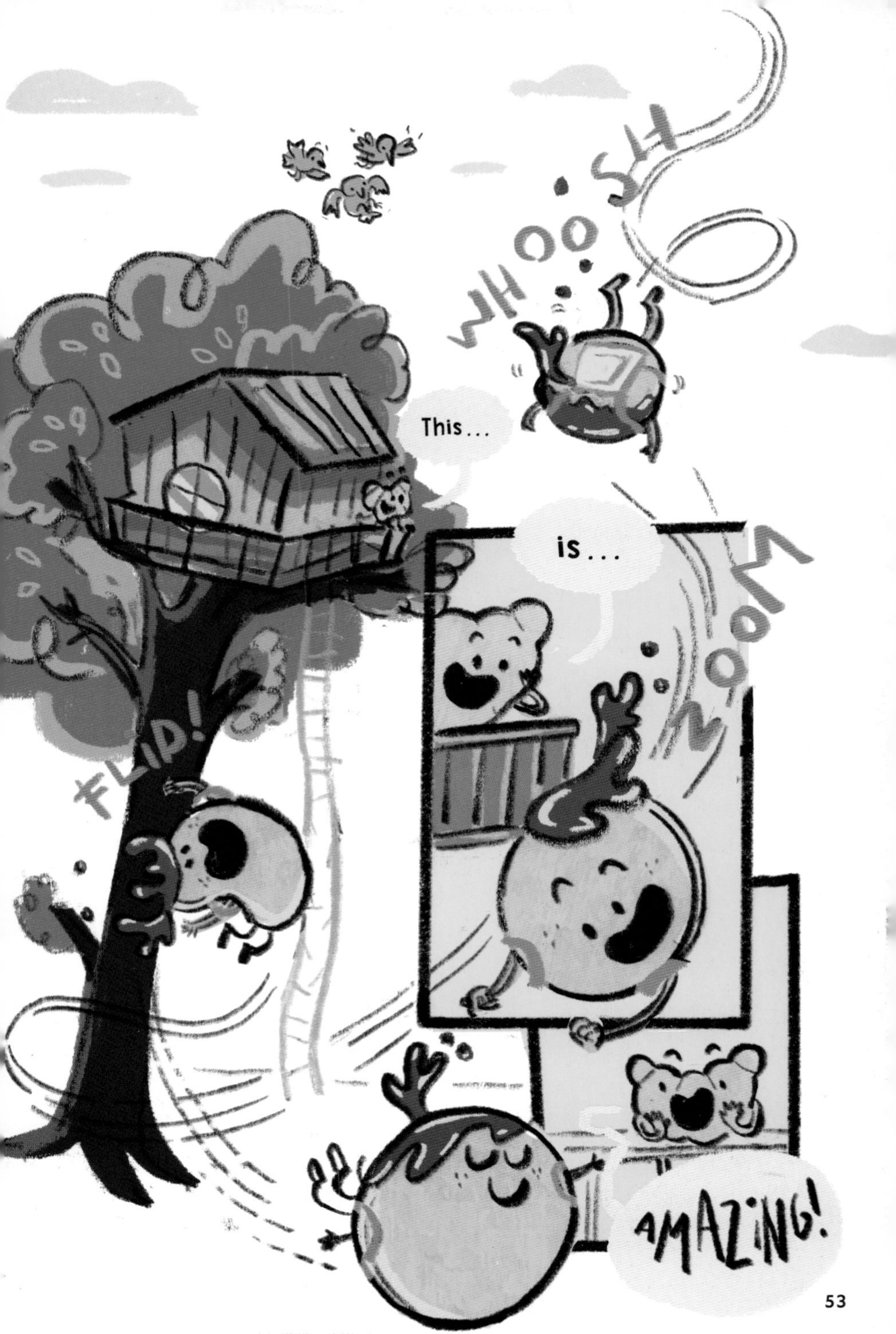
WHOOSH
This...
is...
FLIP!
ZOOM
AMAZING!

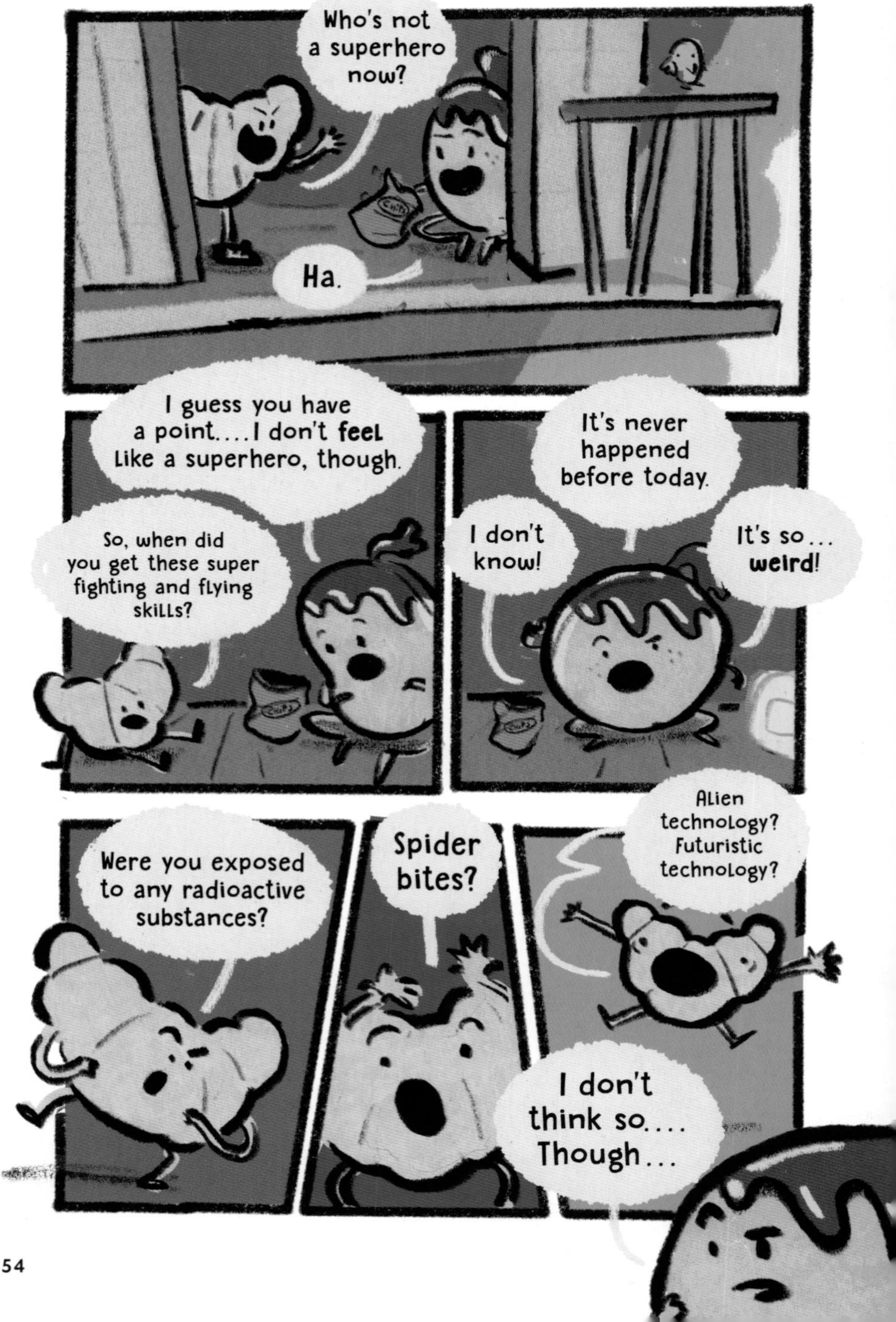
Who's not a superhero now?
Ha.
I guess you have a point.... I don't **feel** like a superhero, though.
So, when did you get these super fighting and flying skills?
It's never happened before today.
I don't know!
It's so... **weird**!
Were you exposed to any radioactive substances?
Spider bites?
Alien technology? Futuristic technology?
I don't think so.... Though...
CHIPS

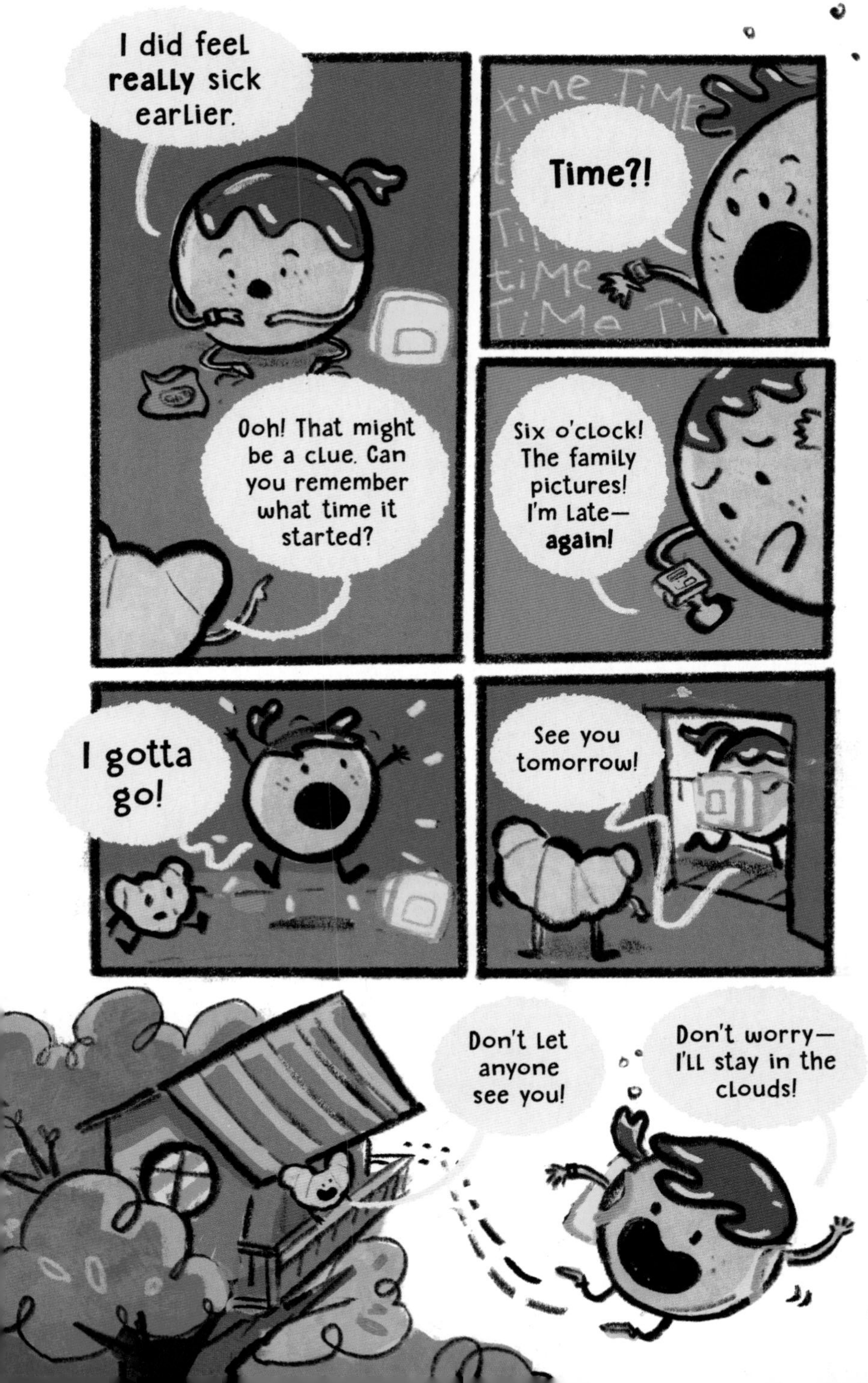
I did feel really sick earlier.
Time?!
Ooh! That might be a clue. Can you remember what time it started?
Six o'clock! The family pictures! I'm late—again!
I gotta go!
See you tomorrow!
Don't let anyone see you!
Don't worry—I'll stay in the clouds!

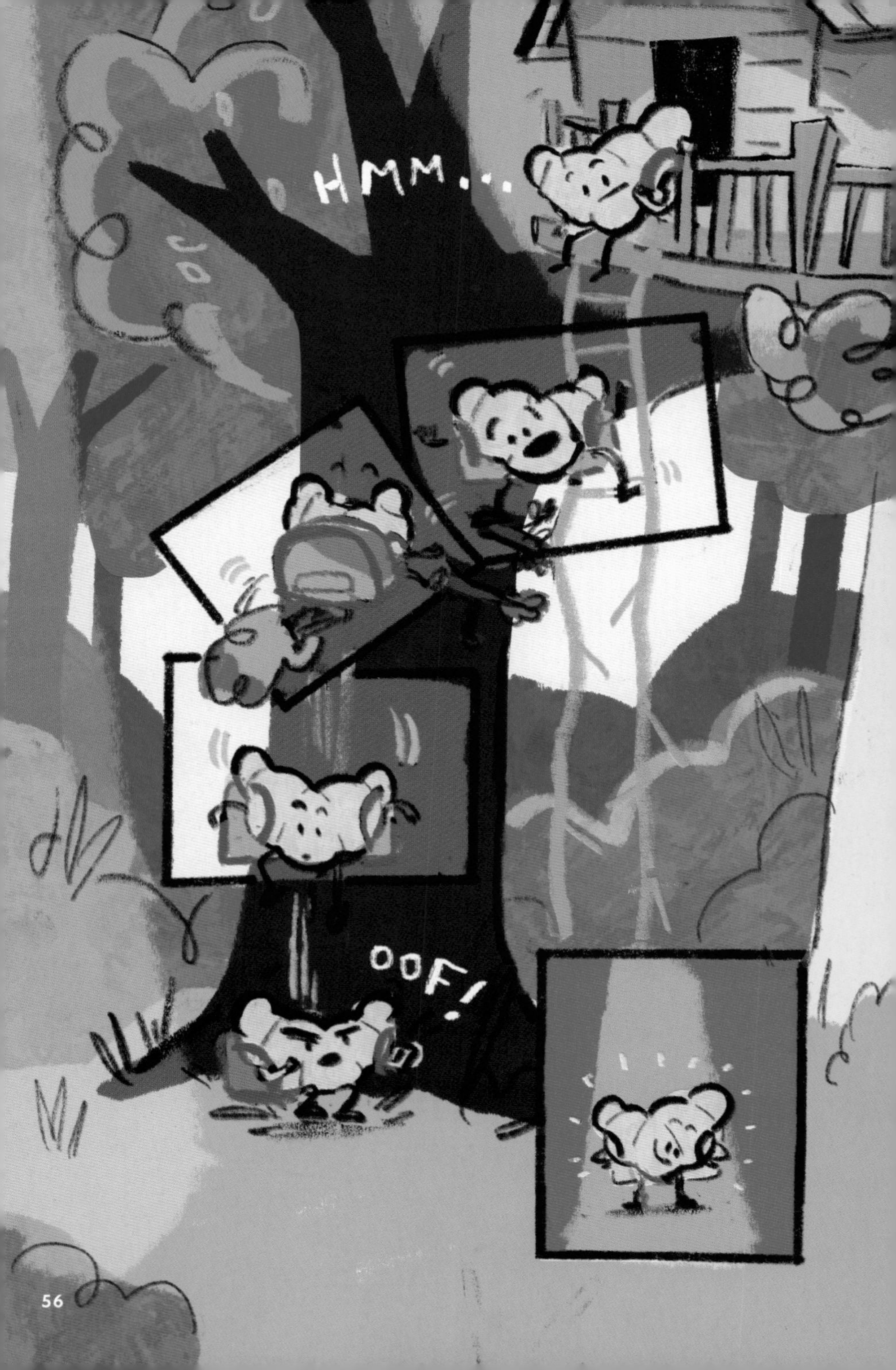
HMM...
OOF!

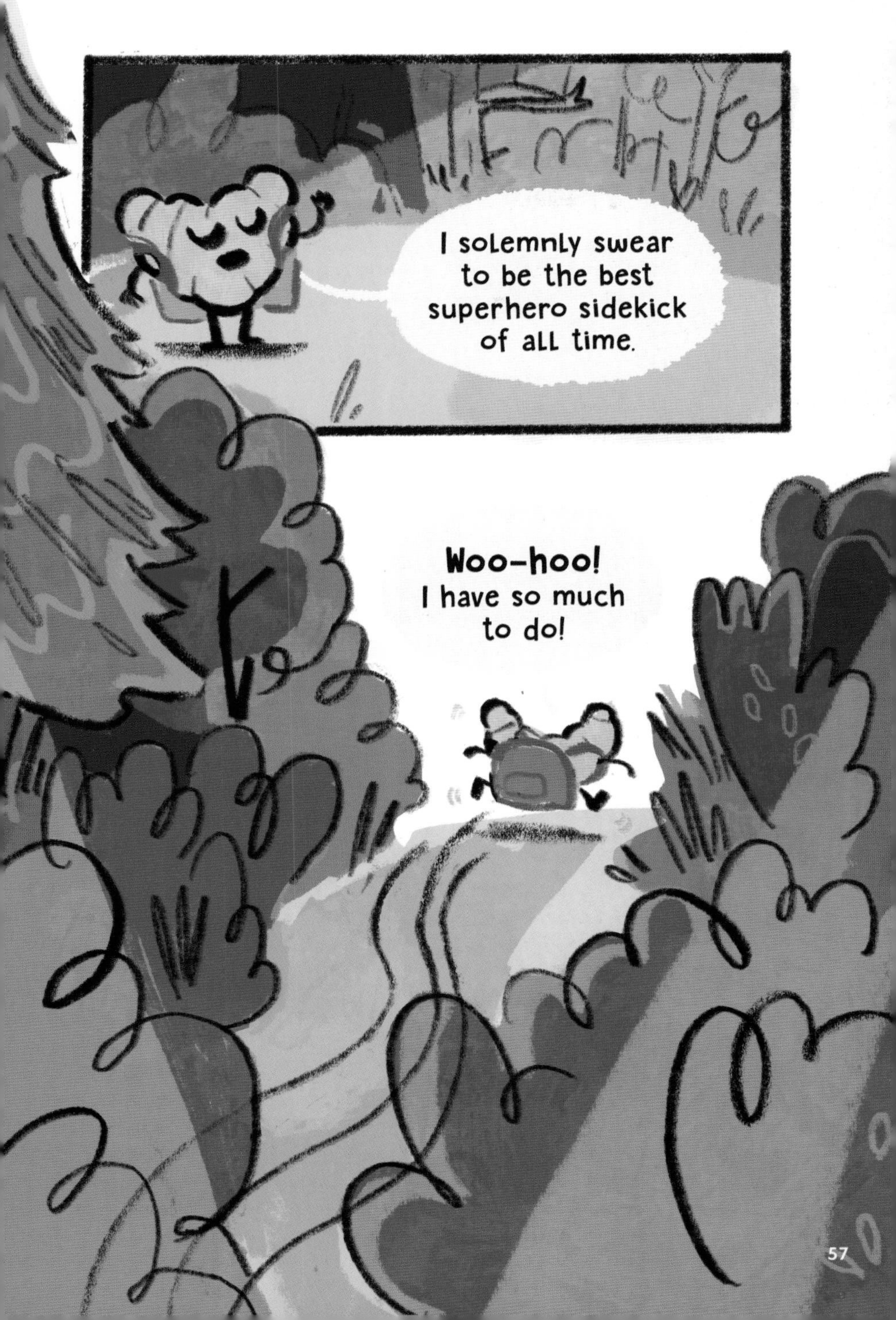
I solemnly swear to be the best superhero sidekick of all time.
Woo-hoo! I have so much to do!

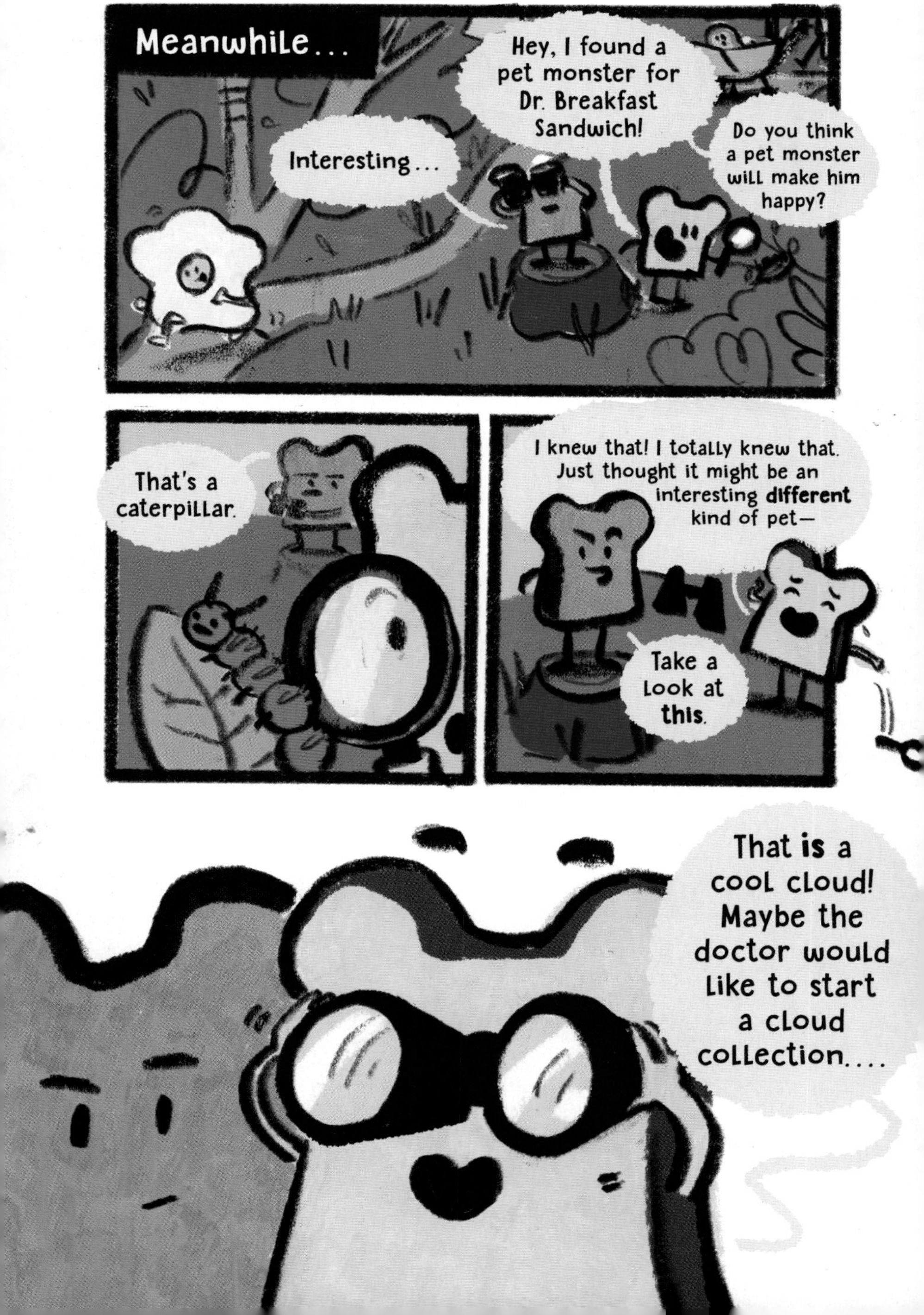
Meanwhile...
Hey, I found a pet monster for Dr. Breakfast Sandwich!
Interesting...
Do you think a pet monster will make him happy?
That's a caterpillar.
I knew that! I totally knew that. Just thought it might be an interesting different kind of pet—
Take a look at this.
That is a cool cloud! Maybe the doctor would like to start a cloud collection....

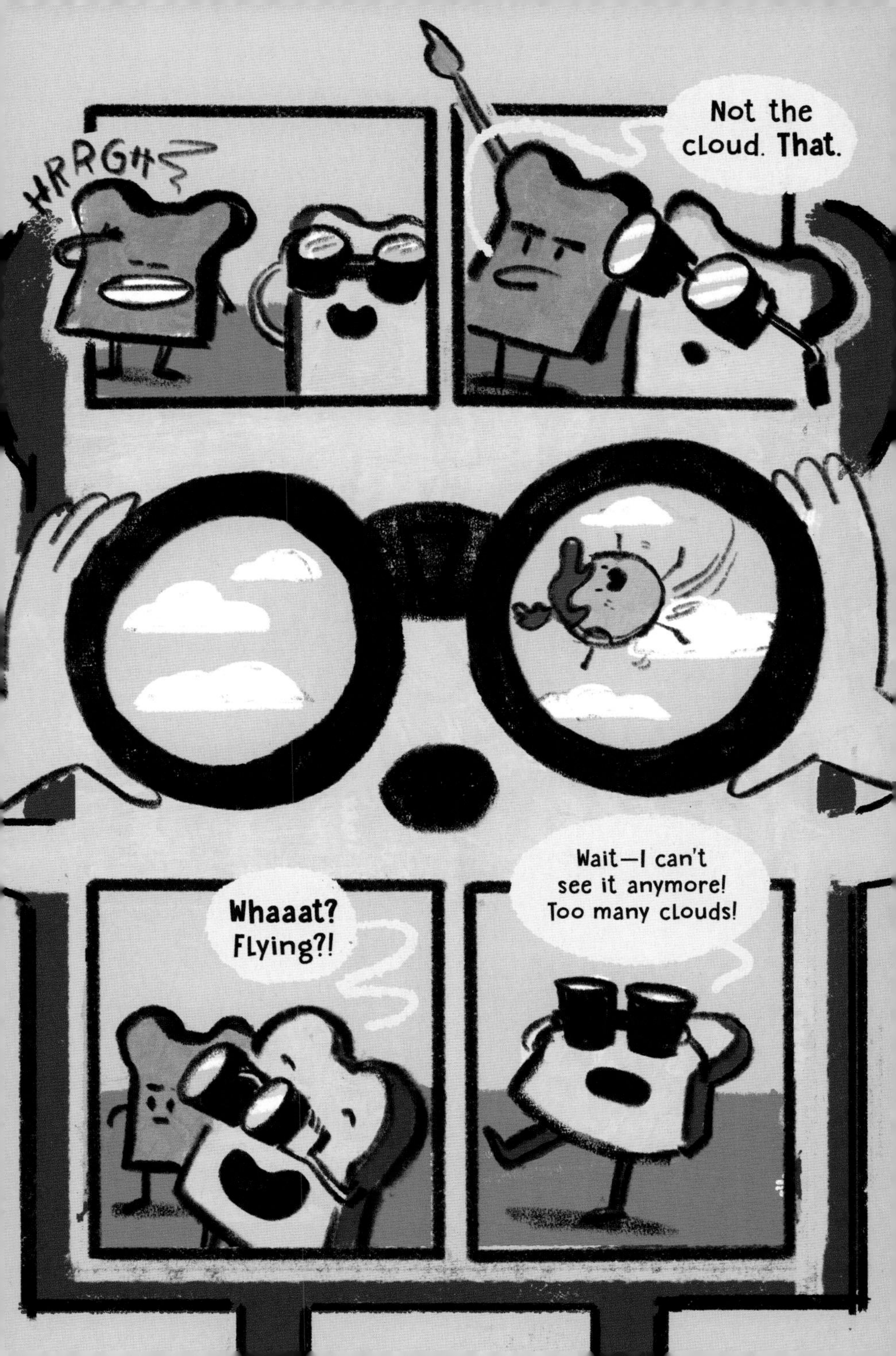
HRRGH
Not the cloud. That.
Whaaat? Flying?!
Wait—I can't see it anymore! Too many clouds!

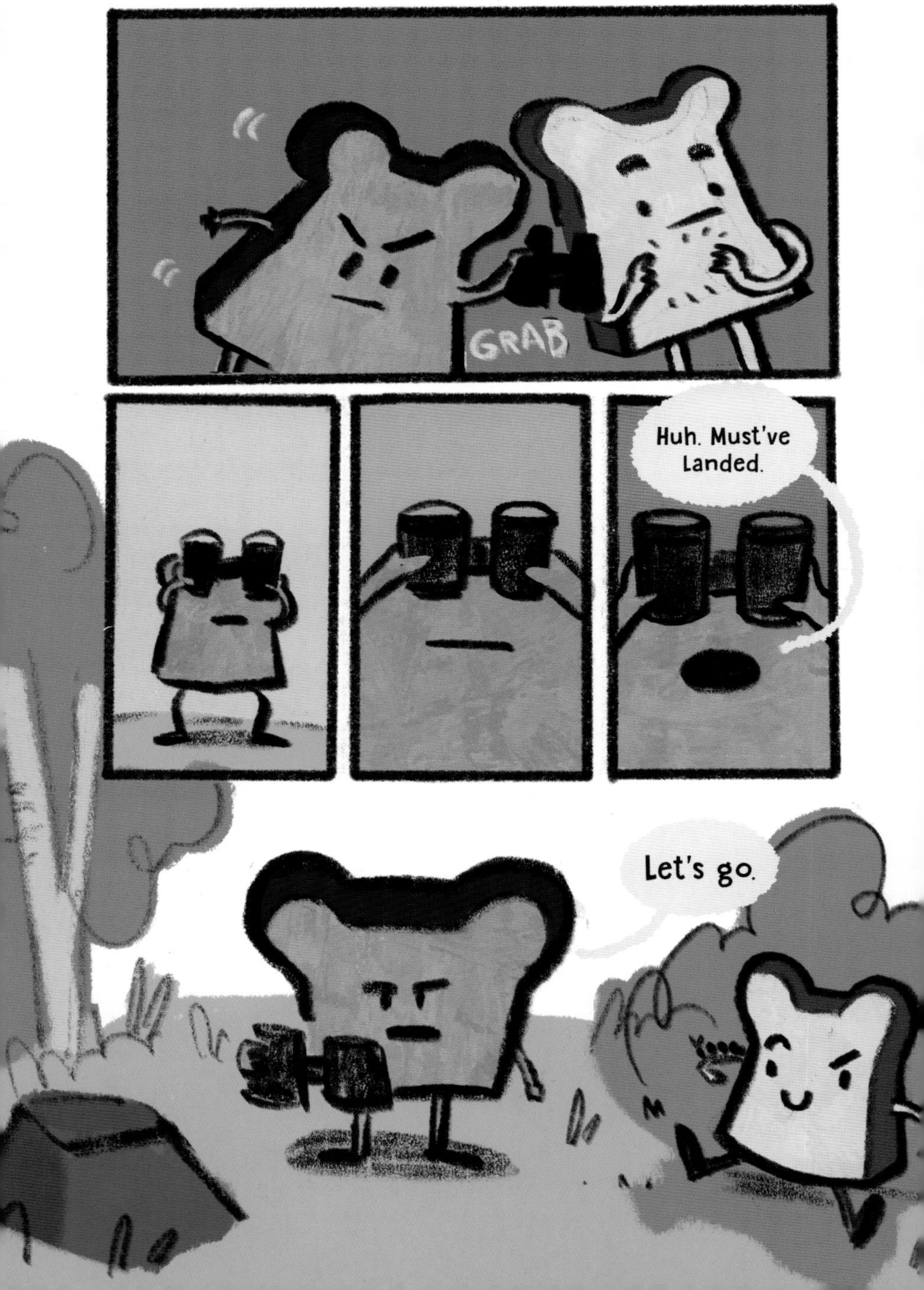
GRAB
Huh. Must've Landed.
Let's go.

CHAPTER SIX

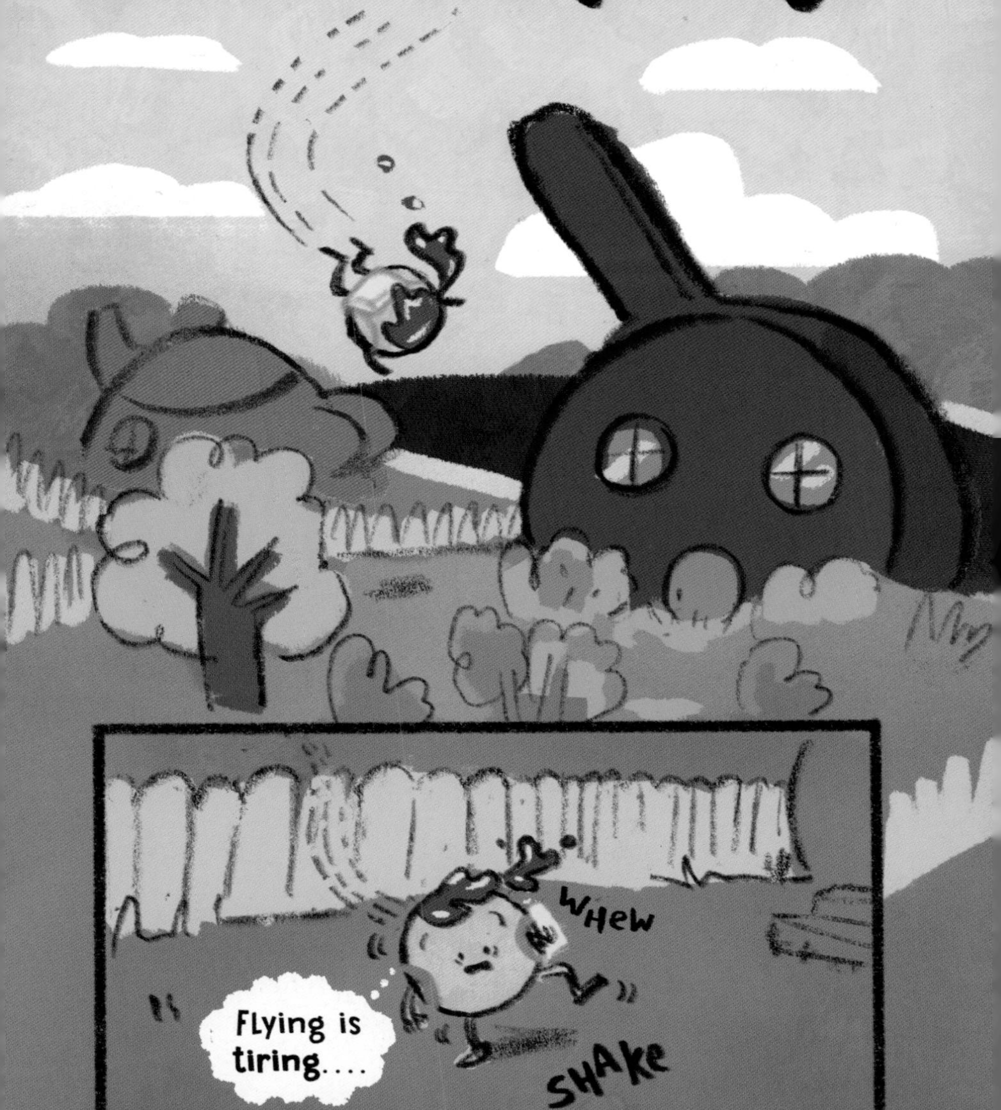
WHEW
Flying is tiring....
SHAKE

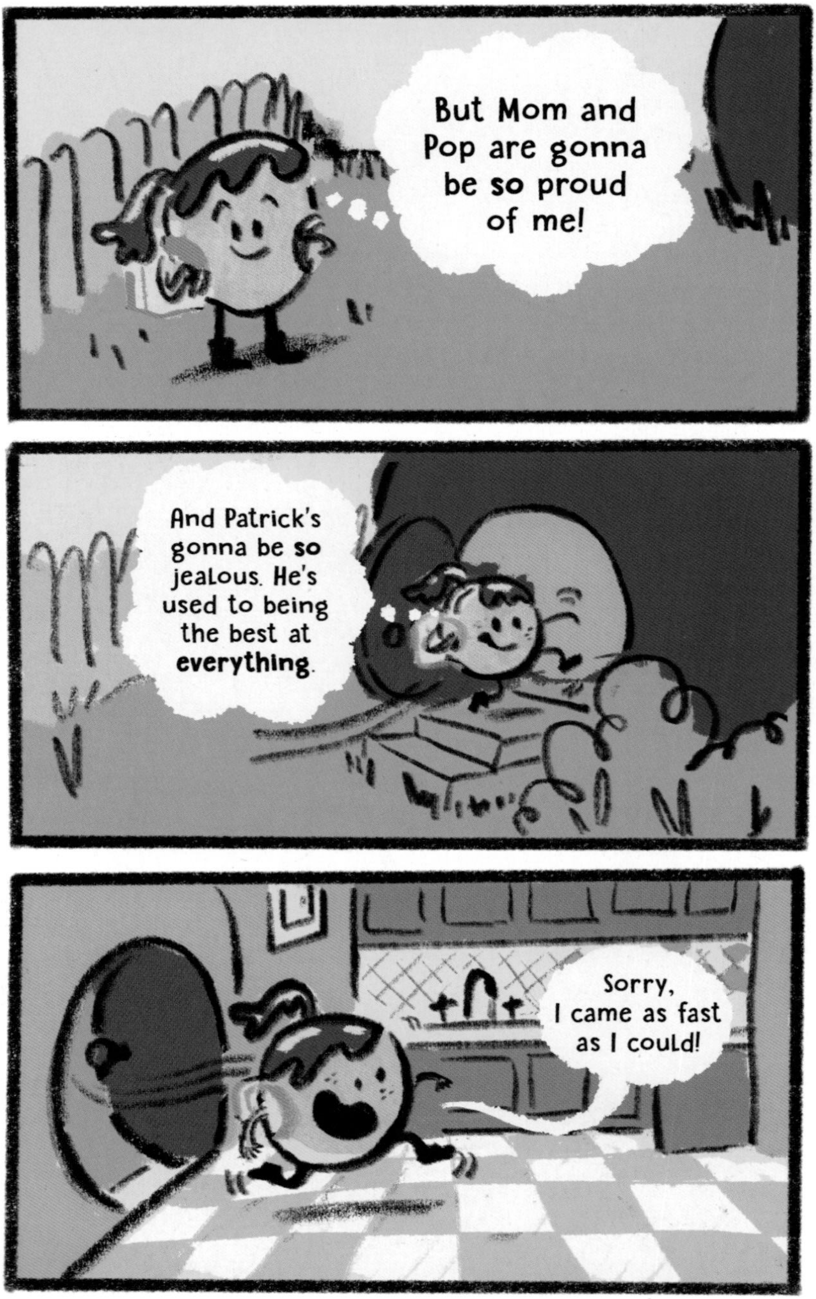
But Mom and Pop are gonna be so proud of me!
And Patrick's gonna be so jealous. He's used to being the best at everything.
Sorry, I came as fast as I could!

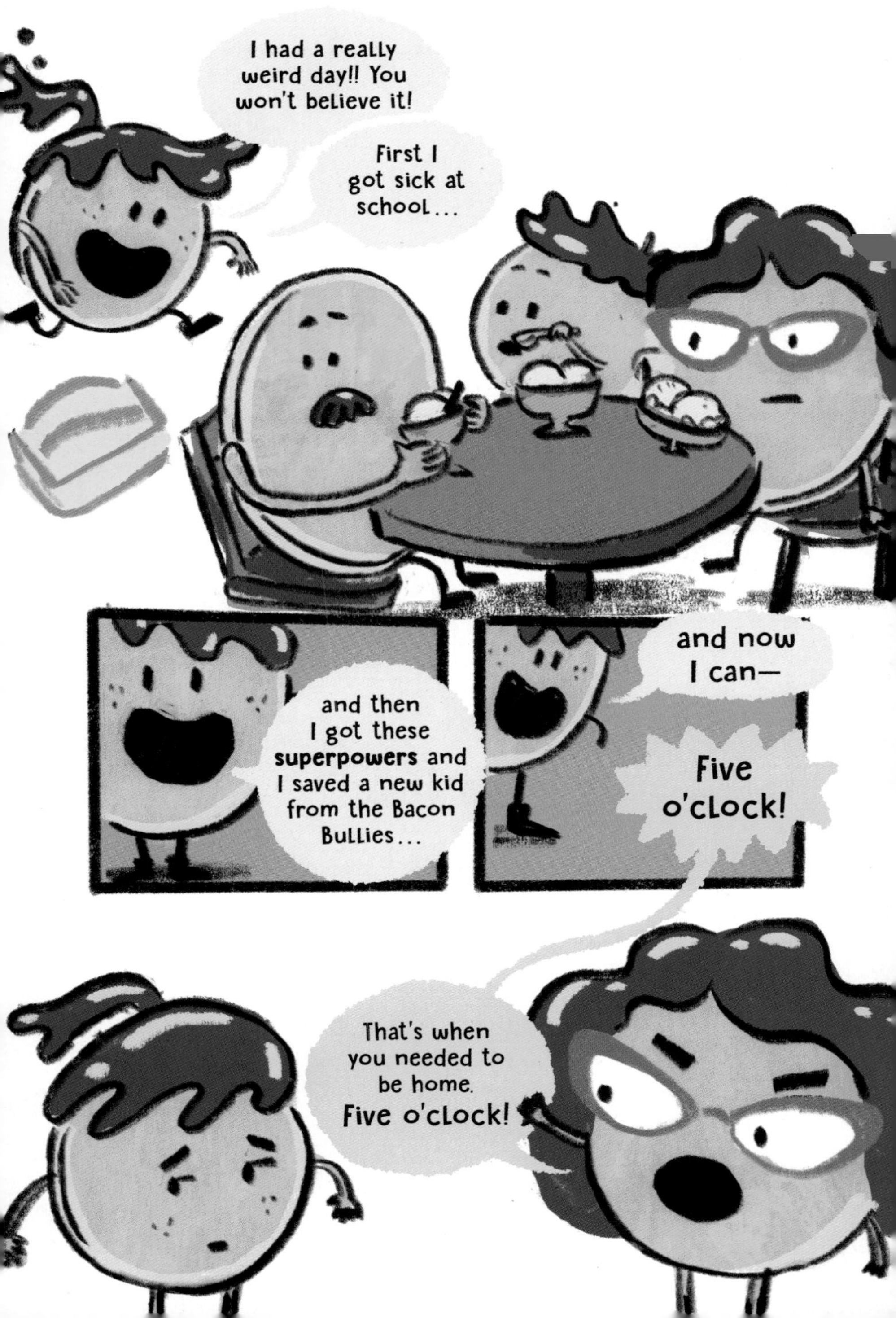
I had a really weird day!! You won't believe it!
First I got sick at school...
and then I got these **superpowers** and I saved a new kid from the Bacon Bullies...
and now I can—
Five o'clock!
That's when you needed to be home. Five o'clock!

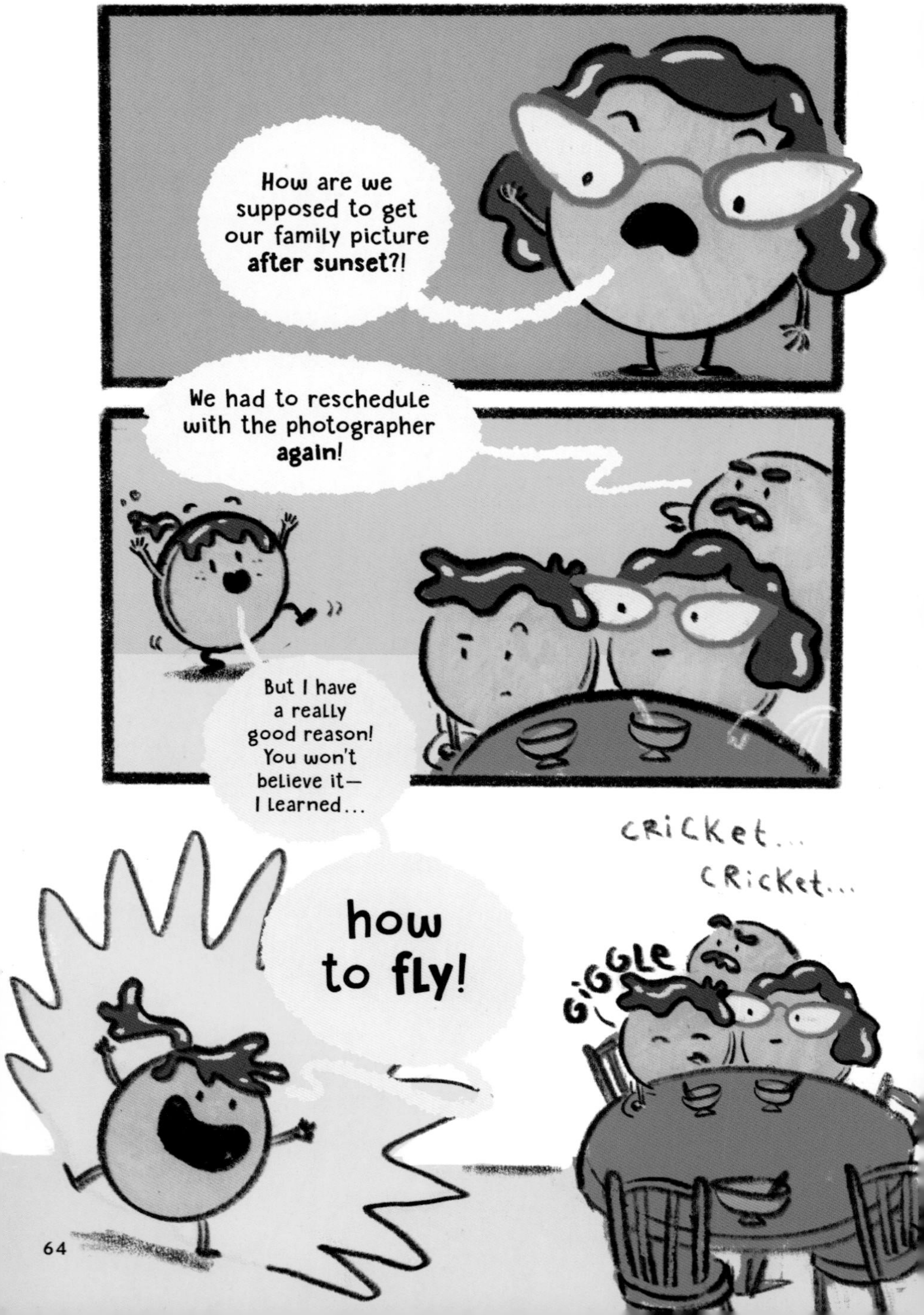
How are we supposed to get our family picture **after sunset**?!
We had to reschedule with the photographer **again**!
But I have a really good reason! You won't believe it— I learned...
how to fly!
CRICKET...
CRICKET...
GIGGLE

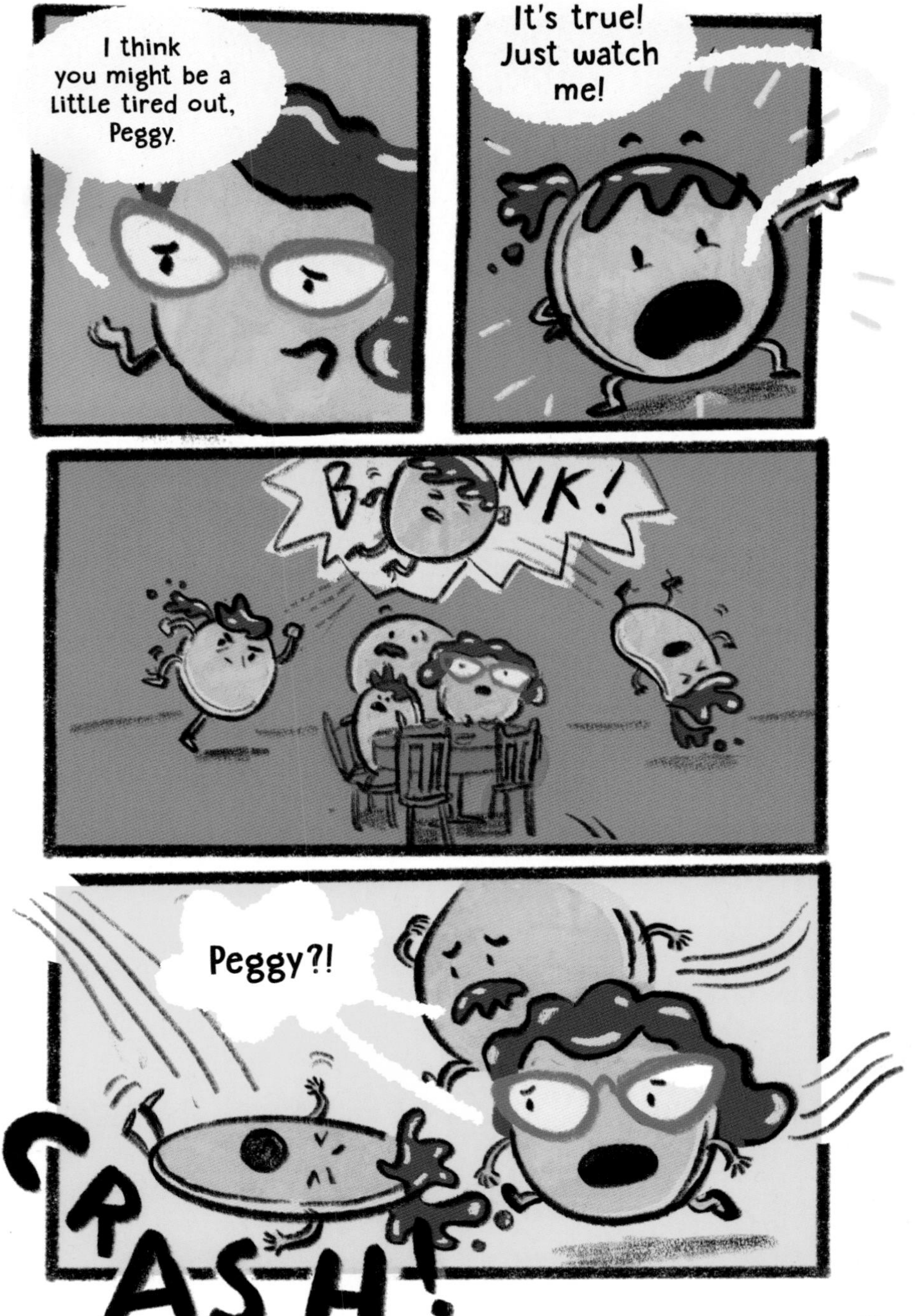
I think you might be a Little tired out, Peggy.
It's true! Just watch me!
BONK!
Peggy?!
CRASH!

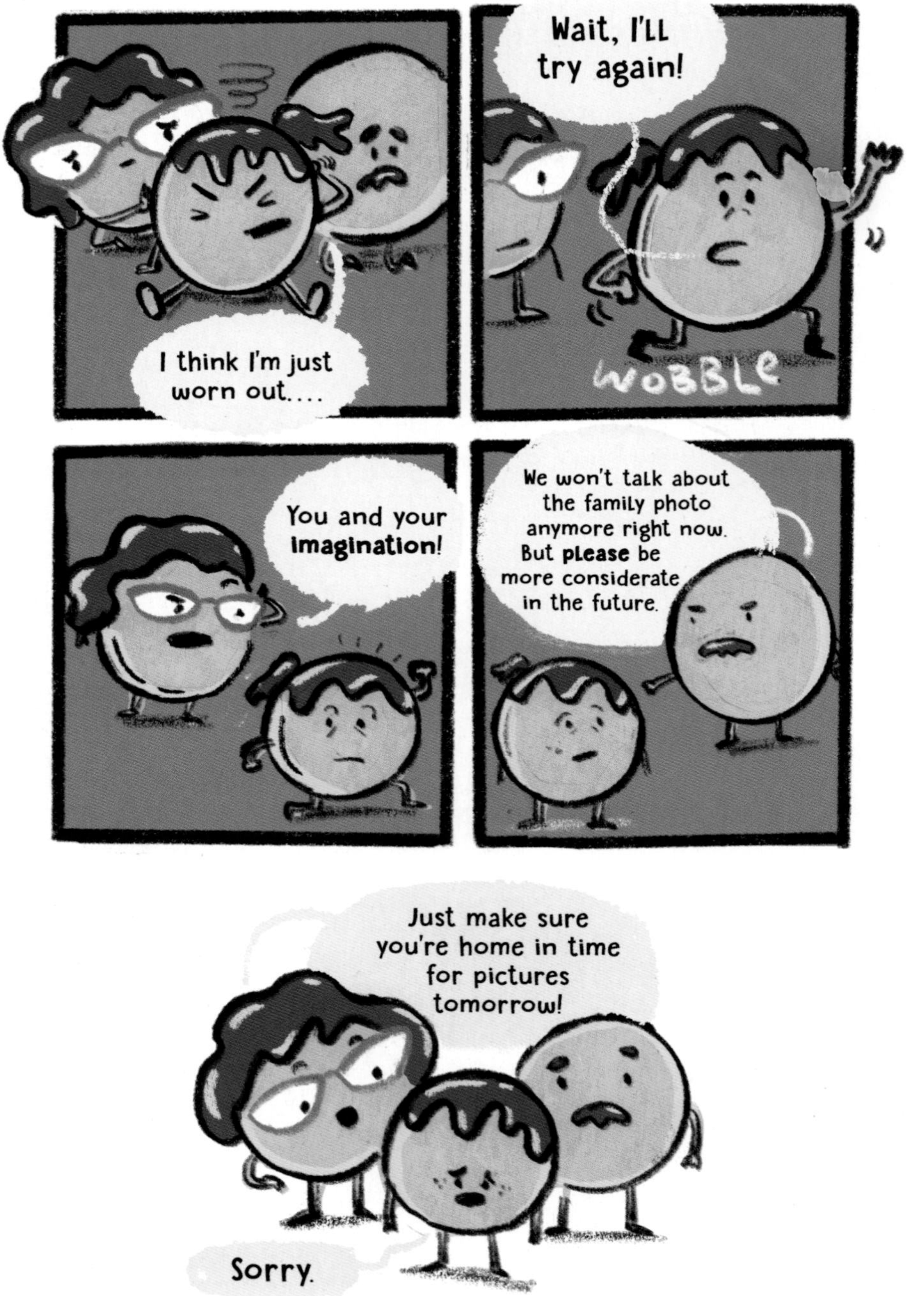
I think I'm just worn out....
Wait, I'LL try again!
WOBBLE
You and your **imagination**!
We won't talk about the family photo anymore right now. But **please** be more considerate in the future.
Just make sure you're home in time for pictures tomorrow!
Sorry.

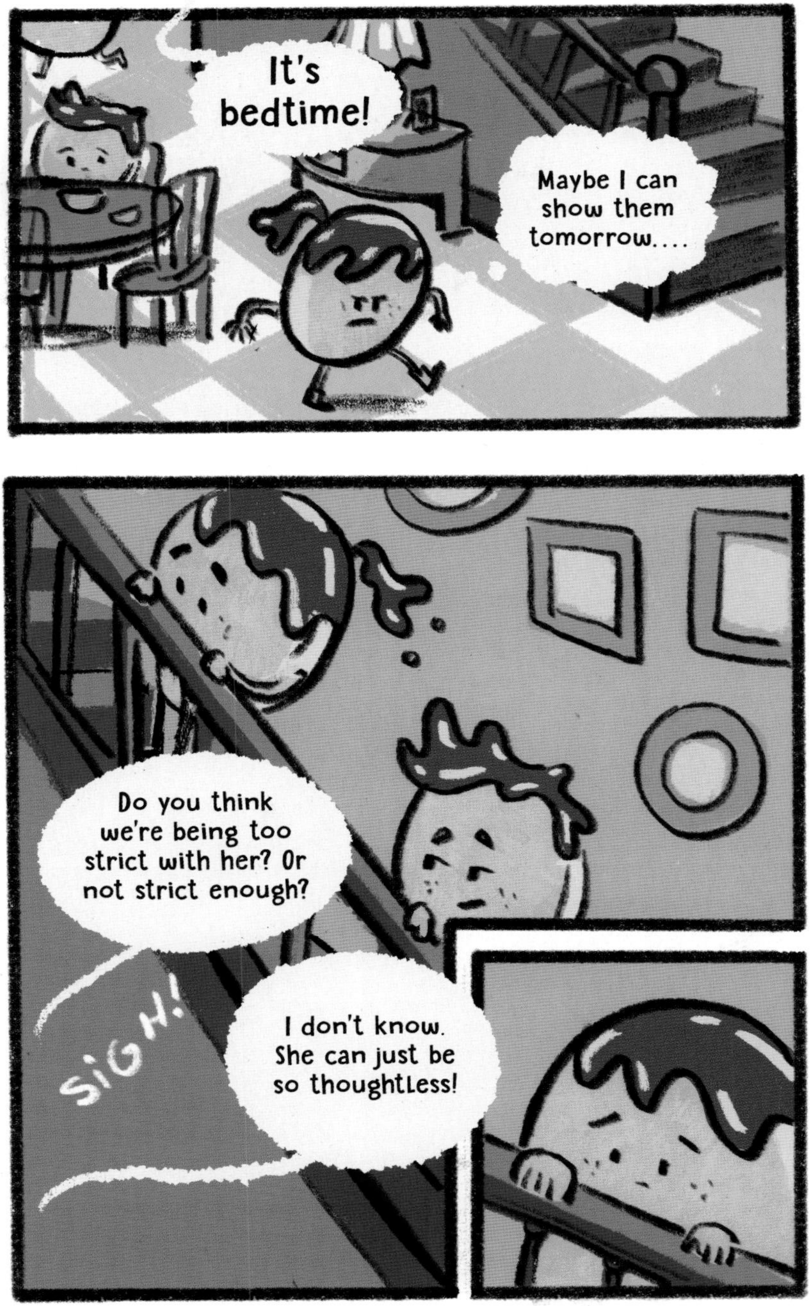
It's bedtime!
Maybe I can show them tomorrow....
Do you think we're being too strict with her? Or not strict enough?
SIGH!
I don't know. She can just be so thoughtless!

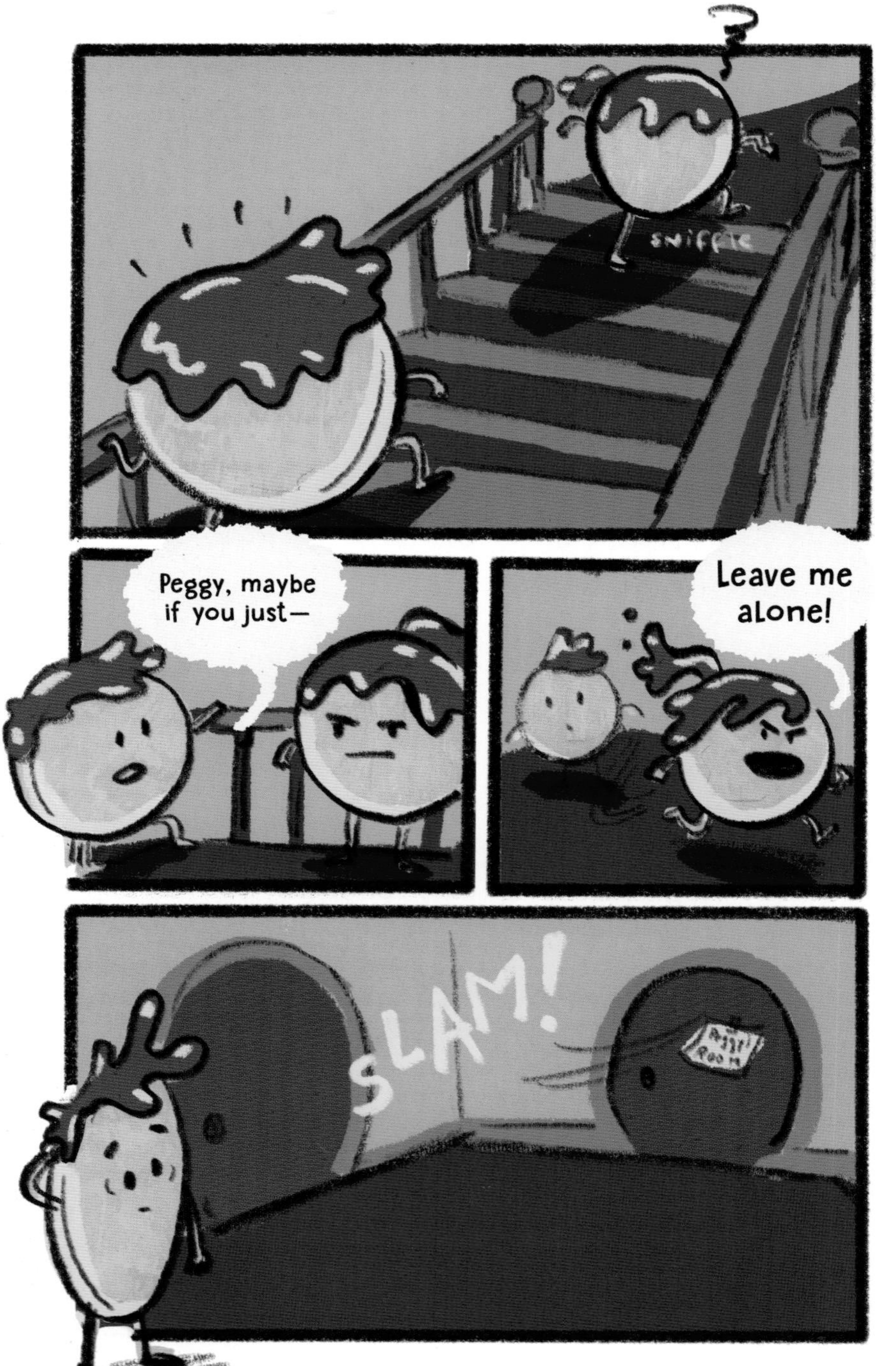
SNIFFLE
Peggy, maybe if you just—
Leave me alone!
SLAM!

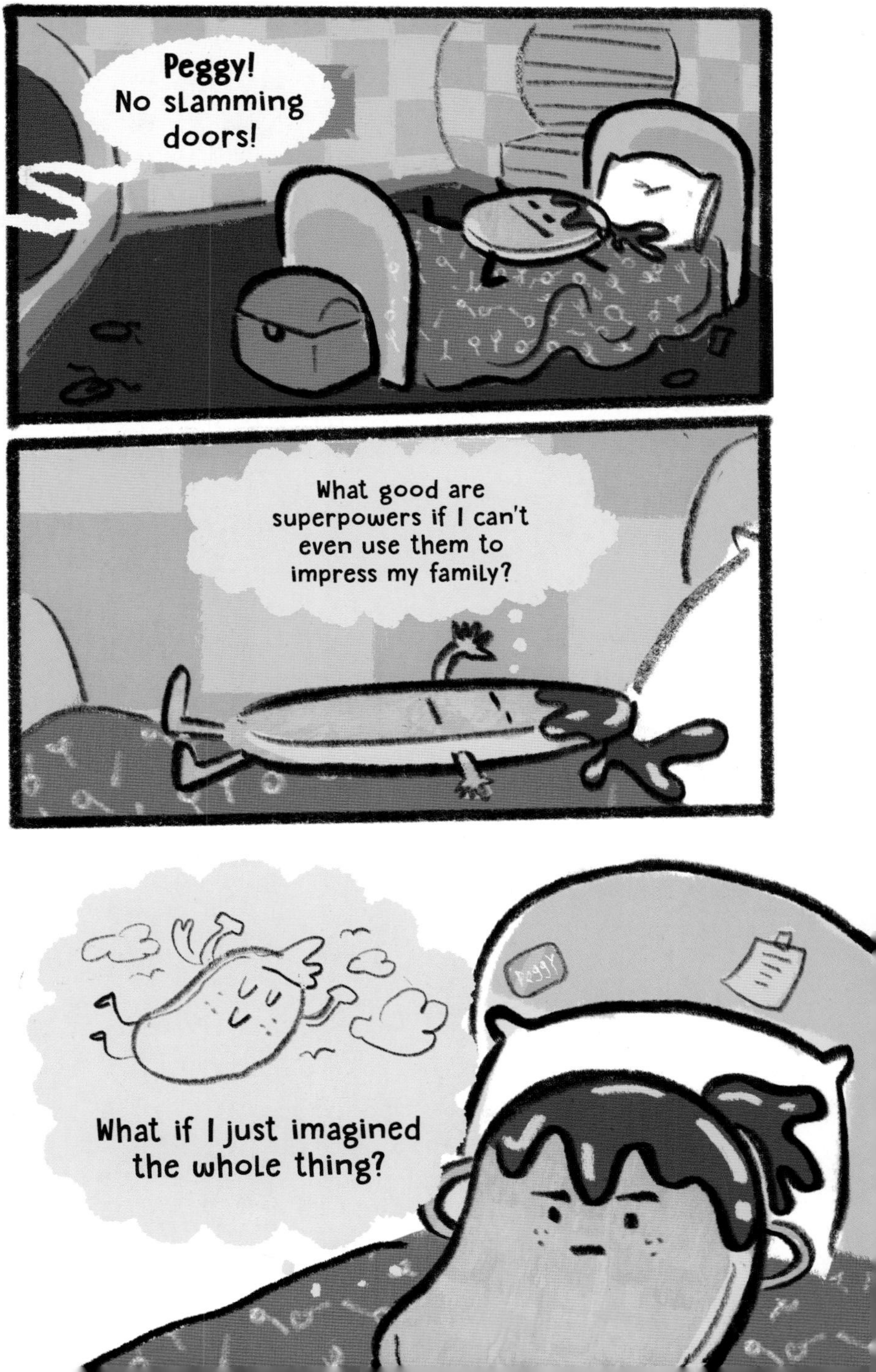
Peggy! No slamming doors!
What good are superpowers if I can't even use them to impress my family?
What if I just imagined the whole thing?

CHAPTER SEVEN

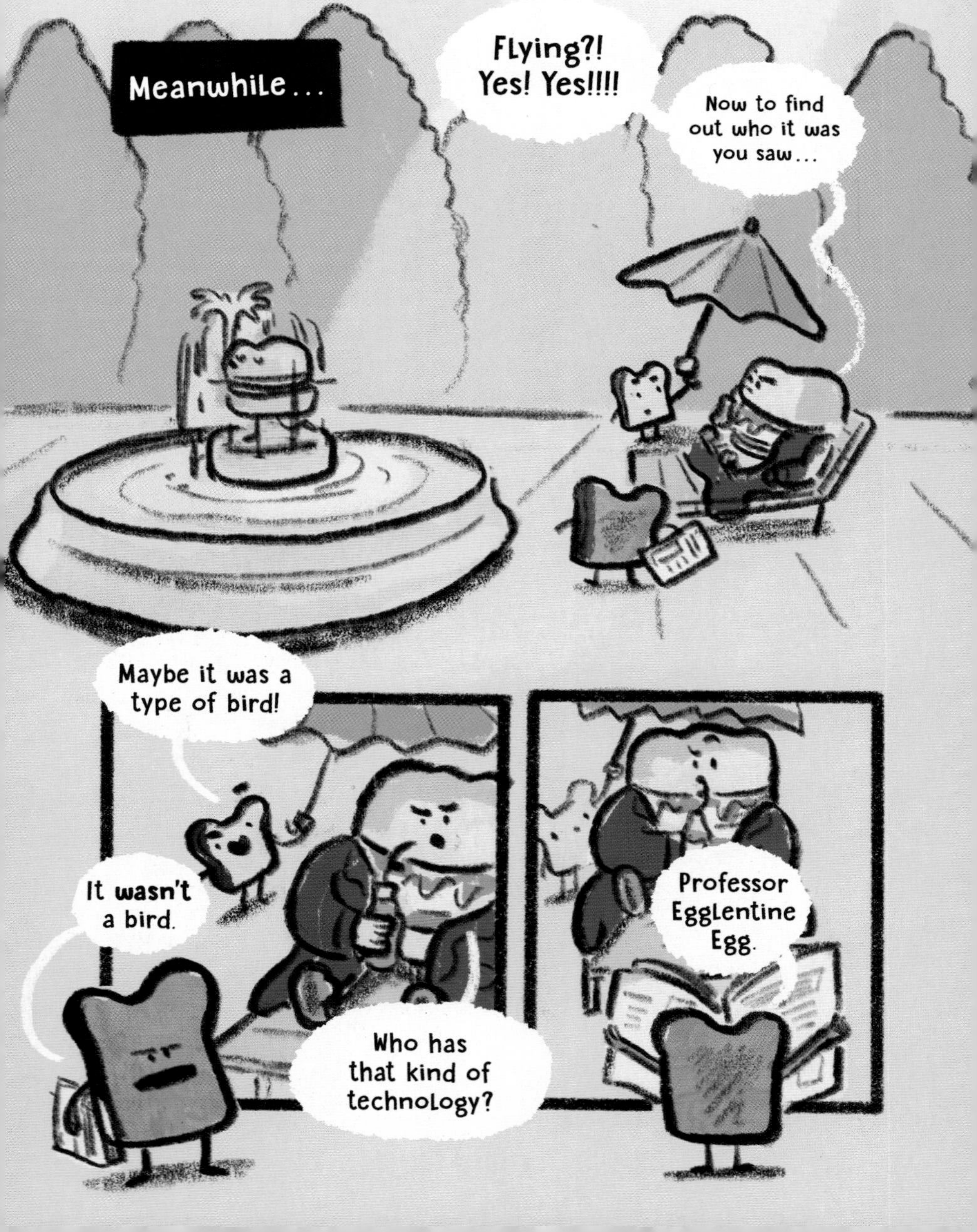

Meanwhile...
Flying?! Yes! Yes!!!!
Now to find out who it was you saw...
Maybe it was a type of bird!
It wasn't a bird.
Who has that kind of technology?
Professor Egglentine Egg.

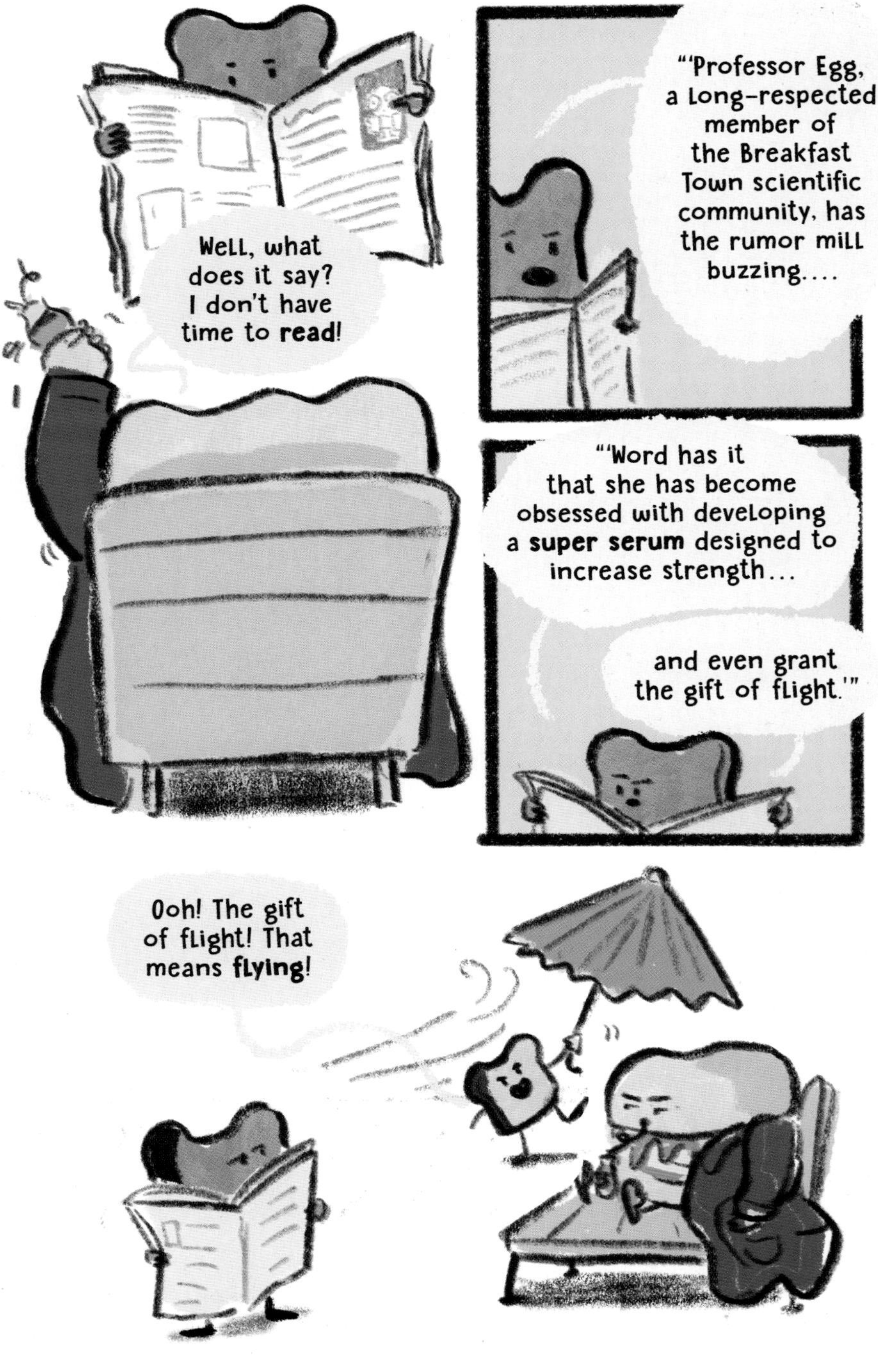
Well, what does it say? I don't have time to read!
"'Professor Egg, a long-respected member of the Breakfast Town scientific community, has the rumor mill buzzing....
"'Word has it that she has become obsessed with developing a super serum designed to increase strength...
and even grant the gift of flight.'"
Ooh! The gift of flight! That means flying!

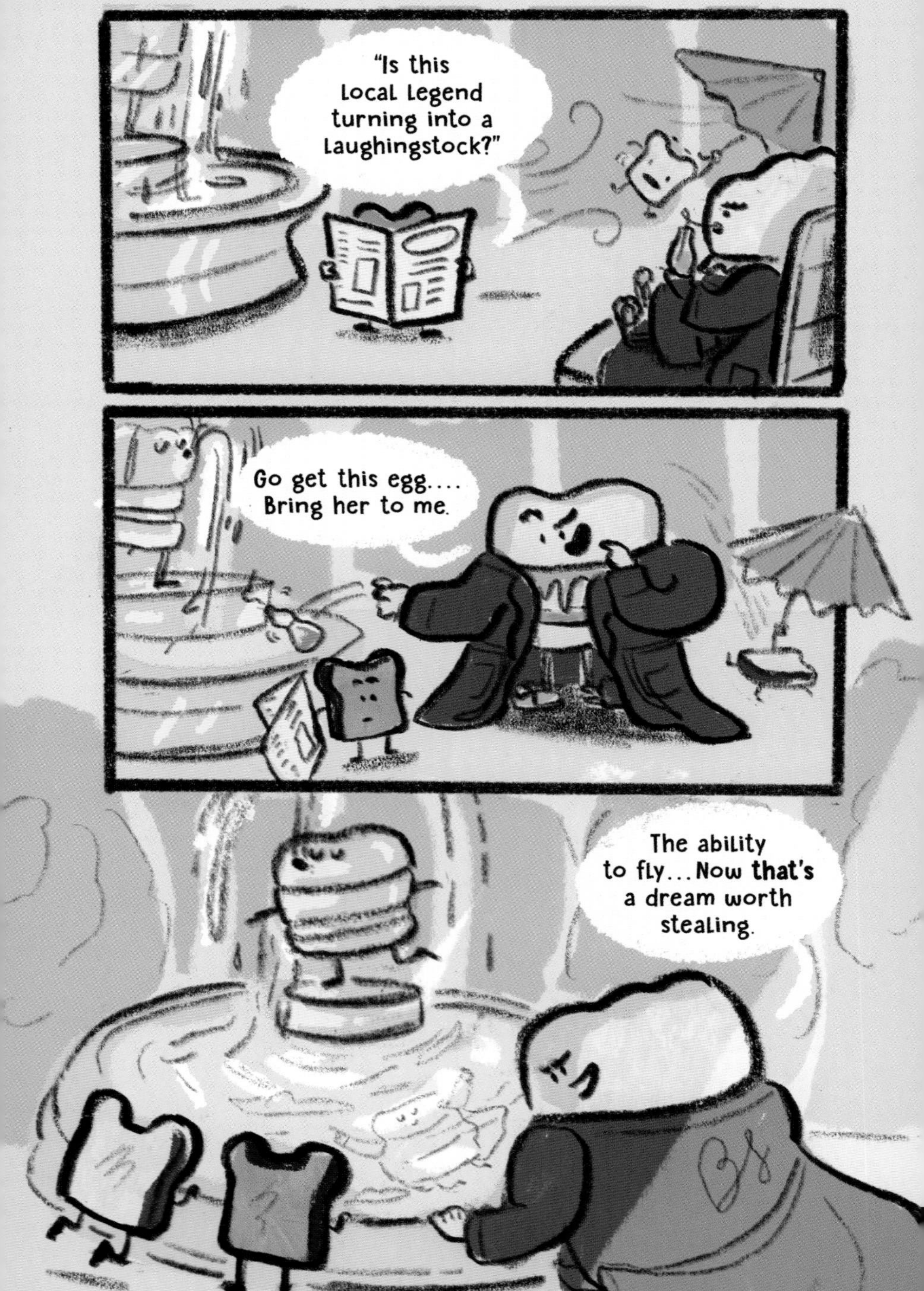
"Is this Local Legend turning into a Laughingstock?"
Go get this egg.... Bring her to me.
The ability to fly... Now **that's** a dream worth stealing.

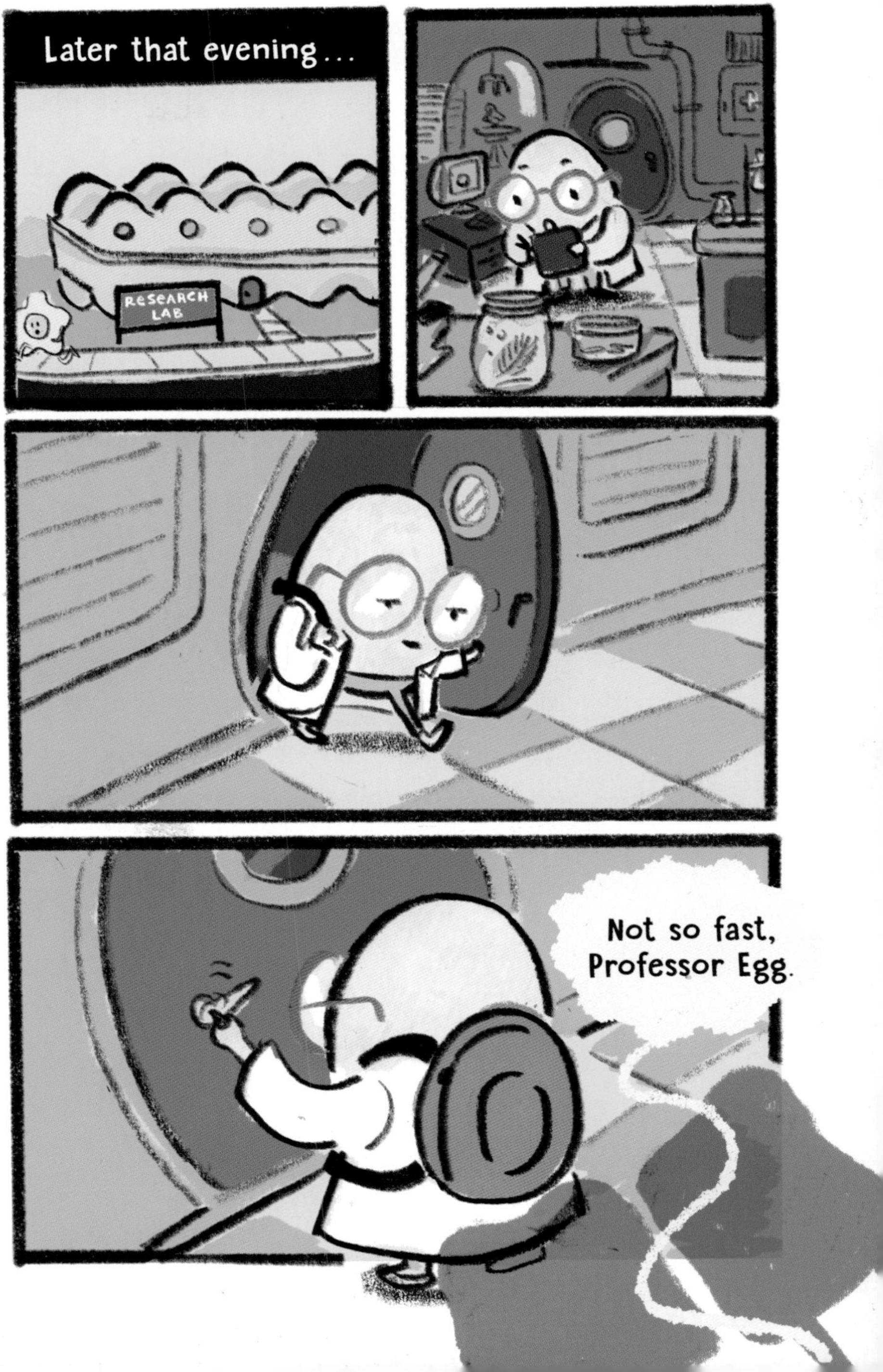
Later that evening...
RESEARCH LAB
Not so fast, Professor Egg.

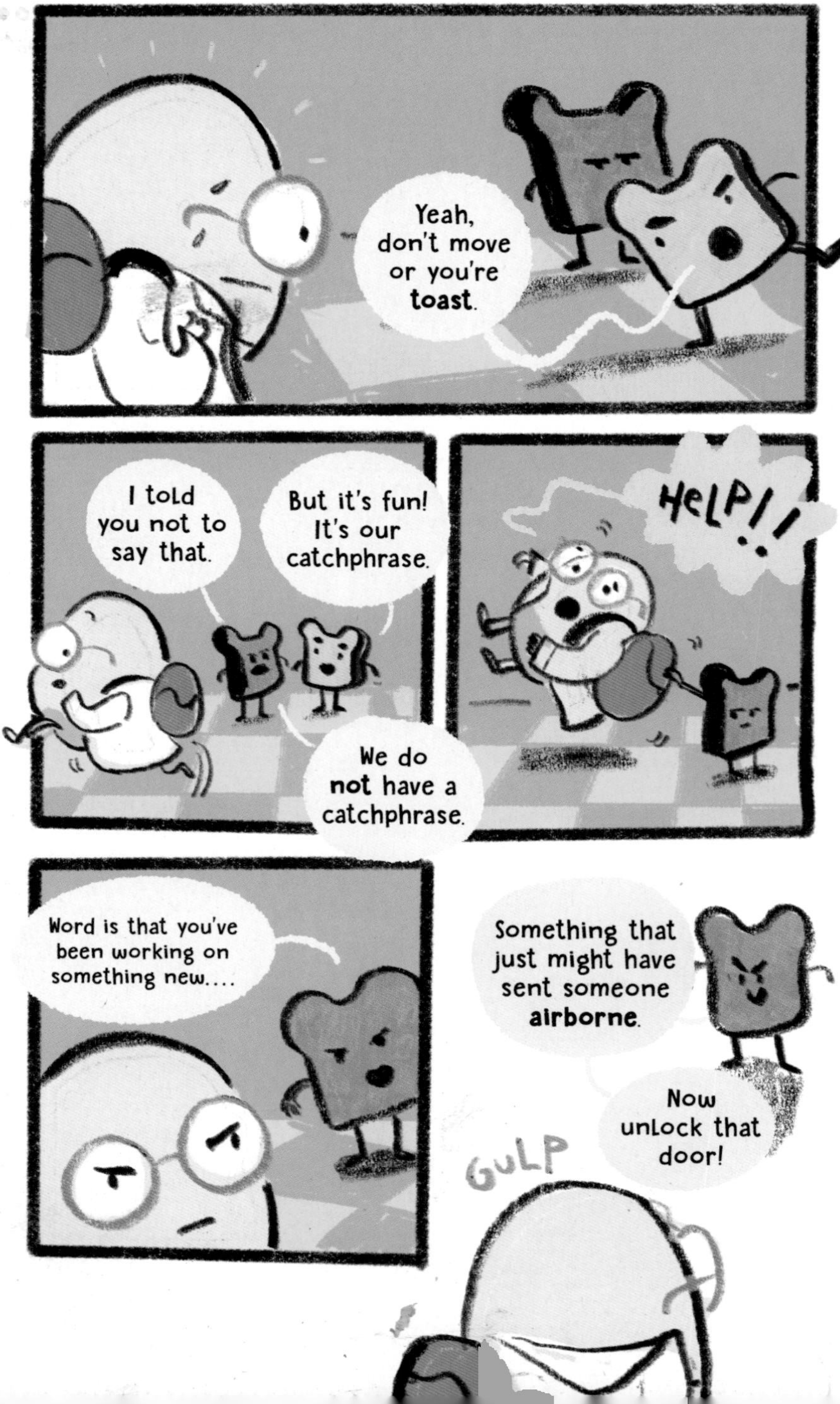
Yeah, don't move or you're **toast**.
I told you not to say that.
But it's fun! It's our catchphrase.
We do **not** have a catchphrase.
HELP!!
Word is that you've been working on something new....
Something that just might have sent someone **airborne**.
Now unlock that door!
GULP

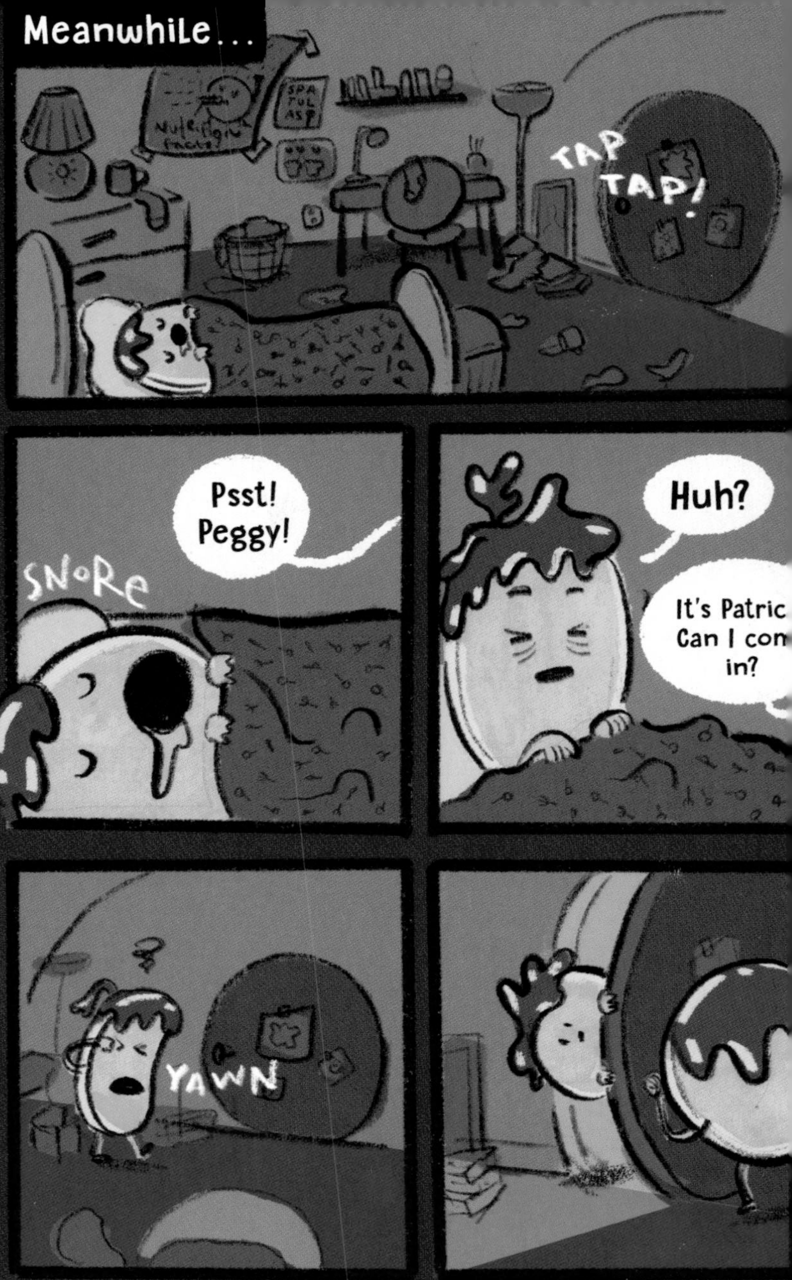
Meanwhile...
TAP TAP!
Psst! Peggy!
SNORE
Huh?
It's Patric
Can I com
in?
YAWN

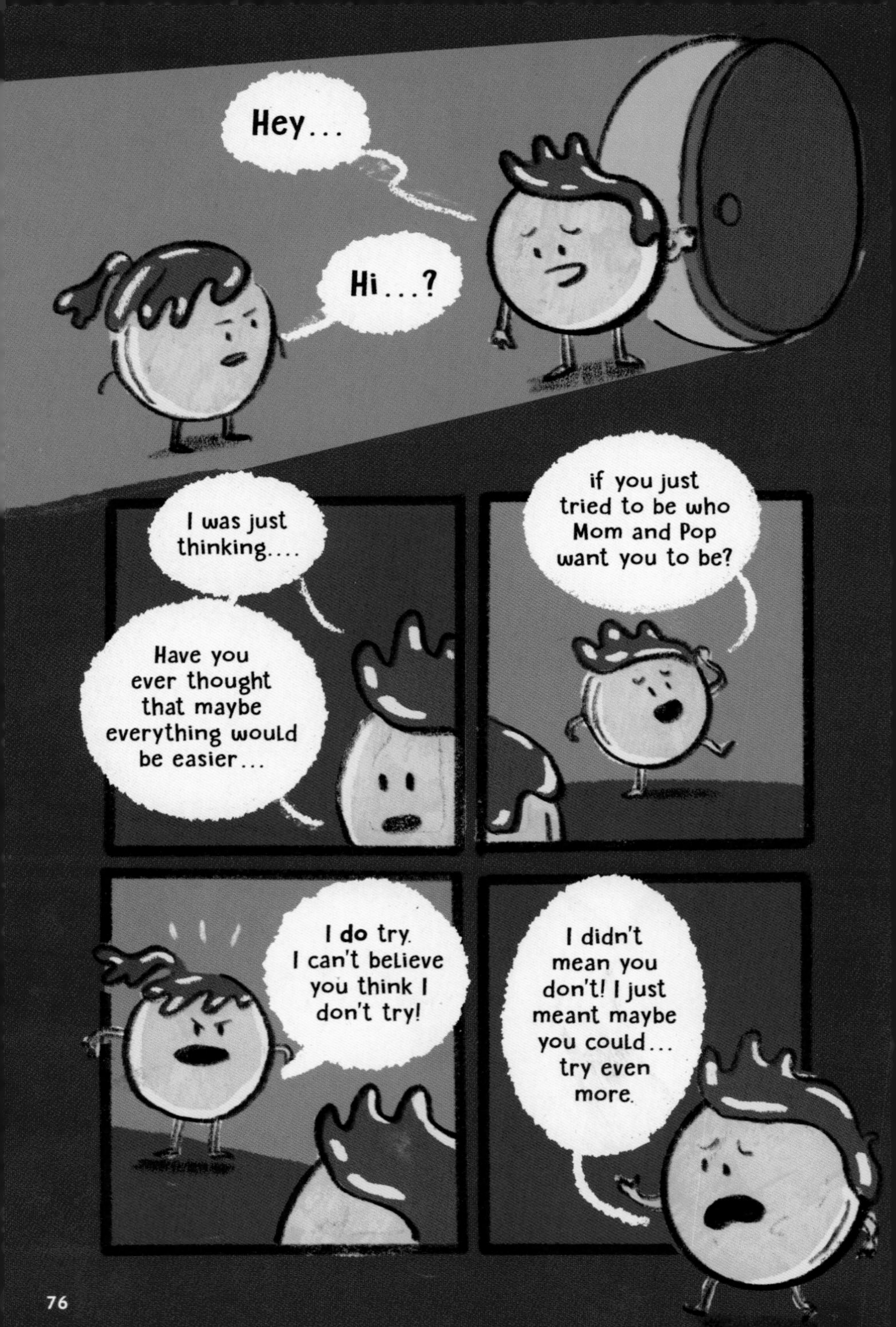
Hey...
Hi...?
I was just thinking....
Have you ever thought that maybe everything would be easier...
if you just tried to be who Mom and Pop want you to be?
I do try. I can't believe you think I don't try!
I didn't mean you don't! I just meant maybe you could... try even more.

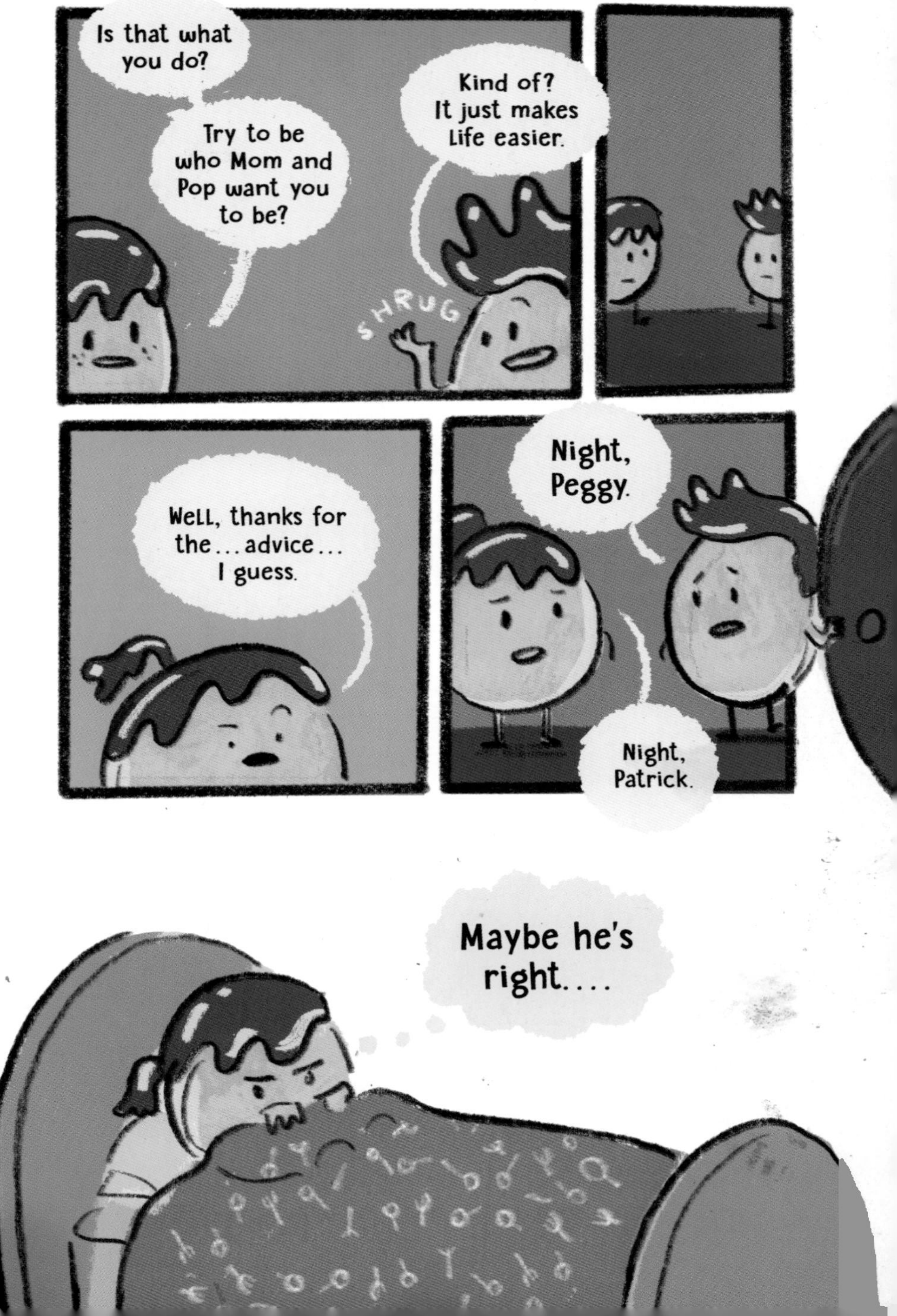
Is that what you do?
Try to be who Mom and Pop want you to be?
Kind of? It just makes Life easier.
SHRUG
WeLL, thanks for the . . . advice . . . I guess.
Night, Peggy.
Night, Patrick.
Maybe he's right. . . .

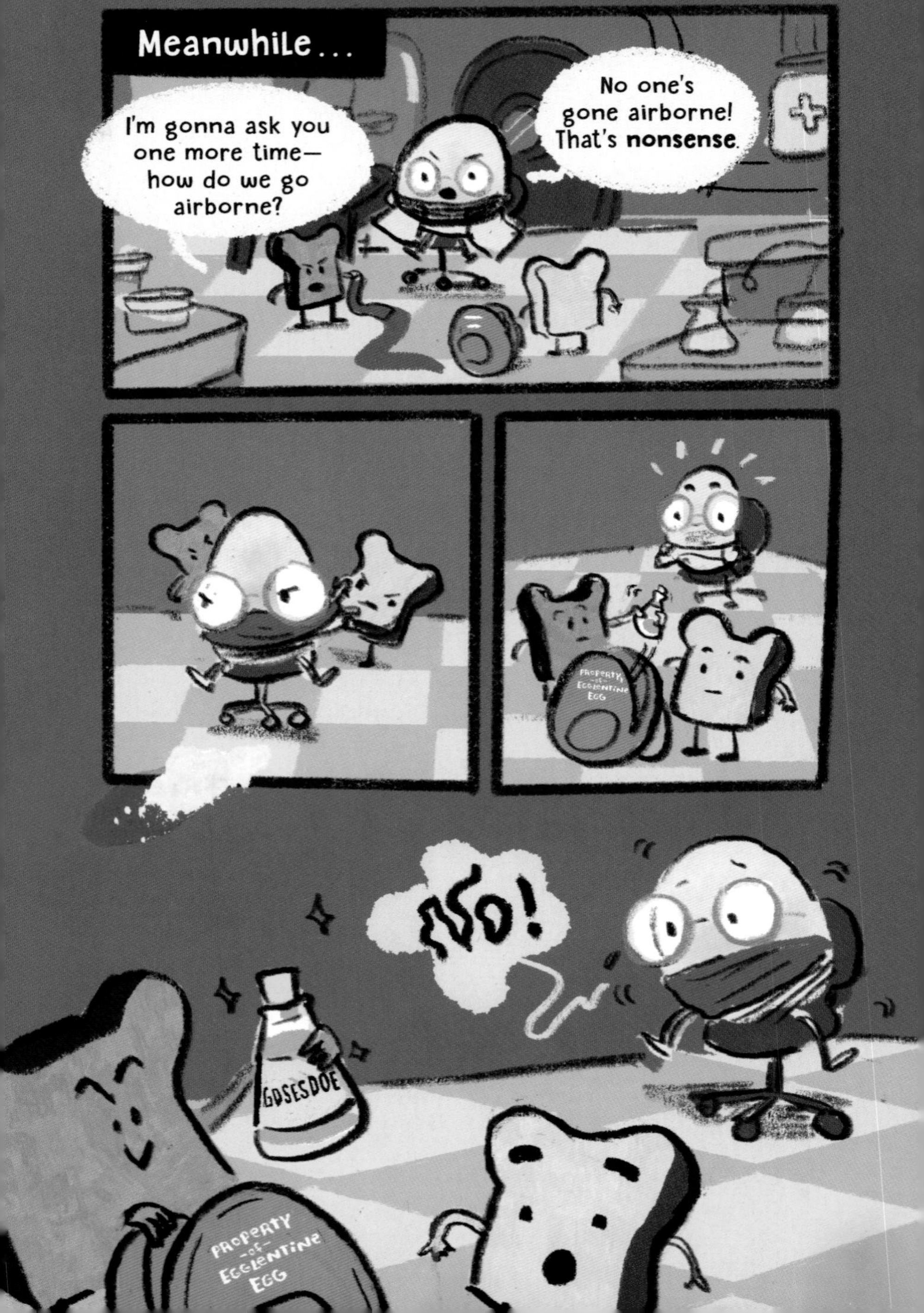
Meanwhile...
I'm gonna ask you one more time— how do we go airborne?
No one's gone airborne! That's **nonsense**.
PROPERTY -of- EGGLENTINE EGG
NO!
PROPERTY -of- EGGLENTINE EGG

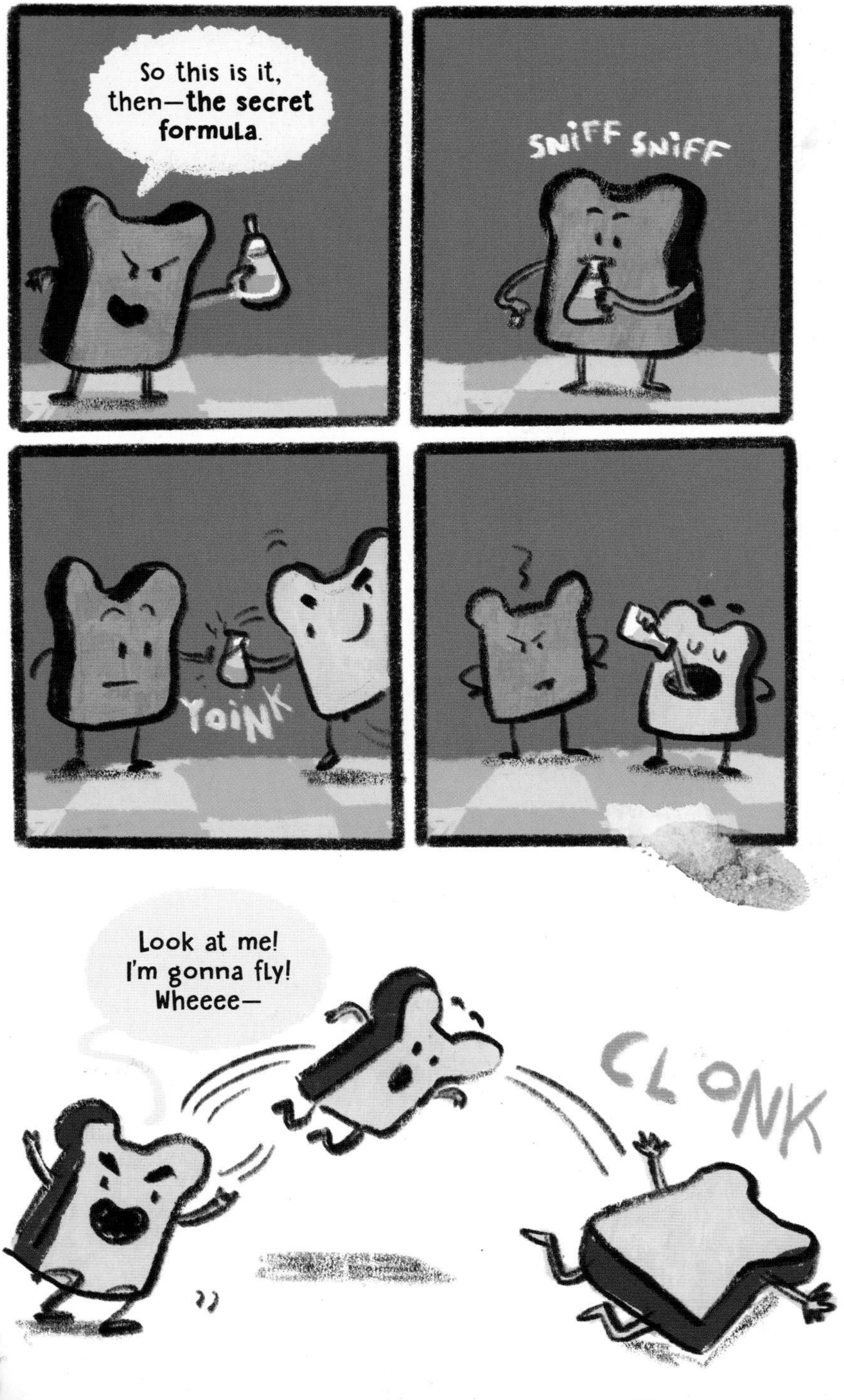
So this is it, then—the secret formula.
SNIFF SNIFF
YOINK
Look at me! I'm gonna fly! Wheeee—
CLONK

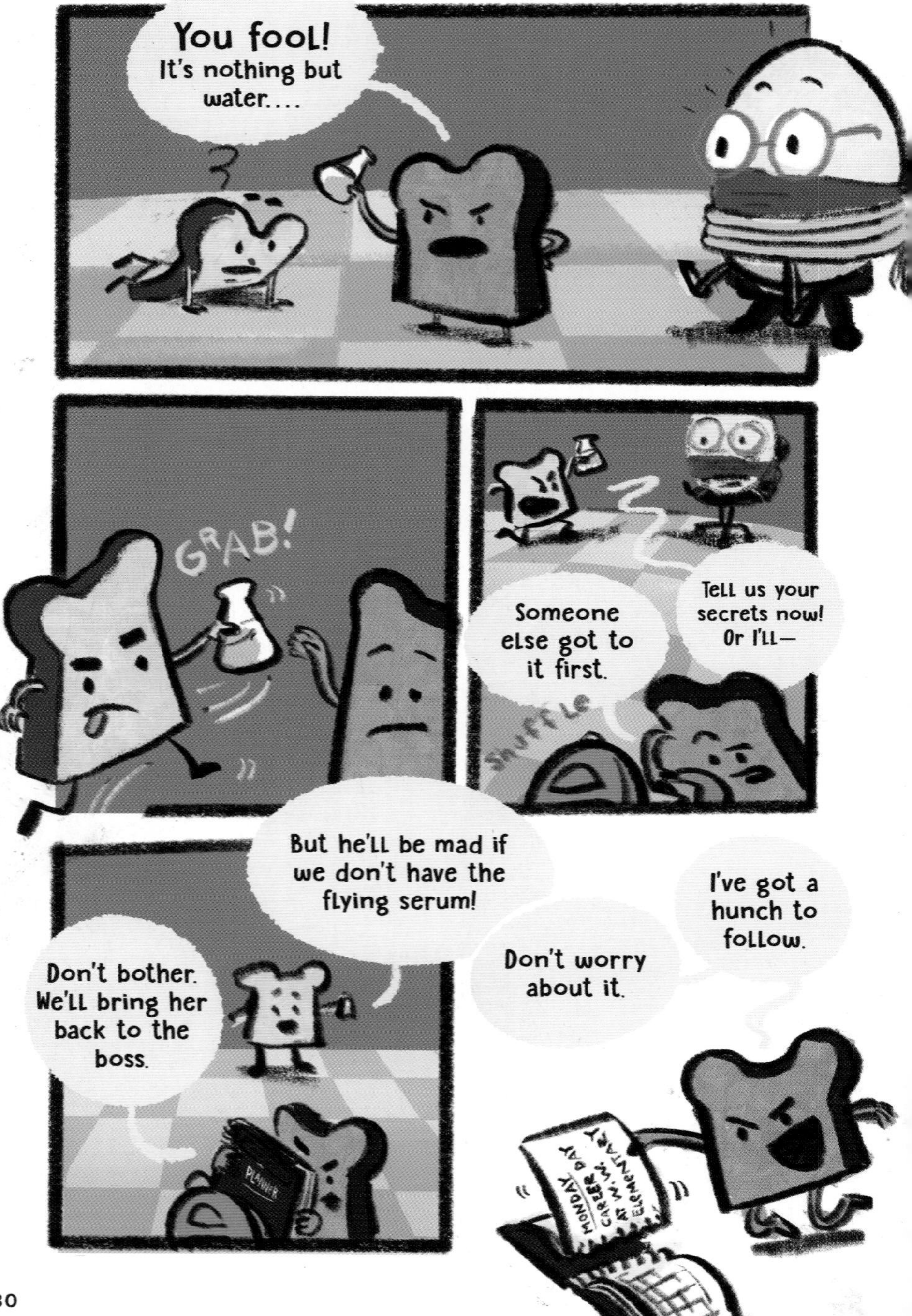
You fool!
It's nothing but water....
GRAB!
Someone else got to it first.
Tell us your secrets now! Or I'll—
SHUFFLE
But he'll be mad if we don't have the flying serum!
Don't bother. We'll bring her back to the boss.
PLANNER
Don't worry about it.
I've got a hunch to follow.
MONDAY CAREER DAY AT W. WATANI ELEMENTARY

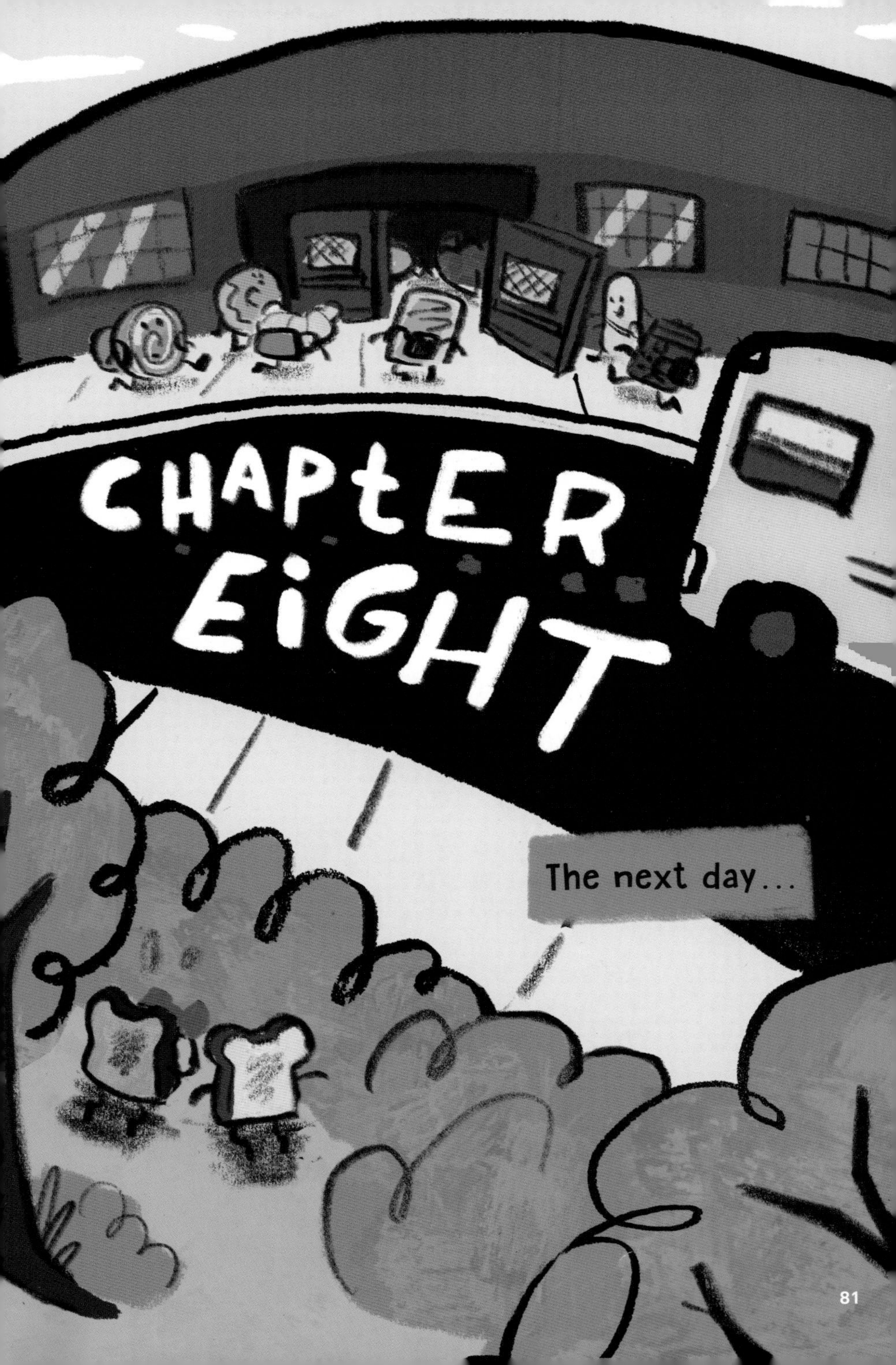
CHAPTER EIGHT
The next day...

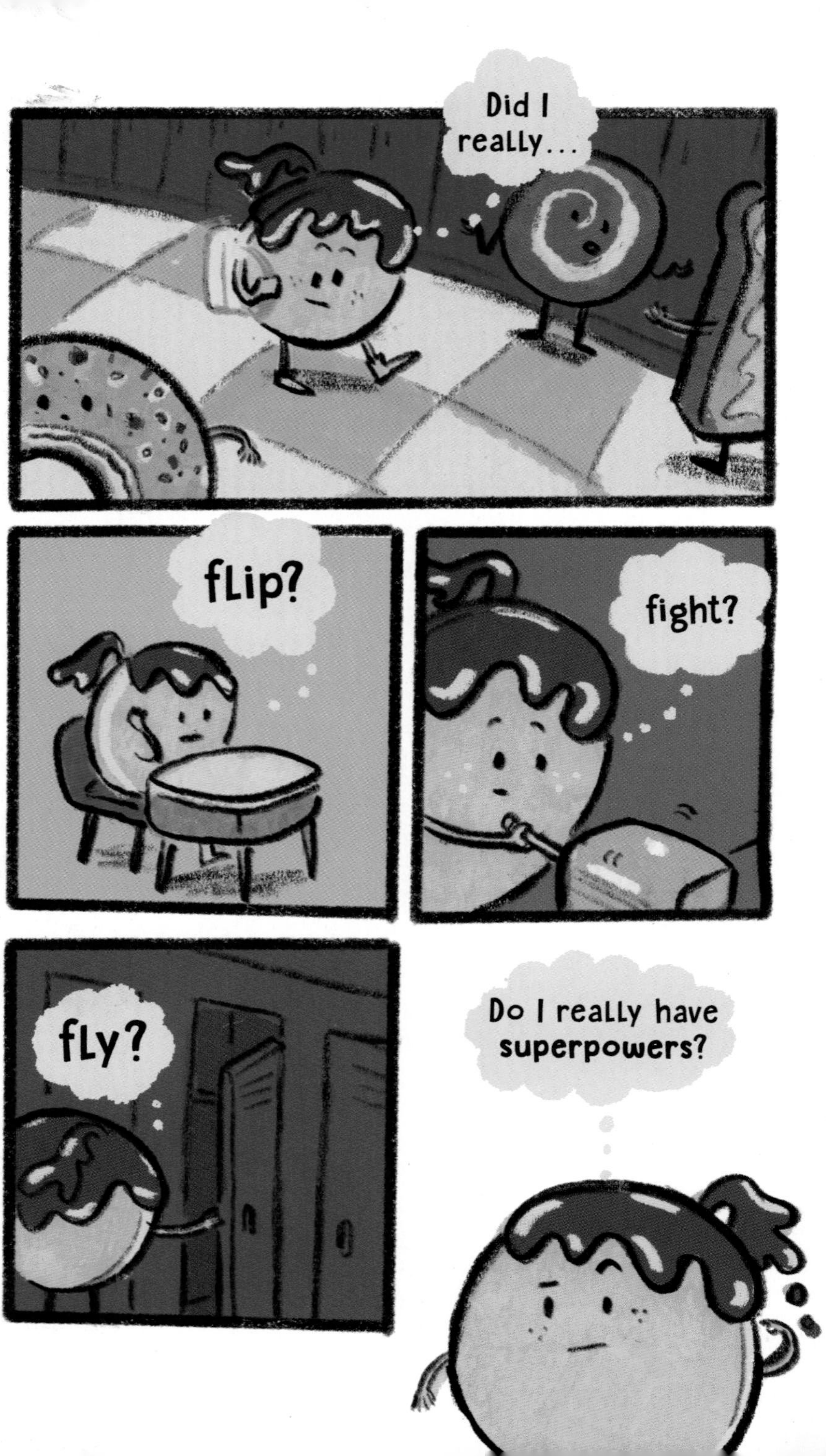
Did I
really...
fLip?
fight?
fLy?
Do I reaLLy have
superpowers?

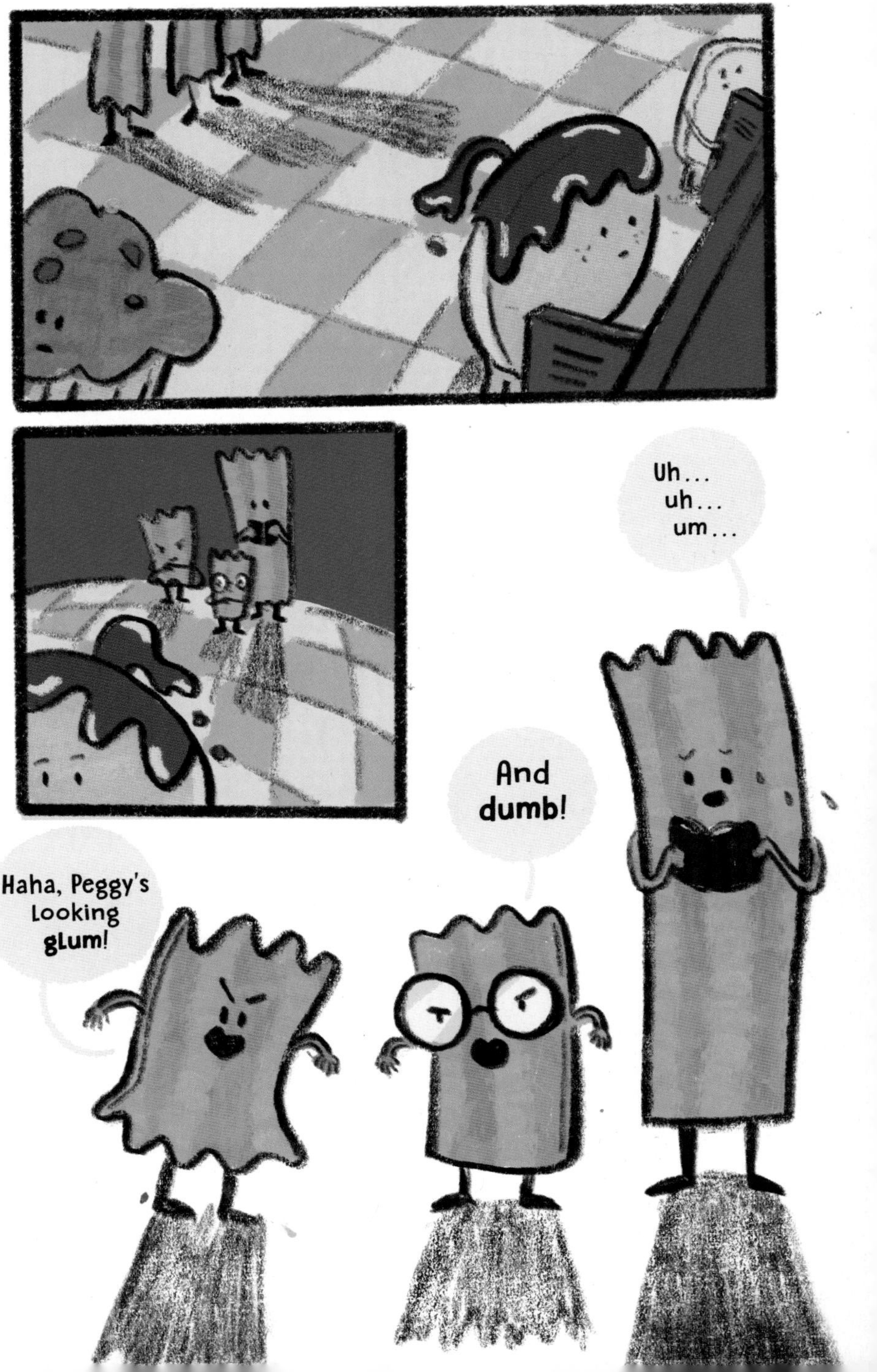
Uh...
uh...
um...
And dumb!
Haha, Peggy's looking glum!

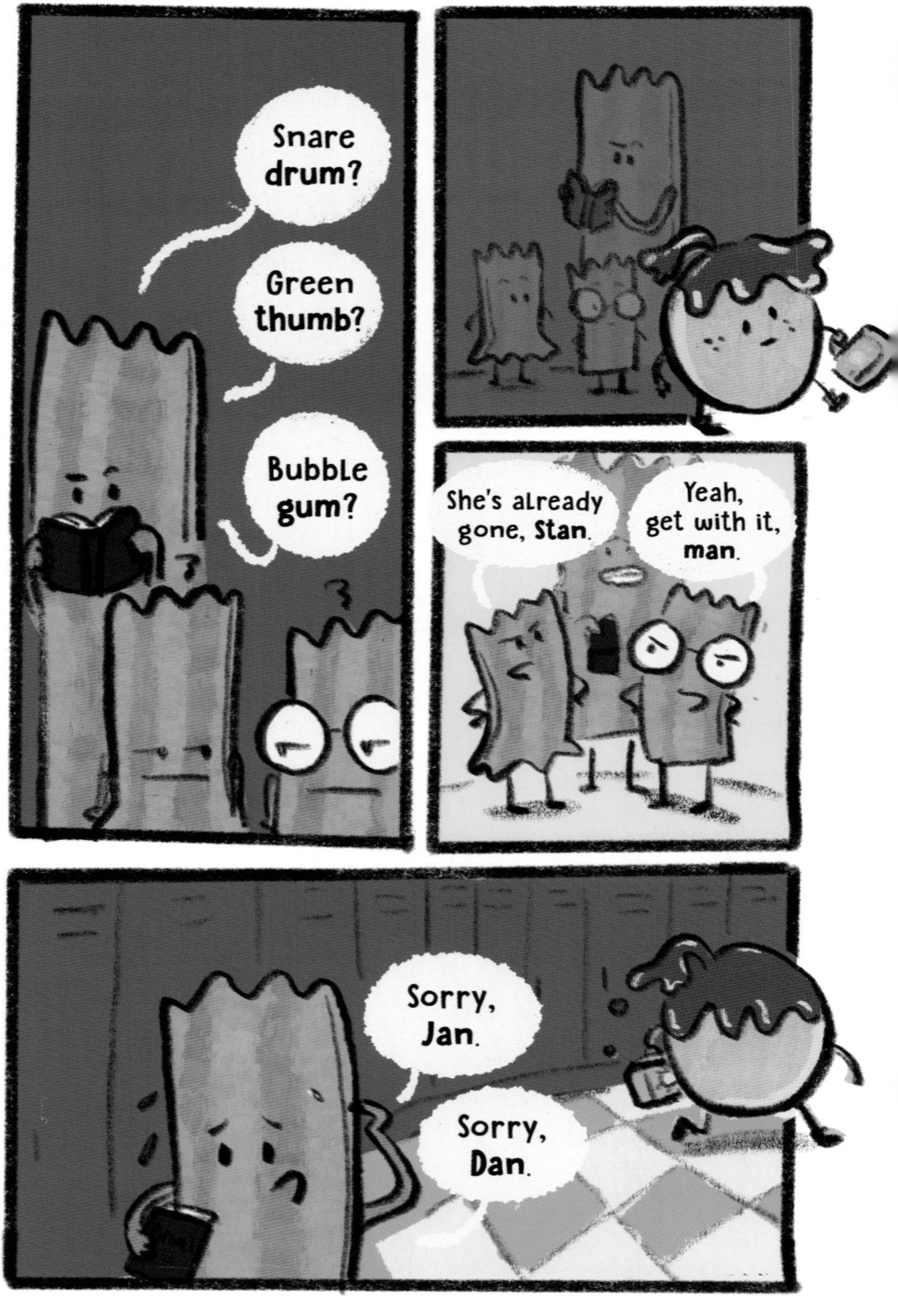
Snare drum?
Green thumb?
Bubble gum?
She's already gone, Stan.
Yeah, get with it, man.
Sorry, Jan.
Sorry, Dan.

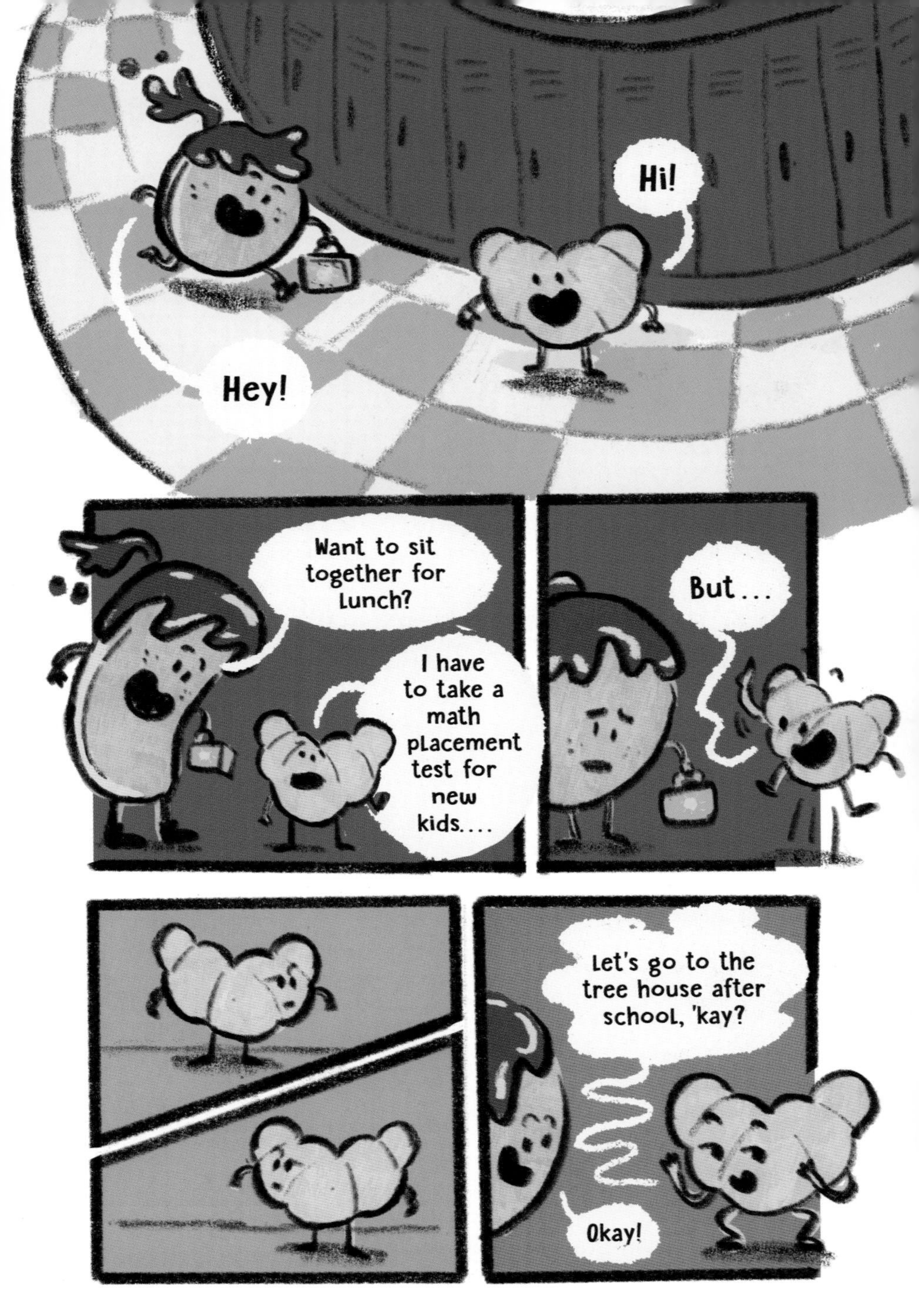
Hey!
Hi!
Want to sit together for lunch?
I have to take a math placement test for new kids....
But...
Let's go to the tree house after school, 'kay?
Okay!

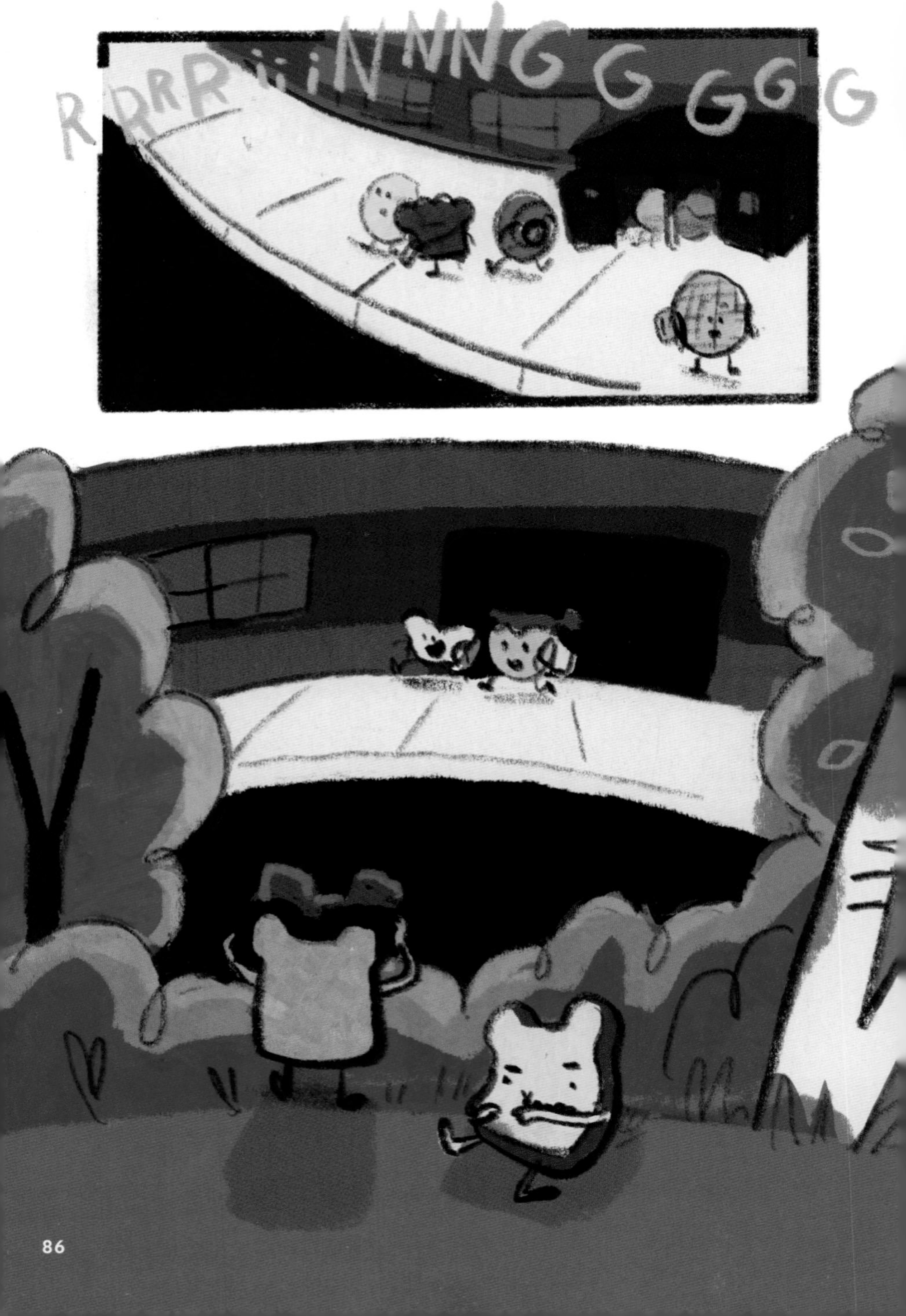
RRRRiiiNNNGGGGG

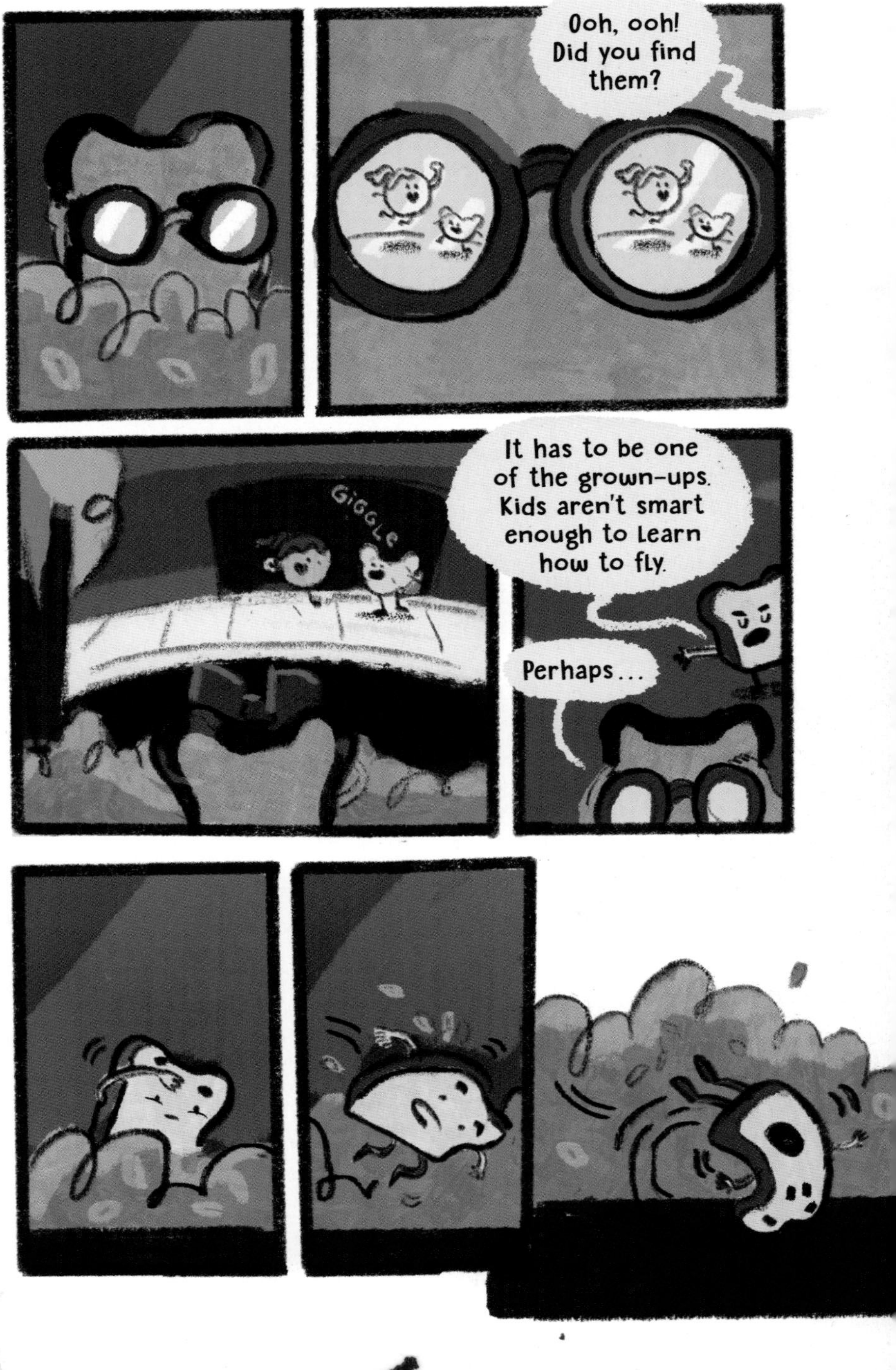

Ooh, ooh! Did you find them?
GIGGLE
It has to be one of the grown-ups. Kids aren't smart enough to Learn how to fLy.
Perhaps...

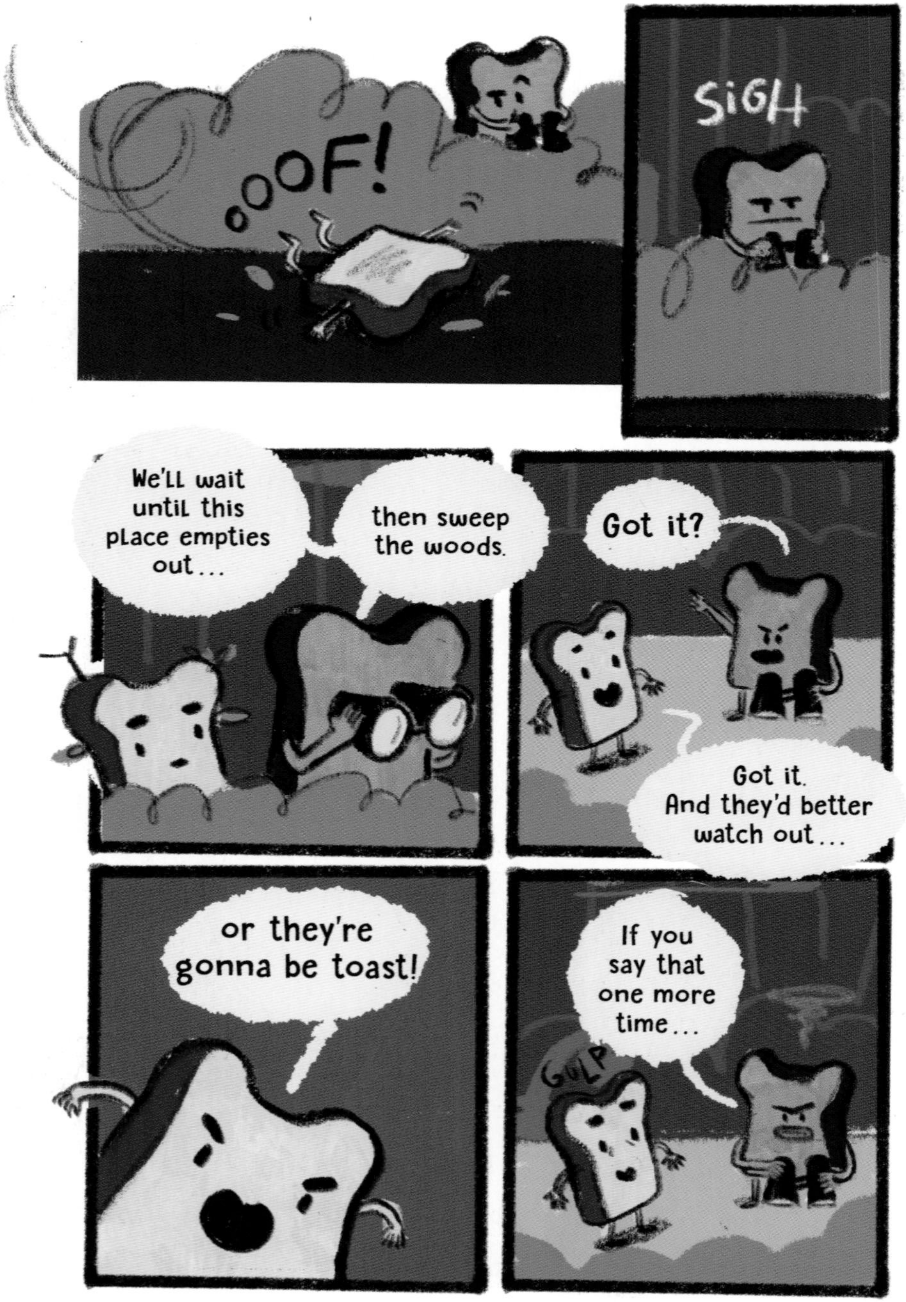

oOOF!
SiGH
We'LL wait until this pLace empties out...
then sweep the woods.
Got it?
Got it. And they'd better watch out...
or they're gonna be toast!
GULP
If you say that one more time...

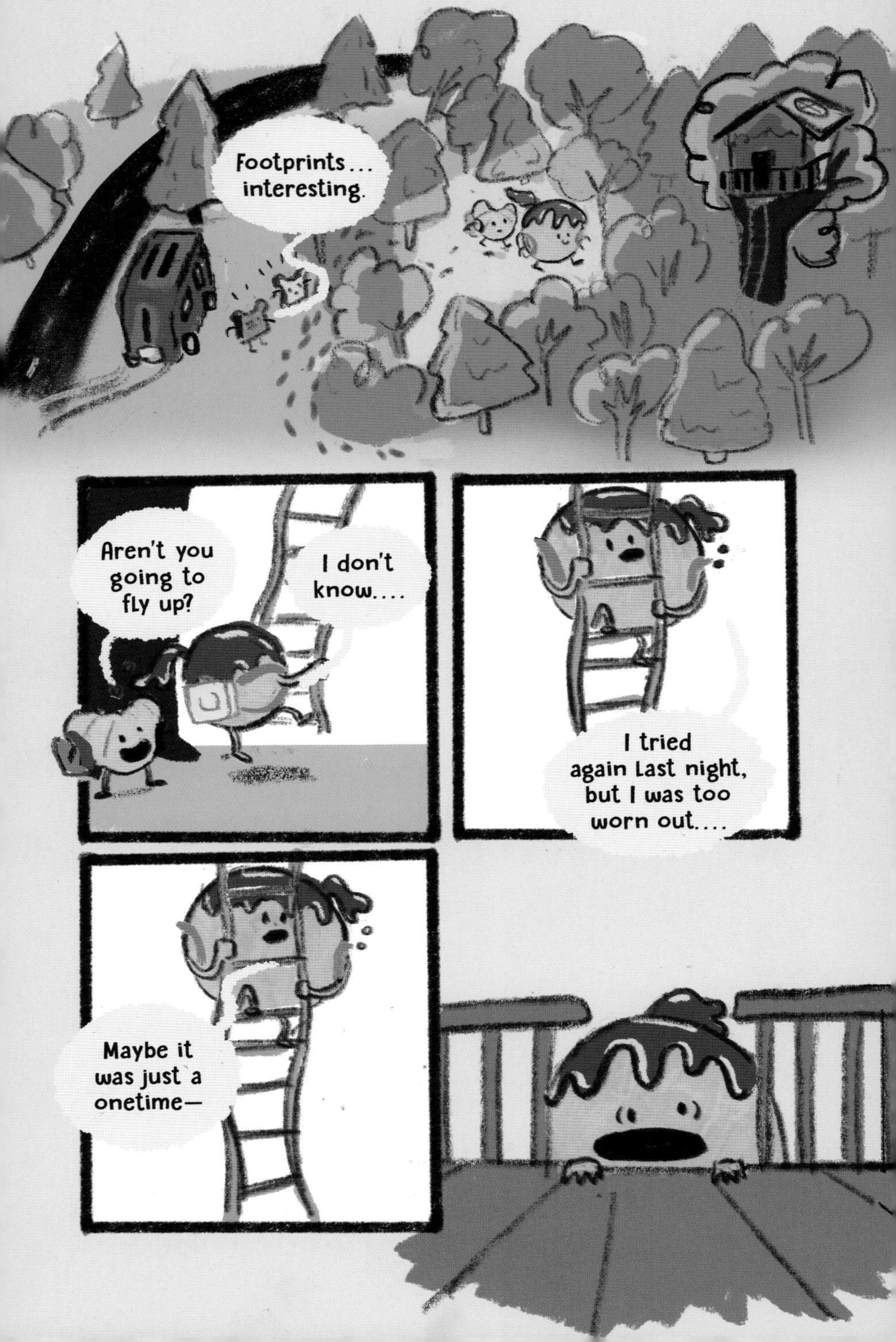
Footprints... interesting.
Aren't you going to fly up?
I don't know....
I tried again last night, but I was too worn out....
Maybe it was just a onetime—

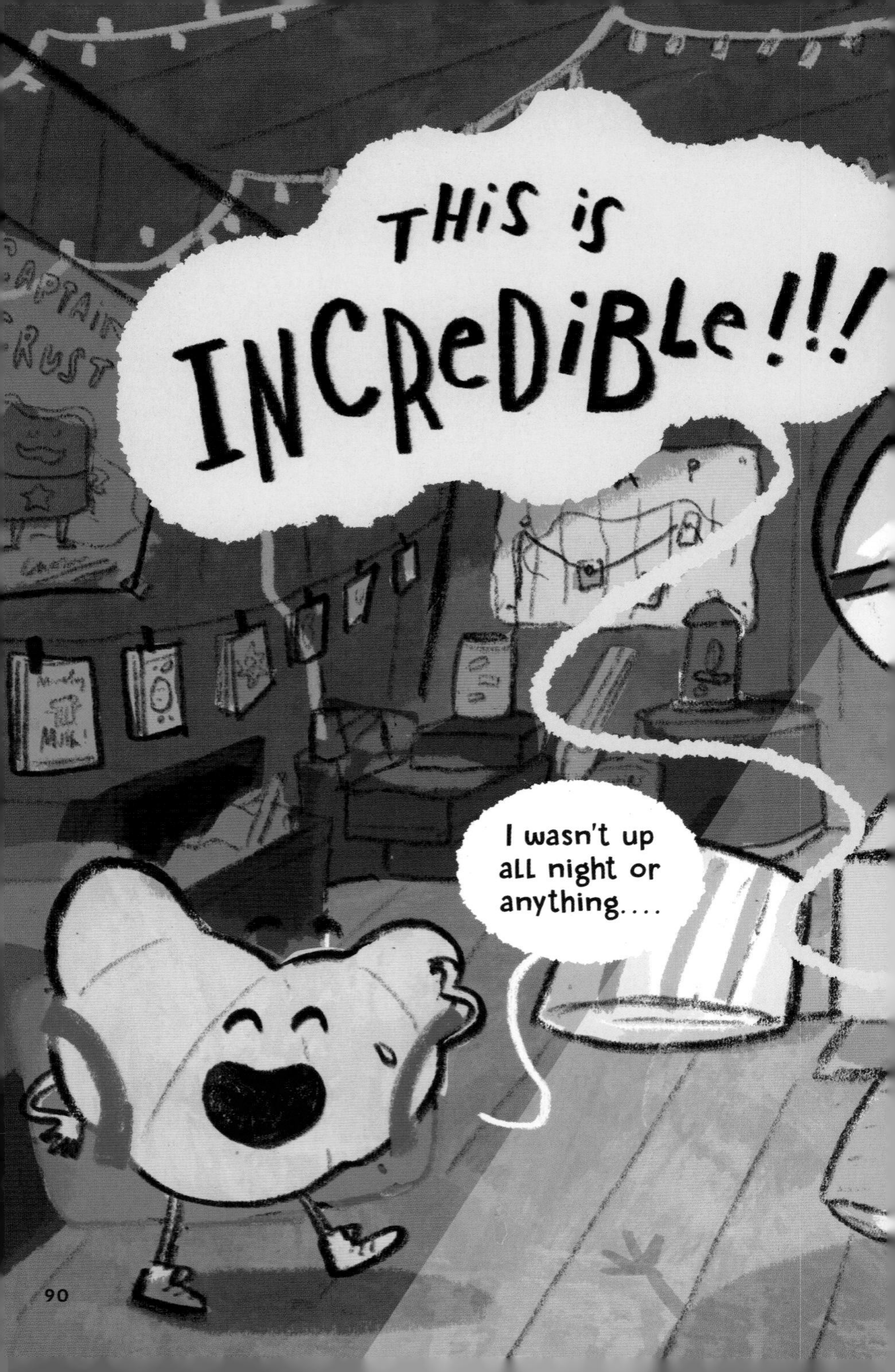
THIS is INCREDIBLE!!!
I wasn't up all night or anything....

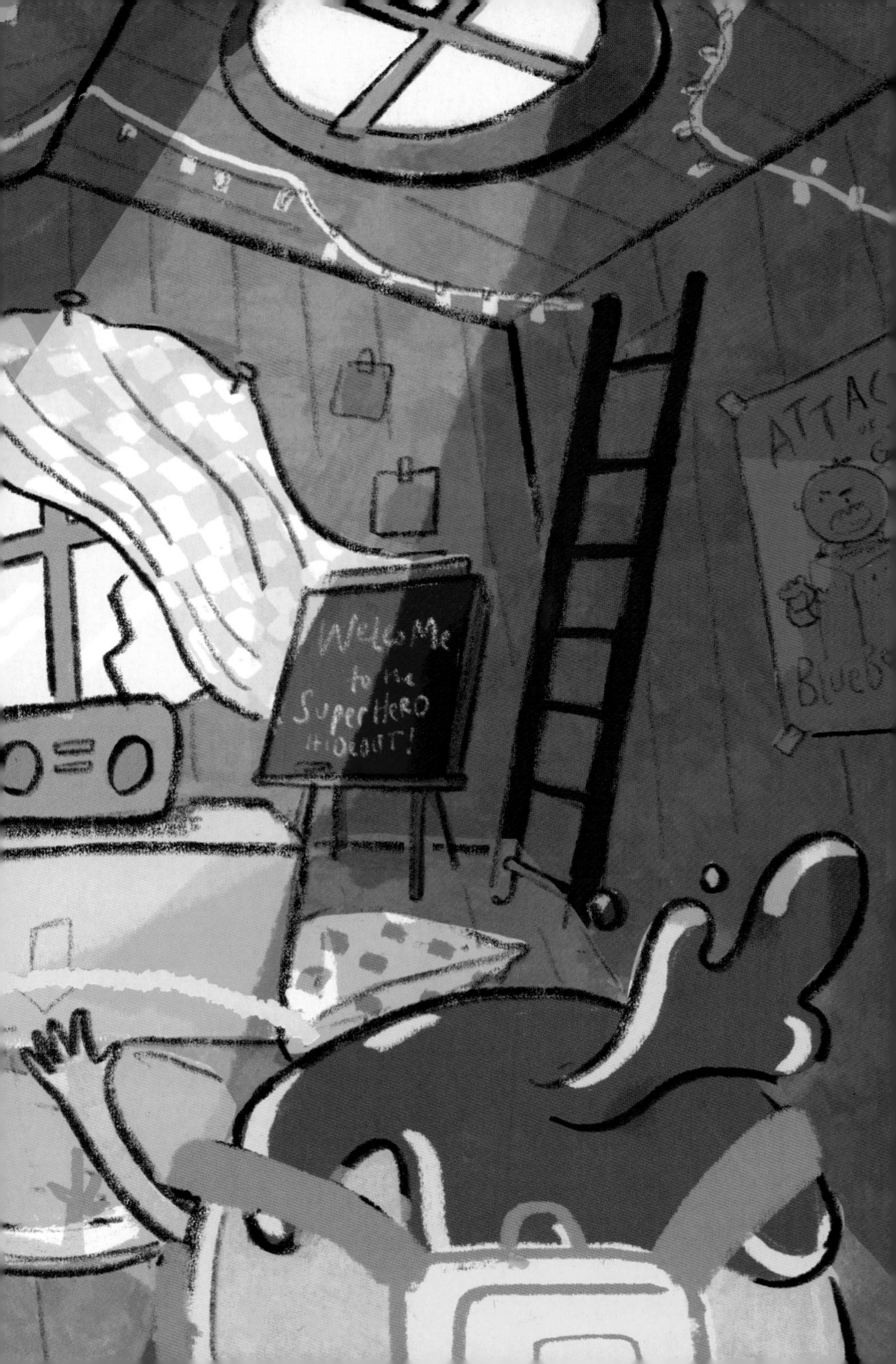
WelcoMe
to the
SuperHERO
HIDEOUT!

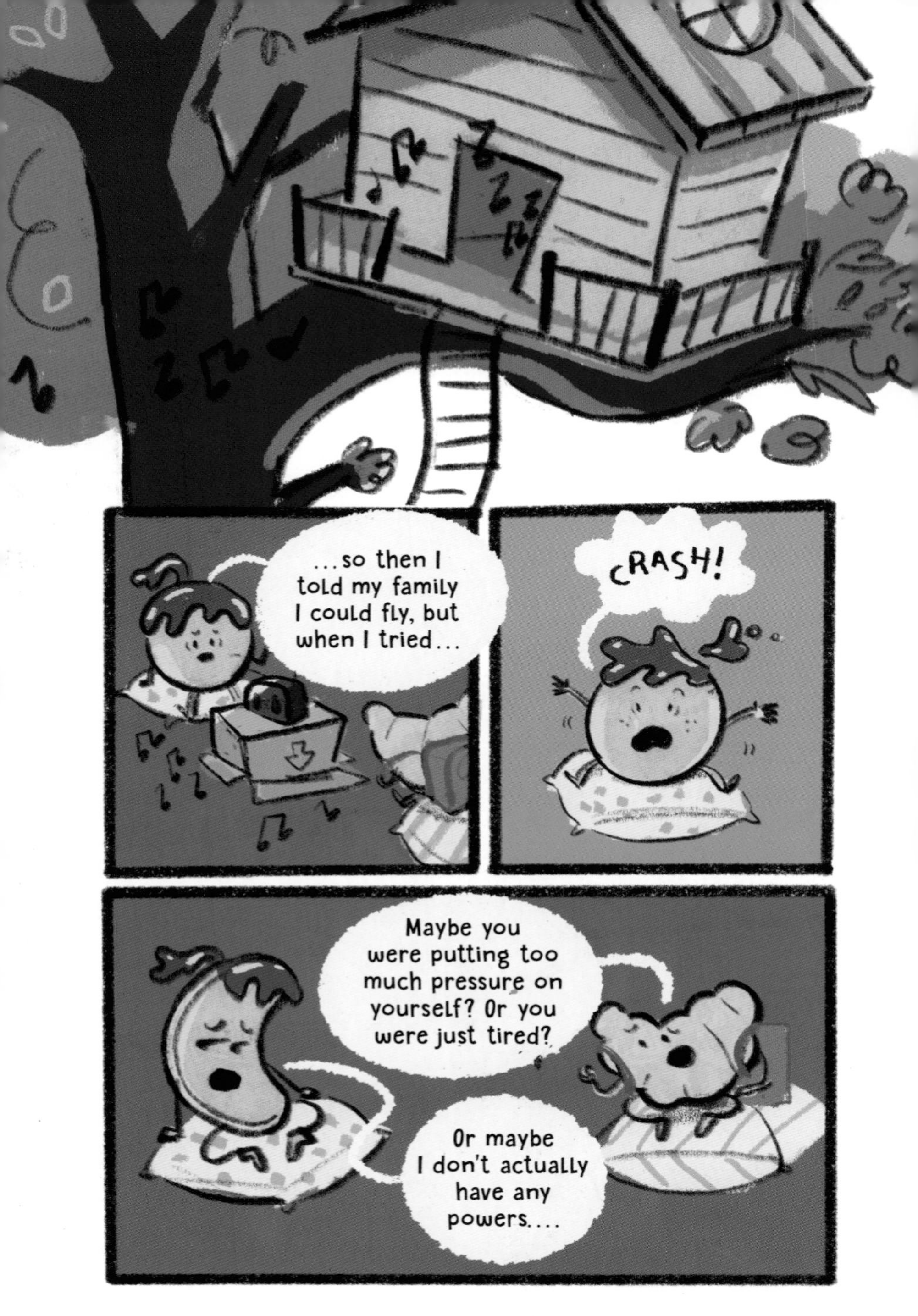
...so then I told my family I could fly, but when I tried...
CRASH!
Maybe you were putting too much pressure on yourself? Or you were just tired?
Or maybe I don't actually have any powers....

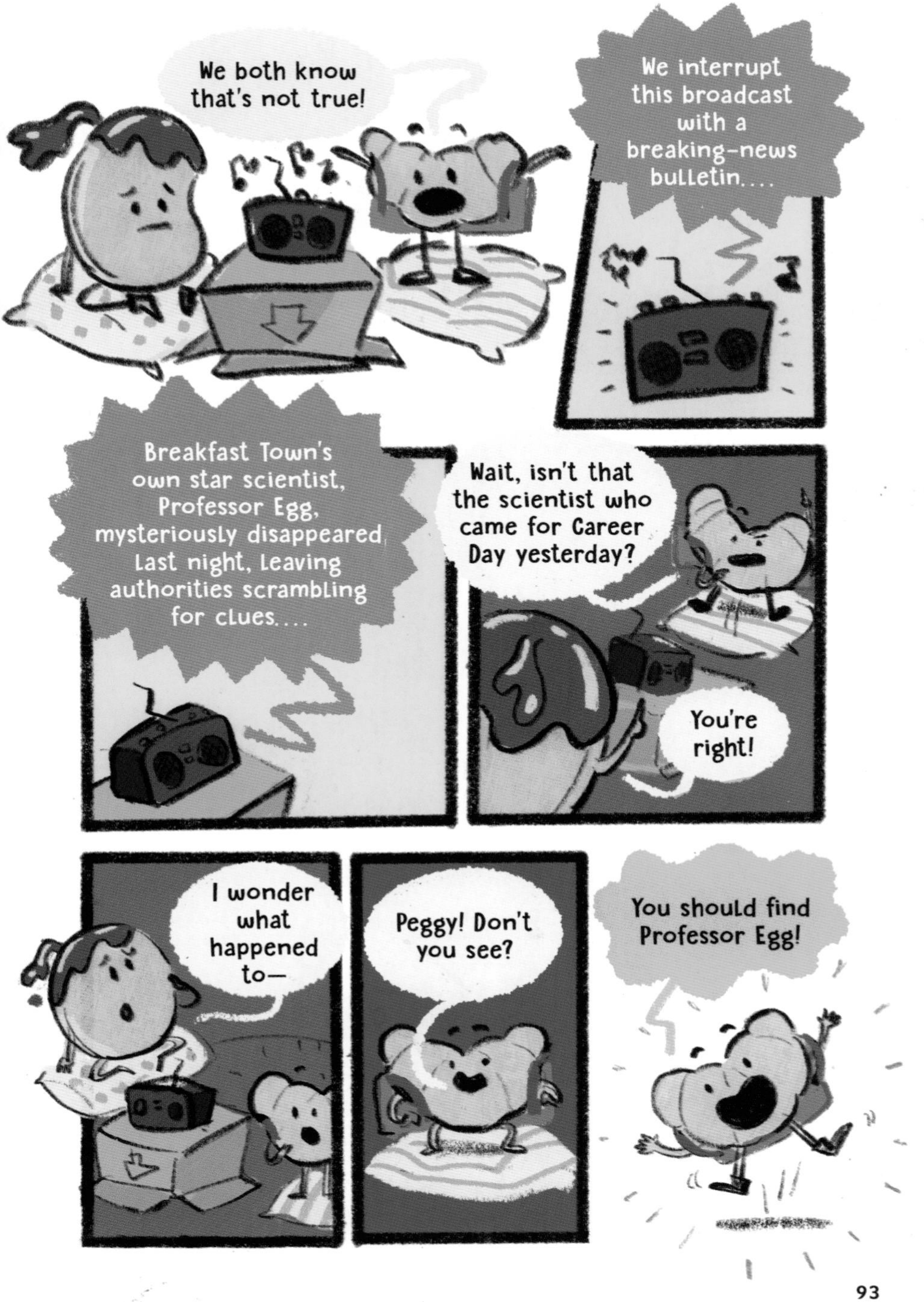
We both know that's not true!
We interrupt this broadcast with a breaking-news bulletin. . . .
Breakfast Town's own star scientist, Professor Egg, mysteriously disappeared last night, leaving authorities scrambling for clues. . . .
Wait, isn't that the scientist who came for Career Day yesterday?
You're right!
I wonder what happened to—
Peggy! Don't you see?
You should find Professor Egg!

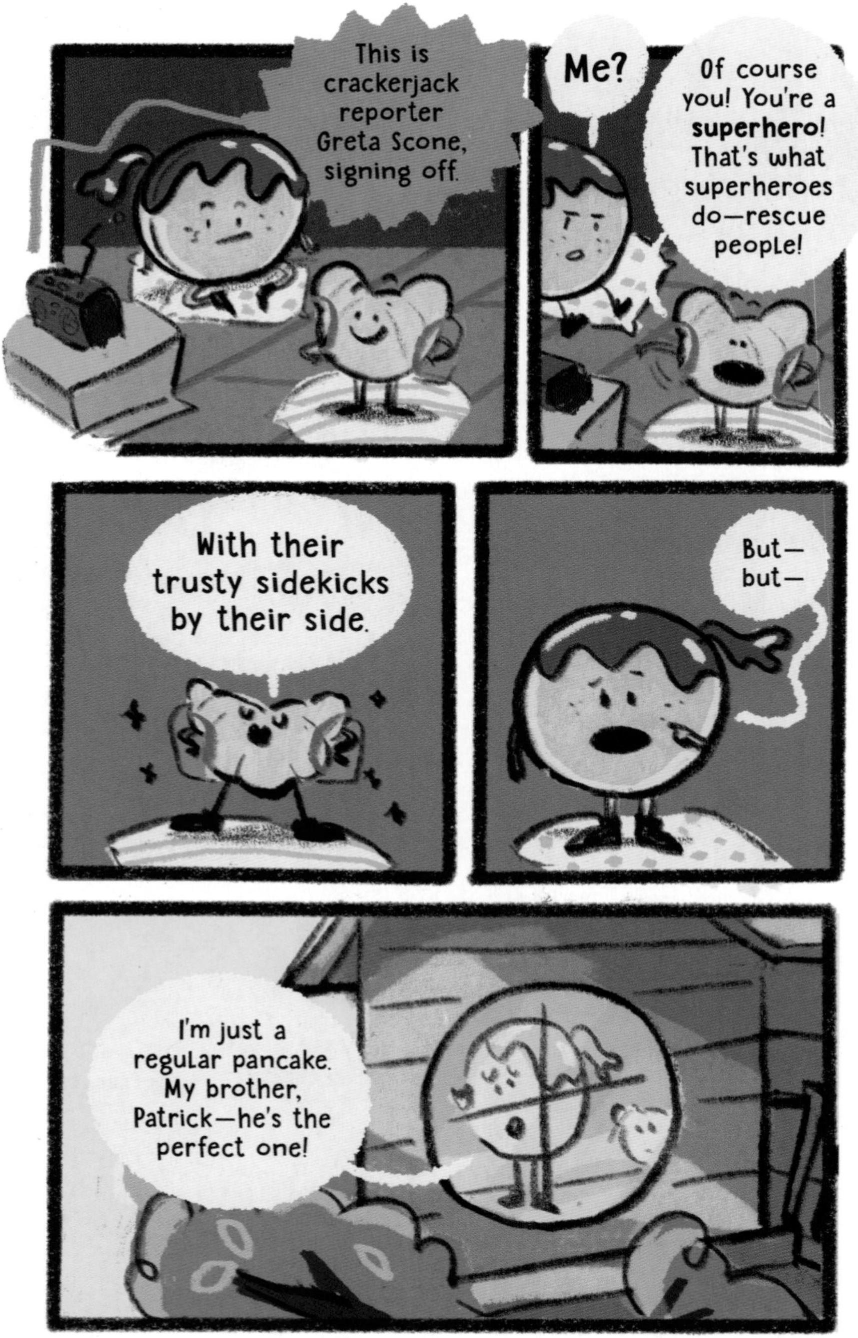
This is crackerjack reporter Greta Scone, signing off.
Me?
Of course you! You're a **superhero**! That's what superheroes do—rescue people!
With their trusty sidekicks by their side.
But—but—
I'm just a regular pancake. My brother, Patrick—he's the perfect one!

You don't have to be **perfect** to be a superhero!

You've just got to **try**.

You've got super fighting skills...

and you can fly!

And—

Anyway, forget about rescuing anyone...for now.

Let's just get outside and see if you can fly again, for starters.

Okay, I'll try.

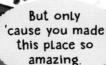

But only 'cause you made this place so amazing.

And don't let me forget to go home in time for the family picture.

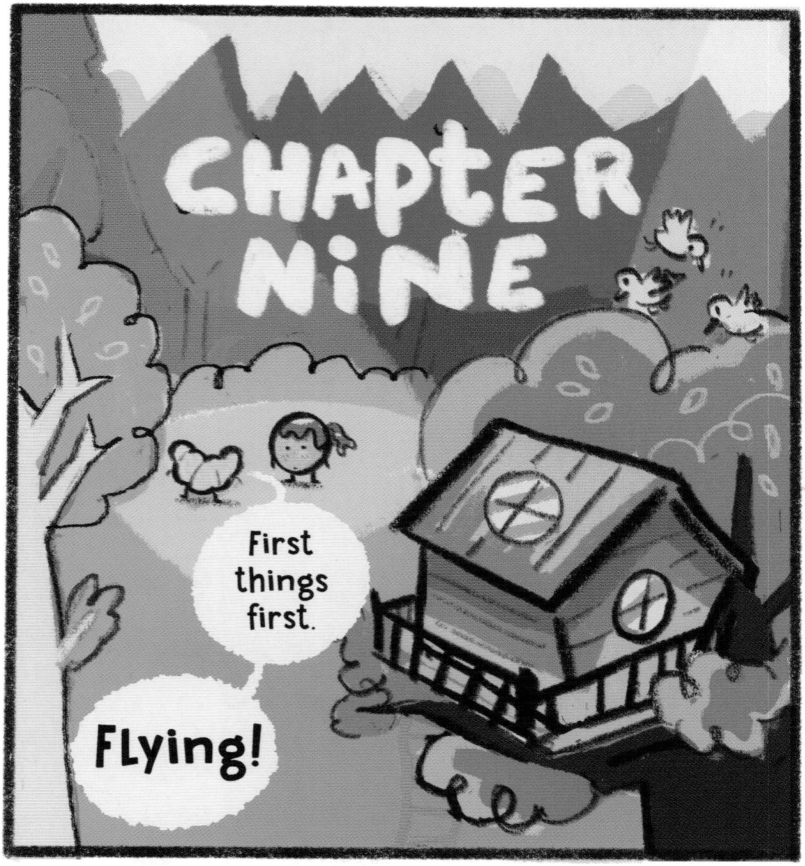
CHAPTER NINE
First things first.
FLYING!

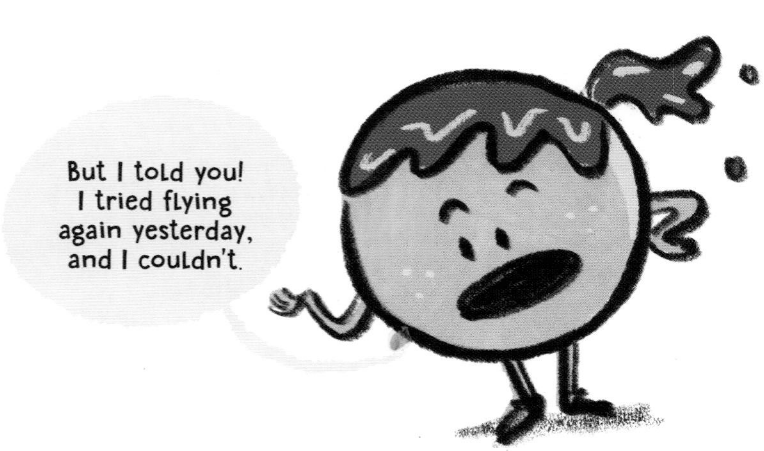
But I told you! I tried flying again yesterday, and I couldn't.

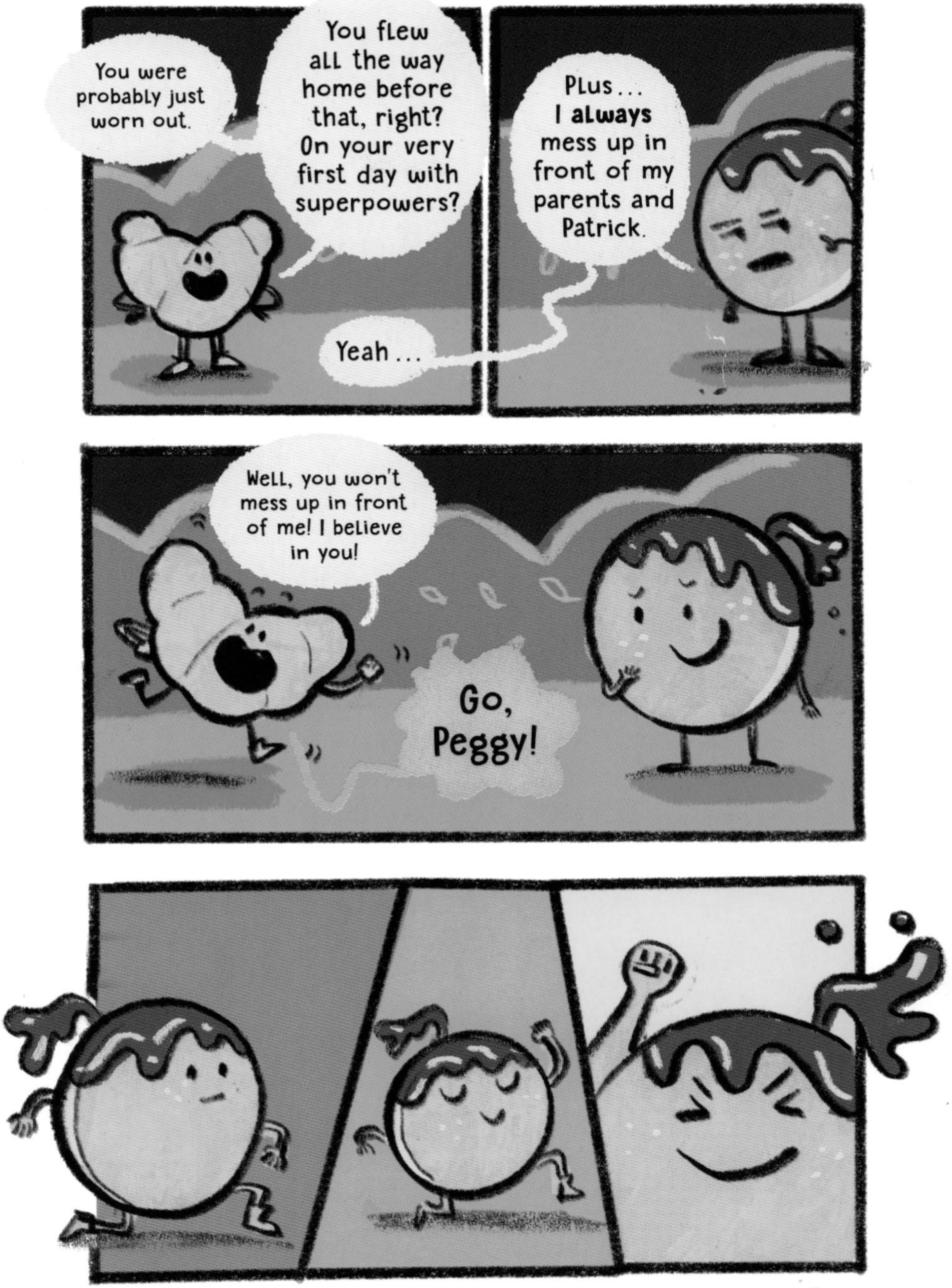
You were probably just worn out.
You flew all the way home before that, right? On your very first day with superpowers?
Yeah . . .
Plus . . . I **always** mess up in front of my parents and Patrick.
Well, you won't mess up in front of me! I believe in you!
Go, Peggy!

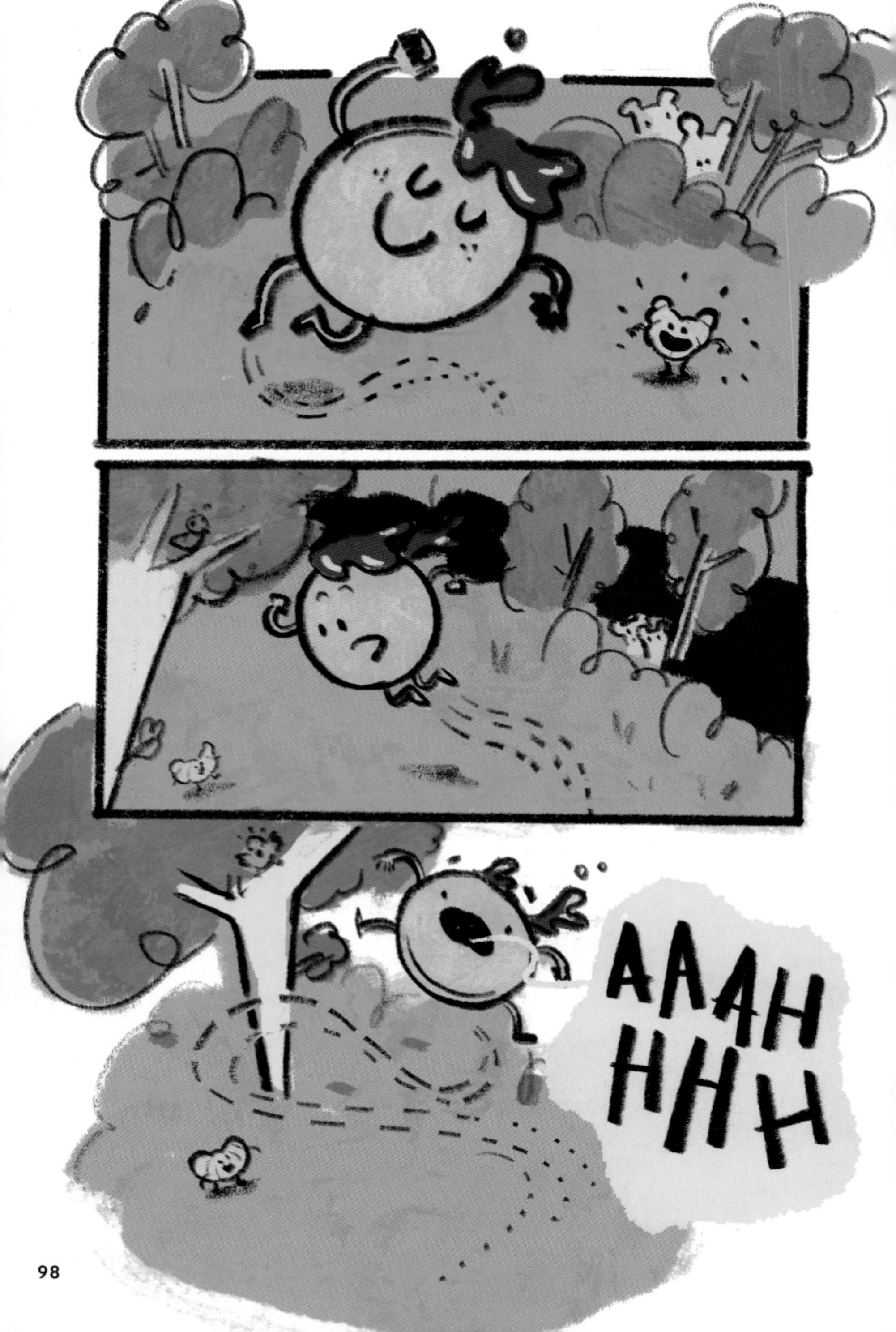
AAAH
HHH

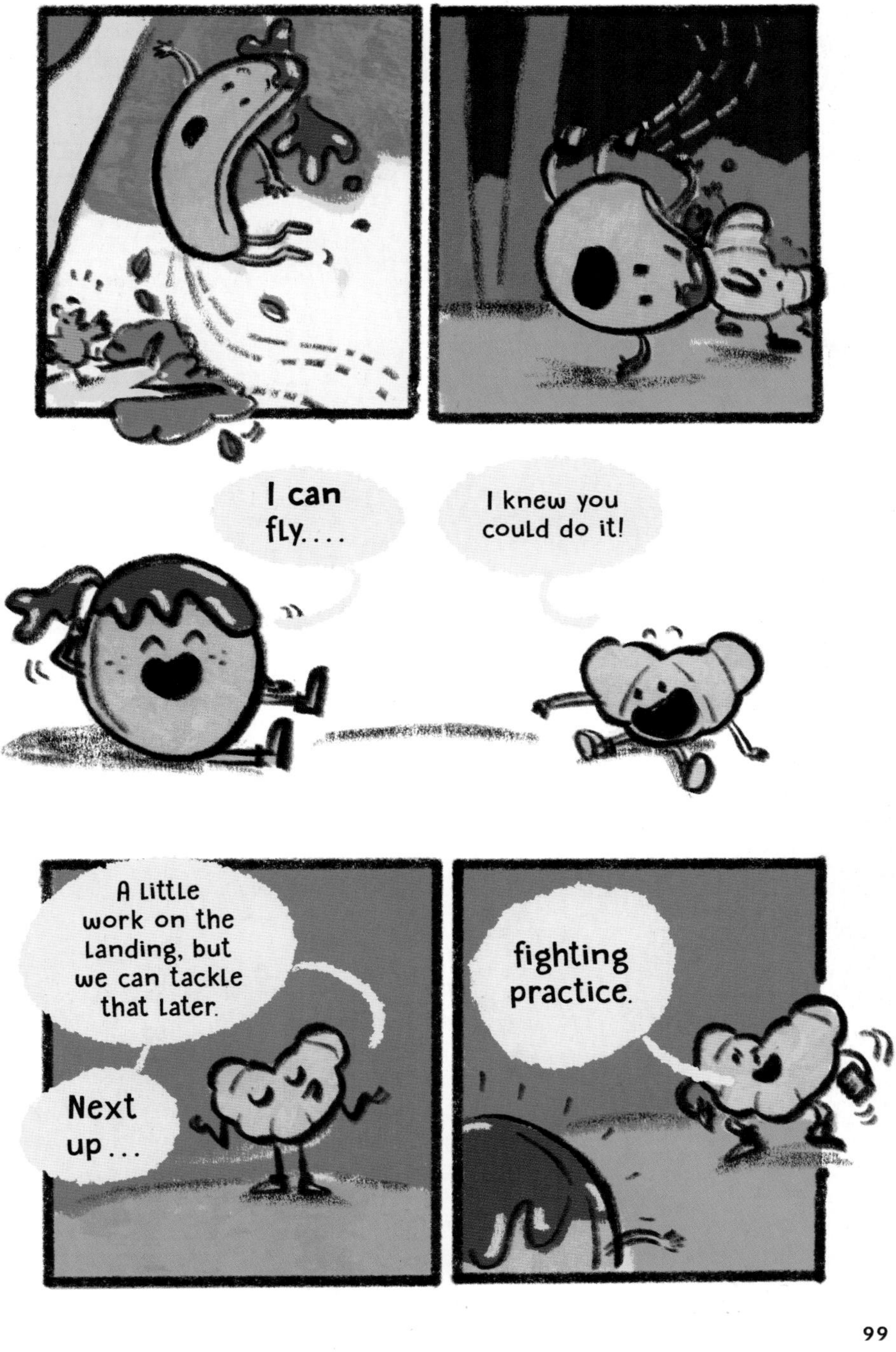
I can fLy. . . .
I knew you couLd do it!
A LittLe work on the Landing, but we can tackLe that Later.
Next up . . .
fighting practice.

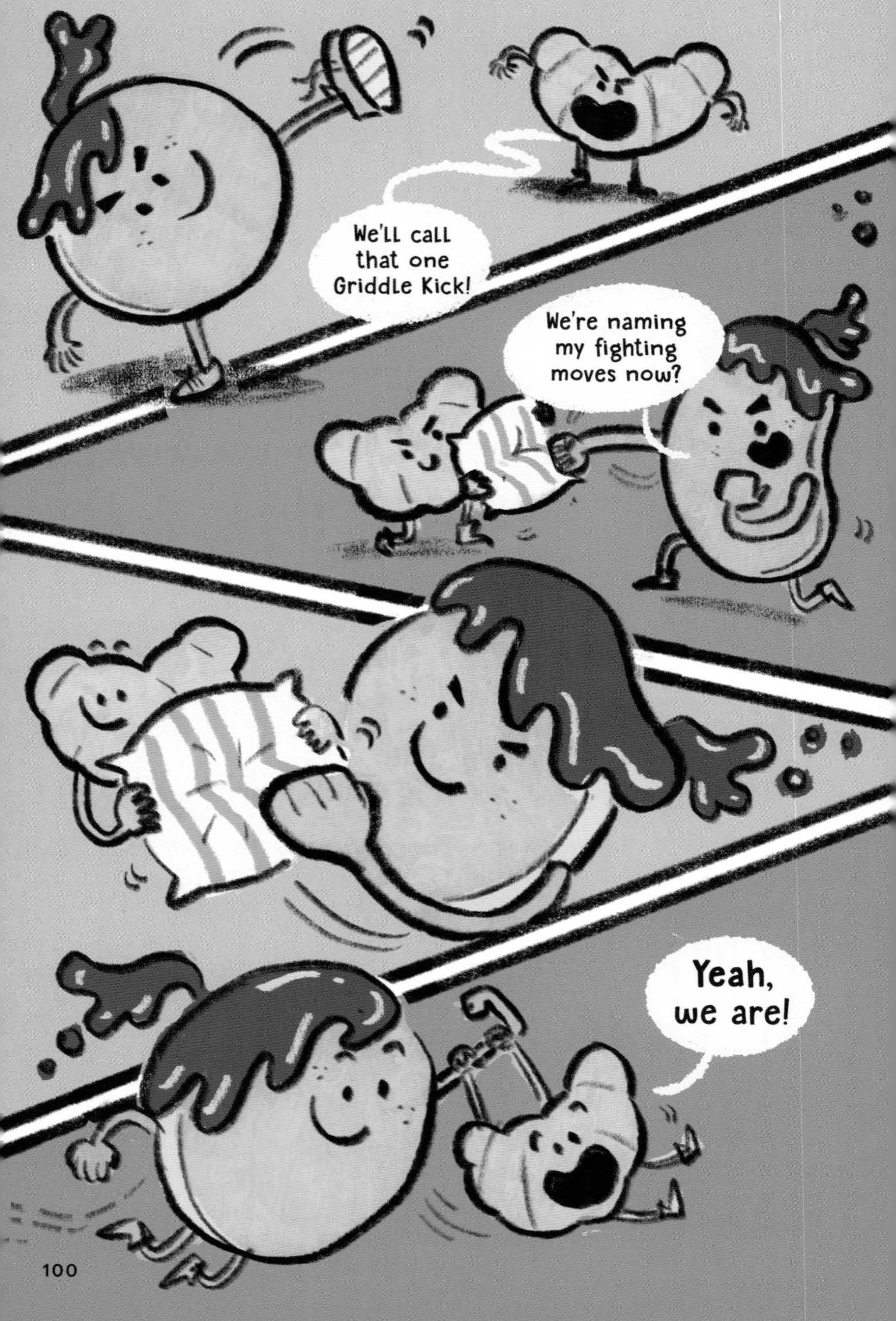
We'LL caLL that one GriddLe Kick!
We're naming my fighting moves now?
Yeah, we are!

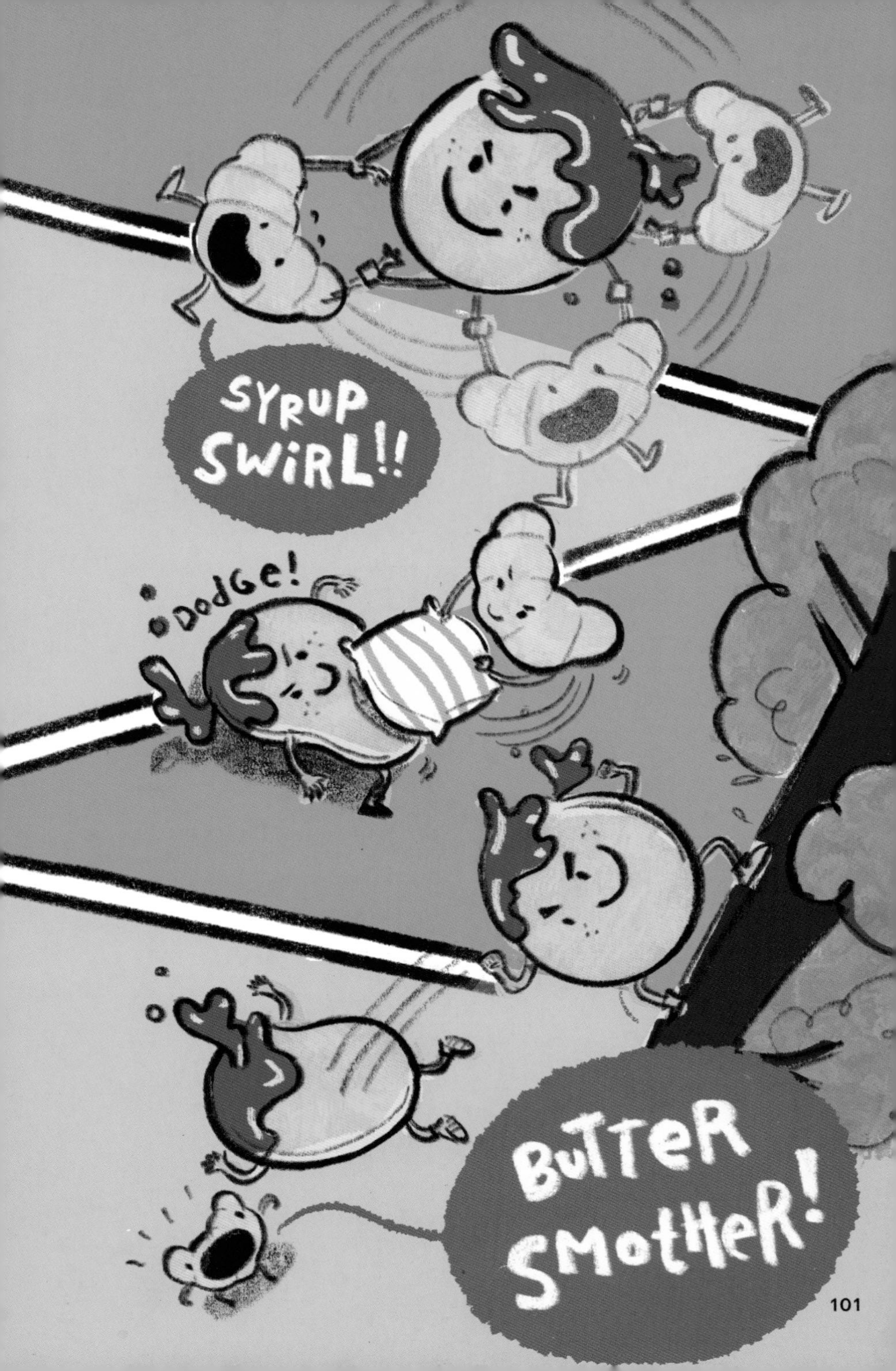
SYRUP SWIRL!!
DODGE!
BUTTER SMOTHER!

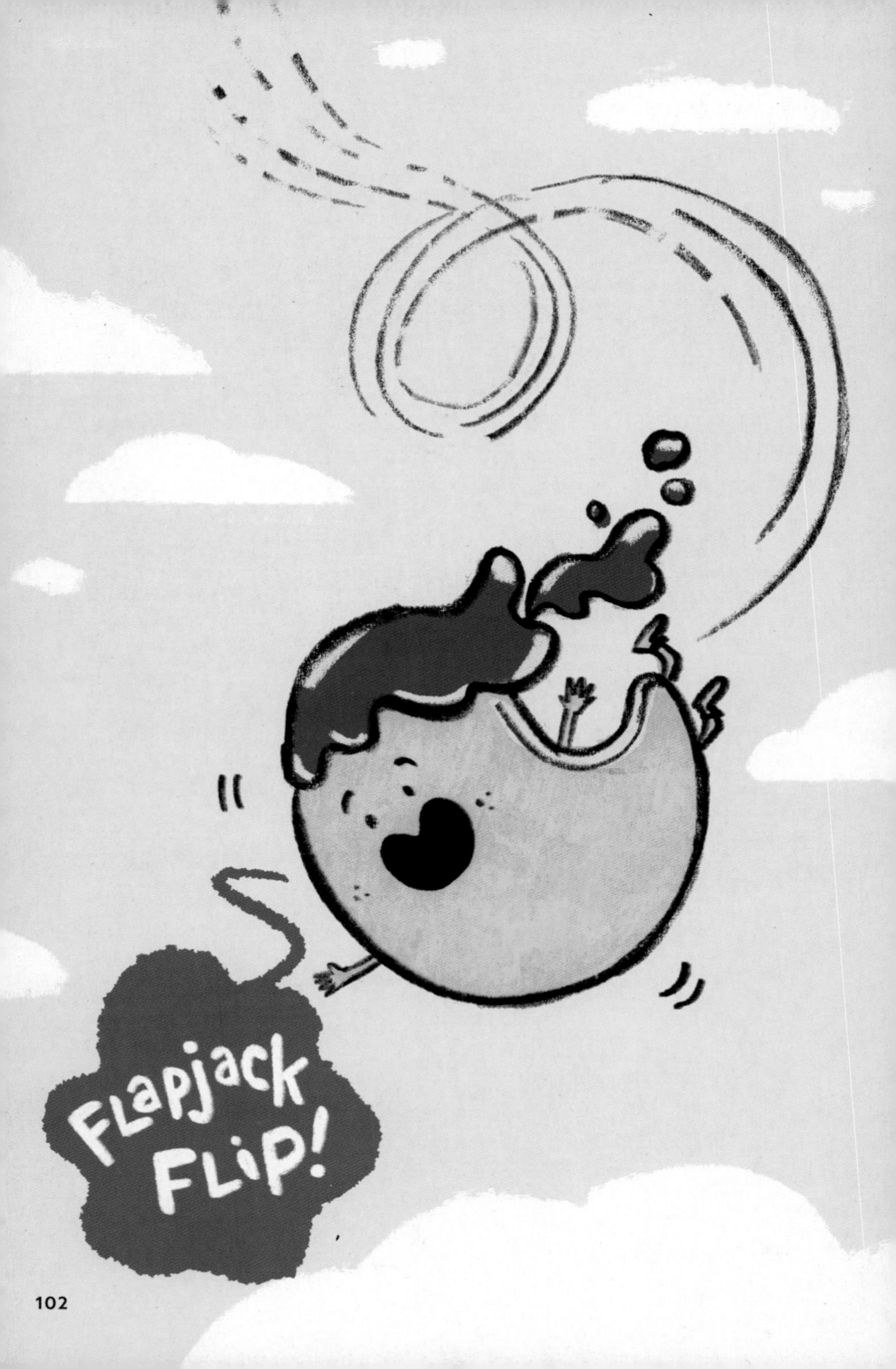
Flapjack
Flip!

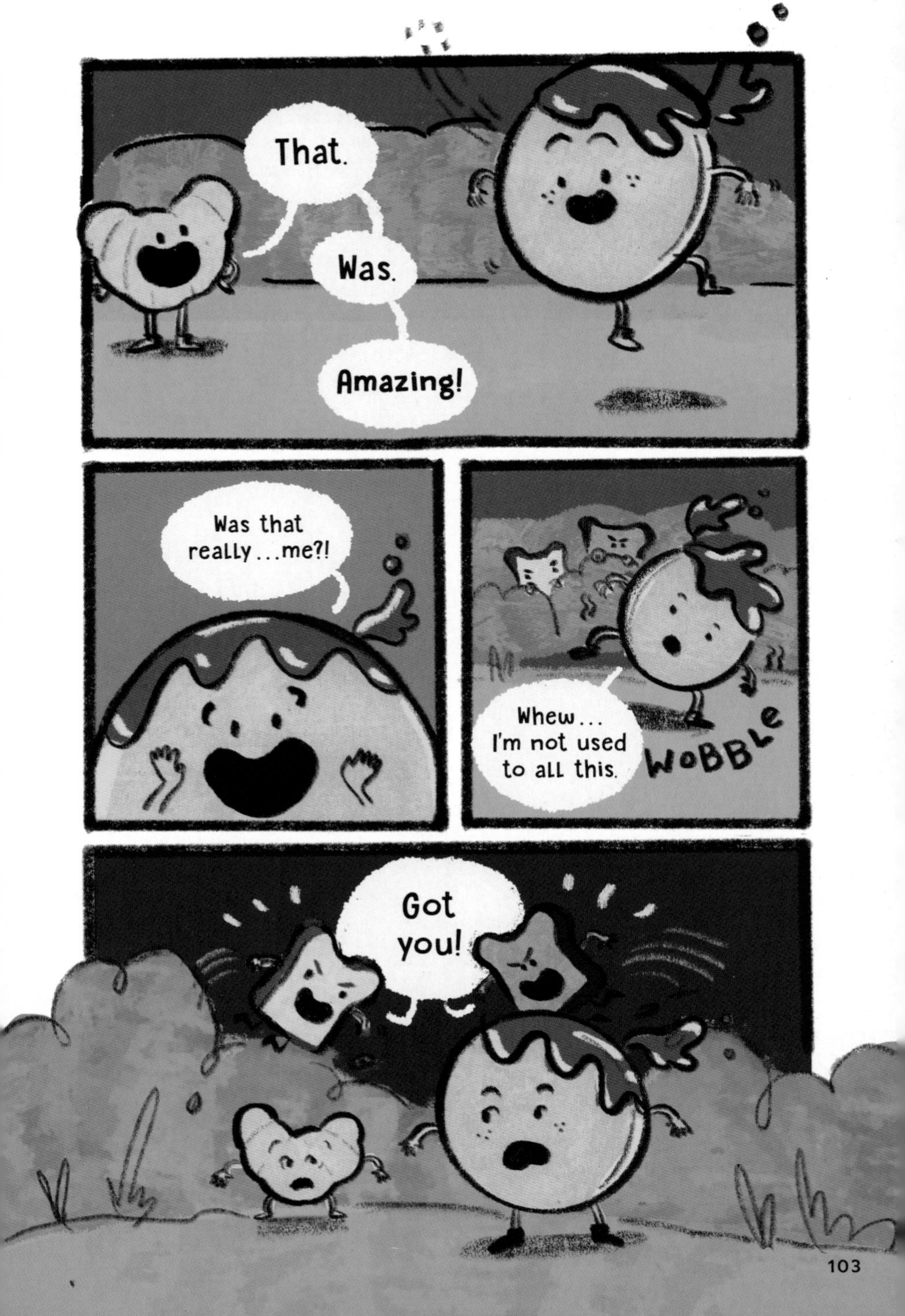
That.
Was.
Amazing!
Was that really...me?!
Whew... I'm not used to all this.
WOBBLE
Got you!

CHAPTER TEN

LEAVE US ALONE!

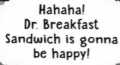

Hahaha! Dr. Breakfast Sandwich is gonna be happy!

Sounds like a supervillain!

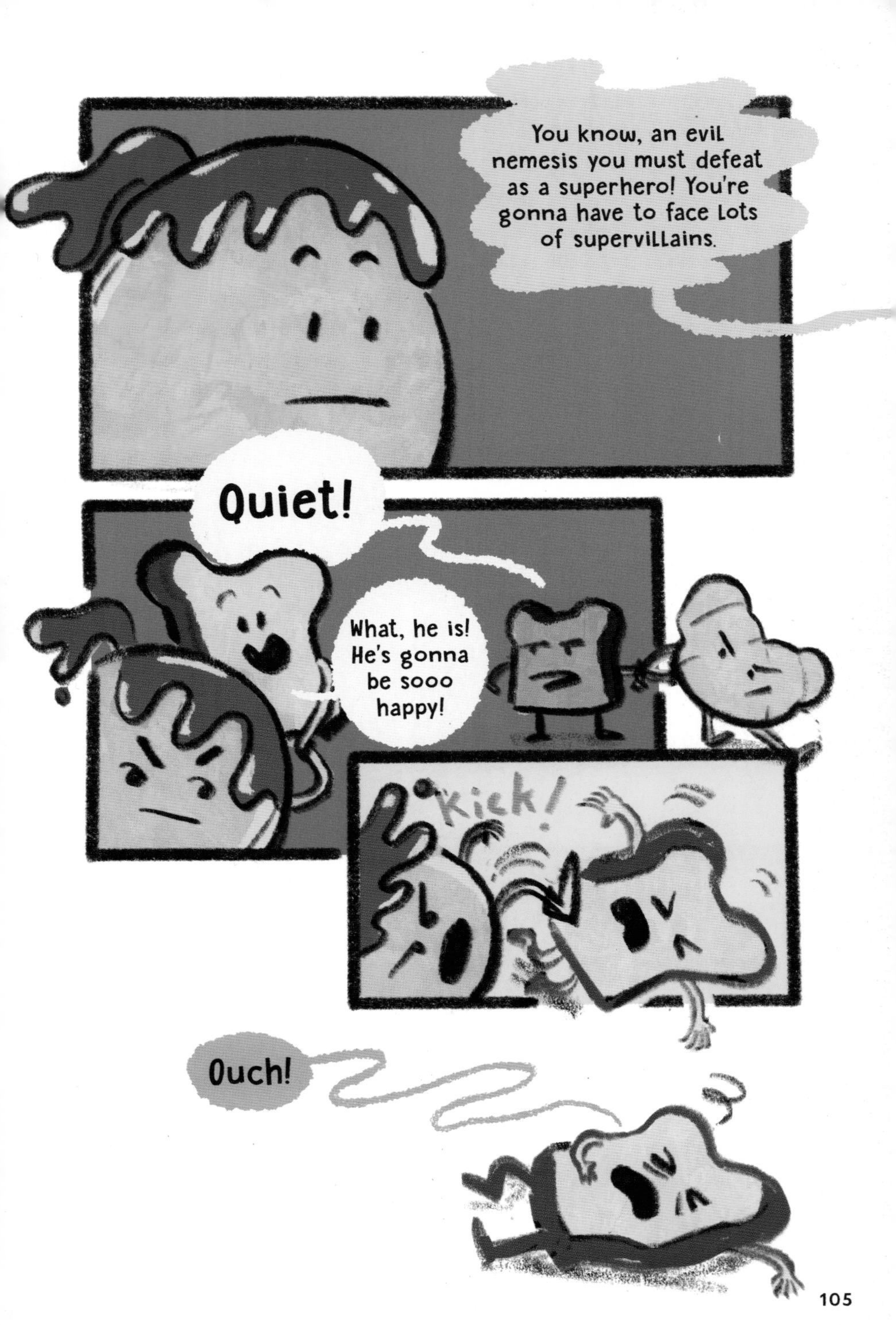
You know, an evil nemesis you must defeat as a superhero! You're gonna have to face lots of supervillains.
Quiet!
What, he is! He's gonna be sooo happy!
Kick!
Ouch!

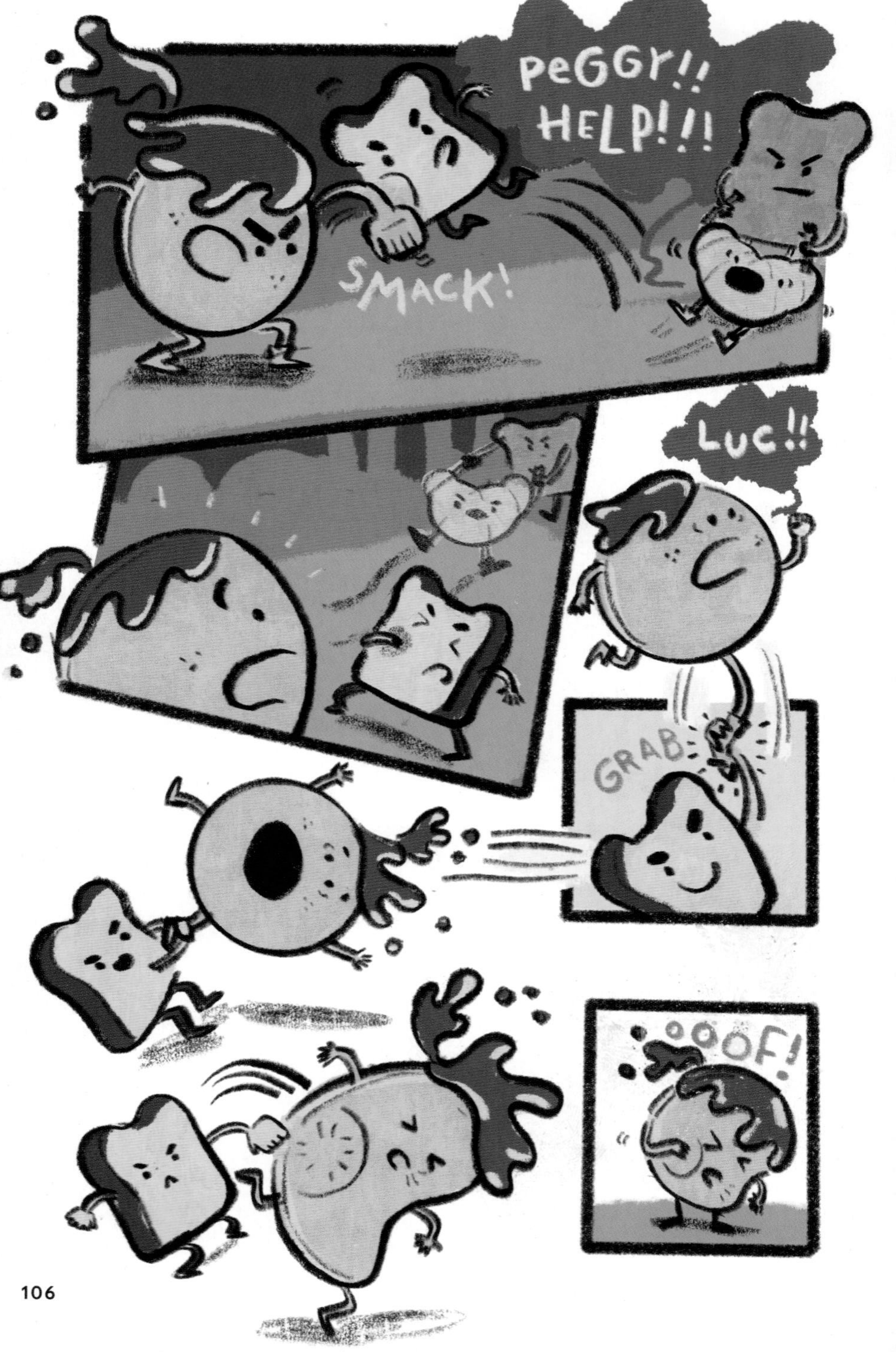
PeGGY!! HELP!!!
SMACK!
Luc!!
GRAB
OOOF!

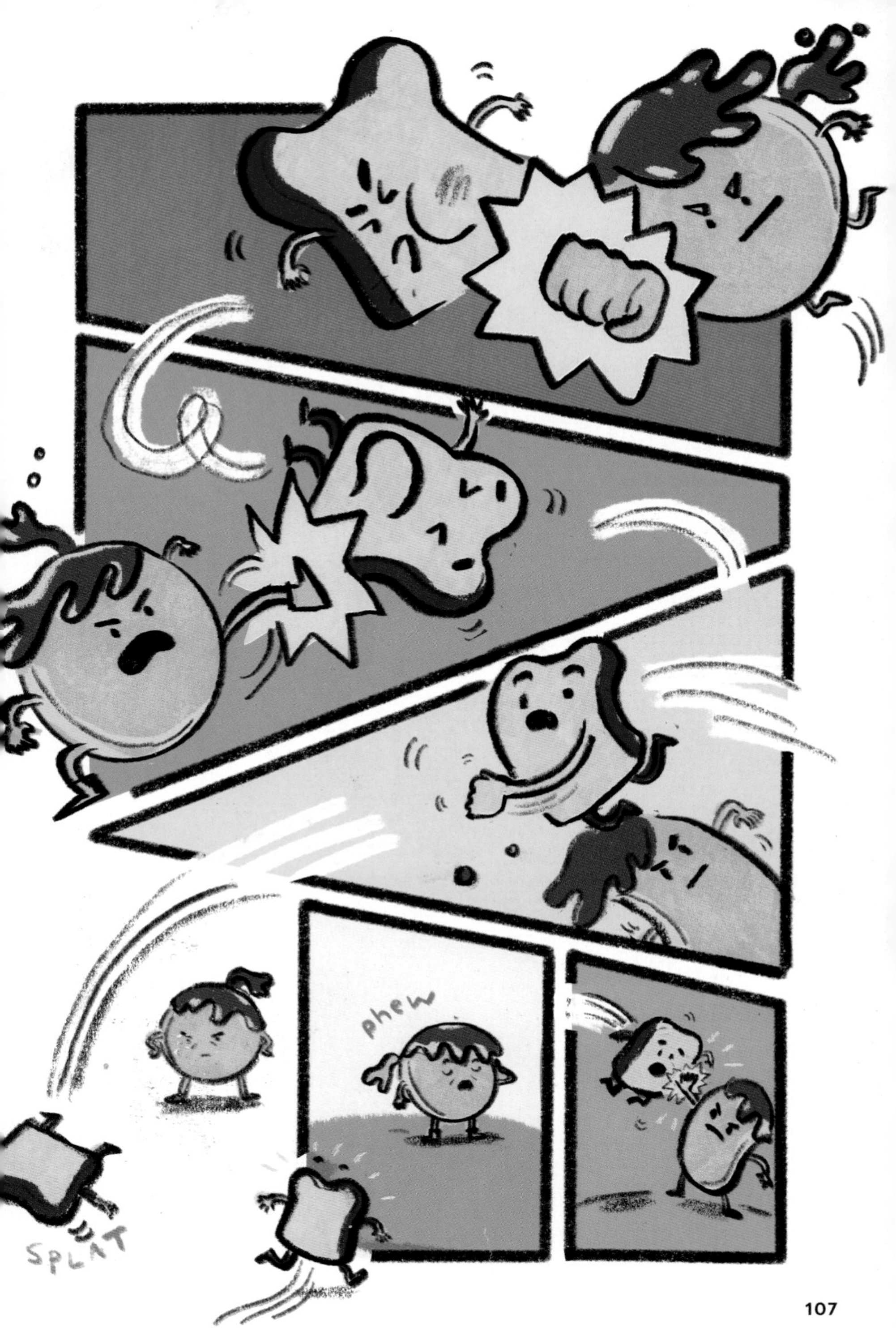
phew
SPLAT

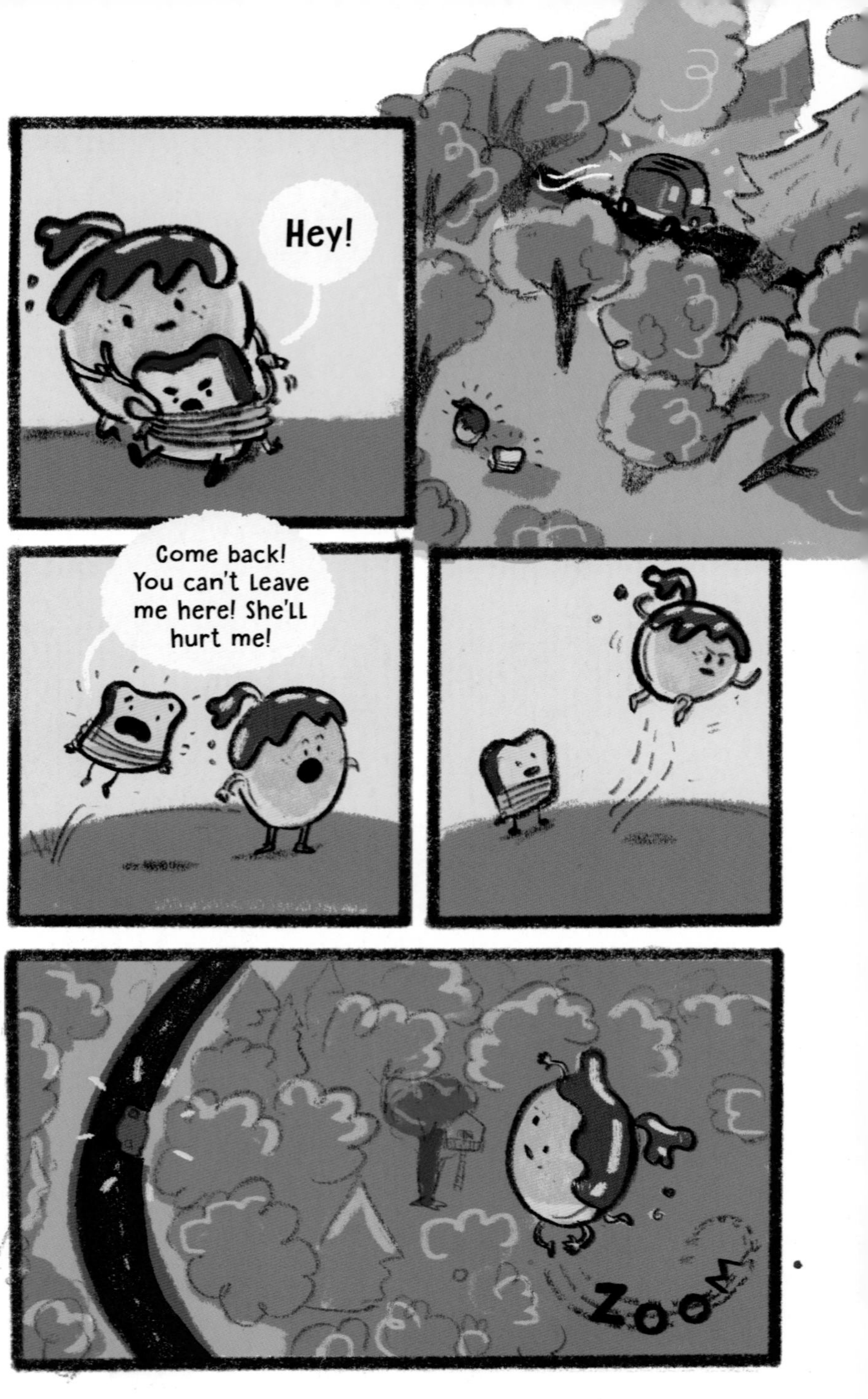
Hey!
Come back! You can't leave me here! She'll hurt me!
ZOOM

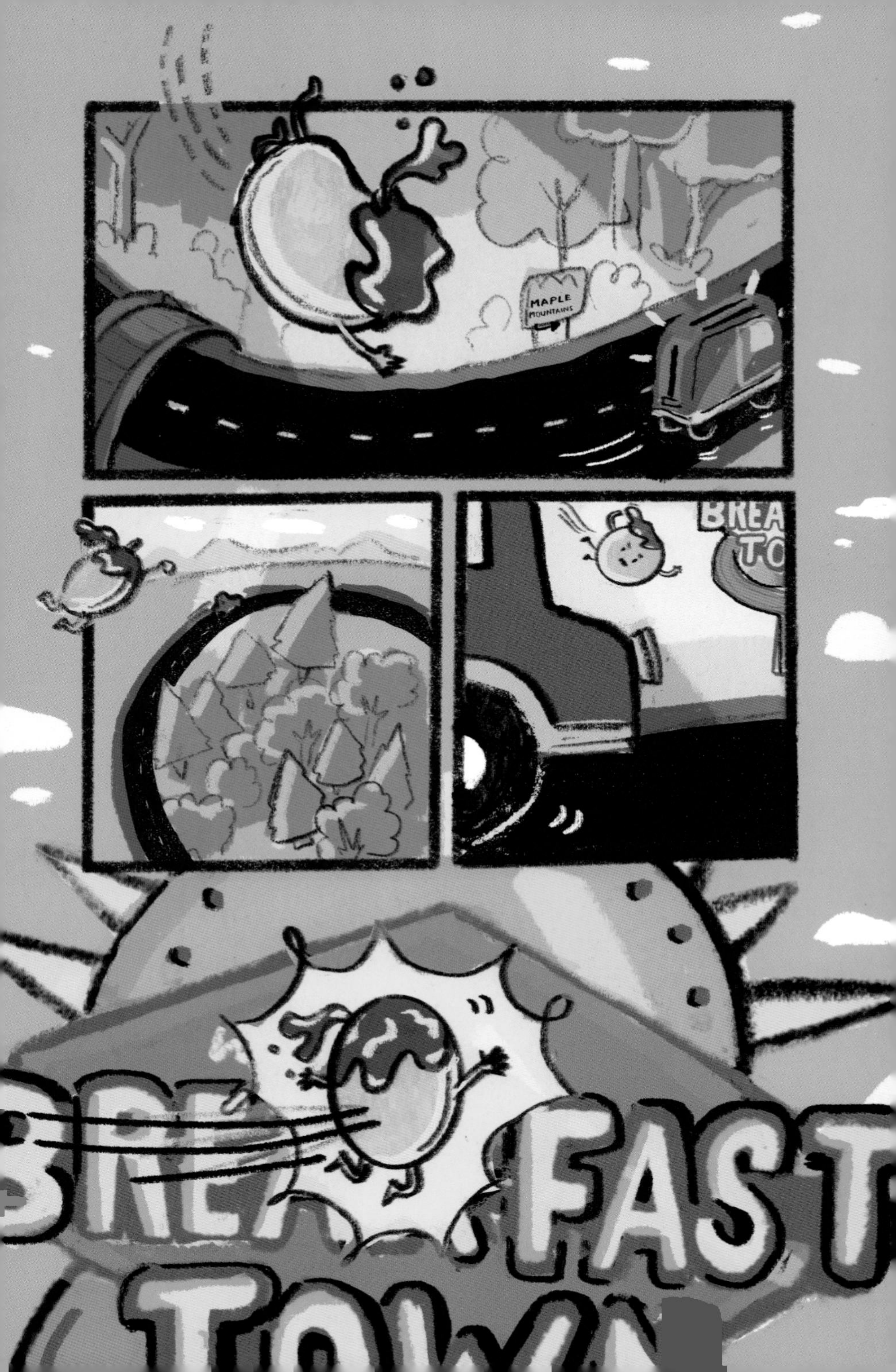

MAPLE
MOUNTAINS
BREA
TO
FAST

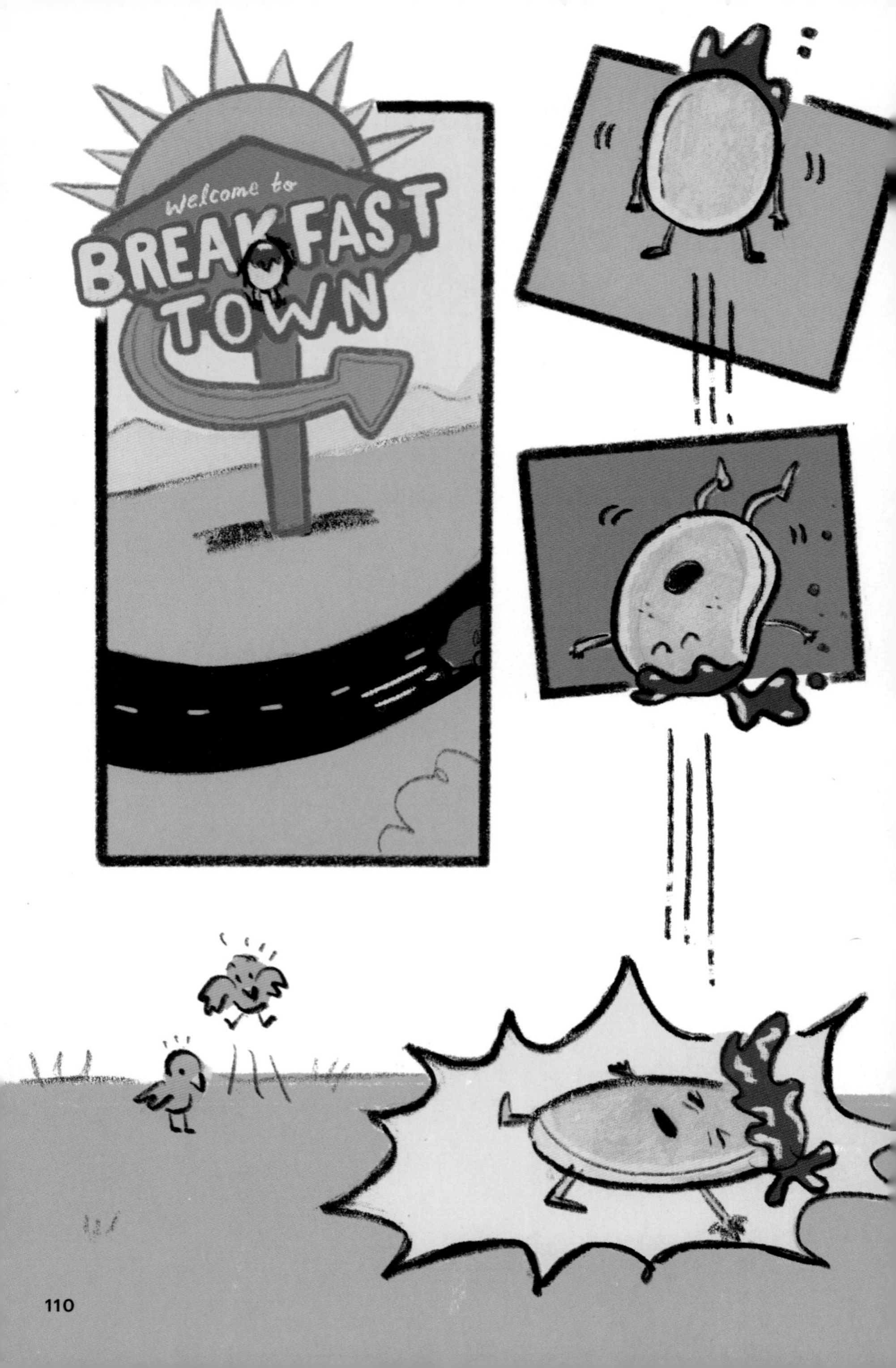
welcome to
BREAKFAST
TOWN

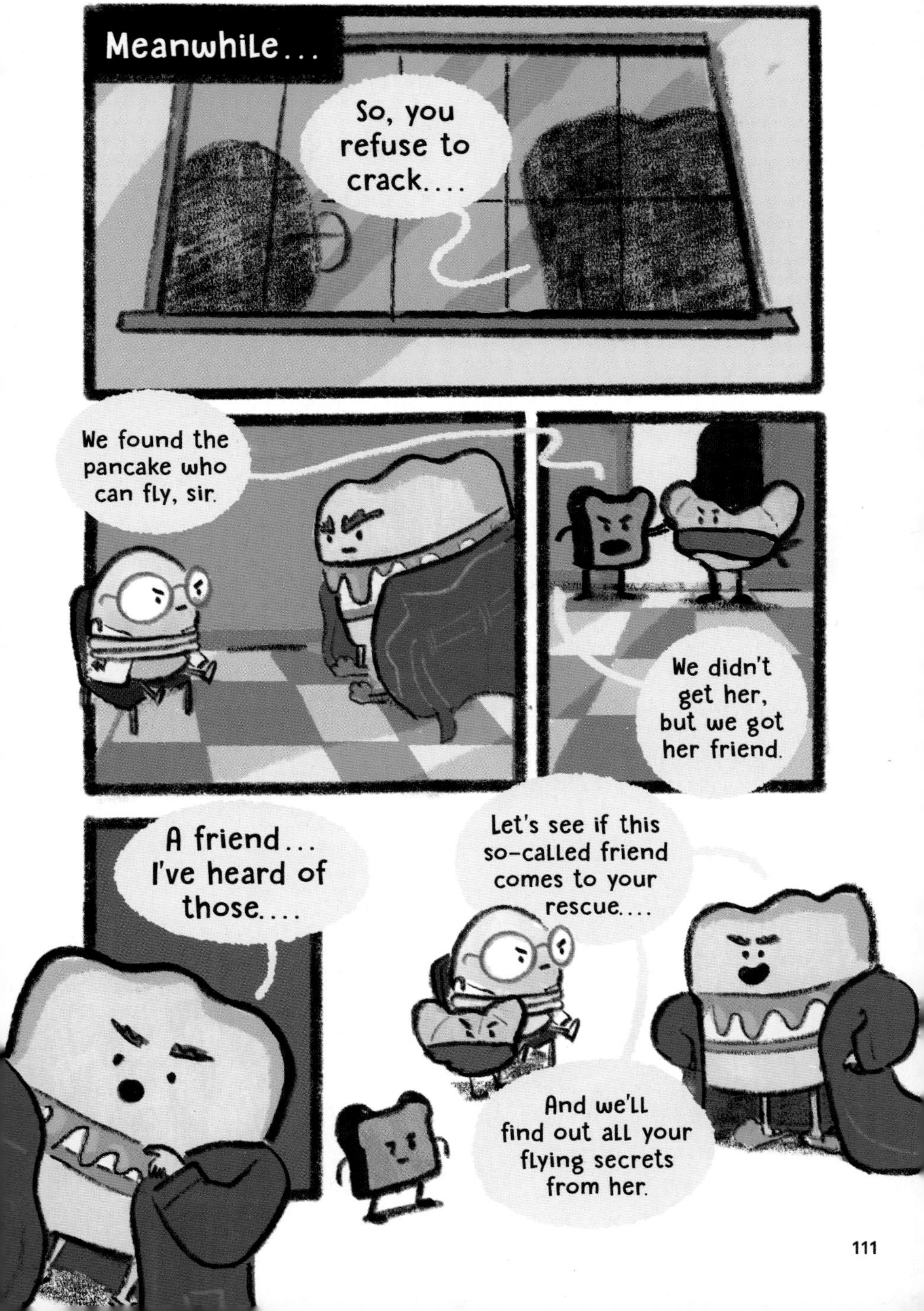
Meanwhile...
So, you refuse to crack....
We found the pancake who can fly, sir.
We didn't get her, but we got her friend.
A friend... I've heard of those....
Let's see if this so-called friend comes to your rescue....
And we'll find out all your flying secrets from her.

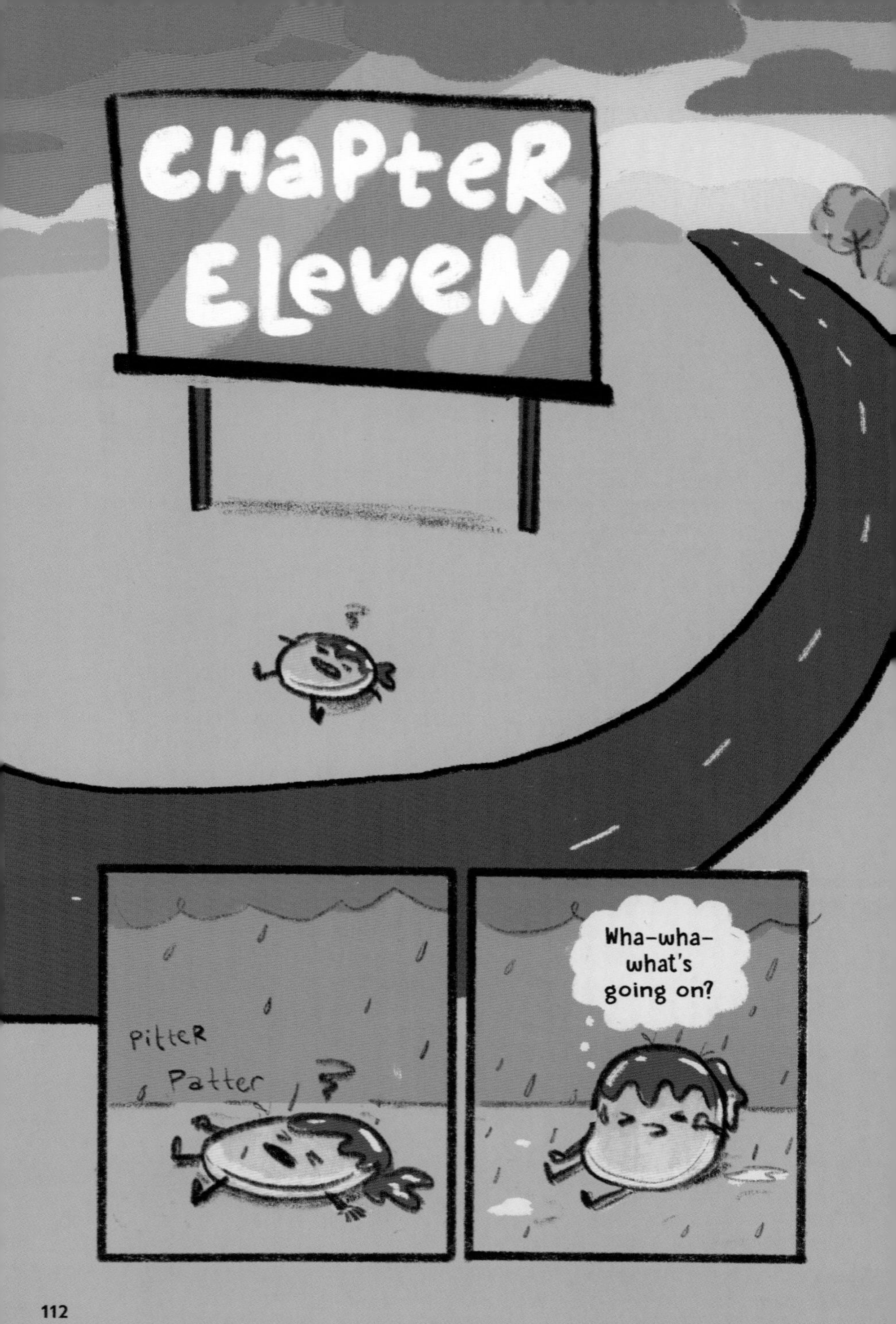
CHAPTER
ELEVEN
Pitter
Patter
Wha-wha-
what's
going on?

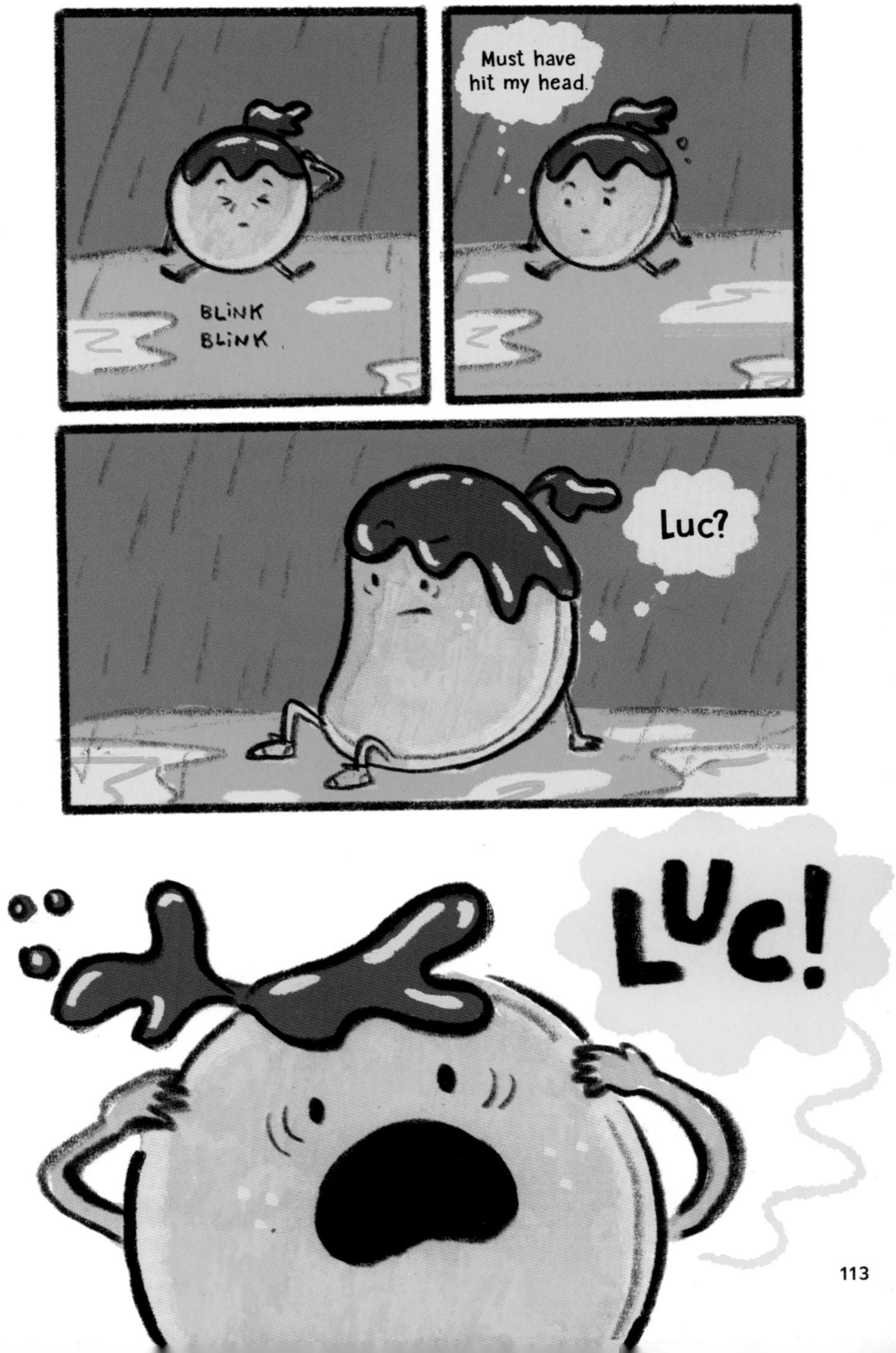
BLINK
BLINK
Must have hit my head.
Luc?
LUC!

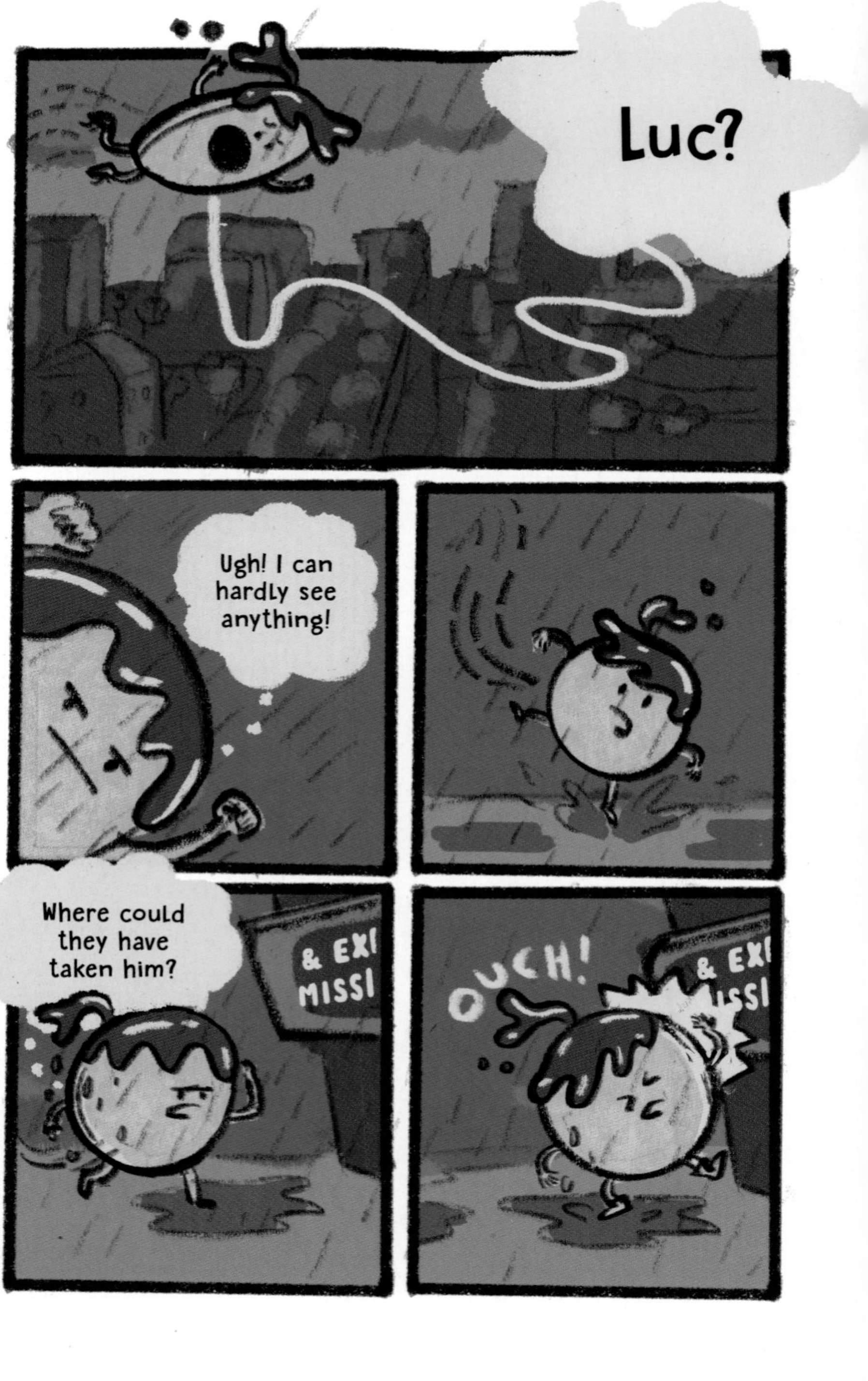
Luc?
Ugh! I can hardly see anything!
Where could they have taken him?
OUCH!

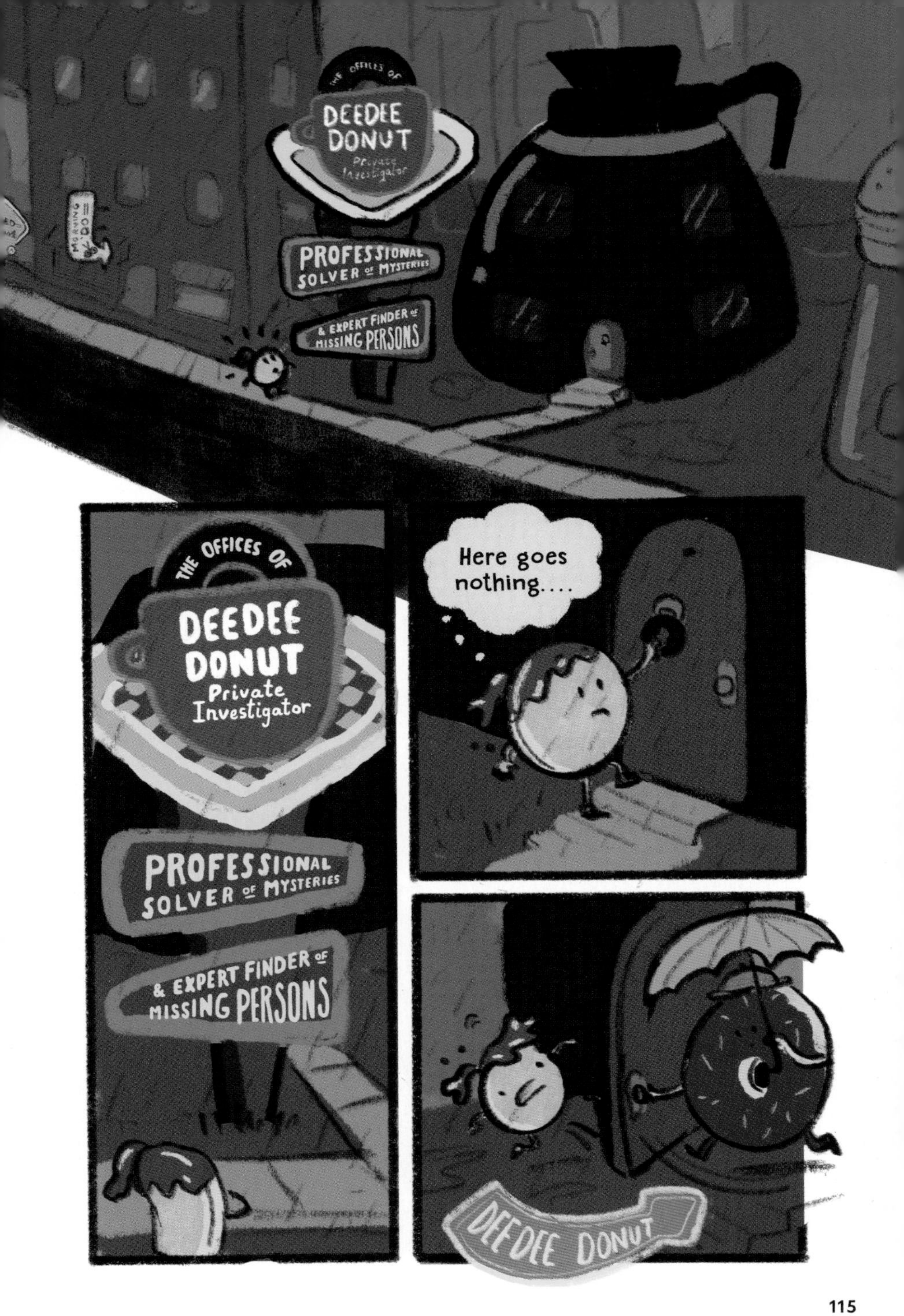

THE OFFICES OF
DEEDEE DONUT
Private Investigator
PROFESSIONAL SOLVER OF MYSTERIES
& EXPERT FINDER OF MISSING PERSONS
THE OFFICES OF
DEEDEE DONUT
Private Investigator
PROFESSIONAL SOLVER OF MYSTERIES
& EXPERT FINDER OF MISSING PERSONS
Here goes nothing....
DEEDEE DONUT

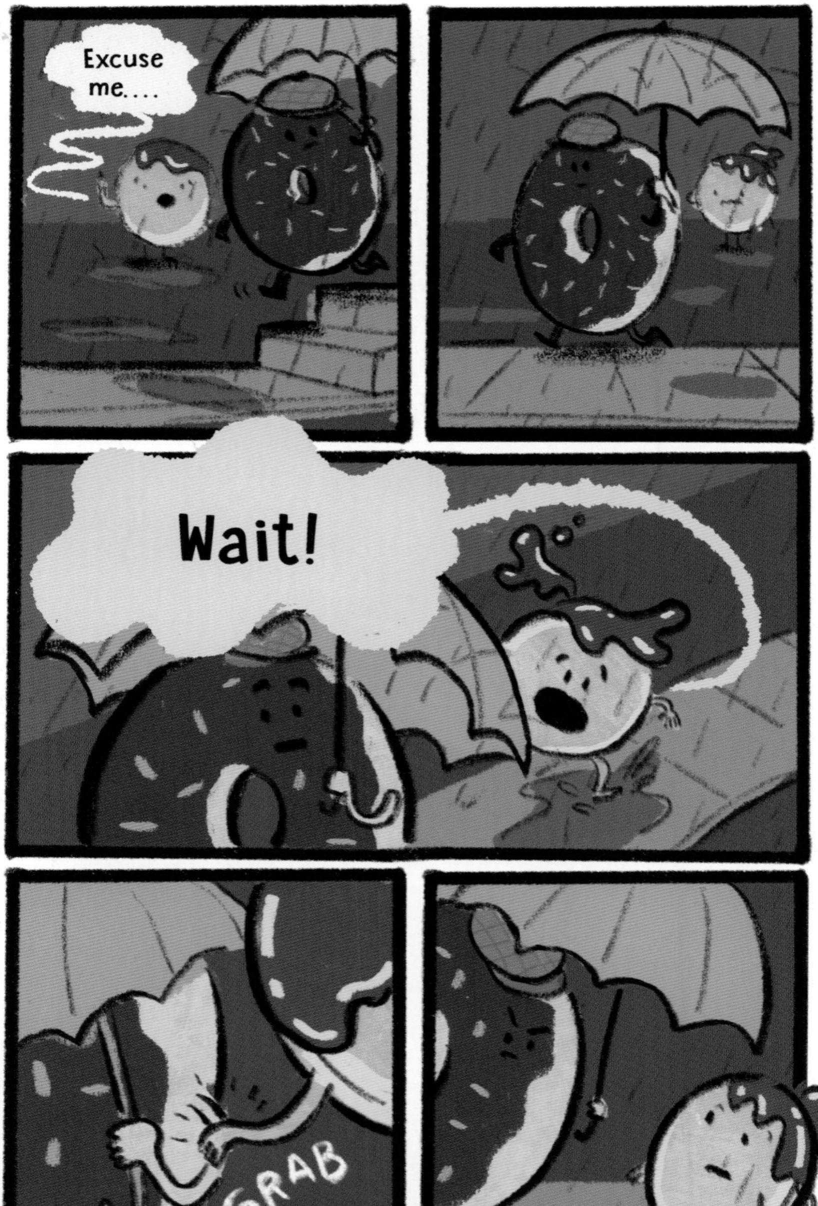
Excuse me....
Wait!
GRAB

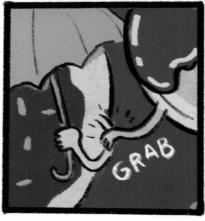

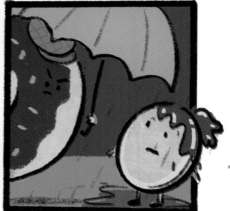

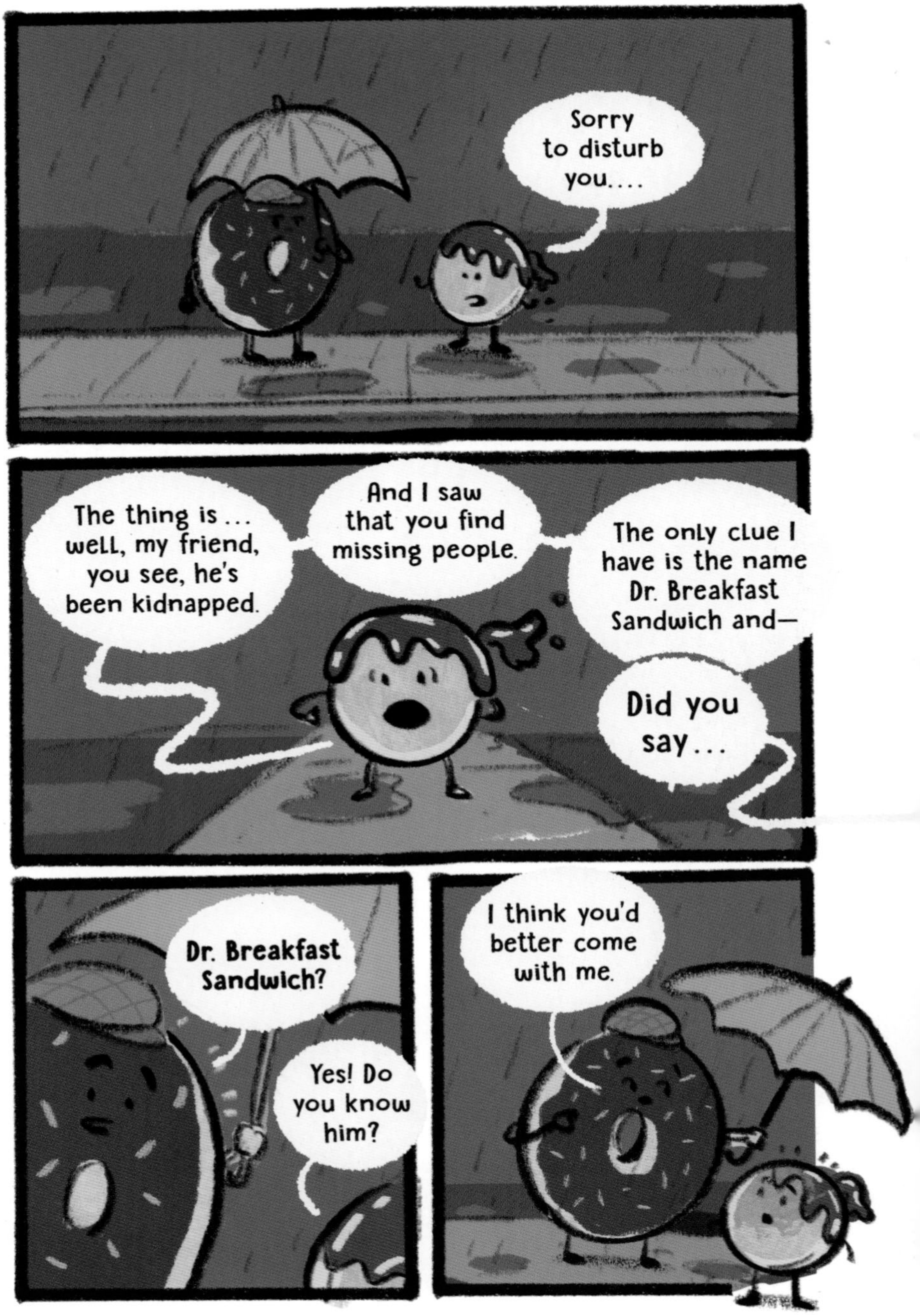
Sorry to disturb you....
The thing is ... well, my friend, you see, he's been kidnapped.
And I saw that you find missing people.
The only clue I have is the name Dr. Breakfast Sandwich and—
Did you say...
Dr. Breakfast Sandwich?
Yes! Do you know him?
I think you'd better come with me.

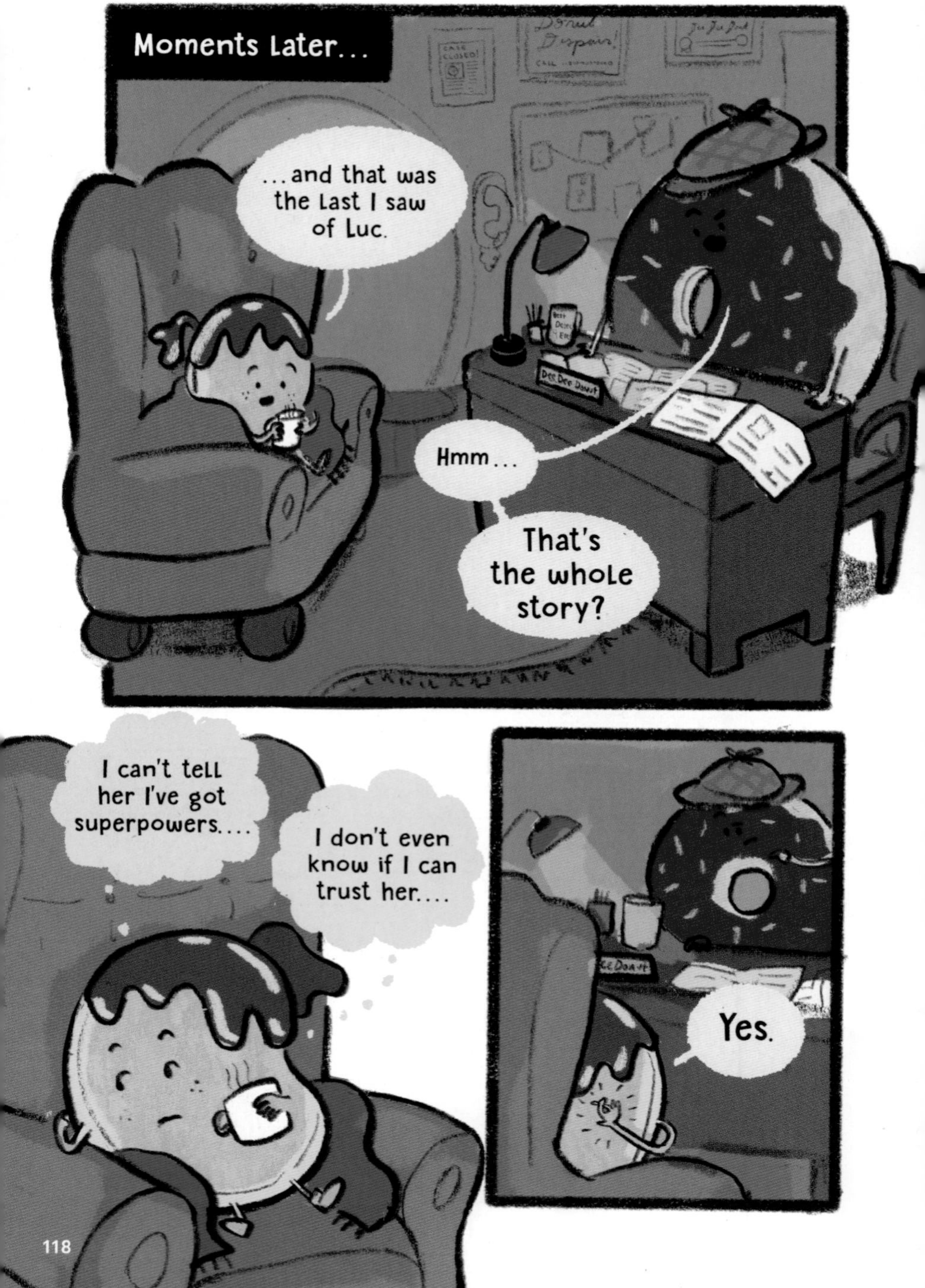
Moments Later...
...and that was the last I saw of Luc.
Hmm...
That's the whole story?
I can't tell her I've got superpowers....
I don't even know if I can trust her....
Yes.

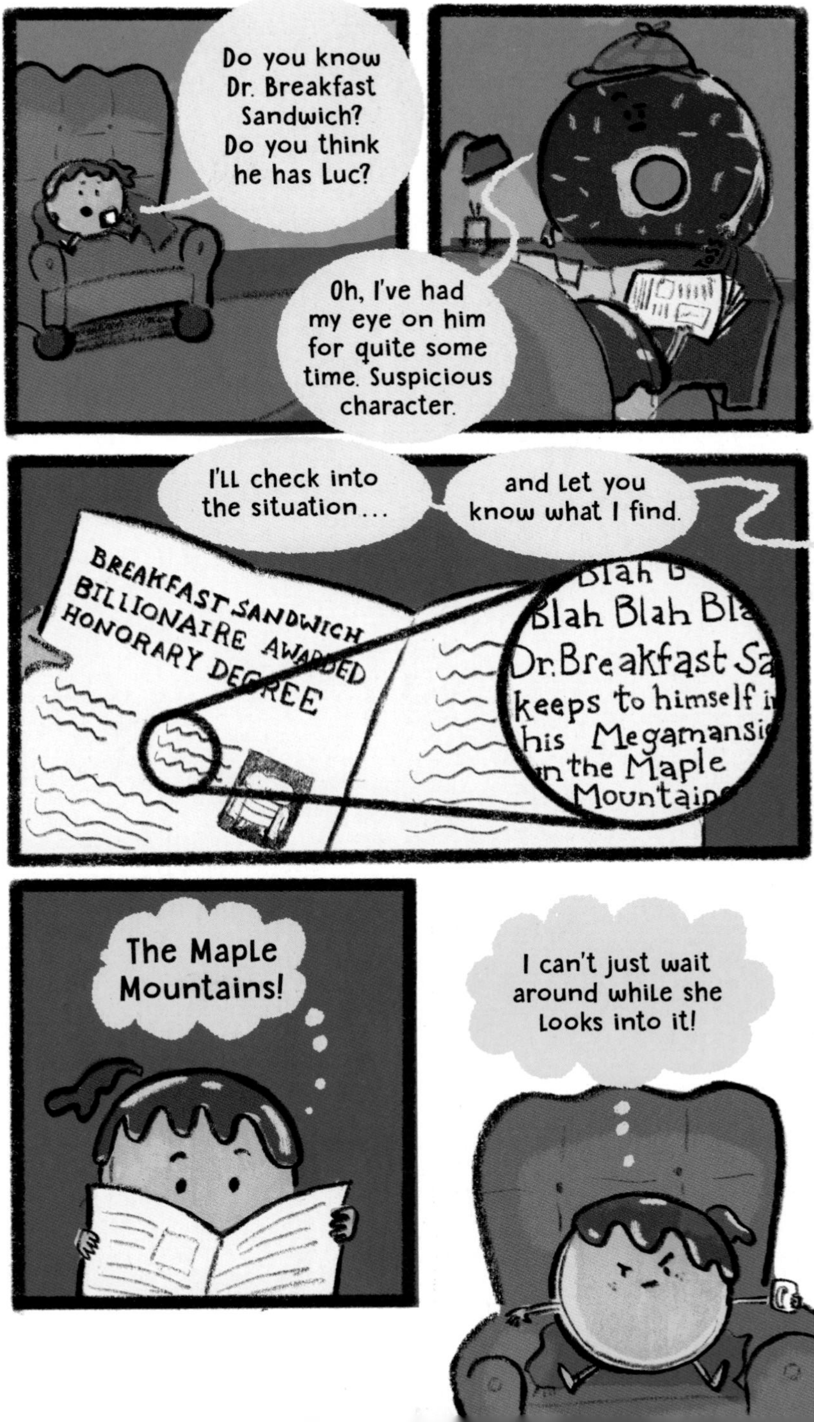
Do you know Dr. Breakfast Sandwich? Do you think he has Luc?
Oh, I've had my eye on him for quite some time. Suspicious character.
I'LL check into the situation...
and Let you know what I find.
BREAKFAST SANDWICH BILLIONAIRE AWARDED HONORARY DEGREE
Blah Blah Bla
Dr. Breakfast Sa
keeps to himself i
his Megamansi
the Maple
Mountain
The Maple Mountains!
I can't just wait around while she Looks into it!

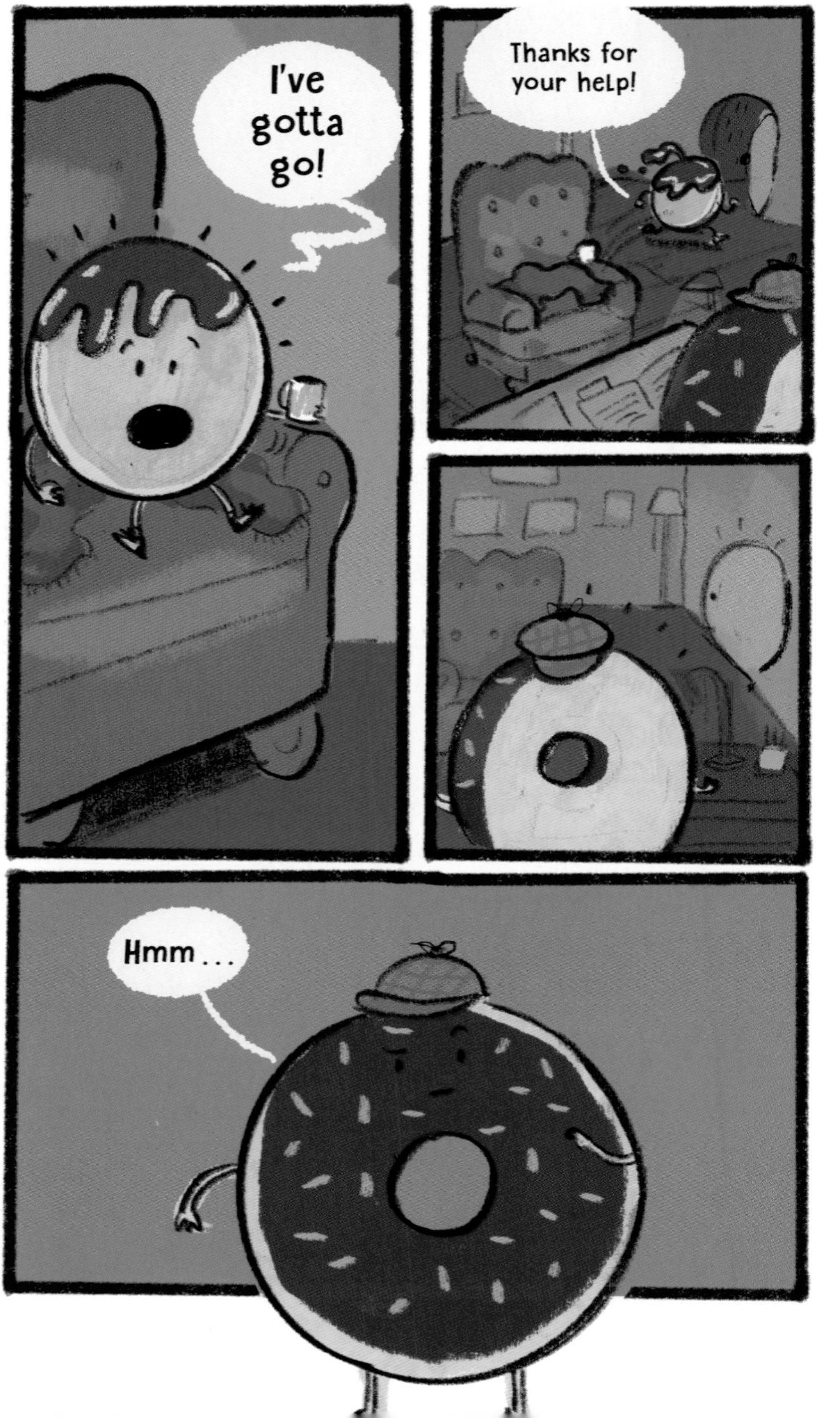
I've gotta go!
Thanks for your help!
Hmm . . .

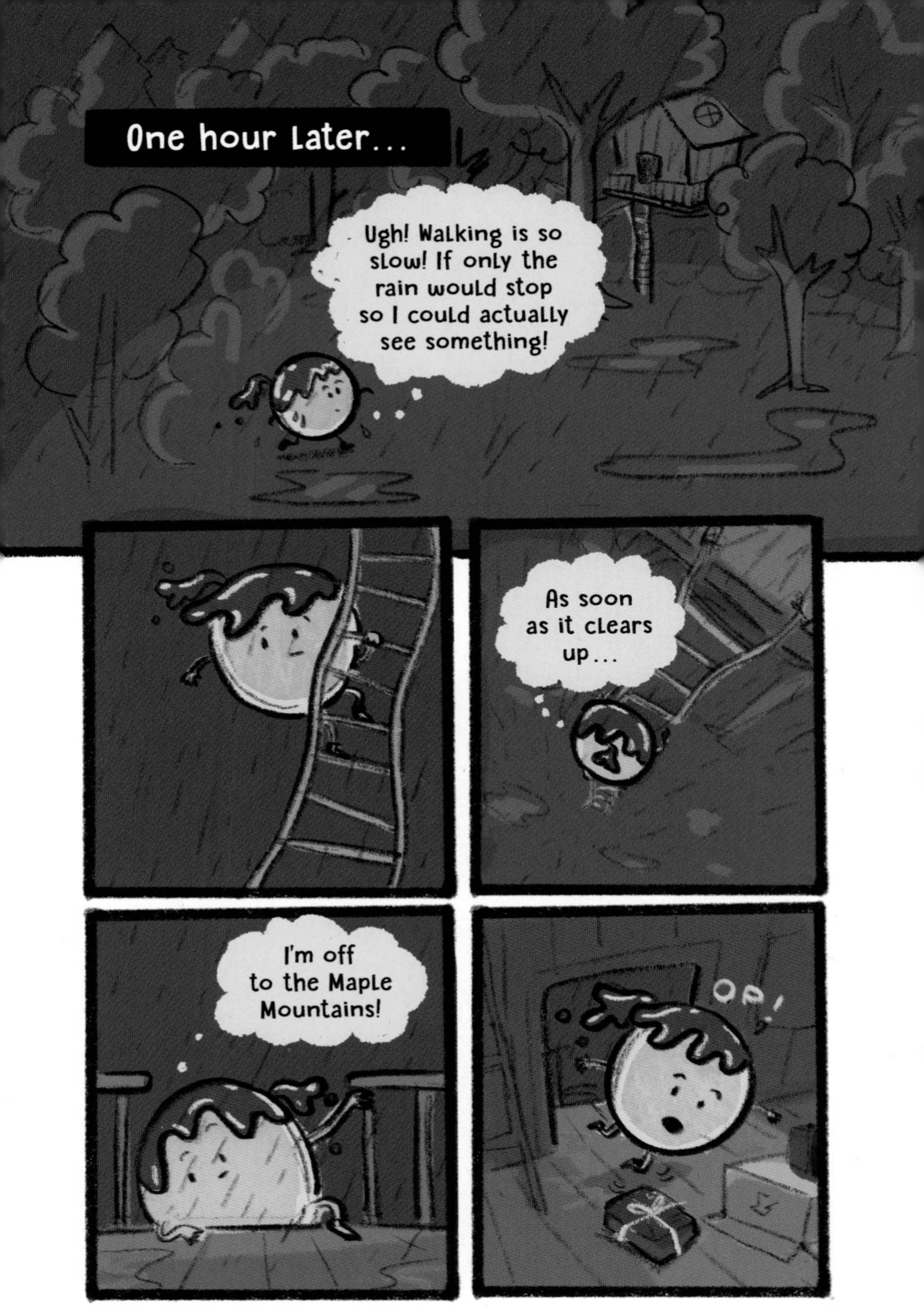
One hour Later...
Ugh! Walking is so slow! If only the rain would stop so I could actually see something!
As soon as it clears up...
I'm off to the Maple Mountains!
OP!

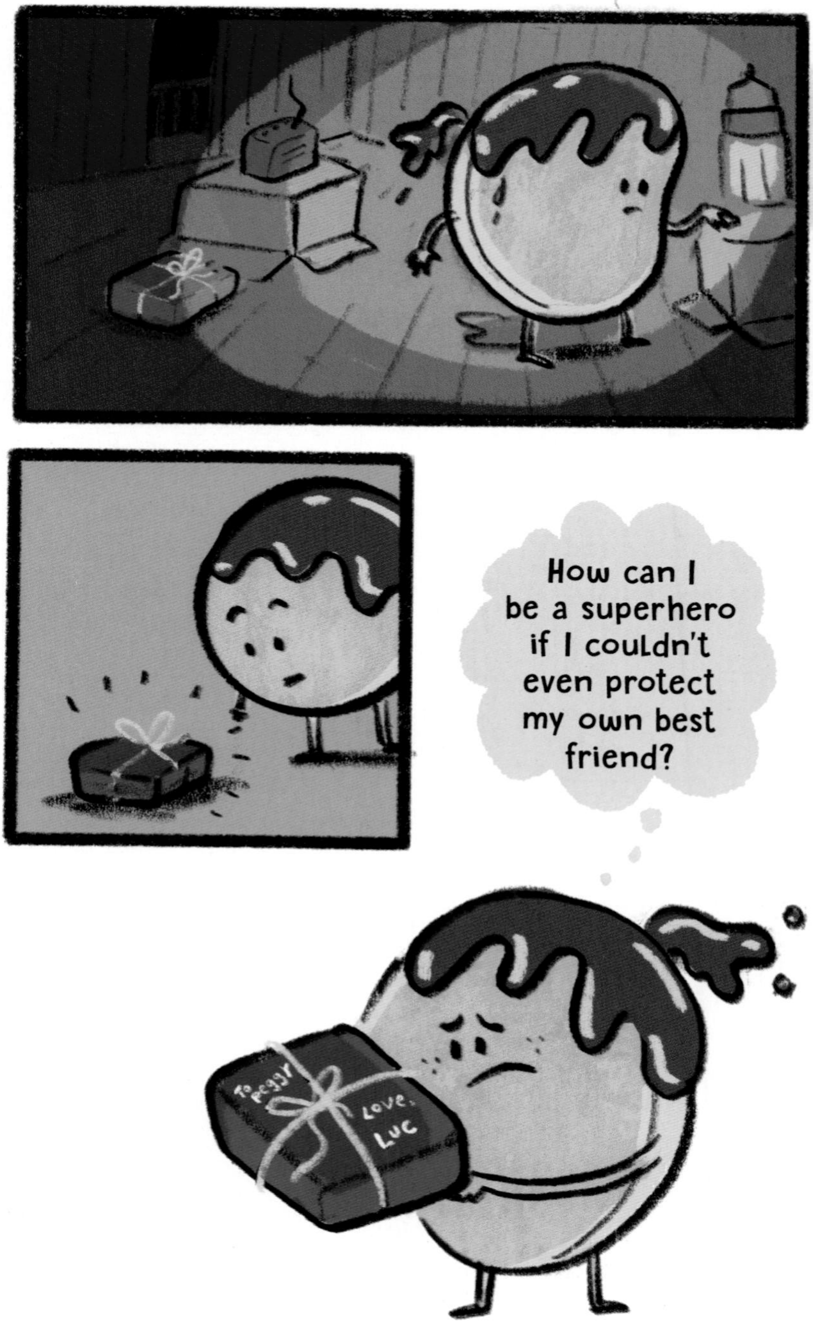
How can I be a superhero if I couldn't even protect my own best friend?
To Peggy
Love, Luc

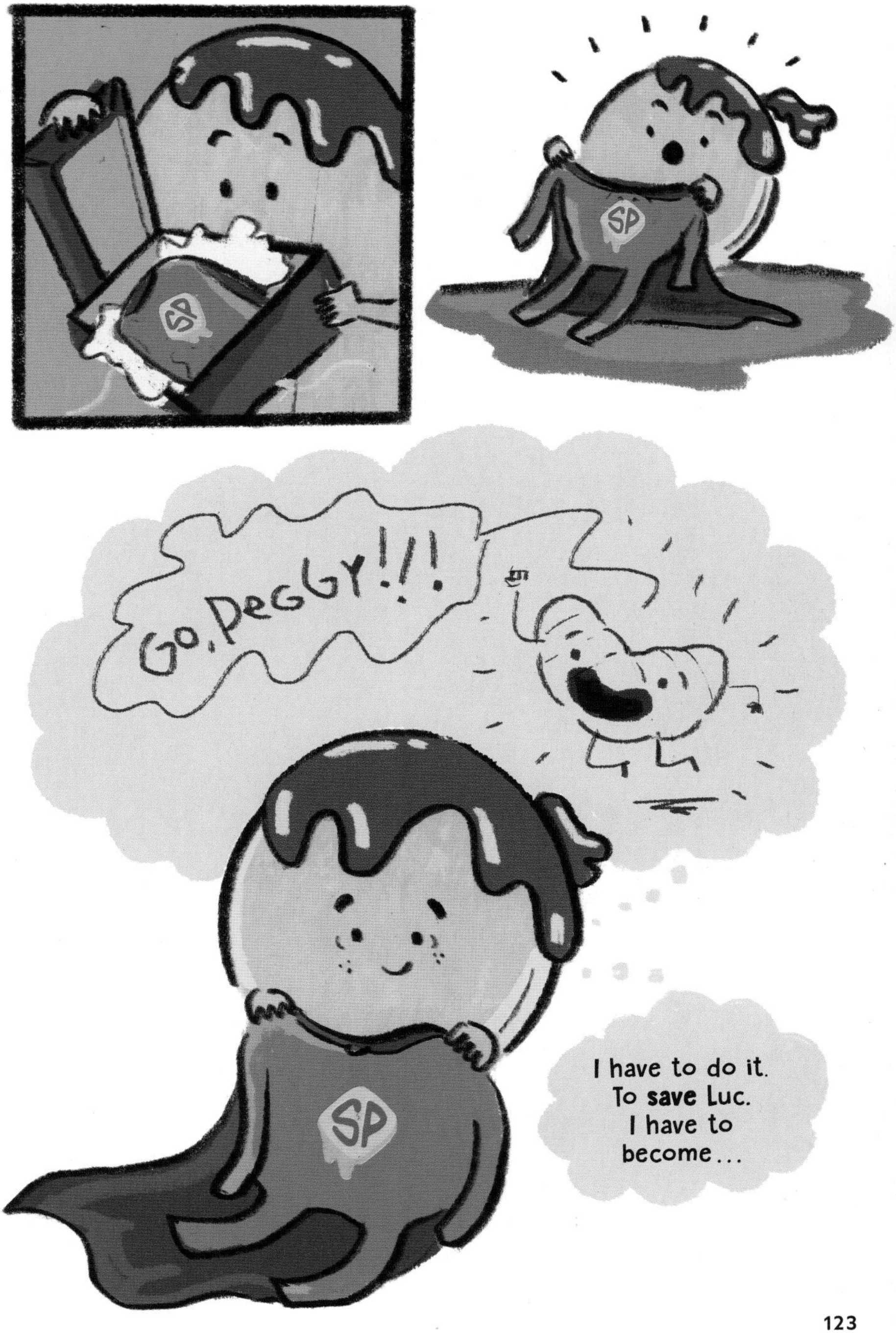
SP
SP
GO, PEGGY!!!
SP
I have to do it.
To **save** Luc.
I have to
become...

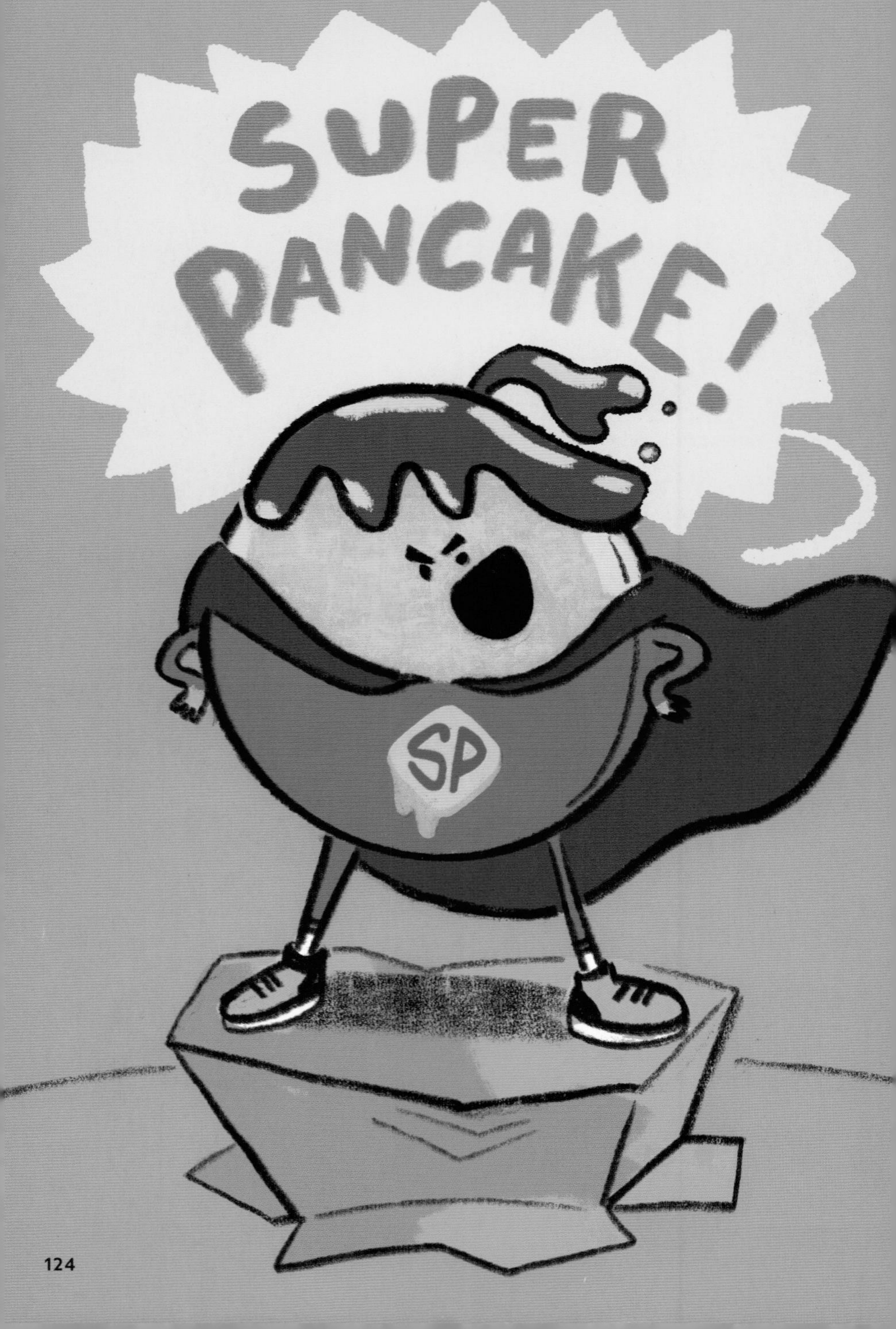
SUPER PANCAKE!
SP

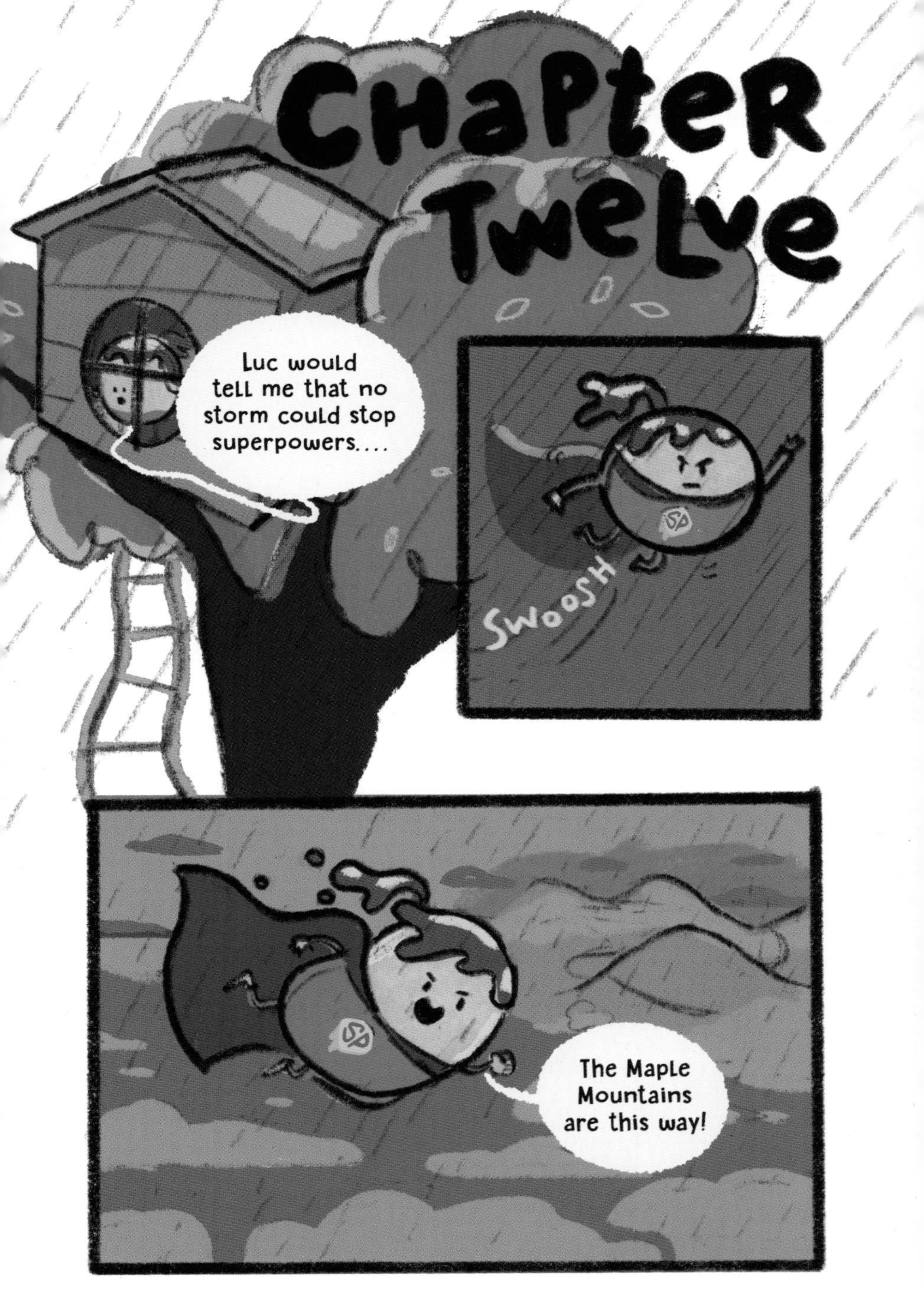
Chapter Twelve
Luc would tell me that no storm could stop superpowers....
SWOOSH
The Maple Mountains are this way!

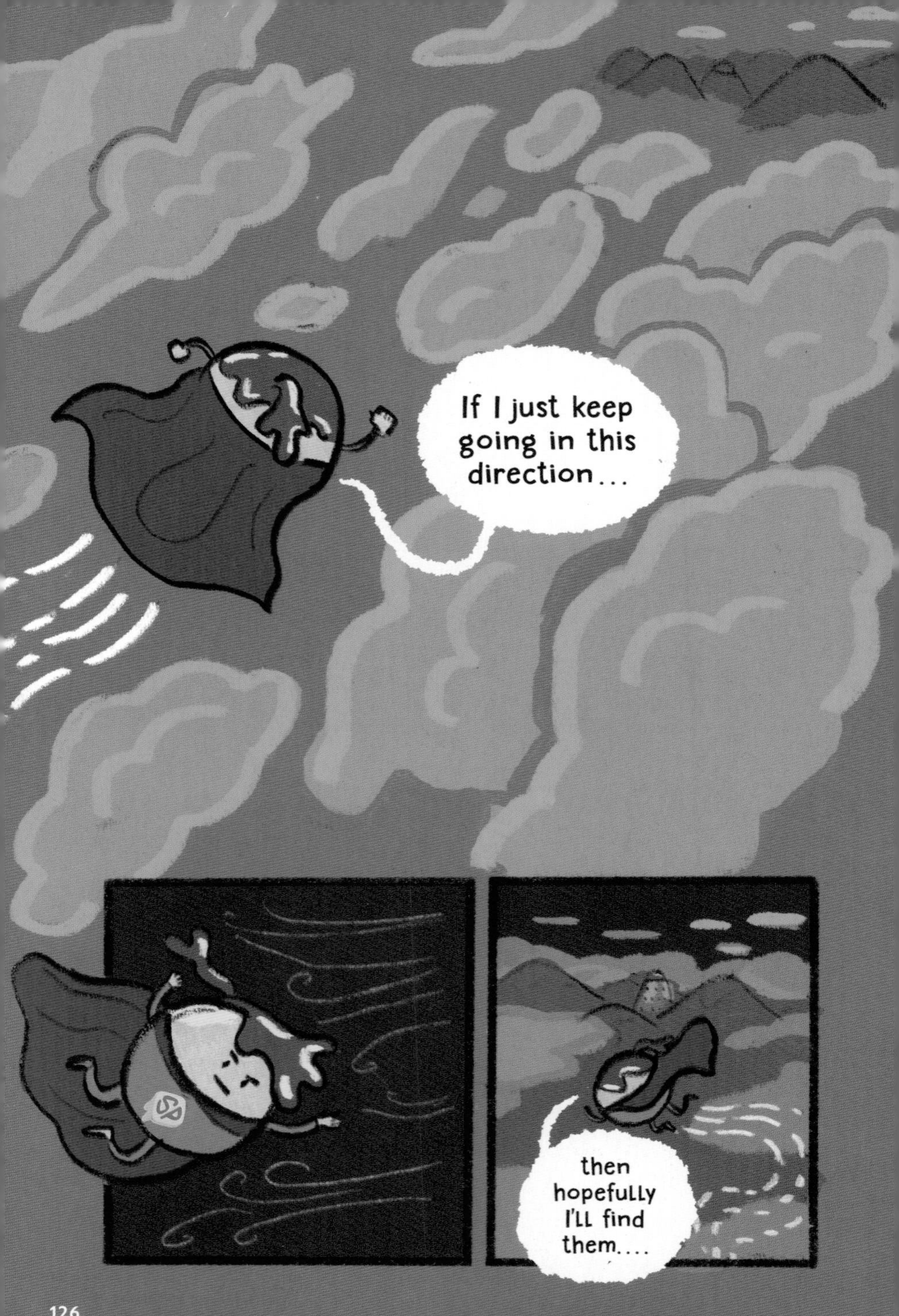
If I just keep going in this direction...
then hopefully I'll find them....

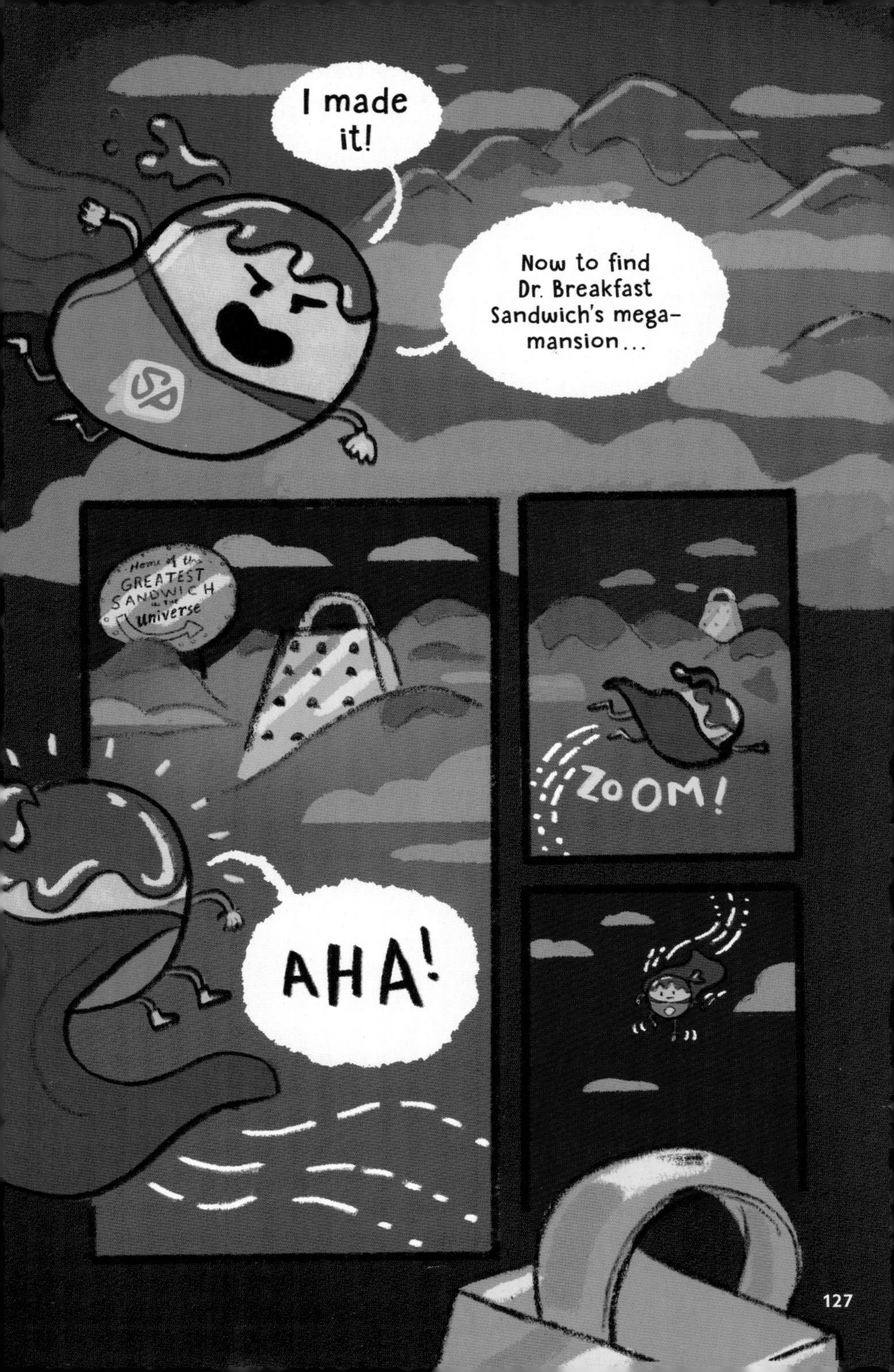
I made it!
Now to find Dr. Breakfast Sandwich's mega-mansion...
Home of the GREATEST SANDWICH in the universe
ZOOM!
AHA!

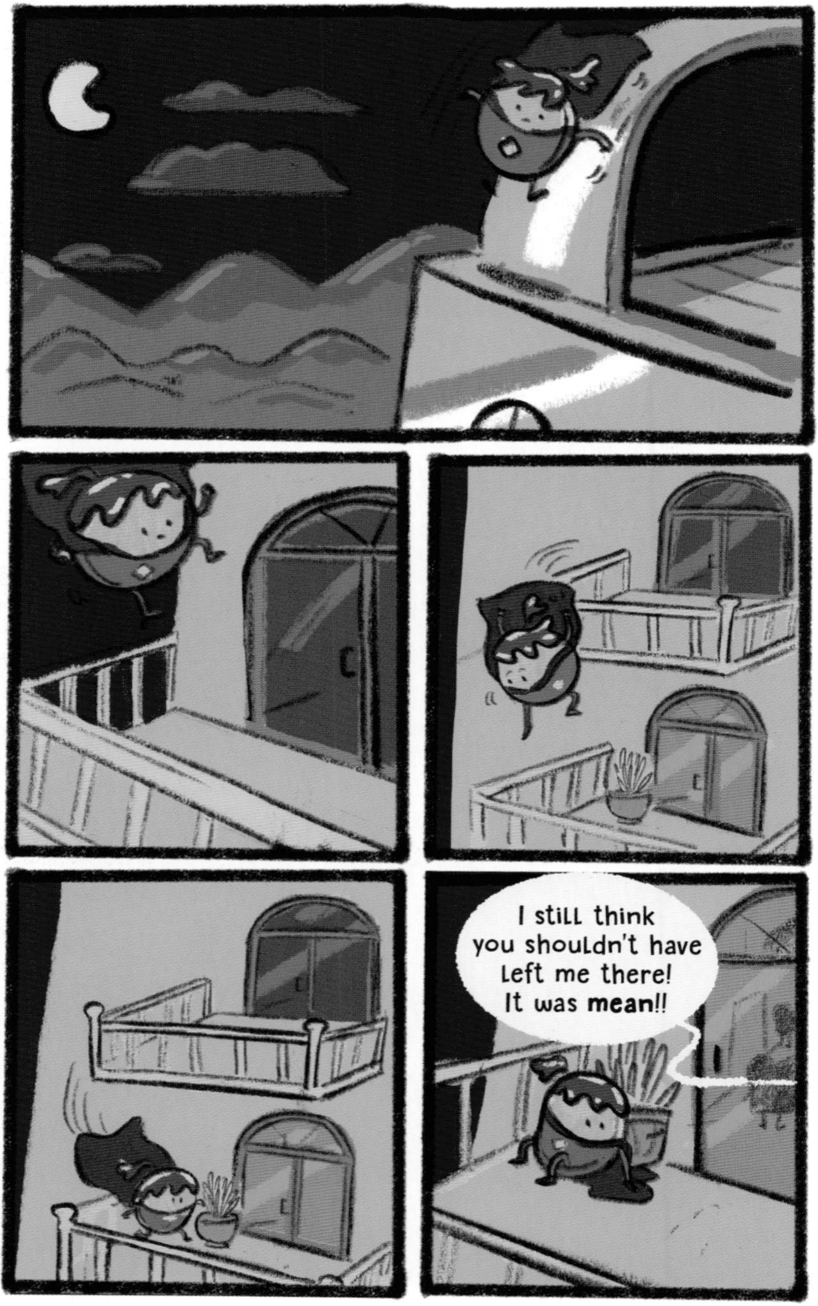
I still think
you shouldn't have
left me there!
It was mean!!

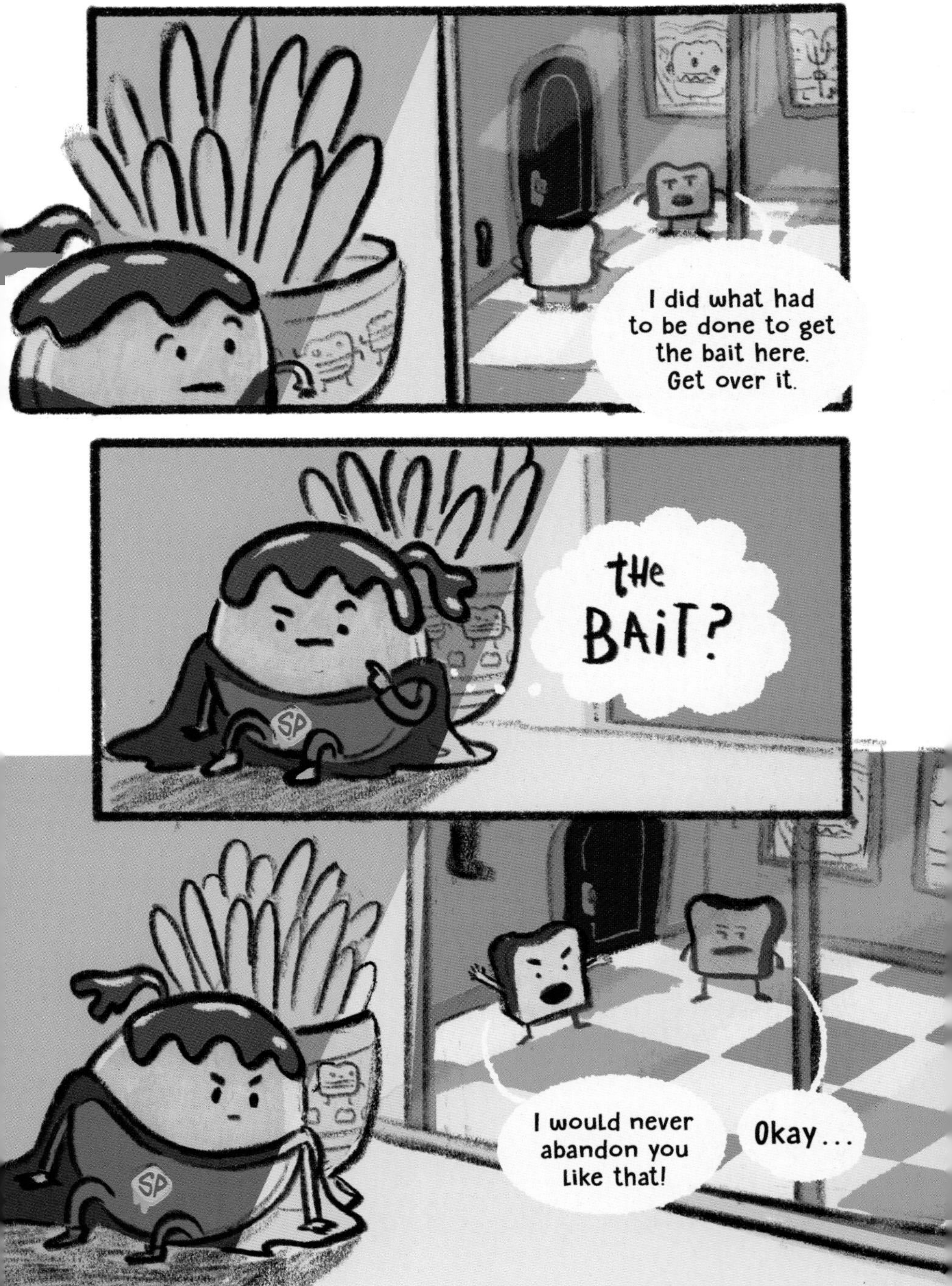
I did what had to be done to get the bait here. Get over it.
THE BAIT?
I would never abandon you like that!
Okay...

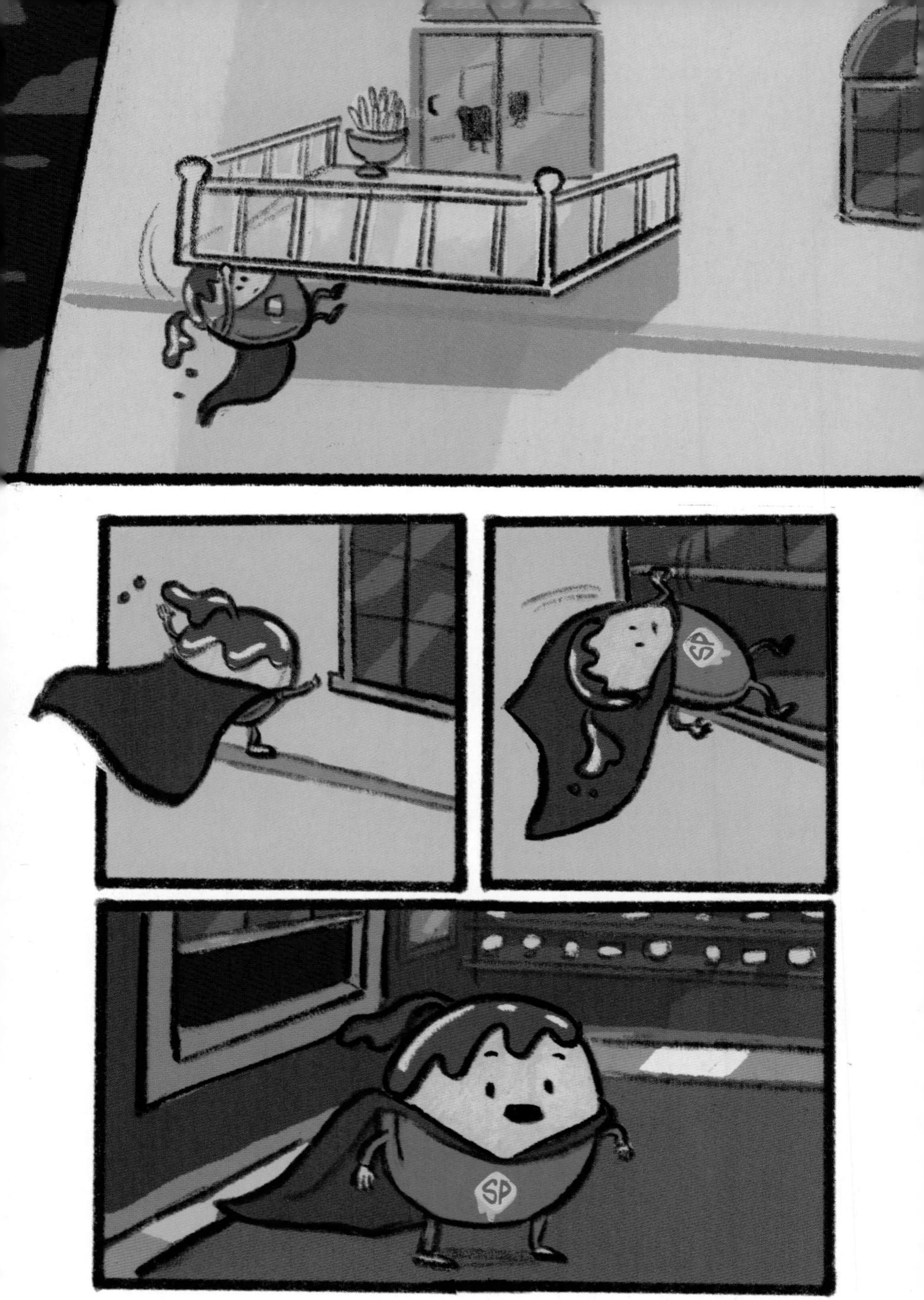

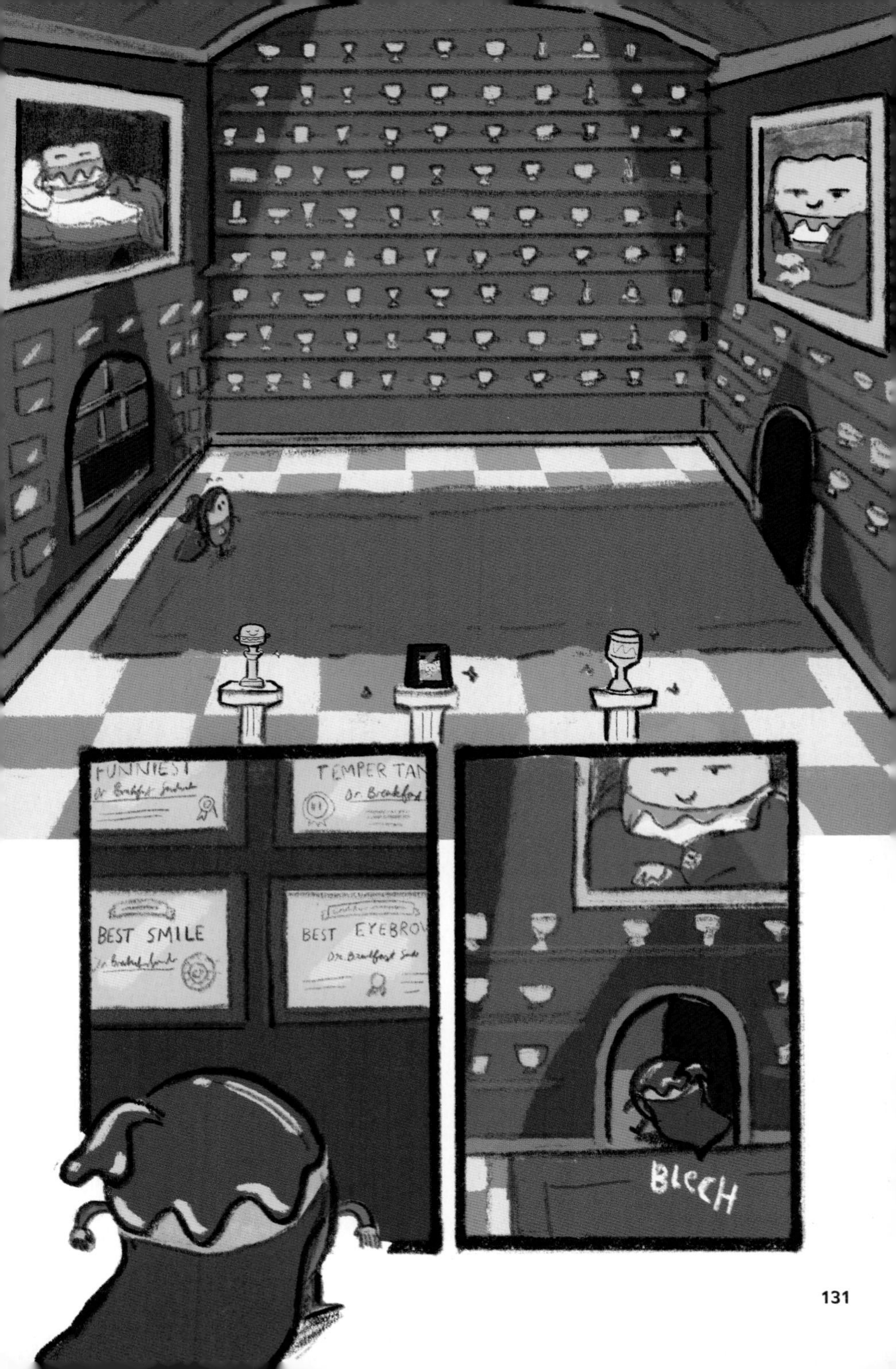
FUNNIEST
TEMPER TAN
BEST SMILE
BEST EYEBROW
BLECH

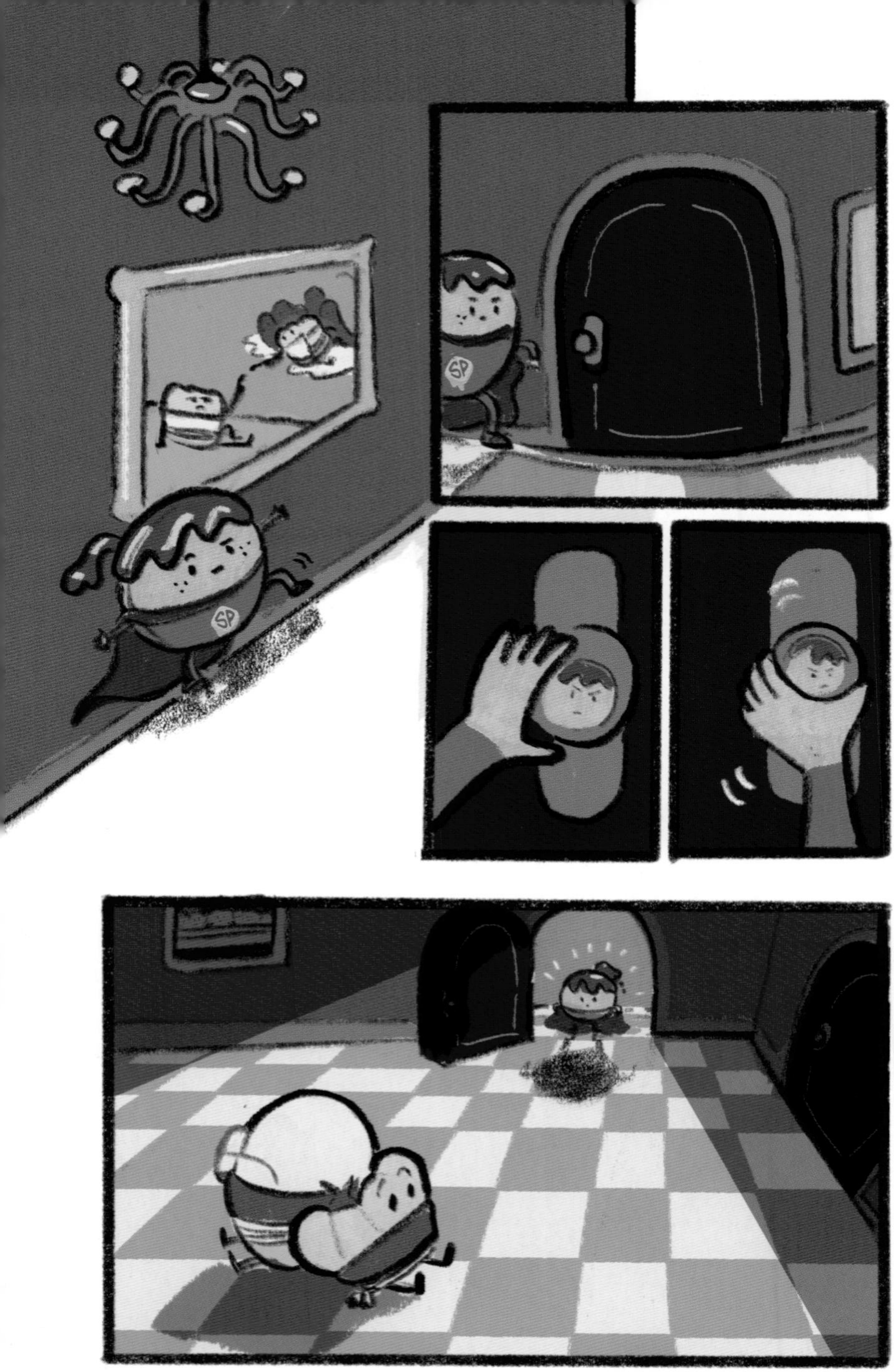

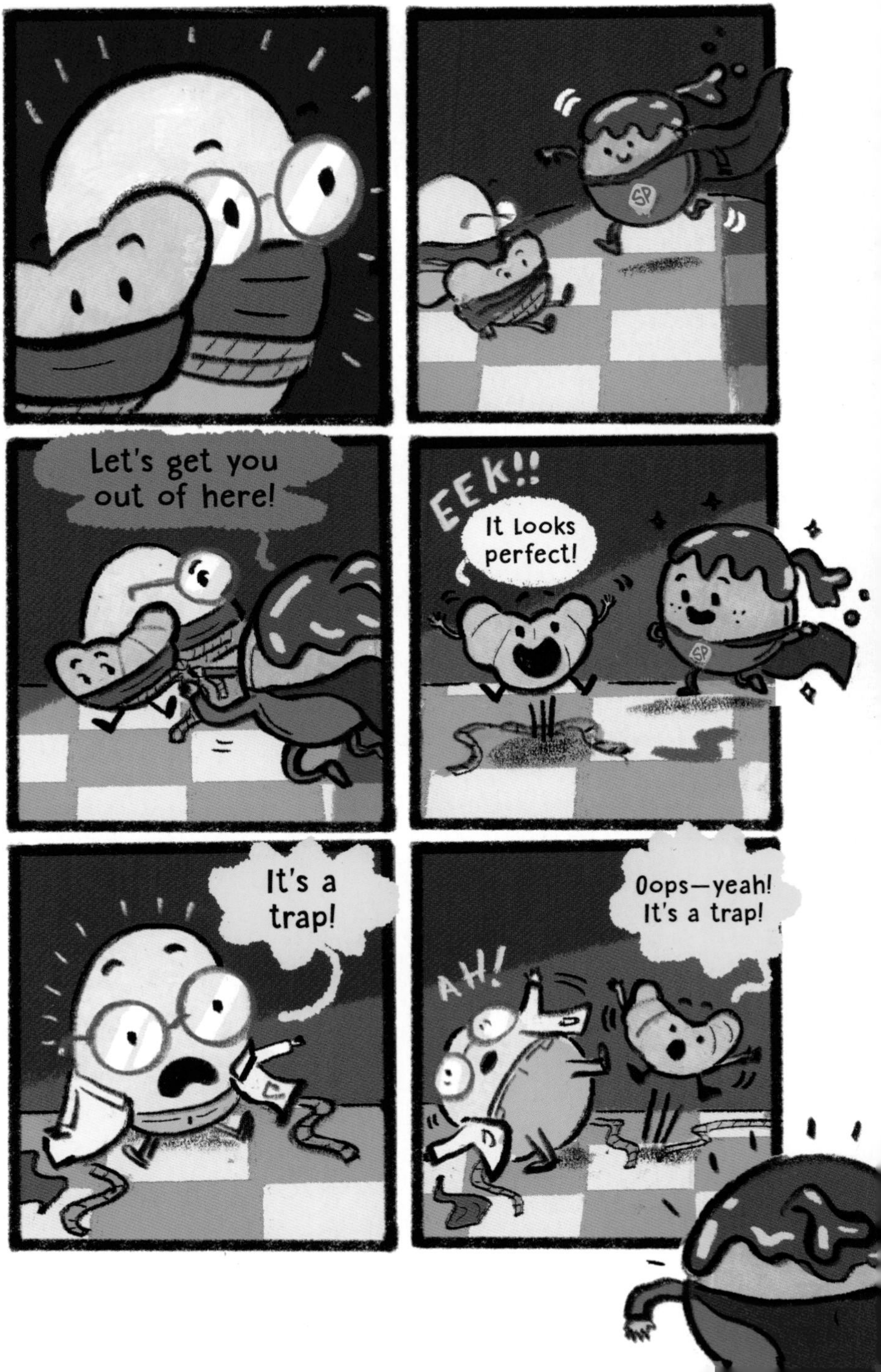
Let's get you out of here!
EEK!!
It Looks perfect!
It's a trap!
AH!
Oops—yeah! It's a trap!

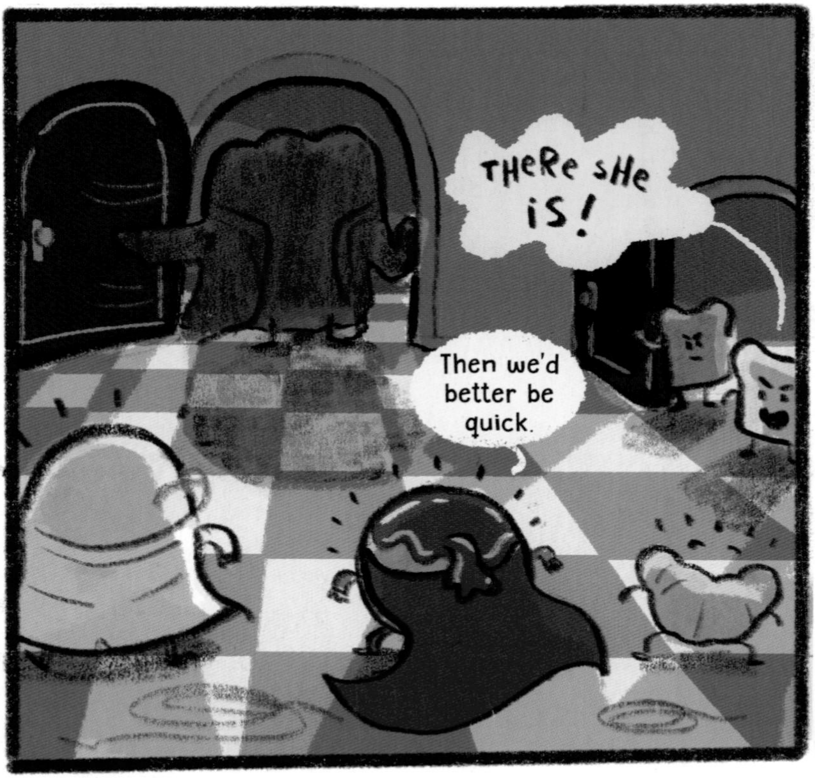
THeRe sHe iS!
Then we'd better be quick.

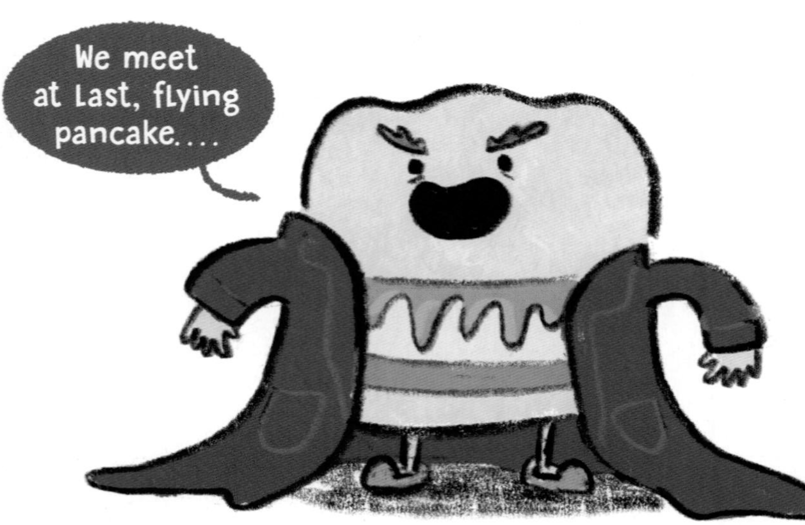
We meet at Last, fLying pancake....

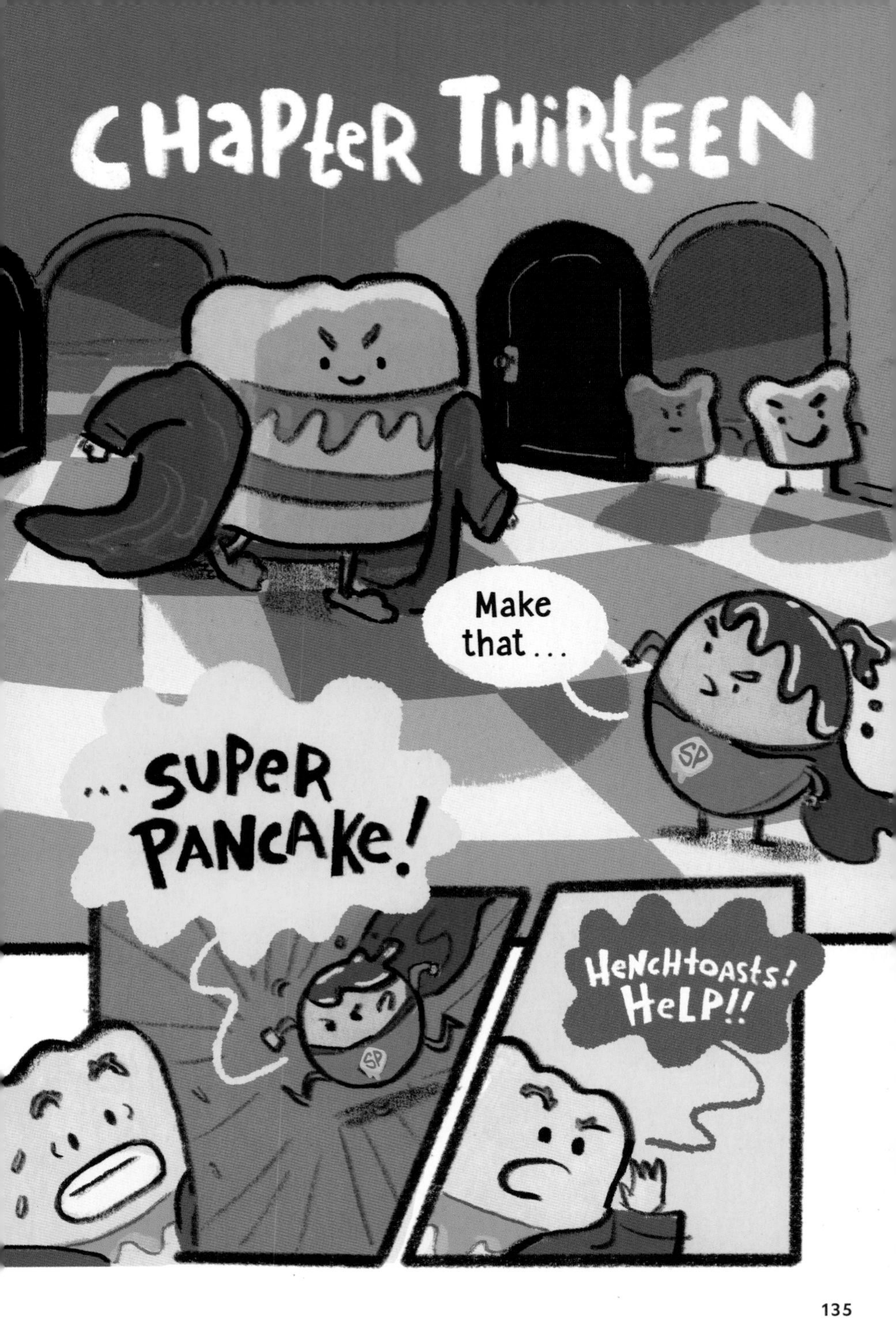
CHAPTER THIRTEEN
Make that . . .
. . . SUPER PANCAKE!
HENCHTOASTS! HELP!!

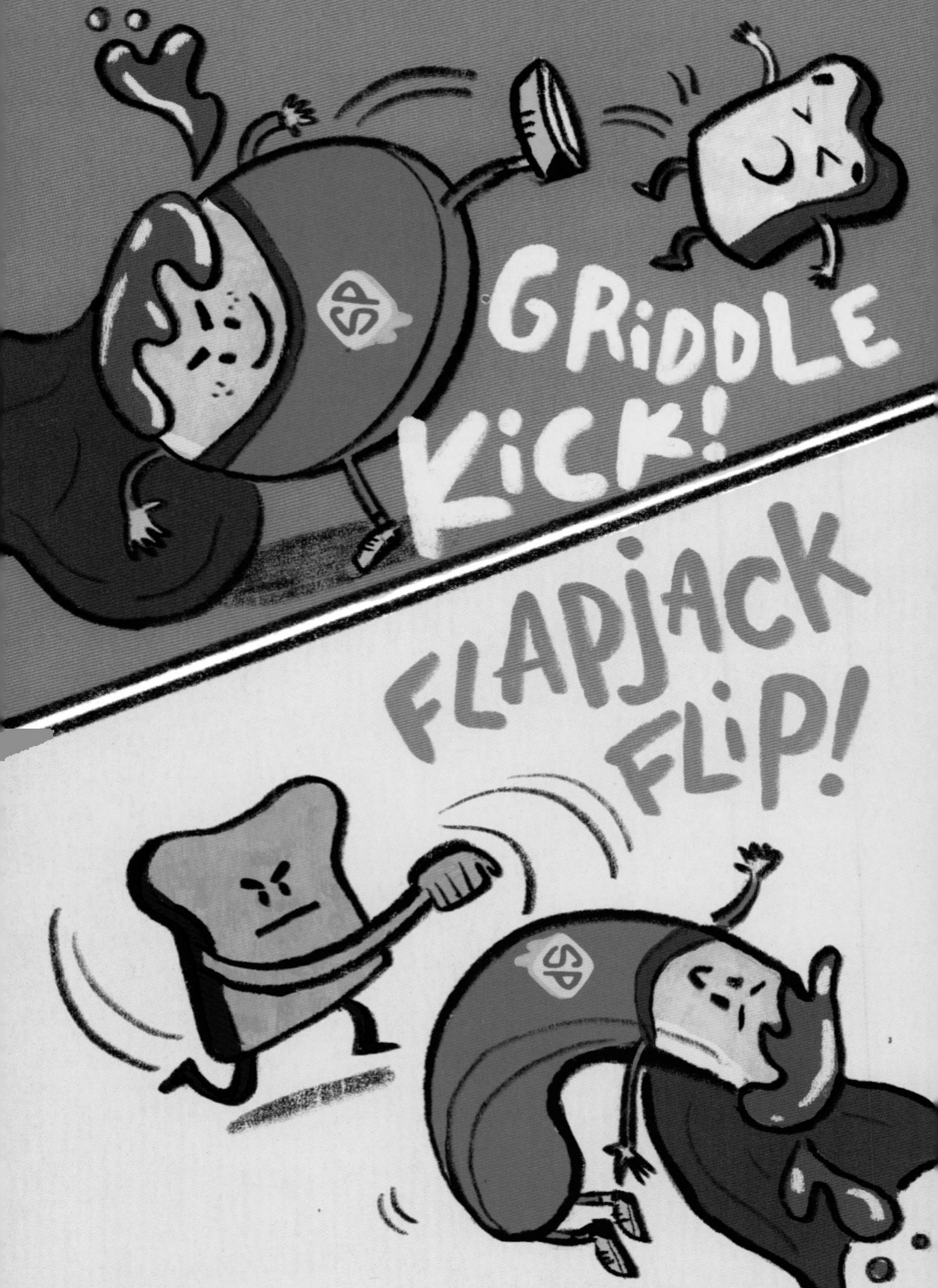
GRIDDLE KICK!
FLAPJACK FLIP!

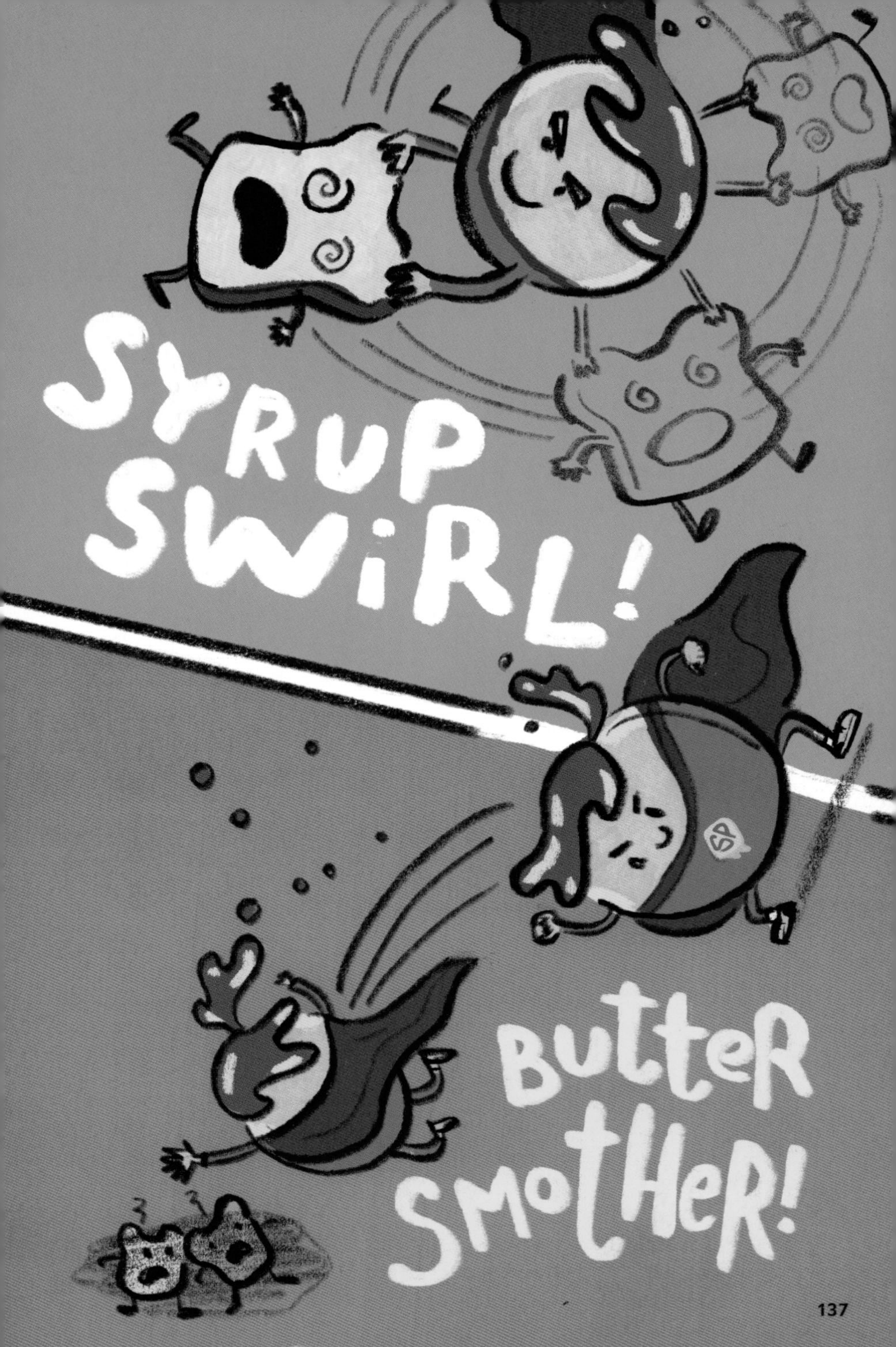
SYRUP SWIRL!
SP
BUTTER SMOTHER!

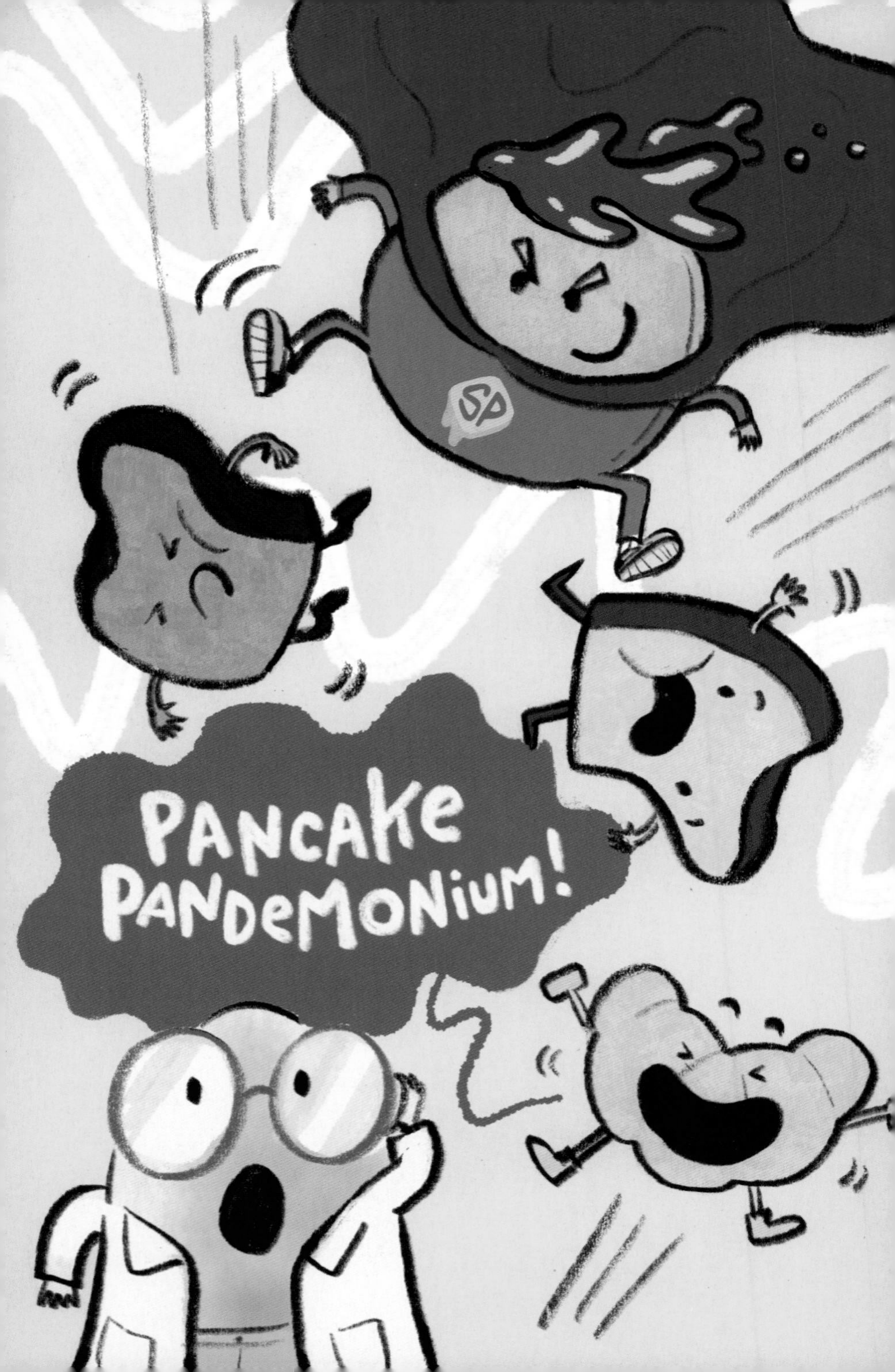
PANCAKE
PANDEMONIUM!
SP

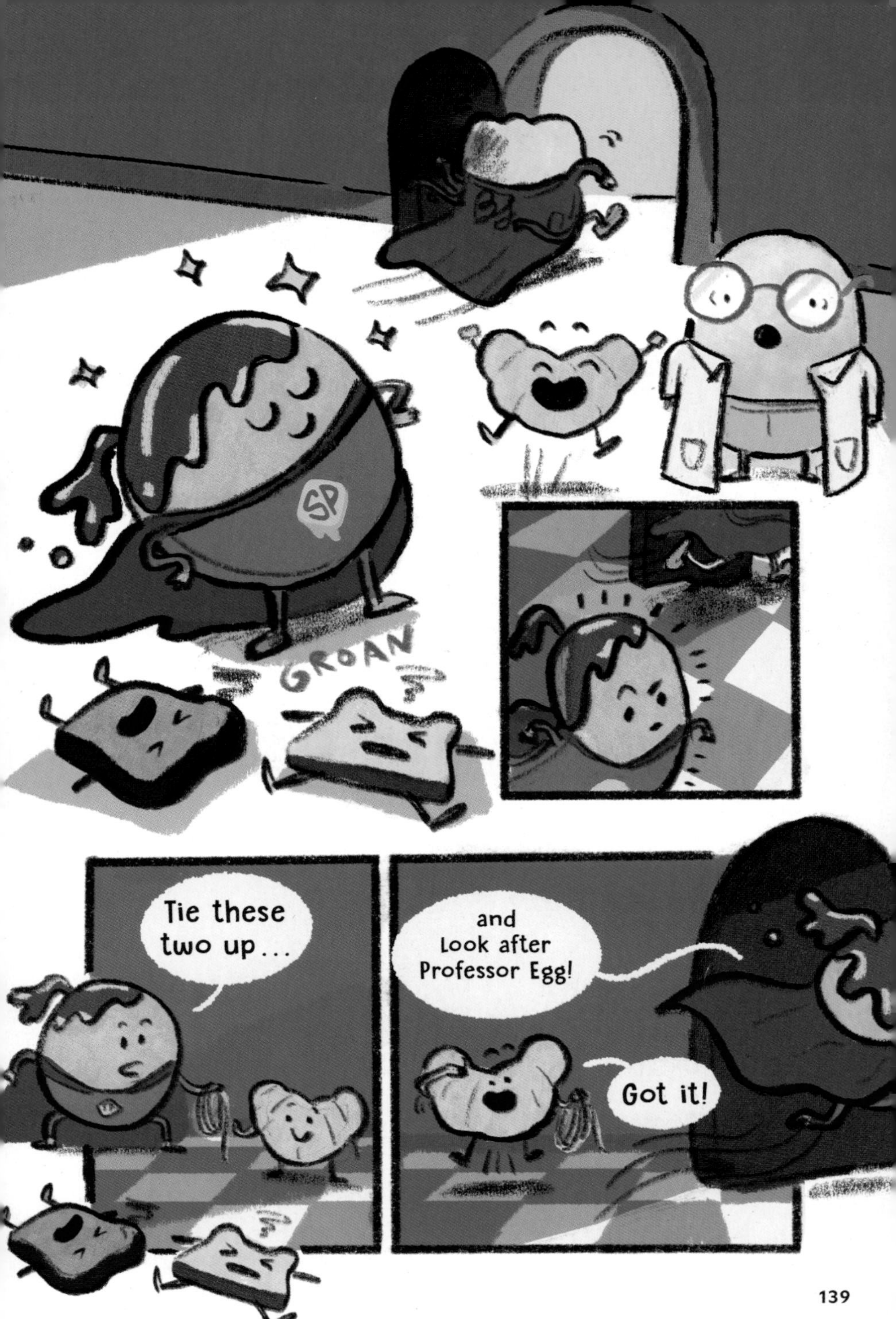
GROAN
Tie these two up...
and Look after Professor Egg!
Got it!

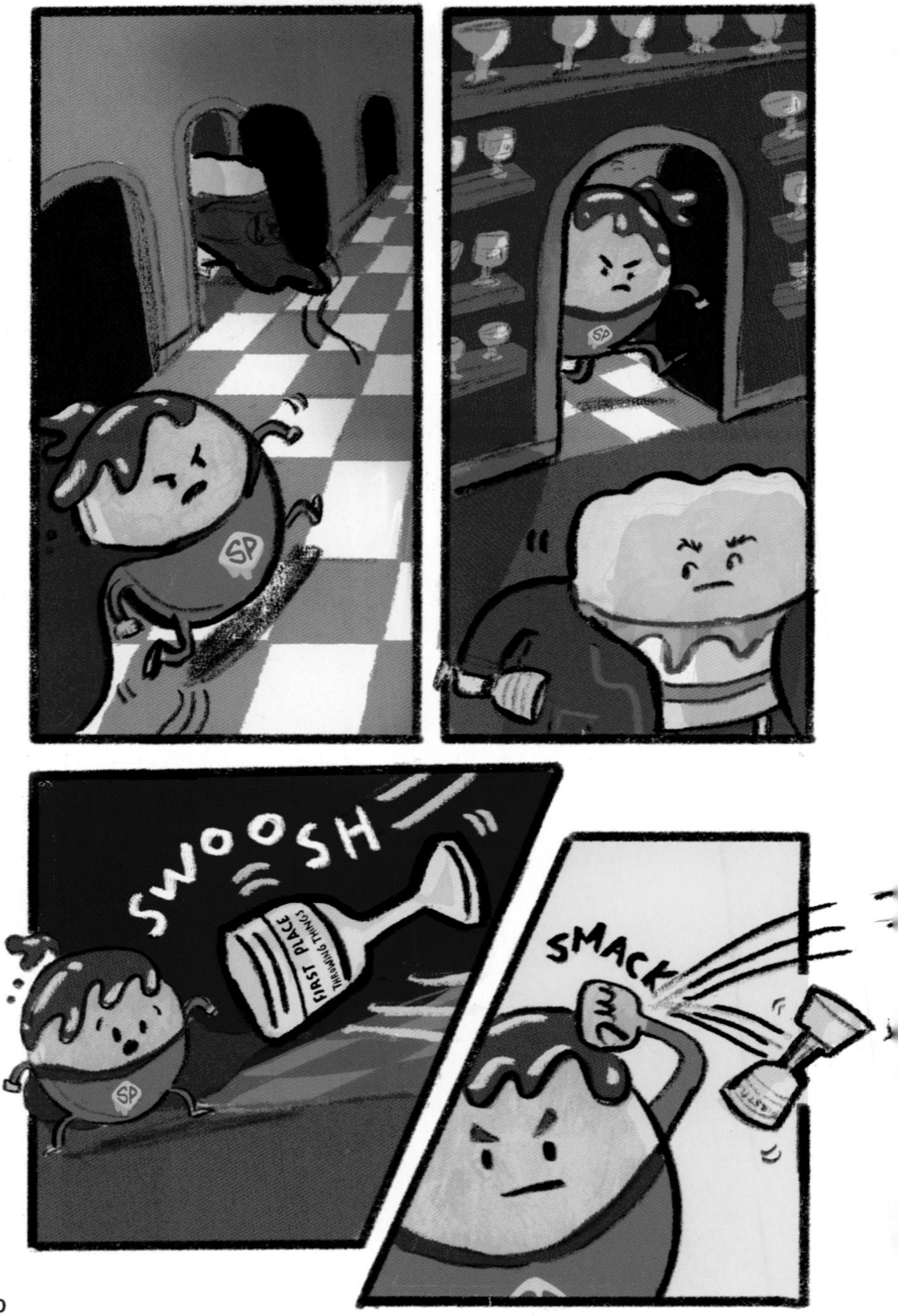
SWOOSH
FIRST PLACE
THROWING THINGS
SMACK

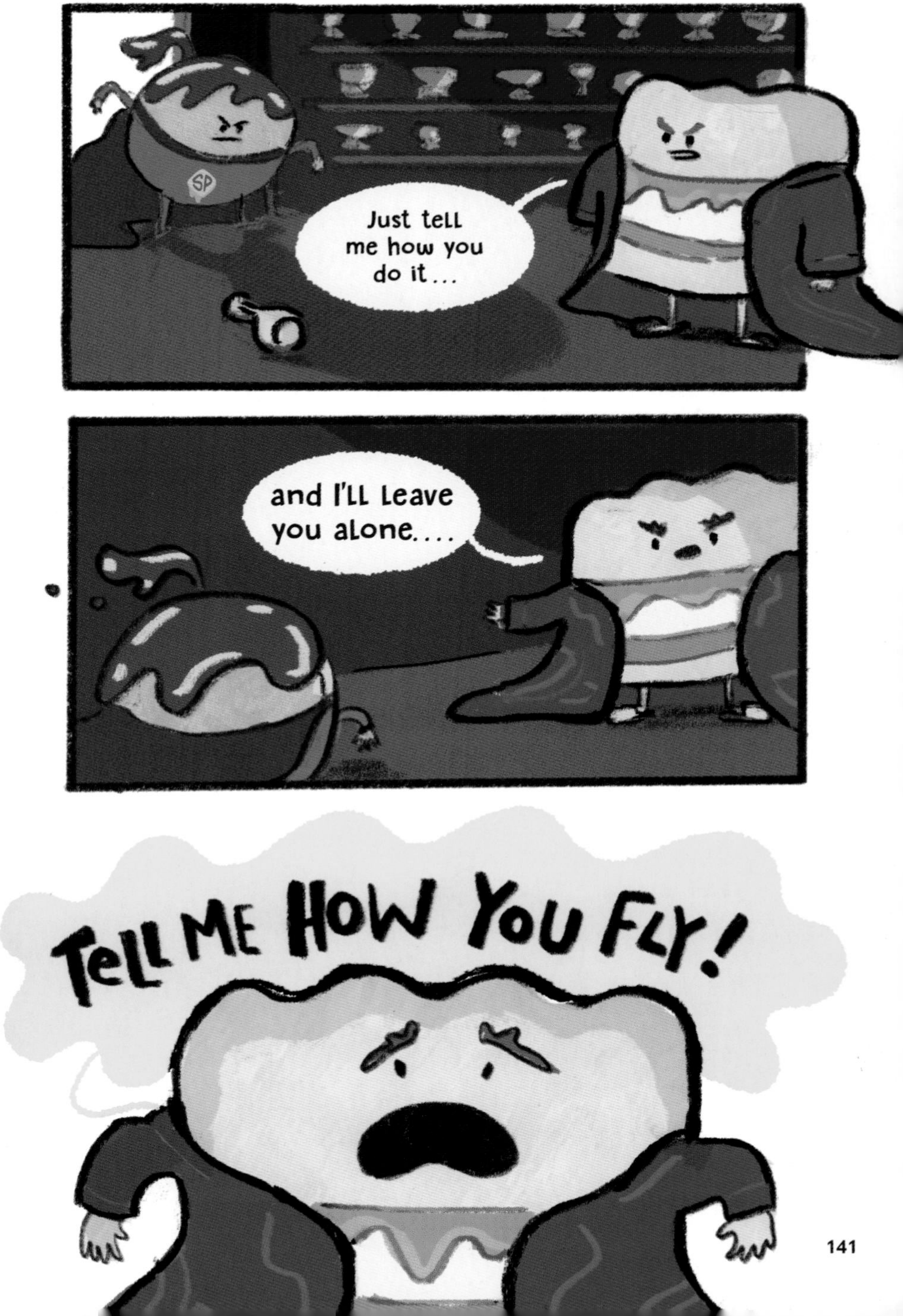

SP
Just tell me how you do it...
and I'll leave you alone....
TELL ME HOW YOU FLY!

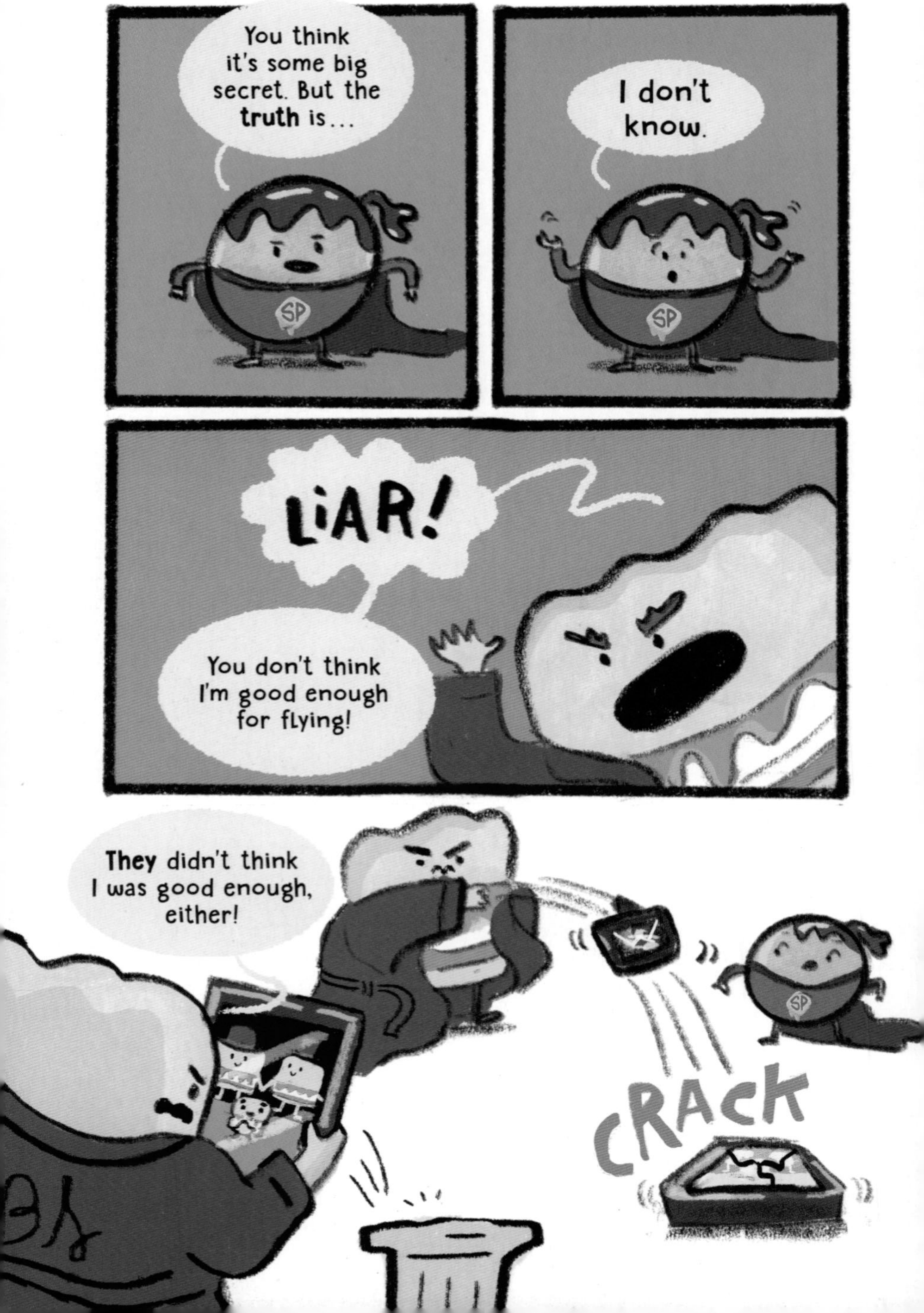
You think it's some big secret. But the **truth** is...
I don't know.
LIAR!
You don't think I'm good enough for flying!
They didn't think I was good enough, either!
CRACK

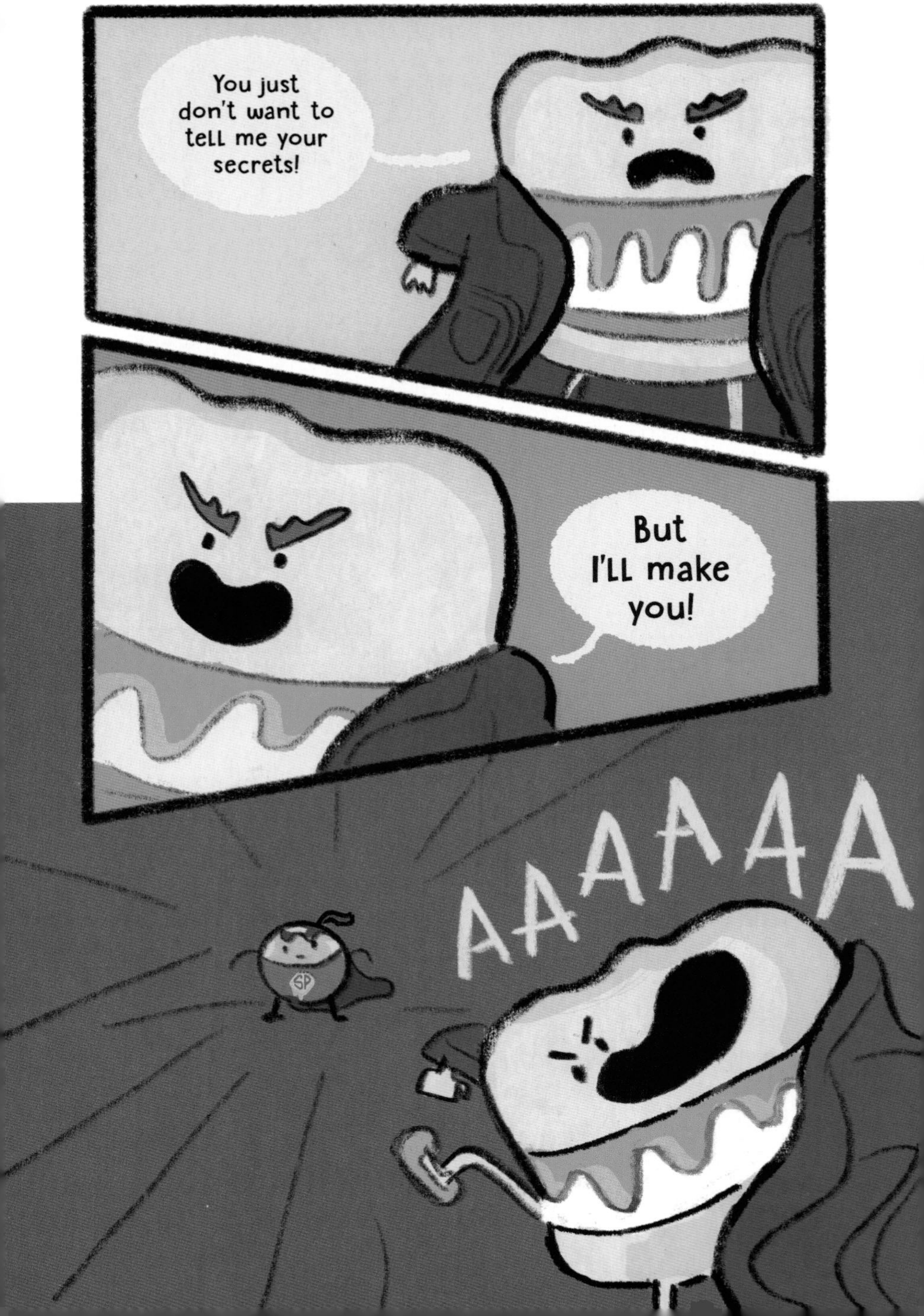
You just don't want to tell me your secrets!
But I'LL make you!
AAAAAA

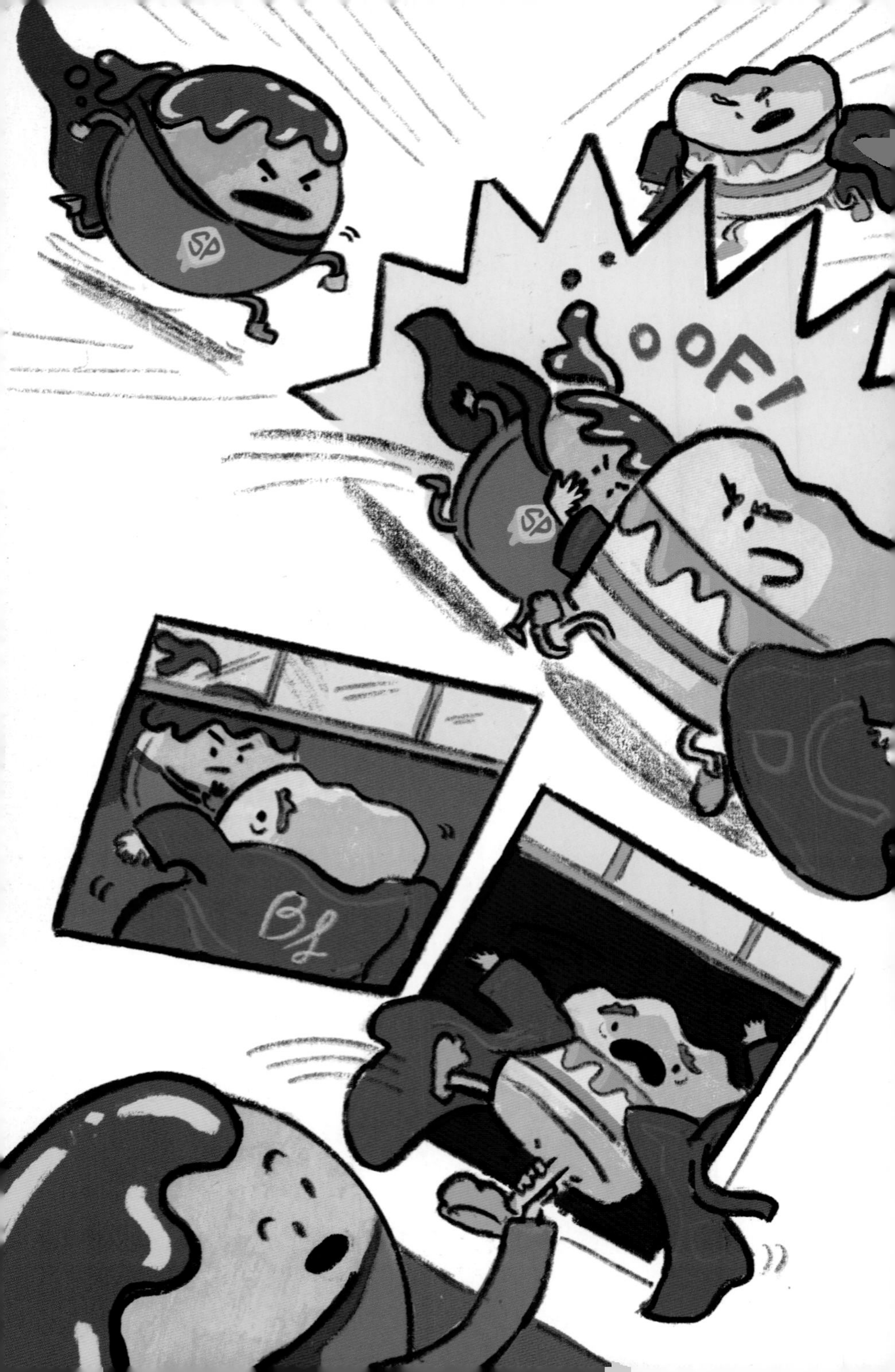
OOF!

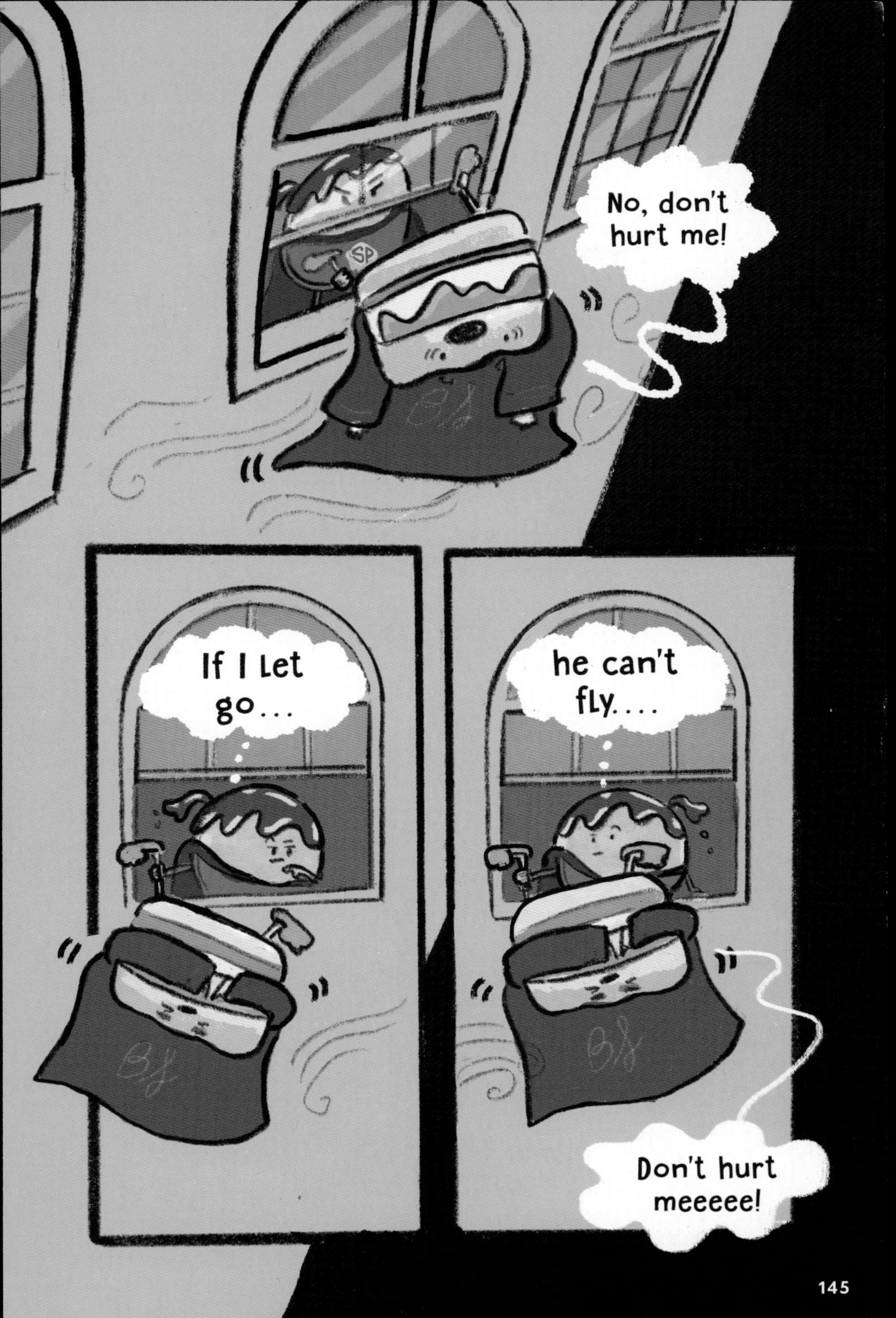
No, don't hurt me!
If I let go...
he can't fly....
Don't hurt meeeee!

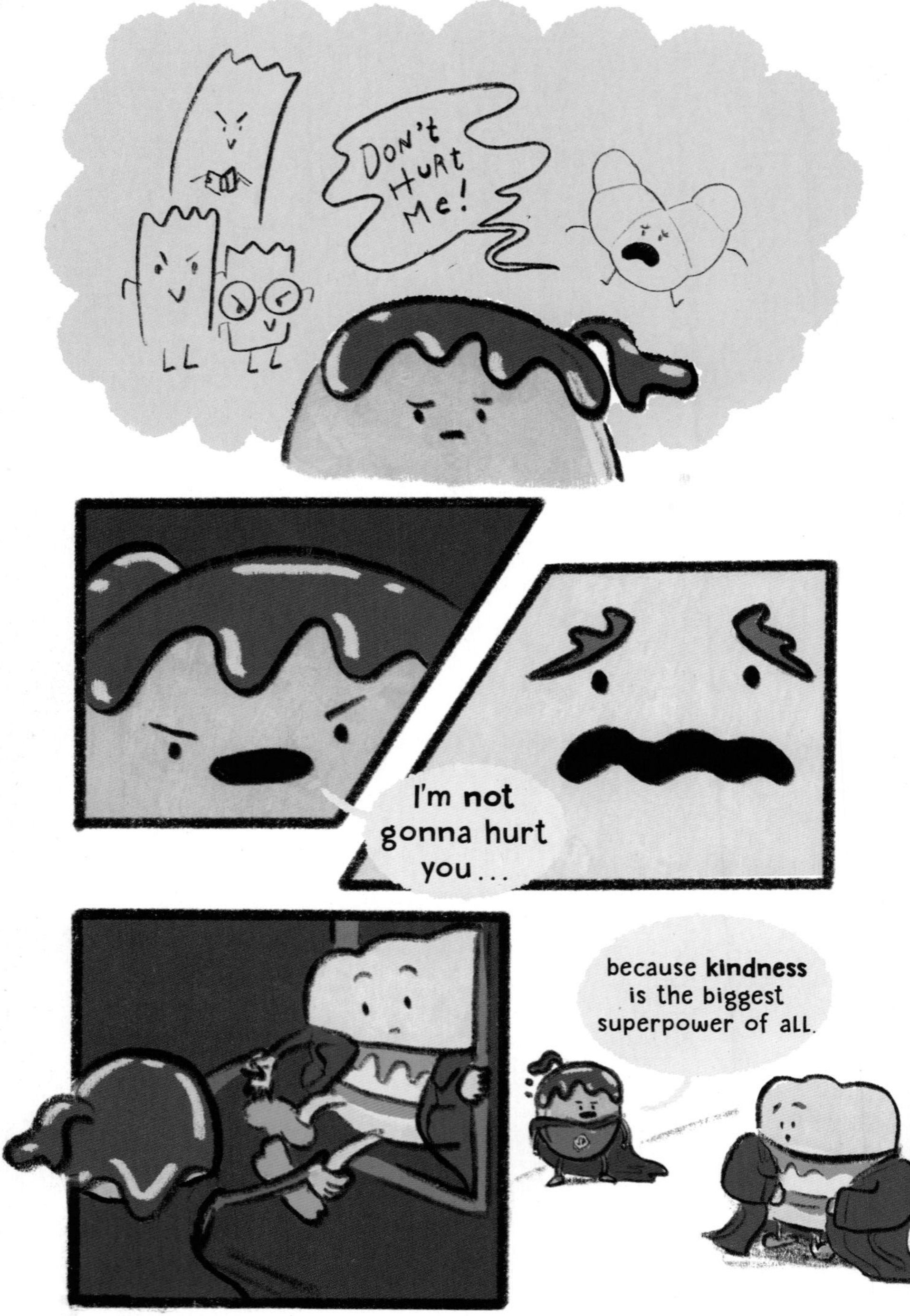

DON'T HURT Me!
I'm **not** gonna hurt you...
because **kindness** is the biggest superpower of aLL.

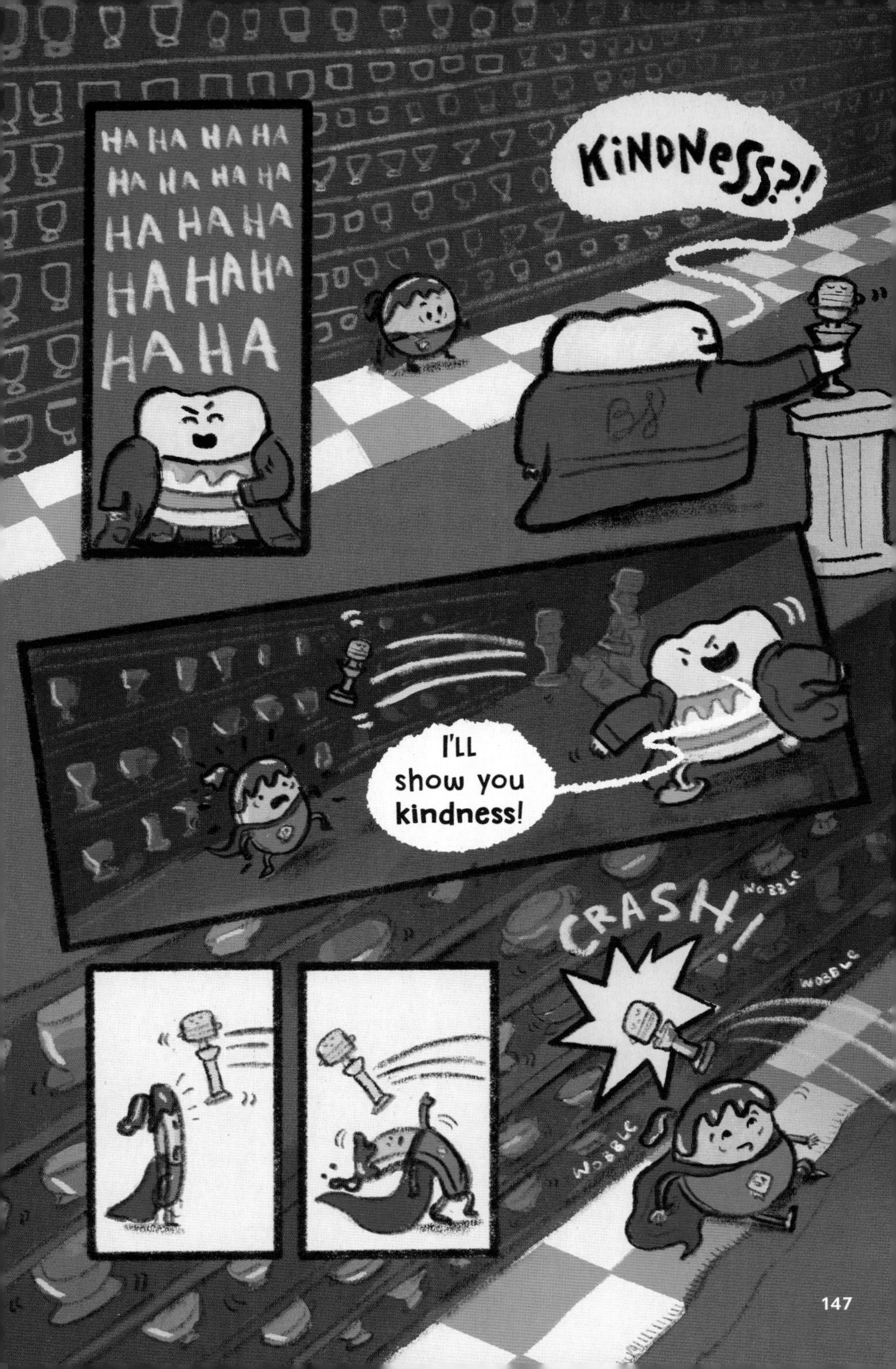
HA HA HA HA
HA HA HA HA
HA HA HA
HA HA HA
HA HA
KINDNESS?!
I'LL show you kindness!
CRASH!
WOBBLE
WOBBLE
WOBBLE

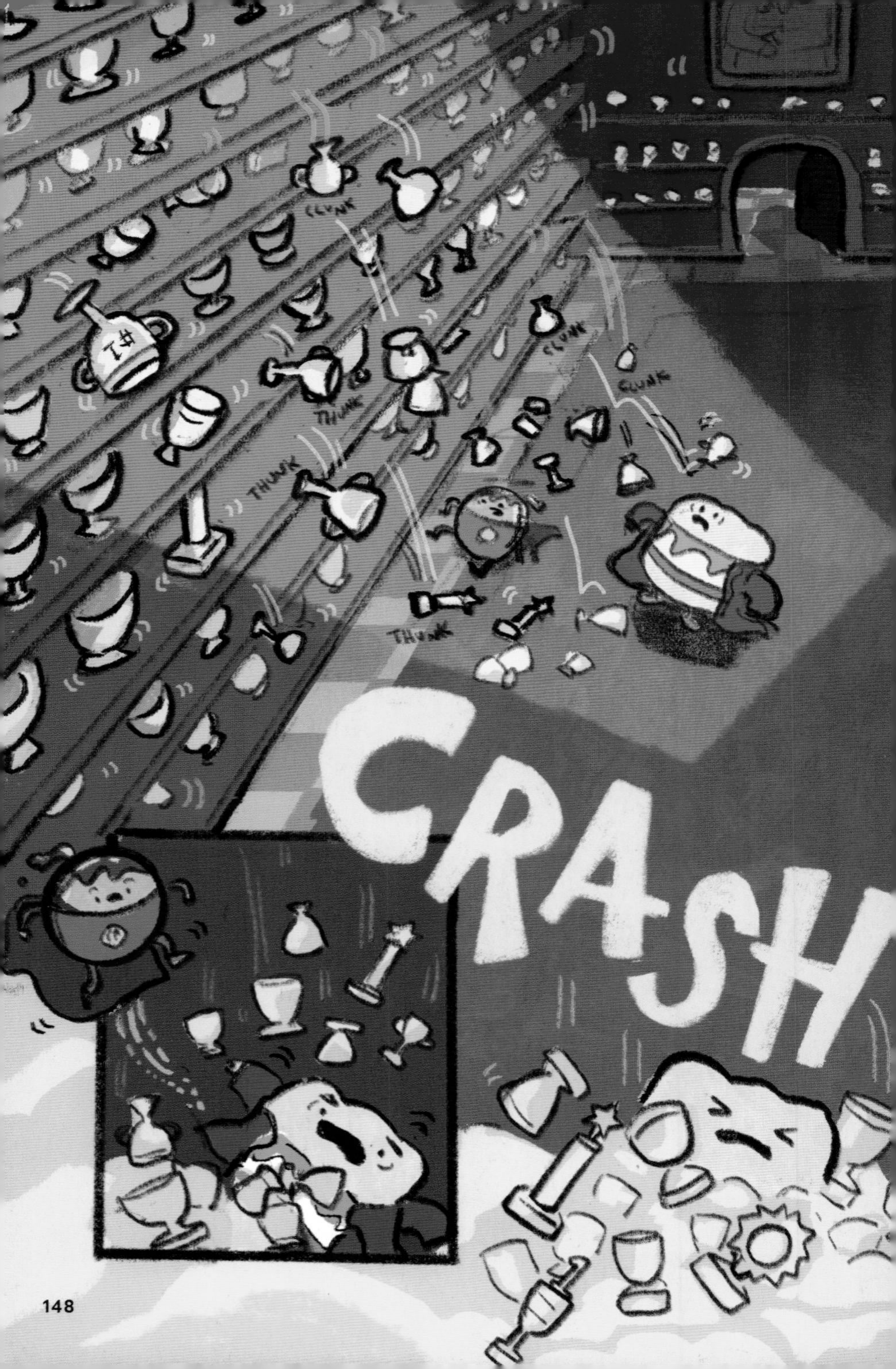
CLUNK
CLUNK
CLUNK
THUNK
THUNK
THUNK
CRASH

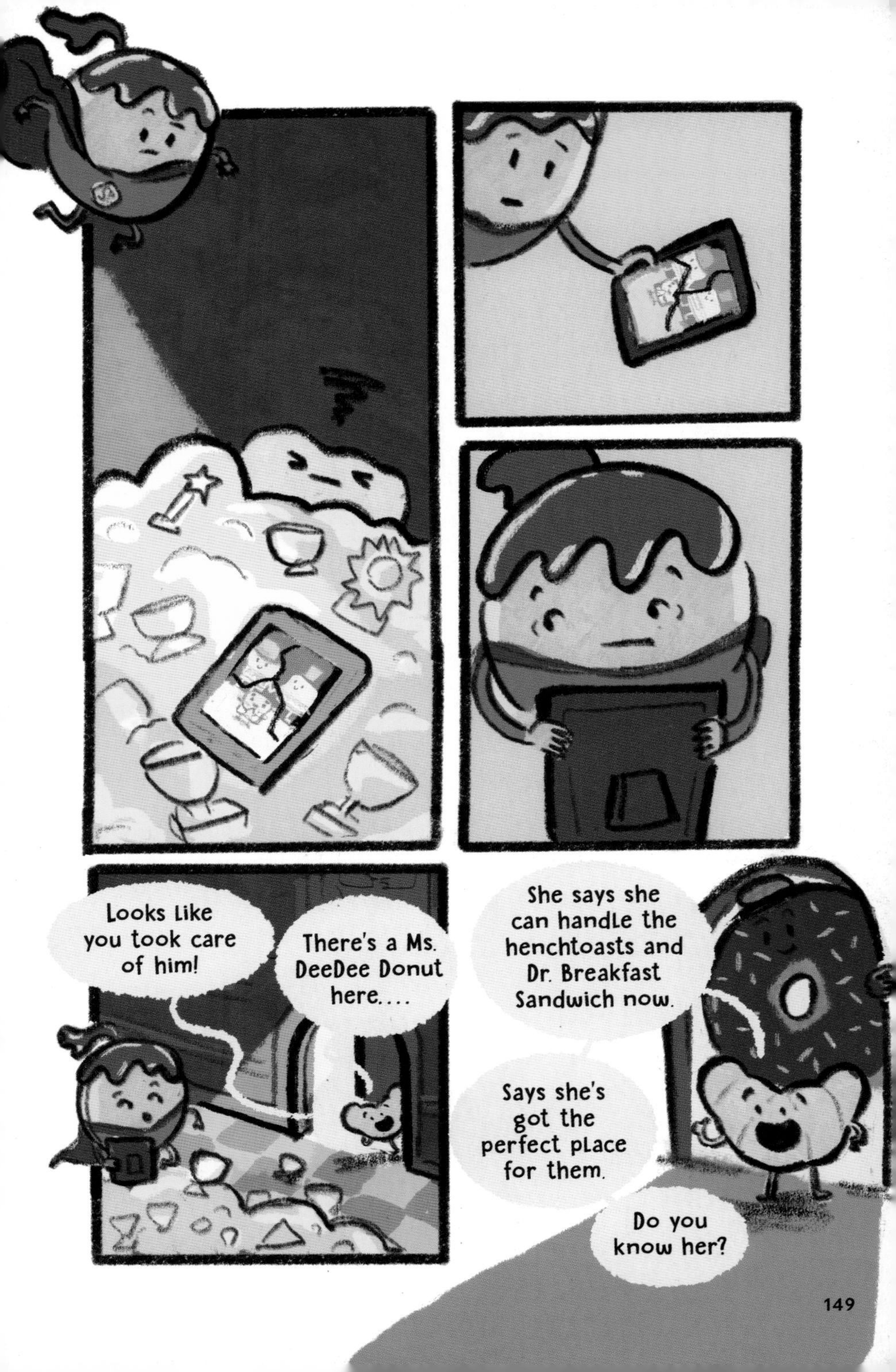
Looks like you took care of him!
There's a Ms. DeeDee Donut here....
She says she can handle the henchtoasts and Dr. Breakfast Sandwich now.
Says she's got the perfect place for them.
Do you know her?

CHAPTER FOURTEEN

Ahhhh! This is amazing!

Incredible!

I have to ask: Did you steal my GDSESDOE formula?

No! I really didn't!

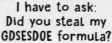

I can tell you are speaking the truth.

Someone must have slipped it to you unawares.

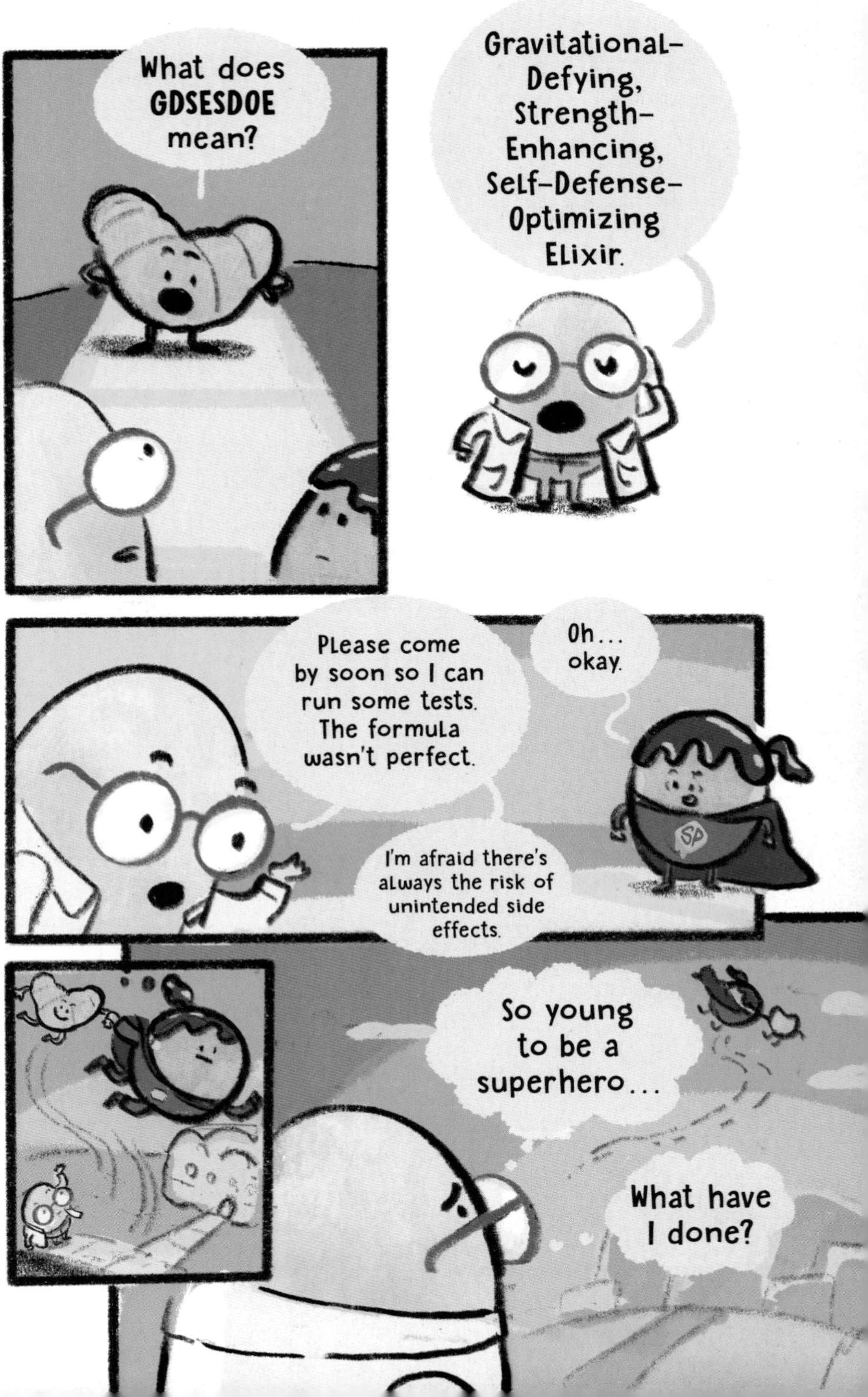
What does GDSESDOE mean?
Gravitational-Defying, Strength-Enhancing, Self-Defense-Optimizing Elixir.
Please come by soon so I can run some tests. The formula wasn't perfect.
I'm afraid there's always the risk of unintended side effects.
Oh... okay.
So young to be a superhero...
What have I done?

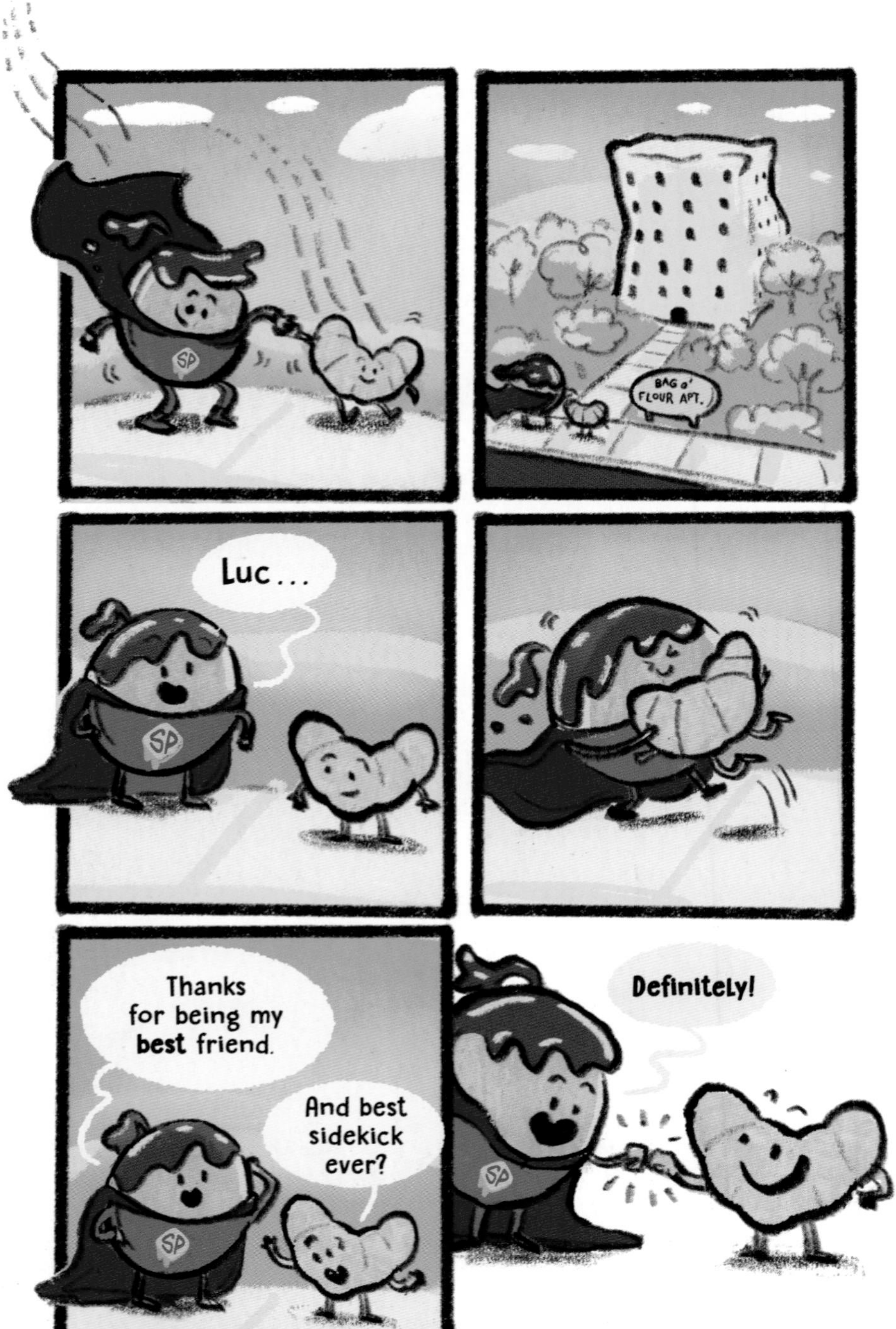
BAG o'
FLOUR APT.
Luc...
Thanks for being my **best** friend.
And best sidekick ever?
Definitely!

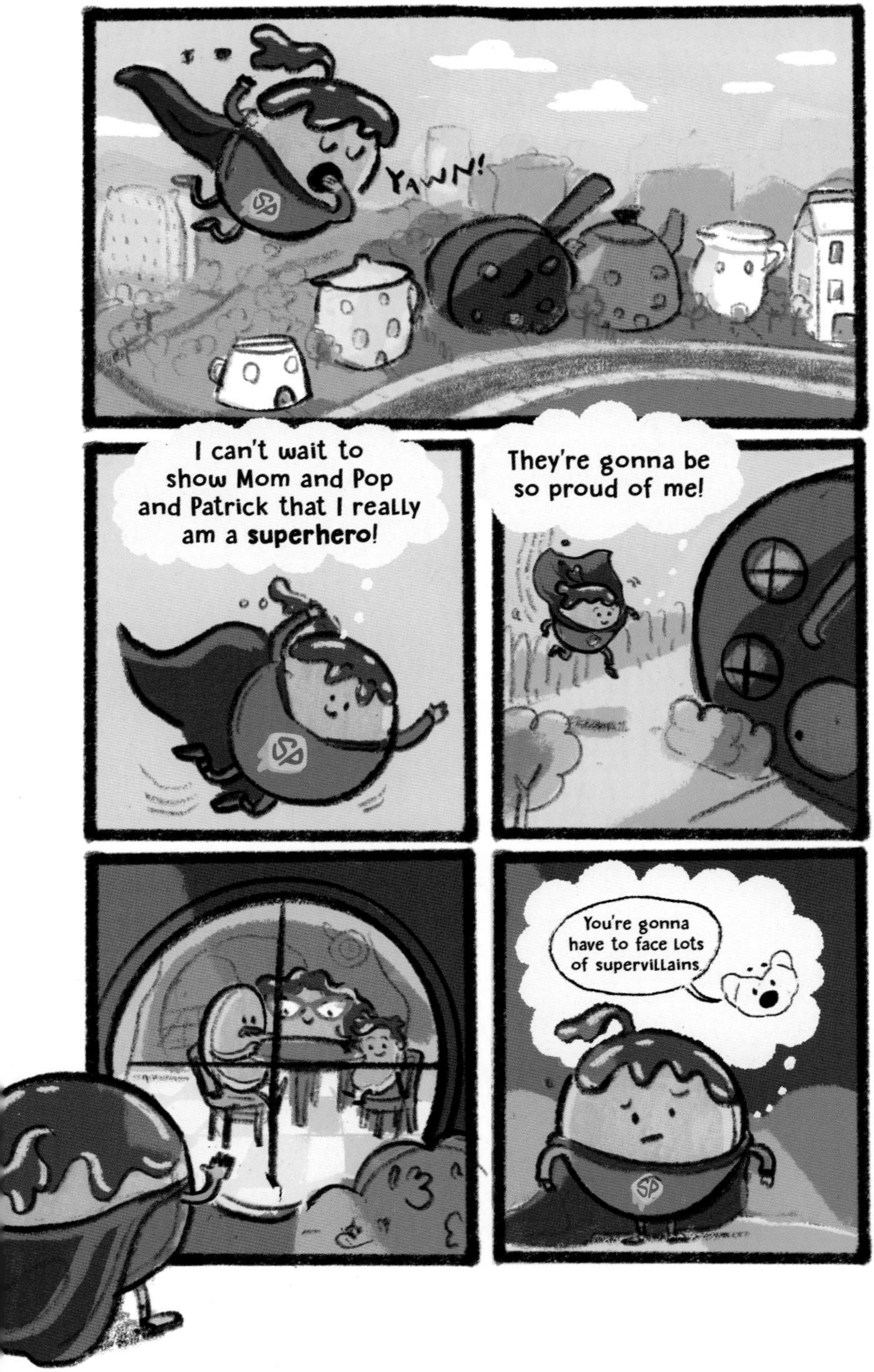

YAWN!
I can't wait to show Mom and Pop and Patrick that I really am a **superhero**!
They're gonna be so proud of me!
You're gonna have to face lots of supervillains.

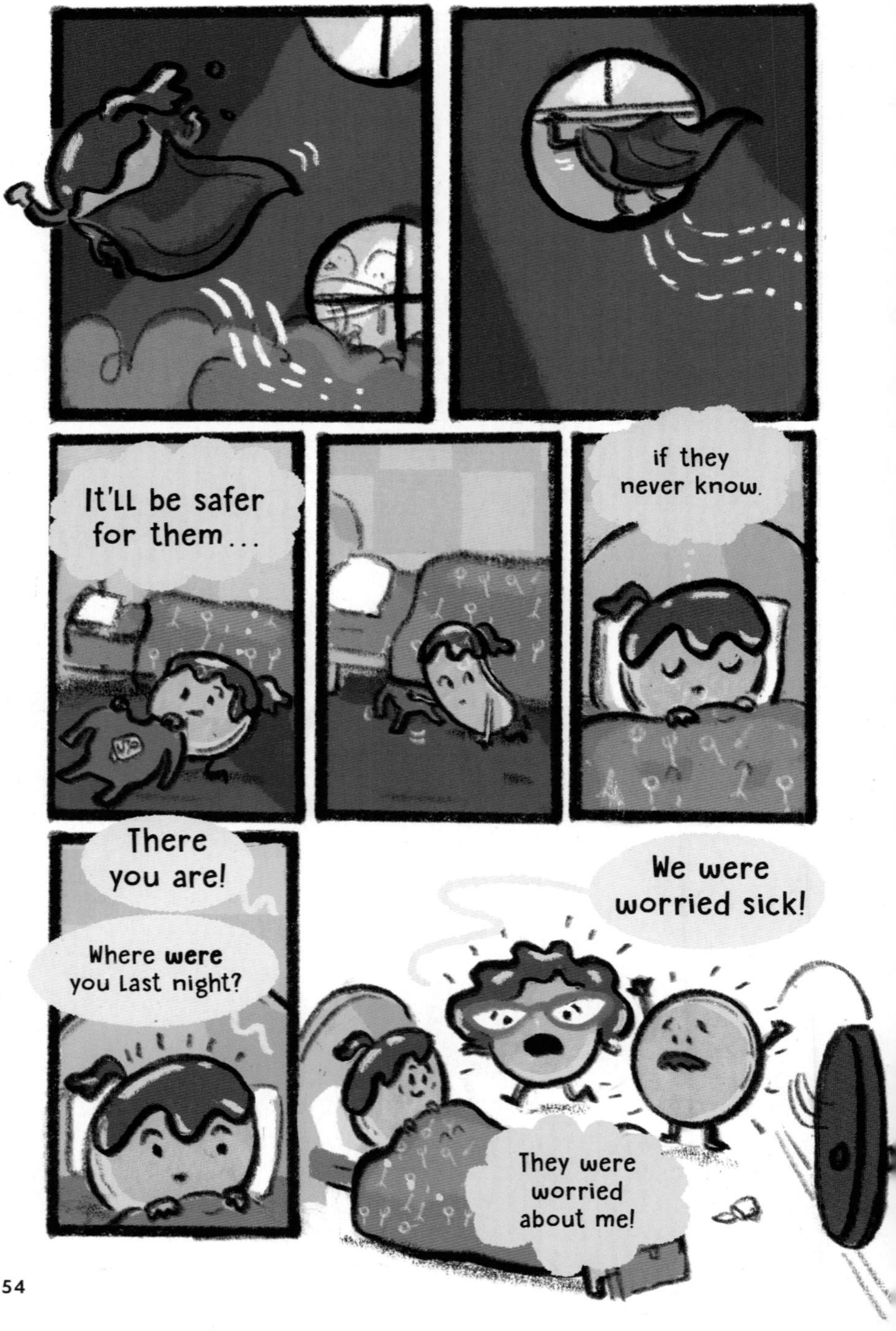
It'LL be safer for them...
if they never know.
There you are!
Where were you Last night?
We were worried sick!
They were worried about me!

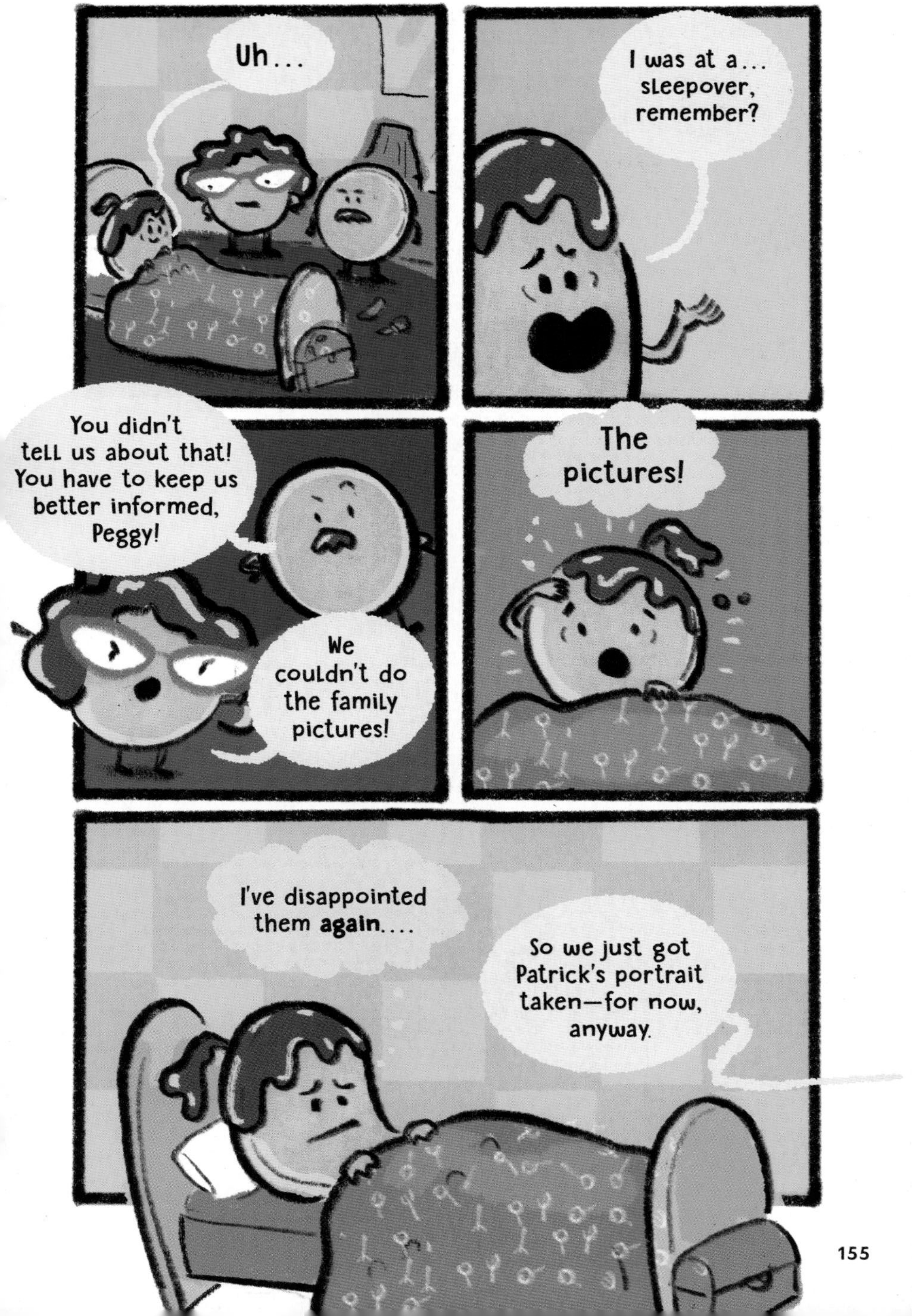

Uh...
I was at a... sleepover, remember?
You didn't tell us about that! You have to keep us better informed, Peggy!
We couldn't do the family pictures!
The pictures!
I've disappointed them **again**....
So we just got Patrick's portrait taken—for now, anyway.

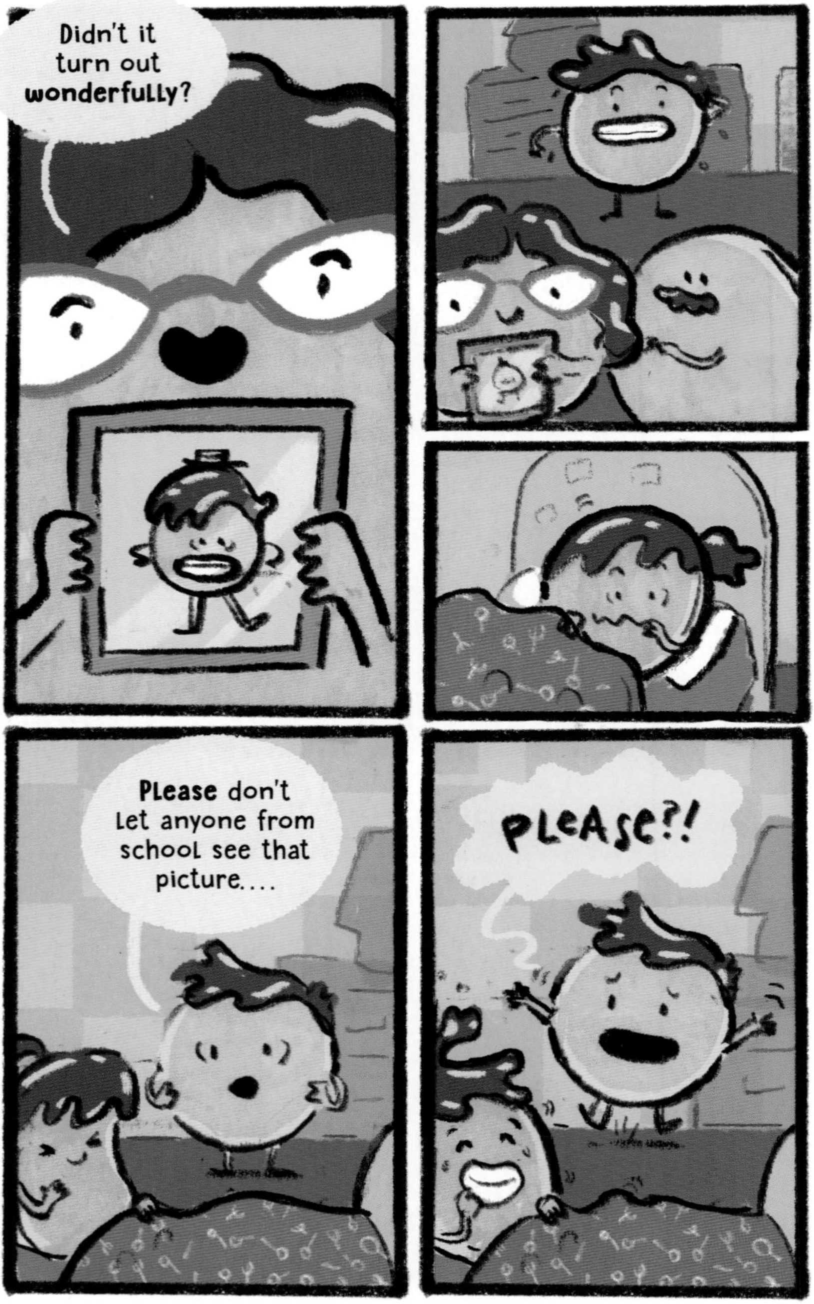
Didn't it turn out wonderfully?
Please don't let anyone from school see that picture....
PLEASE?!

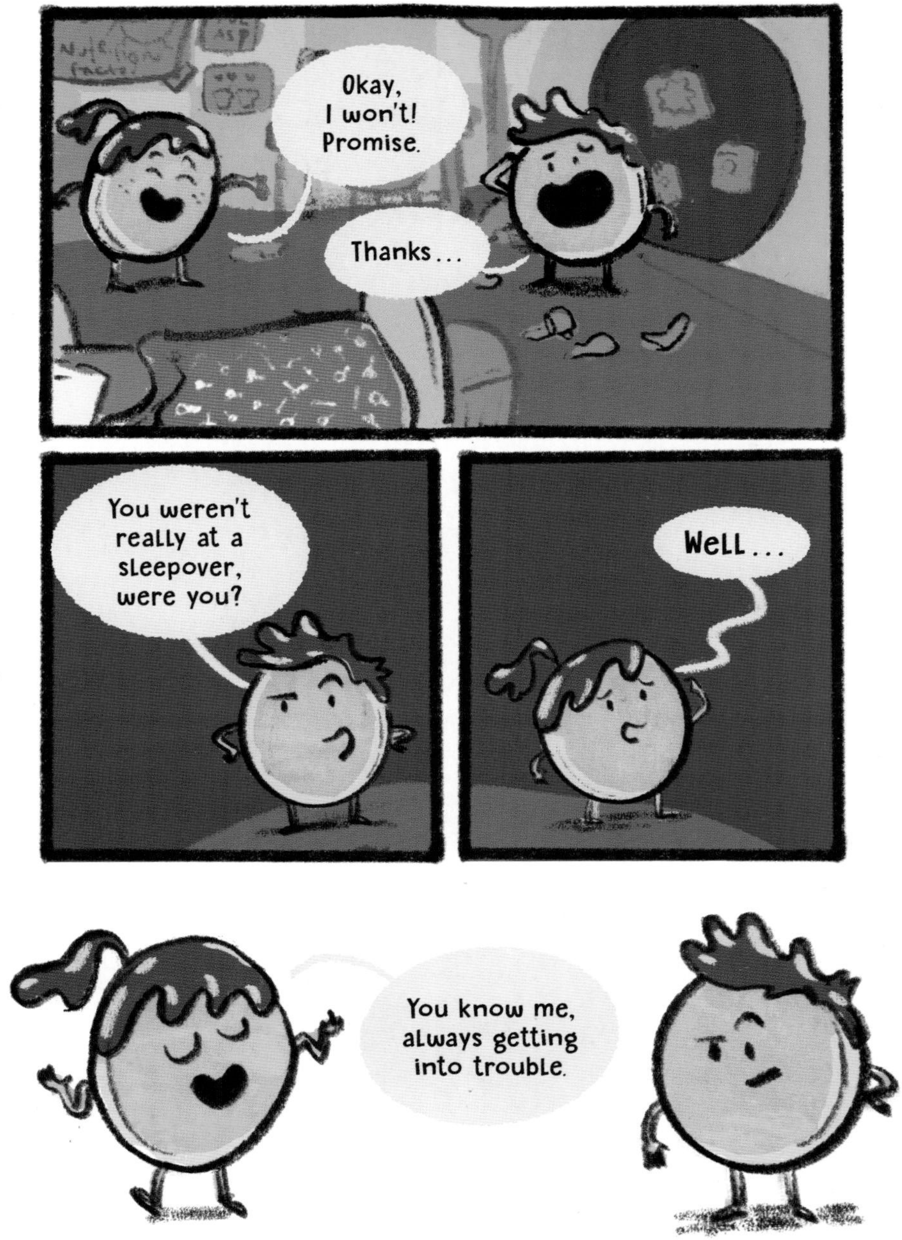
Okay, I won't! Promise.
Thanks...
You weren't really at a sleepover, were you?
Well...
You know me, always getting into trouble.

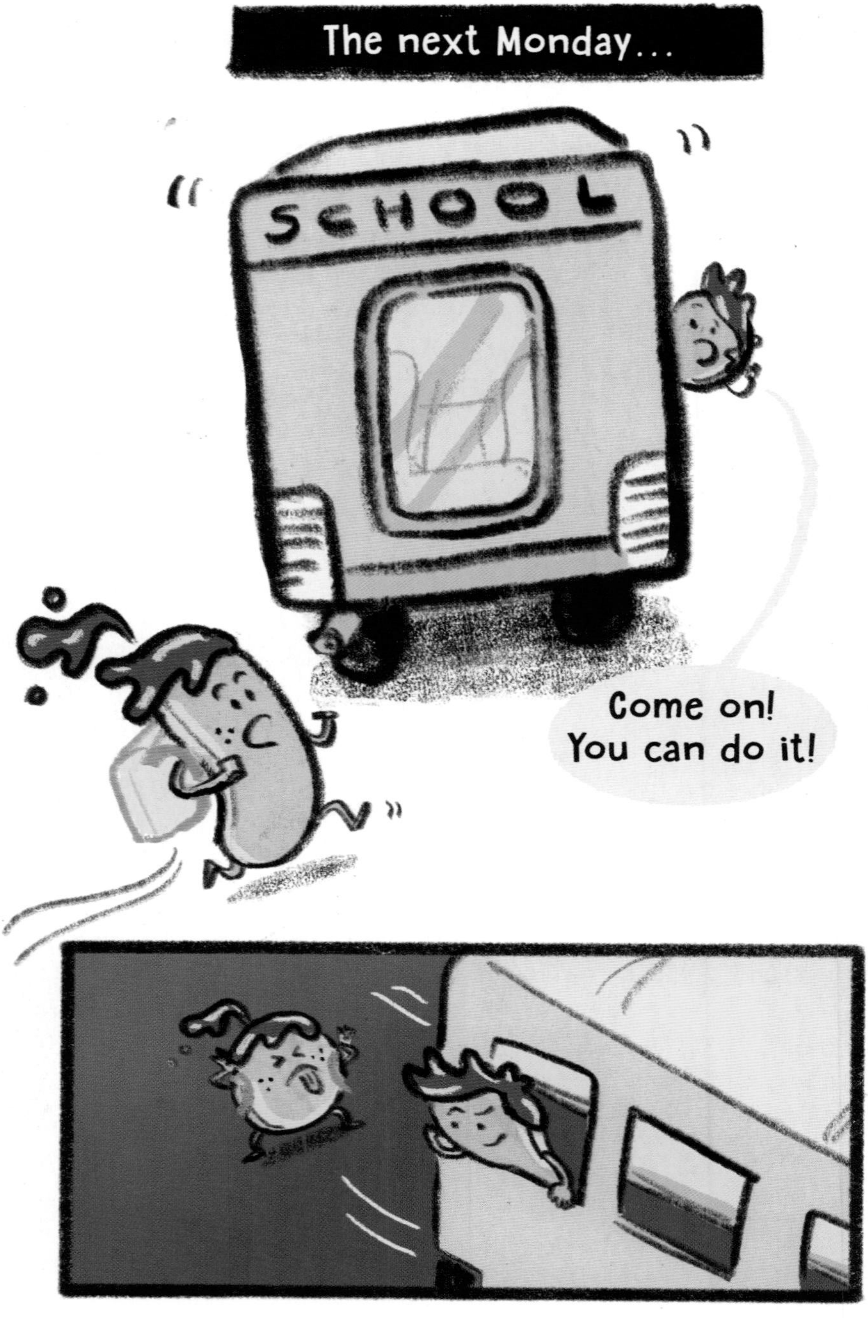
The next Monday...
SCHOOL
Come on!
You can do it!

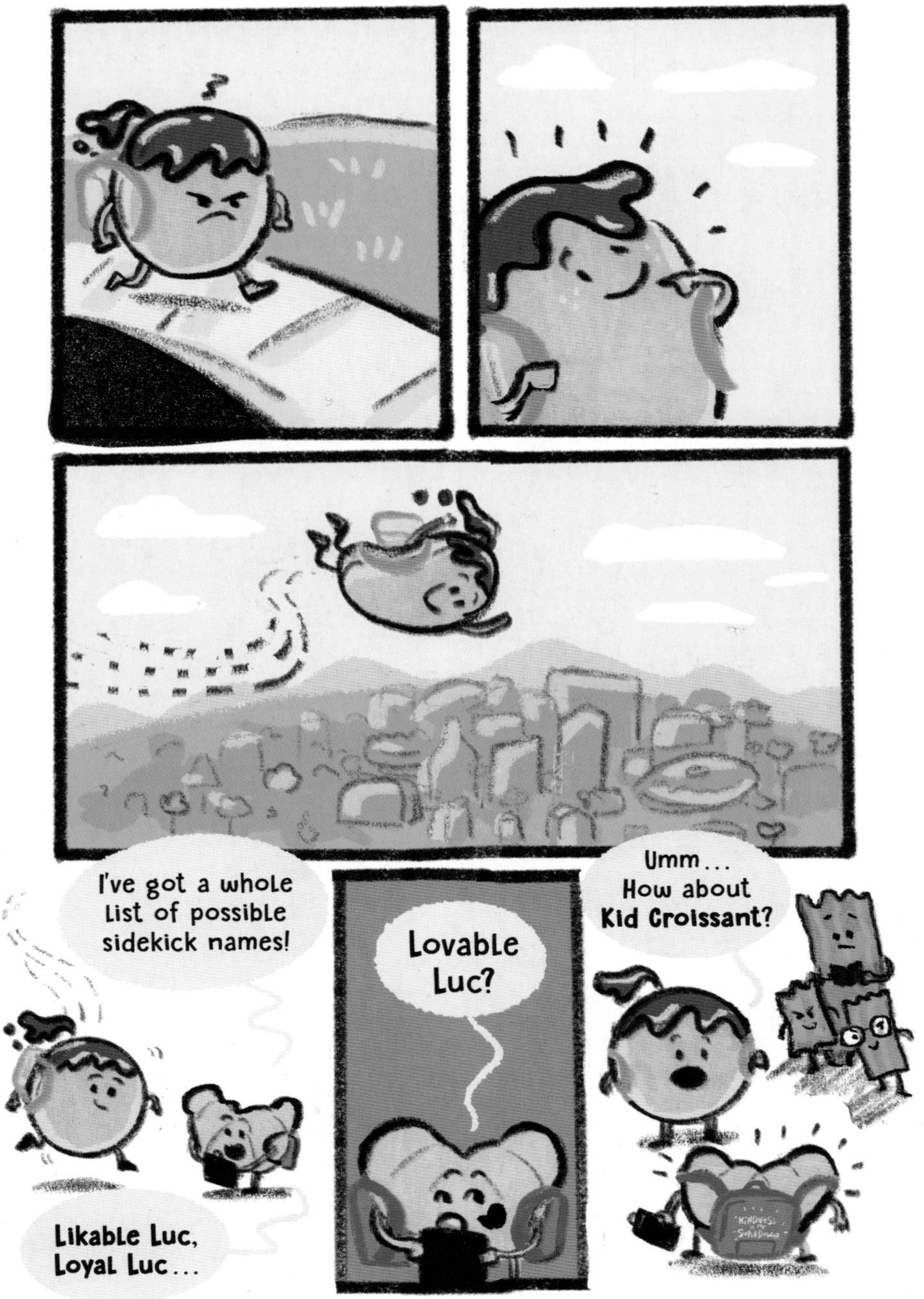
I've got a whole List of possible sidekick names!
Likable Luc, Loyal Luc...
Lovable Luc?
Umm... How about Kid Croissant?
KINDNESS IS THE SUPERPOWER

Peggy and **Luc**...

make me wanna **puke!**

That's it! I'm done!

And you know what? My name's **Stanley!**

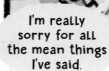

I'm really sorry for all the mean things I've said.

Can I hang out with you guys instead?

SURE!

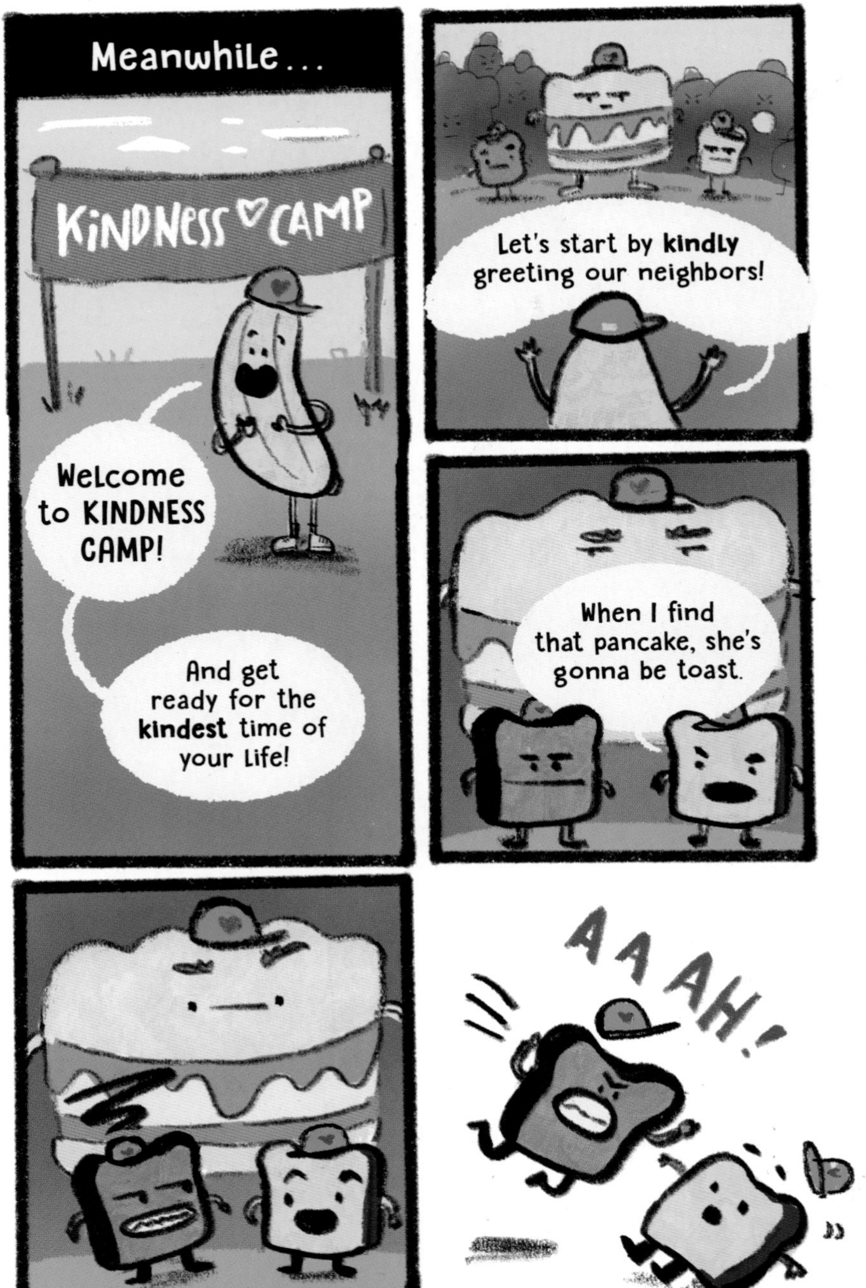
Meanwhile...
KINDNESS CAMP
Welcome to KINDNESS CAMP!
And get ready for the **kindest** time of your life!
Let's start by **kindly** greeting our neighbors!
When I find that pancake, she's gonna be toast.
AAAH!

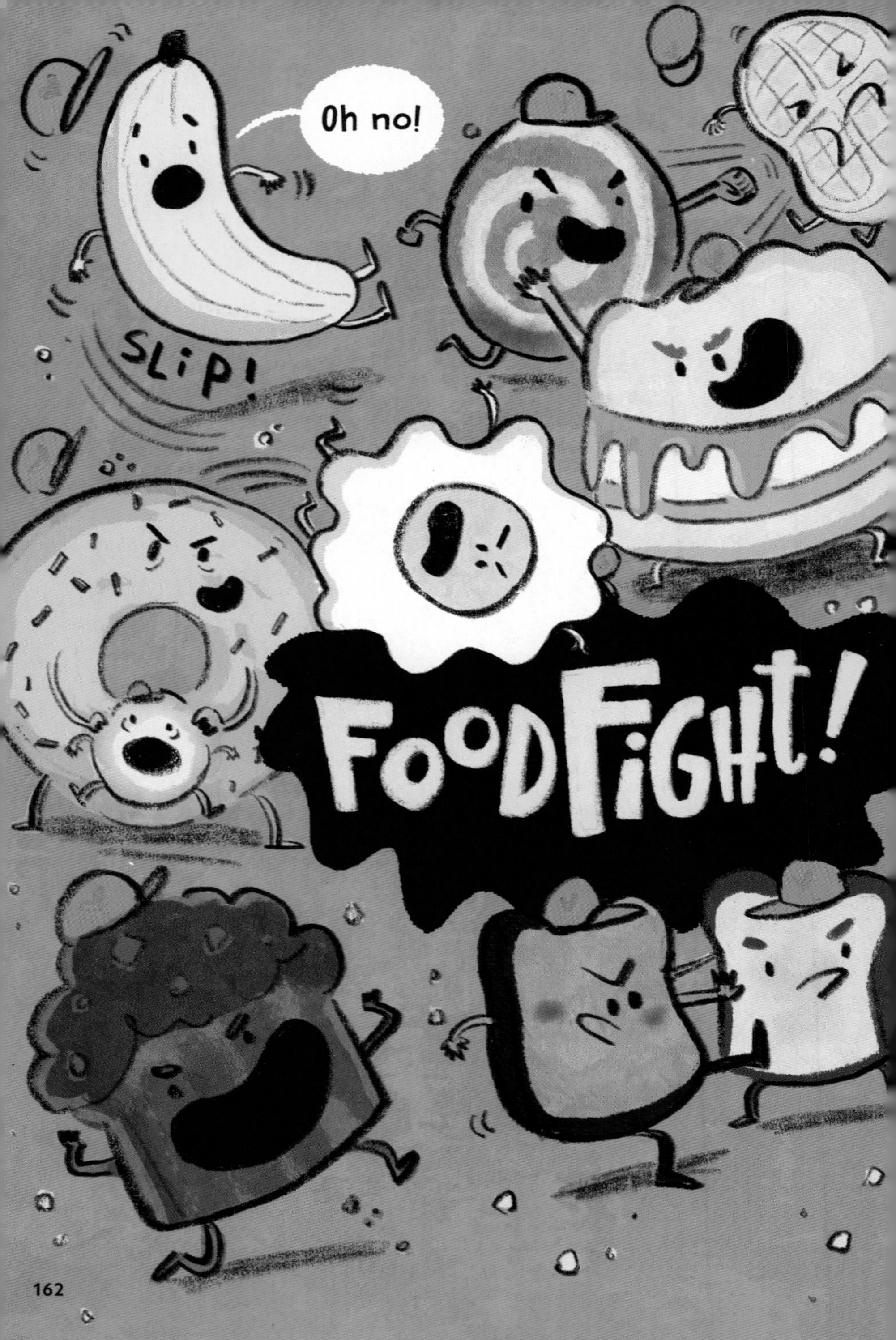
Oh no!
SLIP!
FOOD FIGHT!

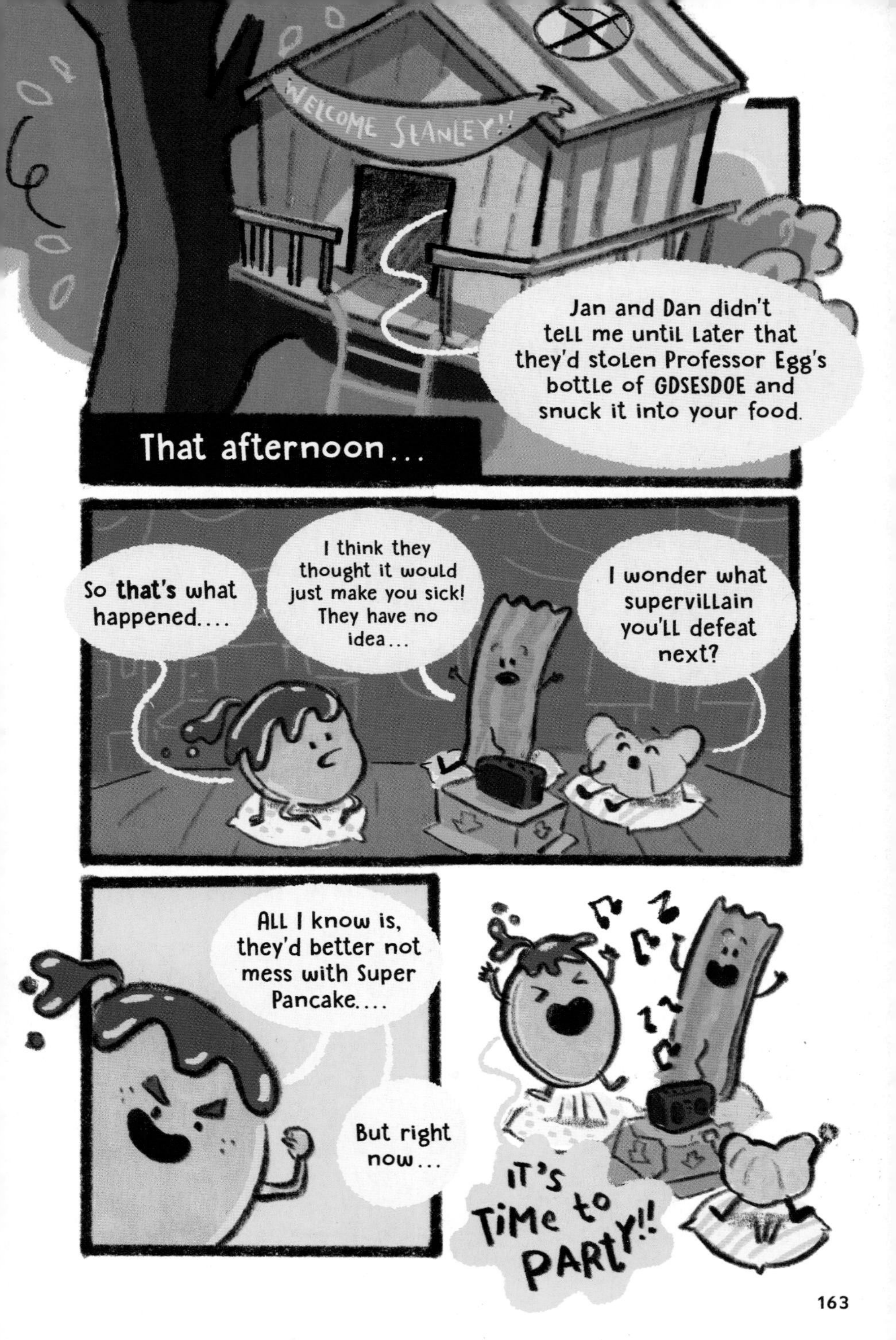
WELCOME STANLEY!!
Jan and Dan didn't tell me until later that they'd stolen Professor Egg's bottle of GDSESDOE and snuck it into your food.
That afternoon...
So that's what happened....
I think they thought it would just make you sick! They have no idea...
I wonder what supervillain you'll defeat next?
All I know is, they'd better not mess with Super Pancake....
But right now...
IT'S TIME to PARTY!!

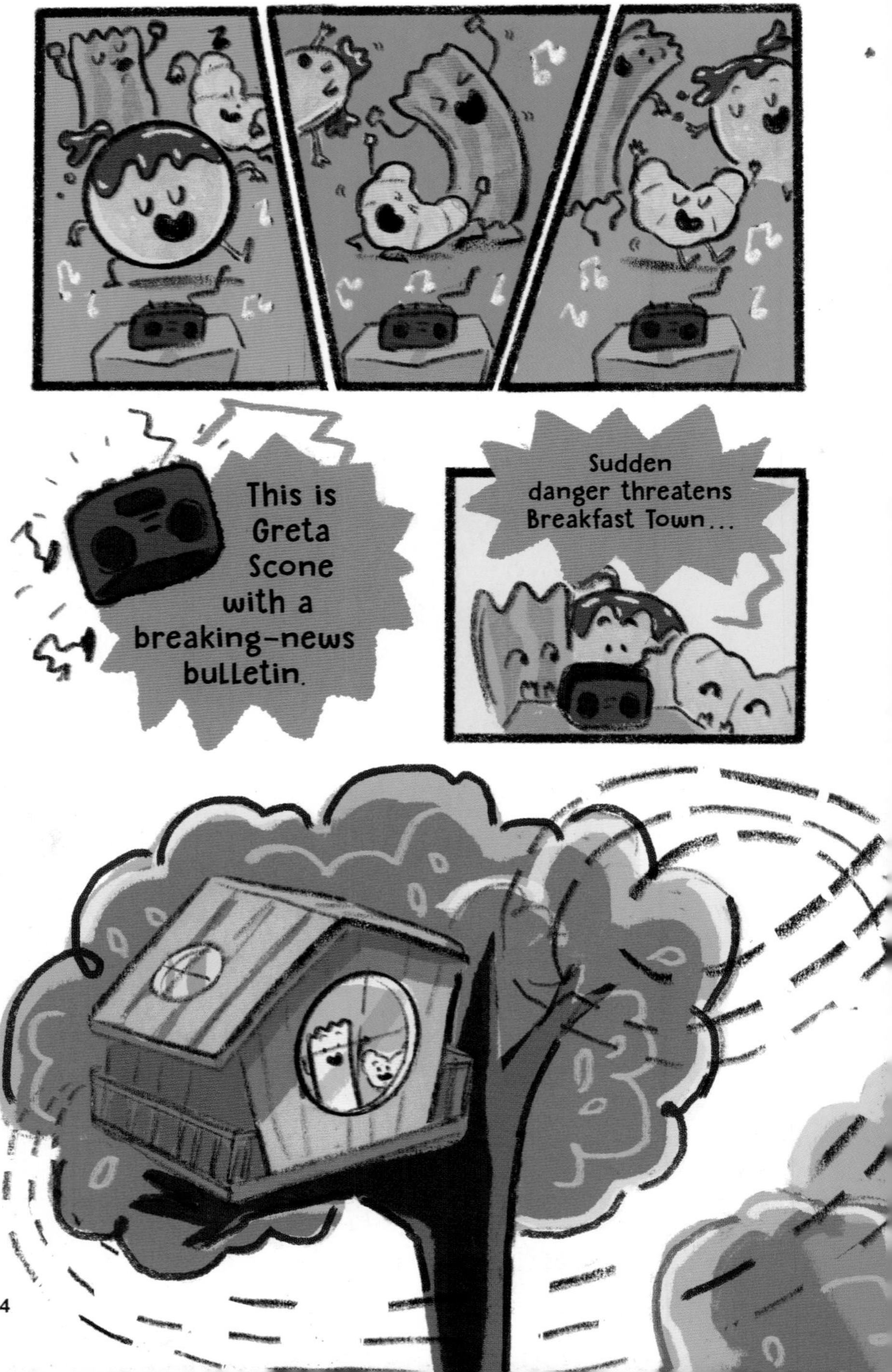
This is Greta Scone with a breaking-news bulletin.
Sudden danger threatens Breakfast Town...

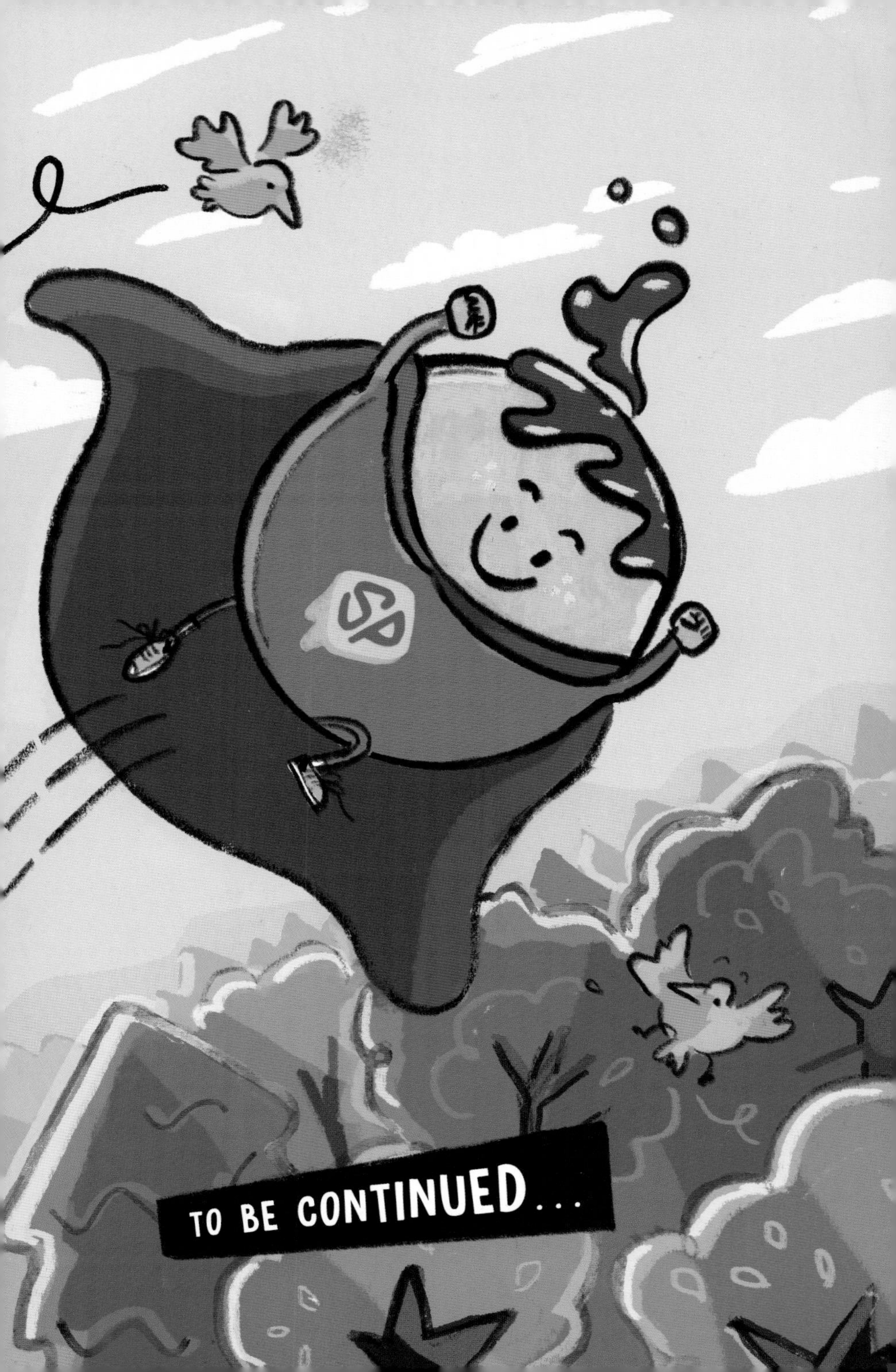
TO BE CONTINUED...

Extra Helpings!

Character Design

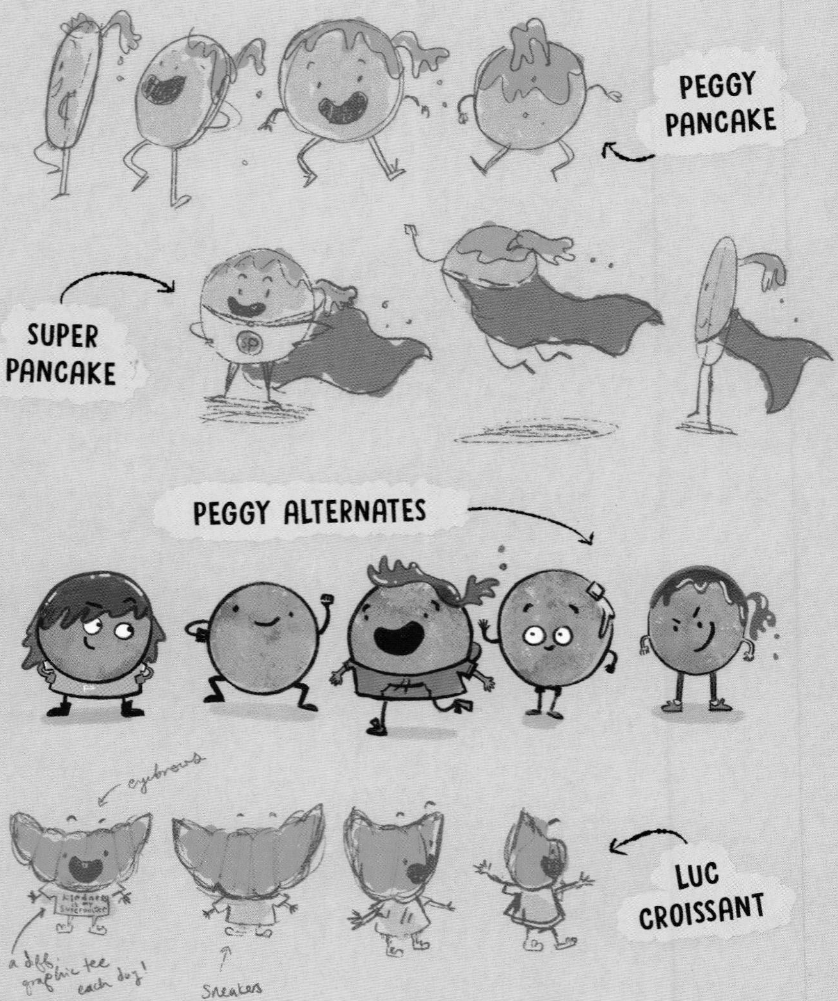
PEGGY PANCAKE
SUPER PANCAKE
PEGGY ALTERNATES
eyebrows
LUC CROISSANT
a diff. graphic tee each day!
sneakers

half of glasses come off even when full frontal

no ears, but glasses stay on head

PROFESSOR EGG

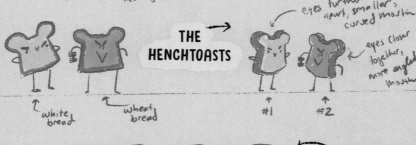

DR. BREAKFAST SANDWICH

↑ we usually see him with his monogrammed silk robe

THE HENCHTOASTS

eyes further apart, smaller, curved mouth

eyes closer together, more angled mouth

↑ white bread

↑ wheat bread

↑ #1

↑ #2

DEEDEE DONUT

COLOR SKETCHES

Environmental Design

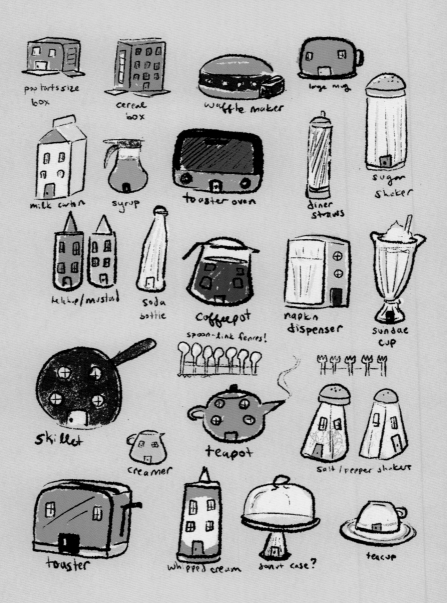

pop tarts size box

cereal box

waffle maker

large mug

milk carton

syrup

toaster oven

diner straws

sugar shaker

ketchup / mustard

soda bottle

coffeepot

spoon-link fences!

napkin dispenser

sundae cup

skillet

creamer

teapot

salt / pepper shakers

toaster

whipped cream

donut case?

teacup

Peggy's home

(a skillet) + a cup?
or could be a teapot!

Luc's apartment
(a cereal box)

aerial
view of
Winifred Waffle
Elementary School
(waffle maker)

B.S. Mansion
= Sugar shaker!

Prof. Egg's Laboratory
(toaster oven)

Detective Donut's
office (coffeepot)

Welcome to
BREAKFAST
TOWN

Winifred Waffle
ELEMENTARY

WELCOME
to
BREAKFAST
TOWN

Welcome to
BREAKFAST
TOWN

THE OFFICES OF
DEE DEE
DONUT
Private Investigator

PROFESSIONAL HOUSE
OF MYSTERIES

NO EXIST FINDER OF
MISSING PIECES

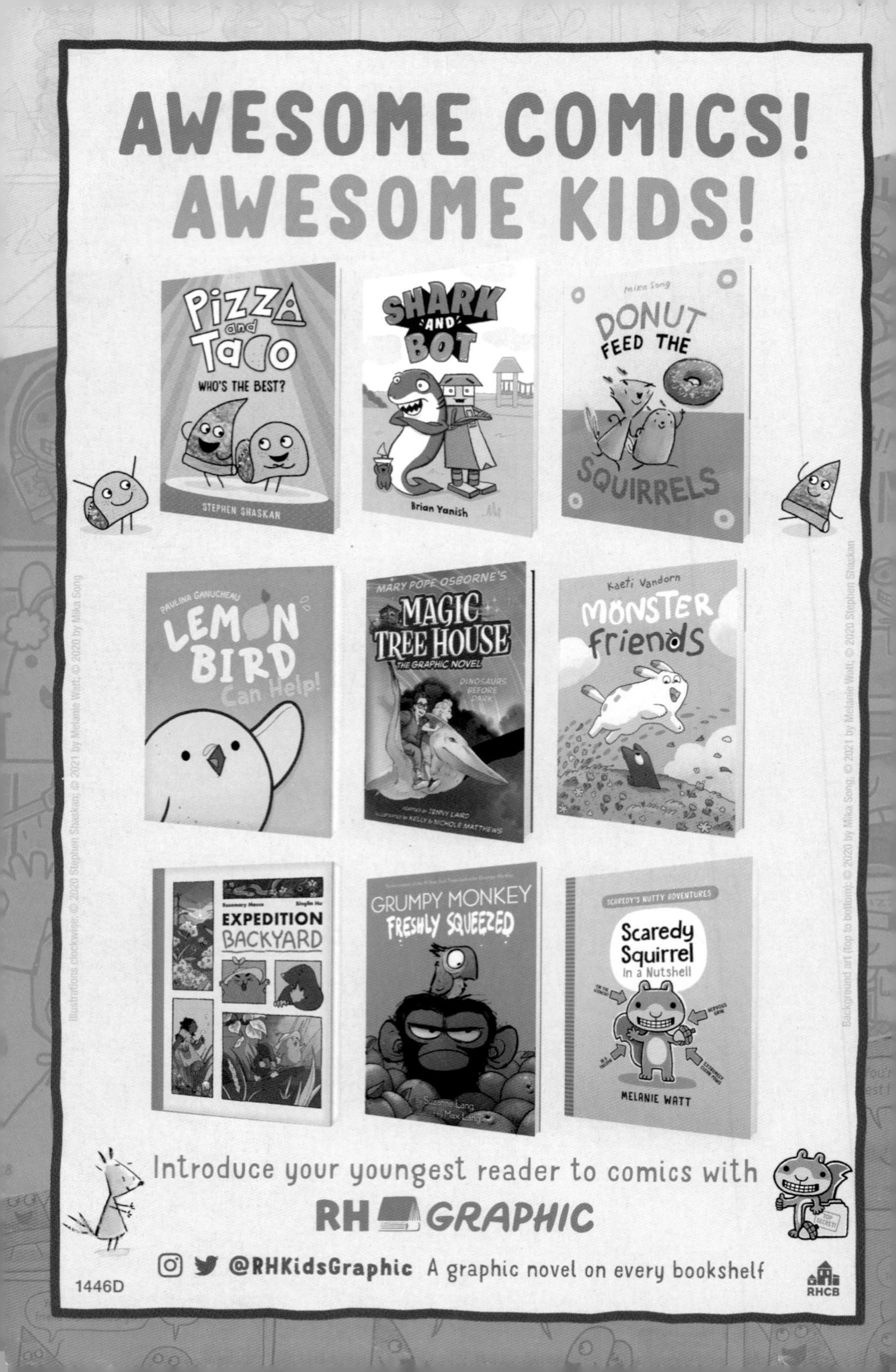
AWESOME COMICS!
AWESOME KIDS!
Pizza and Taco
WHO'S THE BEST?
STEPHEN SHASKAN
SHARK AND BOT
Brian Yanish
Mika Song
DONUT FEED THE SQUIRRELS
PAULINA GANUCHEAU
LEMON BIRD
Can Help!
MARY POPE OSBORNE'S
MAGIC TREE HOUSE
THE GRAPHIC NOVEL
DINOSAURS BEFORE DARK
ADAPTED BY JENNY LAIRD
ILLUSTRATED BY KELLY & NICHOLE MATTHEWS
Kaeti Vandorn
MONSTER Friends
EXPEDITION BACKYARD
GRUMPY MONKEY
FRESHLY SQUEEZED
Suzanne Lang
Max Lang
SCAREDY'S NUTTY ADVENTURES
Scaredy Squirrel
In a Nutshell
MELANIE WATT
Introduce your youngest reader to comics with
RH GRAPHIC
@RHKidsGraphic A graphic novel on every bookshelf
Illustrations clockwise: © 2020 Stephen Shaskan; © 2021 by Melanie Watt; © 2020 by Mika Song
Background art (top to bottom): © 2020 by Mika Song; © 2021 by Melanie Watt; © 2020 Stephen Shaskan
1446D
RHCB